I0825140

THE KINGS' LIST

MORE FROM JADE PRESLEY

THE NEVER LIST SERIES

The Never List

THE SHATTERED ISLE SERIES

Her Villains

Her Revenge

Her Mates

The Assassins

The Reckoning

THE ENCHANTRESS SERIES

The Veil of Blood & Magic

NEW YORK TIMES BESTSELLING AUTHOR
JADE PRESLEY

RED TOWER
BOOKS™

Entangled Publishing, LLC
644 Shrewsbury Commons Ave., STE 181
Shrewsbury, PA 17361
rights@entangledpublishing.com

Red Tower Books is an imprint of Entangled Publishing, LLC.

Visit our website at www.entangledpublishing.com.

Edited by Mary Lindsey
Cover, edge, and endpaper design by LJ Anderson
Cover and edge images by alex_west/GettyImages, AntonMatyukha/Depositphotos, and rozmarina/GettyImages
Endpaper images by CG Trader, AntonMatyukha/Depositphotos, and rozmarina/GettyImages
Original map illustration by Amy Acosta
Case design by Bree Archer
Case image by Nadia Murash/Shutterstock
Jacket design by Liz Wayant

Hardcover ISBN 978-1-68281-669-1
Ebook ISBN 978-1-64937-522-3

Manufactured in the United States of America
First Edition May 2026

10 9 8 7 6 5 4 3 2 1

The Kings' List is a spicy fantasy "why choose" romance (and when we say spicy, we mean extra spicy!) that will take your breath away with royal intrigue, searing passion, and four utterly irresistible princes who—each in their own way—will steal your heart. However, the story includes elements that might not be suitable for all readers, including sexually explicit scenes with one or multiple consenting partners, themes of classism, loss of family members off the page, drowning, hanging, drugging, substance use, death, torture, dismemberment, and violence. Readers who may be sensitive to these elements, please take note.

What do a broody bad boy, a cinnamon roll alpha, a fun-loving tattooed demigod, and an emotionally intelligent prince have in common?

They've each chosen you.

Now, who's ready to get worshipped?

Previously in the Never List series . . .

When I snuck into the palace to search for clues about my missing sister, I expected to slip in and out unnoticed, just another face in the sea of women attending the Choosing Ceremony. Joke was on me, though. Not only was I noticed, I was selected by the four princes of Lumathyst (also called the Legends of Chaos, depending on who you're talking to) to be their mate. *Me*, an Ashlander, a nobody.

The last thing I expected was to fall for them. But I did. *Hard*. Enough to risk my life to become immortal so I could be with them forever. Great plan, right? Yeah . . . no. Everything went wrong. Poison. Death. More power than I could handle. And the discovery that my sister is the leader of the Faders, a rebel group trying to destroy the kingdom.

The kings want me to fail. The princes want to protect me. My sister might be trying to kill me. And me? I'm just trying to survive so I can return to my mates, become their queen, and have my happily ever after.

But first, I have to escape from wherever I am . . .

Bay of Erithmore
Erithmore
N
nw
ne
W
E
sw
se
S
Obsidian City
SILVAC
Sapphire Bay
Sapphire Cove
Ruby Aire
Sea of Cardrayton
Cardrayton
KELESHORE

The Crescent Sea
Royal City
Leaf & Claw
Oak & Iron
Cedar & Silk
Ashlands
Emerald Wood
Lumathyst
Vleyica

CHAPTER 1

Jax

"There are several critical arteries in the body . . ." My voice is low, rough, scraped raw. I spin the knife in my hand, the blade winking in the silver moonlight streaming in through the narrow window near the ceiling of the storeroom. "But the two femoral are my favorites." I lean down, hovering the blade right over said artery.

No longer straining against the ropes binding him to a chair, the steward lets out a whimper. "I told you," he says through his tears. "I didn't touch it. I swear on the goddesses above, your highness, I didn't touch it."

He's trembling with fear. Not that it has anything to do with my power. I have none.

That vacant spot inside me practically weeps at the loss of something I've possessed my entire life. It feels like one of my limbs has ceased functioning. I keep reaching for the phantom power, but more than anything, the emptiness inside me comes from grief.

Rylee. My mate.

I swipe down with my blade, just enough to cut through his cotton pants and nick his skin.

"I swear!" he yelps, eyes widening as he looks down at the shallow cut.

He's lucky that's all it is with what I suspect. I'm desperate for answers. For someone to blame. To punish. Someone other than myself.

"You had access to the Choosing elixir that poisoned her," I snap, smacking him with the back of my hand hard enough to knock the blubbering out of him. "You were charged with caring for the room it was kept in."

"I didn't touch it!" he fires back, pain making him bold with his tone.

I smile. Slow. Deadly.

He goes pale.

"Your highness," he says, tone adjusted. "I would *never* touch the elixir. What need would I have to harm any potential—"

"My *mate*," I cut him off. "She's my mate."

"I celebrate your mate. I want nothing but to serve the kings and princes of Lumathyst," he says, chest heaving. "I pledged my life into service years ago, knowing the Legends would one day ascend the thrones and I would be serving you. I would never do anything to interrupt that progress."

I draw away from him in an instant. I spin around, running my free hand through my hair as I try to catch my breath.

Without my power, I can't be certain he's not lying, but . . .

I know he's telling the truth. Call it a side effect of watching people lie all my life, but, even without my power, I know when someone is being honest.

Fuck.

Despair is a living, breathing thing beneath my skin.

I crane my neck, looking down at him over my shoulder, and take one last shot. "Did you see anyone near it? Were you approached with inquiries regarding it? Were you asked to poison it?" The questions spill out of me at a rapid pace.

Someone tampered with the elixir crafted to send Rylee to meet the goddesses. The key to her becoming immortal.

Someone tried to kill her before she had the chance.

And I will fucking find out who.

Anger erupts inside me, hot as flames, whispering, *begging* me to burn everything around me to ash.

"No, your highness," the man says. "Why would anyone ask me to do that?"

I turn around again, studying him.

Why indeed?

As much as I want to blame my ruthless prick of a father, King Baydel, for my mate's death, I don't think I can. My fellow Legends and I went around in circles about it for days. The motivation behind the attack doesn't make sense. Sure, Baydel may sense that something's off about Rylee—just like Pierce's father did—and not want her as queen of Lumathyst, but he'd gain nothing from killing her. He *only* makes moves if he has something to gain. I haven't eliminated the possibility that he's somehow involved, but without our powers, it's not like the other princes and I can interrogate him. And if he didn't do it . . .

That means someone else wanted her dead.

Everything went wrong in the Athanry, the last phase of the Choosing ceremony. Instead of Rylee gaining immortality, we *lost* her. I felt her death. Our bond severed like a sword shoved through my heart. A pain I can't soothe—not when my mate lies in a bed in the palace, yet to wake up. We sacrificed our powers, giving them to her in order to bring her back, but maybe they were too much for her to handle. Maybe they're the very thing keeping her from waking.

Her voice echoes in the hollow pieces of my soul. *I still choose you . . .*

I rub my aching chest. I can't go back. I can't sit in my room in the royal palace anymore. Can't watch Rylee sleep for one more second. Not when we need answers.

I return my attention to the steward. "Did anyone else have access to the room?"

"A handful of people, your highness," he answers. "The kings, you and the other princes, myself, your mate's handmaiden, and the kings' personal Occuli."

The hair on the back of my neck stands on end.

Too many people had access to a room that should've been sealed.

Why the fuck did the kings allow for such exposure?

I rub my palm over my face.

"Go over it again," I say, waving my hand at him in a circular motion. "Your duties."

He wets his lips but nods, pride overtaking the fear in his eyes. "Daily cleanings of the room, your highness. Each morning, the enforcer on guard would allow me entry. I'd go in and clean the space, taking great care with each artifact in the room. The kings . . . they're adamant I never disturb the treasures, merely keep them clean. One speck of dust would be an insult to the goddesses who entrusted the items to their care."

I close my eyes, trying to breathe around the ache in my chest. I can see the artifact chamber as clearly as I can see him. A room in the palace under constant guard, filled with everything our goddess mothers left behind.

Not just the Choosing elixir for the Athanry, but other treasures—a crown with the finest jewels in Lumathyst, representing each of our cities, for our queen to commemorate achieving immortality. I blink hard, pushing away the image of Rylee unconscious in her bed, far from immortal.

The room also contains tonics and parchments and a few well-loved teacups. I used to visit the room often as a child, right after my mother chose to go to sleep and act as a ward to protect Lumathyst. I'd sit next to the knife she'd left behind, admiring it, feeling closer to her—as if she'd left a piece of herself in the blade.

Once I got old enough to wield the thing, I stole it from the room.

My father, Baydel, punished me for it. Demanded I cut myself with it. But no matter how many cuts he forced me to make, I never let go of that knife.

He gave up, eventually.

I've never gone a day without the blade since.

The same one Rylee so boldly plucked from my harness weeks ago on Axl's boat. The same one I hold now.

Longing streaks through me, tightening my airways.

The steward takes a shuddering breath, head down. He's completely defeated. And so am I. I slip my knife back into the holster at my chest.

What I hoped would be a valid reason for leaving Rylee's bedside has only left me with more unanswered questions. The kings were careless in their limited protection of the elixirs, but could a Fader have possibly slipped by every palace guard and magical ward? Or was it someone on the inside?

Too many possibilities.

And none of them help me with my greatest problem.

My mate still sleeps and shows no signs of waking up.

I'm afraid of who I'll become if she doesn't return.

CHAPTER 2

Rylee

"You need . . . up!" The Goddess Evaluna's voice rings in my ears so sharply, I snap my eyes open.

The obsidian floor beneath me is brutally cold. I suck in lungfuls of air, scanning the area for Kal or Axl or Pierce or Jax.

They're not here.

No one is.

I take in the stillness, the way the space seems in between reality and dream.

Damn it.

"You know, I don't mean any offense," I say as I slowly rise to my feet. My head swims from the motion, but I manage to stand. "But don't you think having me die again is sort of . . . repetitive?"

There's no angry retort. Evaluna's temple is eerily quiet, a soft darkness hovering like a permanent shadow along her statue.

There isn't a sign of Evaluna or the other goddesses.

There isn't a sign of my mates.

Fear slithers into my veins like an oily sludge. Is this some sort of torturous purgatory? A punishment for wasting the gift of a second chance at life? The memory of stepping in front of Jax's blades to save my sister races through my mind.

I walk toward the staircase that leads out of the temple, prepared to walk all the way to Jax's home in Obsidian City. I try and fail to access Kal's power—flight would be really useful right now—but there's nothing there. My insides feel disconnected, like my mind is floating on the Saphire Sea but my body is still in the Ashlands.

The first few steps down are a struggle, my muscles trembling, but I push through. I keep seeing their faces—Kal and Pierce, Axl and Jax—behind my eyes like a beacon calling me home.

If I can get to them, everything will be all right.

After a few more grueling steps down the stairs, I freeze.

It can't be.

I take another step, then another, my heart pounding as I speed up, racing down the stairs. Each stair I take is replaced with a new one. A perpetually growing descent with no end.

No, no, no.

I have to get back to them. They need me. Need their powers back. They need—

"You . . . to . . . wake—!" Evaluna's voice cracks through my mind, her words coming in short, interrupted bursts that are difficult to fully understand.

"I don't know what you mean!" I fire into the ether, knowing it's a fool who speaks to a goddess without tempering her frustrated tantrum. "I *am* awake. I'm trying to go home—"

"No need to yell," Evaluna cuts me off, materializing before me so quickly, I skid to a halt.

I immediately bow, the action almost involuntary.

"Rise," she says.

"Did I die again?" I ask, blinking against her harsh beauty—the flowing blue-black of her hair, the iridescent skin that looks like moonlight itself. "I thought immortality would, you know, prevent that."

"Your immortality saves you from death by illness or old age or other natural causes. Your healing is now accelerated, but a harmful enough physical blow could end your life." She shrugs. "But no, you're not dead. Yet."

"That's encouraging." I do my best to keep the sass out of my tone, but I'm not as effective as I'd like.

"Once you return to the real world, your transition into immortality will be complete."

I blow out a breath.

I'm about to ask her how exactly I get out of here when she says, "War is coming." Her voice is as smooth as the slight breeze that blows through her hair.

I glance around where we stand on the staircase, like a battle might break out right here.

It doesn't.

There's nothing here but the night sky glittering with stars, the endless stairs, and the hint of the Obsidian City far, far away.

My mates are out there somewhere, powerless. My heart clenches in my chest.

"You need to be ready for it," she continues.

I draw my focus back to her. "Me?"

She nods.

I shake my head. "I'm no hero. I'm just an Ashlander. The Legends need me. They need their powers back so they can—"

"They willingly gave them to you, did they not?" she asks, eyes blazing.

I dip my head in submission. "Yes."

"Then it is *you* who needs to be ready." Her eyes trail up the staircase and behind us, toward her temple. Something so human lingers in her gaze—sadness, regret, and a hefty dose of anger. "I hate that we can't assist you more," she adds.

Yeah, me too. The goddesses evidently can't tell me shit. As much as that pisses me off, I keep it to myself and don't interrupt as she continues.

"We should be allowed to tell you everything." She huffs, eyes falling on me. "It's ridiculous, but even *we* are bound by rules."

"Whose rules?"

Her voice remains level, but her fingers ball into fists. "The Fates, devious celestials who happen to outrank myself and the other goddesses, created them. They're always meddling but never allow anyone else to. I assure you, if I could spell it out without jeopardizing the world my son inhabits, I would."

"Thank you?" It sounds more like a question, but I don't really know what to say.

"War is coming," she says again. "You will be vital to its resolution. I hope you don't disappoint us."

"That's the last thing I want to do." I motion toward the never-ending stairs. "Can you help me get home?"

Evaluna shakes her head. "Only you can get yourself out of this place and thereby secure your immortality." She delivers a pointed, narrow-eyed look before she blinks out of sight.

What does that mean? I tip my head back, eyes closed as I search for patience. I'm so damn tired. The Athanry, the battle after, my sister's betrayal, the whole dying thing . . . I need a nap.

I want Jax's arms around me.

I want Kal's assurance whispering in my ear.

I want Axl's playful smile and positive attitude.

I want Pierce in my mind, soothing the panic spiral winding tighter with every breath.

I consider giving in and crying, but I don't really have time to crumble. If I'm the only one who can get myself away from this temple, I need to keep moving.

I take another step down, then another, and another.

I climb down endless stairs until my lungs burn and sweat pops from my brow. My body trembles from exertion and the cold breeze chilling my flushed skin. I lose all sense of time, sliding deeper into a hopeless drift I don't know how to shake.

CHAPTER 3

Jax

I slump back into the armchair next to the bed, take Rylee's hand in mine, and trace the outline of her ruby and emerald rings. Then I make a path to her sapphire bracelet and back. Her chest rises and falls in a slow, steady rhythm—the moon-and-stars tattoo beneath her collarbone peeks from the sheet half-covering her. Even in sleep, she wears our tokens so proudly.

She's alive, she's just not *here*.

"I need you to come back to us," I say, not for the first time. I use my free hand to smooth some of her blond hair off her cheek. She doesn't react to my touch or voice. An overwhelming sense of dread pools in my gut.

What if she never wakes up?

What if—

"Jax, you need to sleep." Pierce's voice cuts through my panic, focusing me. "I can take this shift."

None of us has slept well in the last week, all searching for ways to revive her or hunting for answers about the chaotic Athanry.

"I'll sleep when she wakes up." I shift back in the chair.

"Killing yourself won't help her." He crosses the room and stops near the edge of the bed, eyes raking over Rylee. His longing matches mine, as does his anguish.

I flash him a pointed look. "I'm not sleeping."

"At least eat," he begs. "I can have the kitchens send up something."

"Has it happened again?" I ask, ignoring the worry in his voice.

Pierce leans against the wall next to where I sit and blows out a breath. "No, my power only came back for a blink. Hit me like a hammer." He furrows his brow. "Then it was gone just as fast."

"Tell me again," I request, even though he's told me the story a dozen times now.

Pierce rubs his palms over his face but indulges me. "In the brief moment my power returned, I entered Rylee's mind. She was in your mother's temple. Like she never left the Athanry. She was alone and scared."

"You experienced her having a nightmare." I press my lips together.

"Perhaps," he says. "But it felt real. I've been in her mind enough times to know when she's dreaming." He meets my eyes. "This felt . . . different. My powers were snatched from me before I could explore her mind further." He rubs at his chest, much like I did moments ago.

I know what he's feeling—like if he paws at the spot enough, he might be able to mend the invisible, gaping wound. Without our powers, each of us feels *wrong*. Different. Lesser.

But it doesn't matter. I'll surrender my powers a thousand times if it means Rylee gets to live. That was the deal we made with our mothers.

I swallow hard. "Do you think our mothers played a cruel trick on us?"

"Why would they do such a thing?" Pierce asks.

"I don't know. They seemed angry or jaded when we saw them during the Athanry. Not like how I remember them." Though my memories are painted through the gaze of an adoring, naive child.

"Perhaps they were angry at us for wasting the Choosing elixir?" Pierce offers.

"Maybe. Maybe it's something else. Maybe nothing. I just don't understand why they'd ask for the sacrifice and then not allow Rylee to wake up."

"Maybe she's not waking up because our collective power combining with hers is too much for her psyche. We had years to develop and grow and learn how to control them. She wasn't given the same luxury."

No, we took that choice from her. Made a decision to bring her back, so ensnared by our grief, we didn't stop to think about the consequences.

But our mothers said it would be her choice in the end, whether to return to this life, and she *had* returned.

Only for the weight of our powers and the strike of my blades to put an end to that.

"Any word on the Fader she defended?" I ask, lowering my voice. We didn't tell our fathers about the specifics—that Rylee had repossessed our powers soon after she'd returned them to us and then stepped in front of two of my blades to protect a Fader.

"No," Pierce answers. "I was on the hunt earlier today. Kal and Axl are out there now. Searching for her—" He cuts himself off.

Her sister.

That's what he doesn't say. What he *can't* say.

Because there's no one else in Lumathyst Rylee would protect.

Right?

She never spoke of anyone else important to her, beyond Ivy and Layce, and they've been here at the palace since the Athanry. They aren't Faders.

But her sister? The one who's been missing for over a year? I don't want it to be true, but nothing else makes sense. Rylee wouldn't put her life at risk for just anyone. Especially not with how intertwined all our lives are now. I squeeze her limp hand, willing her to respond.

"Has there been another attack?" I ask, gently placing her hand back on the bed by her side.

"Thankfully, no," Pierce says. "The people are on edge enough with the stories spreading about the Athanry. The kings, naturally, are doing their best to assure them all is right and well, but I fear once news inevitably leaks that our mate is unconscious and possesses . . ." He glances over his shoulder, ensuring no one lingers beyond the closed door. We're alone. No one is listening. "All our powers," he continues in a whisper. "There will be an increase in attacks. Quite possibly a play from one of our enemies across the seas."

I pinch the bridge of my nose. "Rylee was only ever meant to gain the ability to balance us should we be a danger to each other when our powers reached their full strength. Now that she has full control of all of them? We're in uncharted territory. So, having Erithmore finally take a swing at us because they hear about our *situation* is the least of my concerns."

"I understand that, Jax," Pierce says, his tone rough. "But you have to consider the possibilities. We all want Rylee back. *Need* her back. But we must protect the people of Lumathyst, too—"

"I don't give a shit about Lumathyst!" I growl, gripping my knees. "*Nothing* matters if she doesn't wake up. Do you think for one second that I wouldn't burn this entire damned royal city to the ground if I thought it would bring her back?"

Pierce cocks an eyebrow, silently urging me to calm the fuck down.

I try.

It's impossible.

"And the people in the Obsidian City?" he challenges. "Would you throw them in the flames as well?"

I glare at him.

"You wouldn't," he answers when I cannot. "Because Rylee returning to us won't come down to a blood sacrifice." He rolls his eyes. "She's the most brilliant, strong, capable woman we've ever met. Do you think she won't snap out of whatever is holding her back?"

Tension uncoils at the hope and certainty in his voice. "She will," I say, nodding.

"She will," he echoes. "And it's up to us to ensure that this realm is at peace when she wakes. What sort of mates would we be if we allowed her to return to war and ruin?" Pierce asks, a small, broken smile on his face.

I can't return it, but I nod in understanding.

A knock on the door sounds, and Pierce crosses the room to check who's on the other side. After a few seconds, he swings the door open, and Mirren—one of our oldest, most trusted friends and Rylee's handmaiden—comes in, a tray of food in her hands.

"You will eat, Jax Lavine," she says in a stern, motherly tone. "Or I will drag you out of this room by your ear."

I press my lips together, a fleeting moment of levity dissolving in my chest as quickly as it rises.

Pierce manages a true laugh. I wonder if that's because he's so sure Rylee will return to us, where I'm riddled with nothing but doubt. I've loved very few things in my life, and each of those things has been taken from me. Hope is a dangerous game I rarely play.

Mirren places the tray on the table near the bed. "You too, Pierce."

"Understood," Pierce says.

Mirren lingers near Rylee, looking down at her with just as stern a look. "You'd better be ready for my lecture when you awaken, girl. I'm not fond of all this waiting. You're being dramatic." She turns back to me. "Eat," she demands.

"I don't take orders well." I arch a brow at her. "From anyone—"

"Oh, enough with that," she cuts me off, scooping a bread roll off the tray and holding it toward me, a look of challenge in her eyes. *"Eat."*

I take the bread, immediately biting into it to satisfy the woman.

"Good." She nods toward the food. "I want that tray empty by the time I get back."

Pierce bows deeply as she passes him on her way out of the room, and it's all I can do to force myself to take more bites.

Silence fills the space as Pierce and I eat, both of us looking to Rylee with a ridiculous hope that she'll magically wake up and chide us for staring—

Kal bursts into my room, panicked. *"Jax."*

CHAPTER 4

Immediately, I'm on my feet. Kal's wearing our Legend jacket, his cloth mask in his hand.

"What's happening?"

"Faders," Axl says, coming in right behind Kal. He pulls his hair back before securing his mask.

"Where?" I ask, anger slicing through me.

"Yours."

Shit.

I glance down at Rylee, a war tearing through me.

"We must go," Pierce implores, rounding out our group. "If we have a shot at finding . . ."

Her sister.

This is our chance to bring her in alive.

"I can't leave her here," I say, hesitation clear in my tone.

"You can't leave your city unprotected, either," Mirren chides, storming into the room as if she's about to don a mask and join us in the fray. "I will stay with her, Jax."

It's a little comfort.

"You left before," she adds.

"They were here," I say, motioning to my friends. "Maybe one of you should stay behind."

"If things were normal, of course we would," Kal says, silently pleading with me. "It's going to take all of us."

Without our powers.

Fuck. We've all been trained in combat since we could walk. But we've leaned on our powers for so long, fighting without them will be a challenge.

"It's been a week, Jax," Mirren challenges. "She hasn't awoken. The odds are she won't in the few hours you're gone. I will stay with her. I won't let anything happen to her."

"We need to go," Axl says, urgency in his tone.

"Your people, Jax," Kal adds. "They need you."

She needs me.

I want to say the words, but I can't choke them out. She sleeps, safely in my room in the palace. Mirren won't let anything happen to her, not that anyone has made an attempt in the last week, though that could be because one of us has always been with her. I can't help but worry whoever tainted the elixir will try to kill her again.

"None of us wants this," Axl presses. "Trust me. But think of how pissed she'd be if she knew we let a Fader attack go unchecked."

Fuck, he has a point. My little liar would be *livid.*

"Go," Mirren implores before taking my seat at Rylee's bedside. "She'll still be asleep when you return."

That doesn't offer much hope, either.

But she's right. They're all right.

I can't leave my people unguarded.

Rylee wouldn't want that.

I growl and grab my jacket off the back of the chair, slipping it on in a hurry before securing my mask. "Let's make this quick."

CHAPTER 5

Rylee

I don't know how long I've been on these stairs. Could be minutes, hours. It feels like an eternity. Evaluna said I can free myself from . . . wherever I'm trapped. I've tried everything I can think of, except for one possibility.

Jump.

At the far left of Evaluna's temple, there's a steep drop-off. The fall would be enough to kill me, but I'm certain I'm asleep. That none of this is actually real. It's all happening in my mind. Some post-Athanry effect of becoming immortal, or a result of holding all the Legends' powers. Either way, it's not real.

And the best way to wake up is to *fall.*

Right? I stop trying to go down the stairs and take a step toward that edge.

My nerves twist as I peer over it. It's just a dream. I'll wake up if I'm scared enough. I'll wake up.

I scoot my toes over the lip, my heart in my throat.

Please tell me I'm right. Please tell me I'm not about to fall to my death. They'll be so angry with me.

Evaluna said I need to wake up. This must be right.

I picture my mates' beautiful faces and step off the ledge.

And plummet so fast, my heart stops and restarts. The ground approaches, growing larger and larger as I pick up speed.

Shit. I was wrong.

The ground is a breath away. Will it hurt when I break every bone in my body? Will it—

I jerk awake, sucking in a sharp breath as I sit bolt upright. My head throbs, my vision blurry. Rubbing at my eyes, I do my best to slow my racing heart.

Fuck, there's an overwhelming weight against my bones I've only felt once.

Power.

Eons of undiluted power.

It swarms me, fills every inch of my soul—

She lives. She's stronger than I thought.

The voice slithers through my mind.

Thank the goddesses. She's alive. I'm going to kill her for putting us through this. Another voice.

I cringe against the thoughts, against the onslaught of emotions storming my senses—relief and anger and pride and confusion.

Those voices. I *know* them.

I peel my eyes open, heart hammering as I try to focus. I'm in Jax's room in the palace. In his bed . . . *our* bed. I blink rapidly, body trembling, eyes filling with tears.

A hand squeezes mine—Mirren.

But it's not her I'm worried about. It's the second voice.

I look to my other side and jolt so hard, my head smacks the headboard.

"Hello, little bug," Baydel says from way too close. He's sitting on the bed, almost touching me. Reflexively, I shift away.

Mirren grips my hand tighter in what I interpret as a warning.

Or maybe I'm tapping into Jax's gift and I can feel the warning from her emotions?

My four mates' unearthly powers swell inside me like ocean waves, and I can hardly breathe around them.

"Jax," I blurt. "Kal. Axl. Pierce?" It's hard to form a coherent sentence with my mind whirling so fast.

Why aren't they here?

Why did they leave me with *Baydel*?

Fear and panic swim in a rapid current swirling inside me.

My stomach roils.

"They just left," Baydel answers, curiosity rippling over his features. For once, he doesn't look at me with hatred. I don't feel any coming off him now, either, though I could be interpreting Jax's power incorrectly.

Shit. I need to get a grip.

"Where?"

"The Obsidian City," Mirren says.

"A Fader attack is underway," Baydel offers, and Mirren dares to glare at him for the briefest of seconds.

Faders.

Erin.

My mates. They're vulnerable.

Panic has me moving before I can comprehend what I'm doing. Too quickly, I throw off the covers, slide off the bed, hurry to the wardrobe, and fling it open.

All black, of course.

"What are you doing?" Baydel asks, still seated.

"They fight, *I* fight," I say, doing my best to clamp down on the power rising inside me, begging me to *fly* to them as fast as I can. "Mirren, my boots? Please?" I ask as I stare at the wardrobe filled with Jax's things.

Mirren nods, racing out of the room as I slip a too-large black jacket over the long nightgown I wear. The jacket smells like smoke and leather and all things Jax. It fills my fragmented soul with hope and clears my mind.

"Really?" Baydel asks, tilting his head. "You've been unconscious for seven days."

That fact brings me up short as Mirren hurries back, my boots in hand. I shove the thought away, slipping my shoes on just as fast, the connection to my mates feeling stretched by the distance between us. It's an itch, a painful nagging that's urging me to move faster.

"I'm fine," I say despite the dizziness threatening to lay me on my ass.

"Rylee," Mirren chides me. "You should stay here. Let the healers look at you—"

"I can't," I say over her, and I don't know what she sees in my eyes, but she stumbles back a step. For the first time since I met her, she looks afraid.

Of me?

I flash her an apologetic look, then remember decorum and dip my head to Baydel. He's still king, and the last thing I need right now is for him to pull a power card and force me to stay.

Without their powers, the Legends are weakened. The Faders could kill them.

I can't let that happen.

"I'm sorry," I say to Mirren. "Please, can you take me to a velomage?"

She nods a bit too quickly, bowing to Baydel before the two of us race out of the room.

"Pierce's backup," she says once she's led me into a stable-like building on the palace grounds, filled with the princes' conveyances—velomages and carriages alike.

"Thank you," I say.

"You owe me answers," she says as I mount the velomage.

"I know." Something sharp lodges in my chest.

She steps closer as the magic roars to life beneath my grip on the handles. "Protect them."

"I will," I say. "I promise."

I take off, hoping I can stay true to my word, but as the chaotic clash of power roils inside me, I'm not sure how I'll control it.

CHAPTER 6

Pierce

"What's our strategy?" I ask, voice lowered as we linger just outside the center square of the Obsidian City.

"To not die," Axl says in that gruff way he does—half serious, half joking.

I arch an eyebrow at him, unamused.

There's an apprehension lingering in my bones I don't recognize. A foreboding, even if a small one.

We'd faced the Faders without our powers at the Athanry from a place of pure, grief-fueled adrenaline.

Now?

We're fully aware of the missing powers we've relied on our entire lives.

And, more than ever before, we have something to lose.

"We use a split maneuver," Kal says, ever the optimist, though his eyes are full of dread as he looks on the scene happening a few blocks ahead of us.

Mayhem.

Chaos.

The Faders, clad in their signature white canvas uniforms and full-face masks, are breaking into shops that line the center square, smashing anything they can, hurting anyone who gets in their way. And, being the

Obsidian City, the Nightmare's city, his people are fighting back. They're known for their wild desires, impulsive behavior, and unflinching courage. They aren't taking the attack lightly.

"Axl, you and I can flank the right side, come up from the third block over," Kal continues, and I nod, the plan already laying a clear visual in my mind despite him not finishing. It seems I haven't lost my ability to strategize—a small comfort.

"Jax, Pierce, you two go to the left, take that street there, and sneak up on them from behind."

Jax nods, more eerily quiet than usual. There's a twinkle in his indigo eyes that sends an icy chill over the back of my neck. He's been dying to unleash his barely controlled anger since Rylee went down.

I fear for any Fader he may get ahold of tonight.

"No killing," I say immediately. The rule never stood in the past, not when they were actively trying to blow us to bits with the blasters they use, not to mention that odd substance they possessed that nullified our power whenever it touched us.

But now? How could we? After what we suspect?

"Agreed." Kal immediately supports me.

"I'll do my best." Axl shrugs.

"I make no promises," Jax says, low and cold.

Shit.

I catch his gaze, imploring. "And what if you cross that line tonight with the wrong one?" I lean forward a little on my velomage. "How are you going to tell Rylee that you killed her sister? Do you think she'll ever forgive you? Regardless of the circumstances?"

Jax glares at me, then the scene ahead of us. He turns to Kal. "We'll go left." He revs his velomage and takes the lead.

I spare Kal and Axl an encouraging nod, then take off after Jax. I'll have to stick close to his side, not out of need for protection, but to ensure he doesn't kill anyone.

We slip off our velomages as we near the scene, not wanting to give away our position. A strange feeling, certainly. Under normal circumstances, we wouldn't have bothered to be stealthy, let alone split up.

But we're not in normal circumstances, and we may never be again.

Fear slips in like a cold blade, corrupting my usual calm, calculated approach to Legend business.

This will be a challenge.

I feed off adrenaline as we creep closer, keeping to the shadows of the buildings, my muscles bracing for a fight.

Booms of magic blasters and the cries of Jax's people fill the night air. Jax and I mimic each other, falling into that rhythm we've practiced since we were young, ducking low as we approach a group of Faders converging on a legal enhancement shop—the place is known for its mind-altering teas and smoking herbs. Nothing that pushes the boundaries too much, but still enough to not be legal anywhere but the Obsidian City.

I recognize the shop owner. He's unconscious on the pavement outside his store, blood dribbling from a split lip and a gash on his head.

Anger ripples beneath my skin, ridding me of the last lingering dregs of worry.

Jax must feel it, too, because one moment, we're being quiet, careful about how we approach the five Faders currently wreaking havoc on the store, and the next, he's racing up to the closest Fader, wrapping his arm around their neck from behind.

Shit.

I leap into the fray, backhanding one Fader and landing a kick to the gut of another. Forcefully, I make my way in front of the shop, pushing back the remaining two, who are doing their best to set it ablaze.

"Fuck," Jax groans, releasing the Fader.

A fine white dust coats his face, turning the skin beneath his eyes red as he paws at it.

The Fader joins the four closing in on me as Jax stumbles forward, tears of blood streaking down his cheeks.

I spare a glance to my right, down the block, where Axl and Kal are fighting hand to hand with three Faders.

"Eight," I say to Jax, chest heaving and fists raised.

"We can take eight," he says, flashing his teeth at the five creating a horseshoe formation in front of us.

They aren't reaching for their blasters. How curious.

I'll puzzle that out later. For now—

"Took you Legends long enough," one of the Faders, a man, says. "Are you losing care for your people now that you've secured a mate to fuck whenever you want?"

A low growl comes from Jax, but I hurry to jump in.

"Where is your leader?" I ask, scanning the five before us. None of them have the slight build of the one Rylee stepped in front of at the Athanry. Maybe she's off fighting Kal and Axl? Or perhaps she's lying low after last week's disaster.

"We'll take you to her," a masculine voice says from beneath one of the Faders' masks. "In pieces!"

They converge on us as one, like fire nips at their heels.

Jax and I go back-to-back, fighting and fending off as many as we can. Fists and boots and that damned white dust fly so quickly I can't keep track. It's a small relief they don't know we're without our powers. If they did, they wouldn't keep hitting us with the concoction to try to nullify them, and they'd resort to using the blasters. Survival instincts take over, focusing on what I can defend against.

Block, punch, duck, kick.

Over and over again.

Until my muscles feel like hot rubber and my breath comes too quick. If I had my powers, I'd use my energy bands to render each of them unconscious in seconds or dive into their minds and force them to sleep. But I don't have my powers. And I've never tired this quickly before. For a split second, genuine fear snaps through me—

The butt of a magical blaster hits me in the temple. White-hot pain bursts down the left side of my face, my ears ringing.

I go down like a stone.

"Pierce!" Jax hollers, but it sounds muffled.

I blink until the black bleeds out of my vision.

Arms snake under my shoulders, and my boots drag against the cobblestone road as someone hauls me back.

They have Jax pinned to the ground. He looks feral, thrashing beneath the three Faders it's taking to subdue him.

Fuck.

I still haven't reconnected to my limbs, the mental lock broken as they drag Jax and me to the center square.

"Kal," I groan when the Fader drops me in a heap next to his unconscious body. His brown hair looks black on the back of his head, soaked in blood.

Axl is on his stomach, his wrists and ankles bound with ropes, his skin red and puckered beneath them. He hisses when the binding cuts deeper as he struggles.

Is this how we go? Powerless and weak against a rebel group?

Jax snarls as the three hold him down next to me. He looks wild, like an animal ready to rip out their throats with his teeth.

My fingers twitch, the adrenaline in my blood forcing life back into my limbs. I can't give away my hand just yet, can't let them know feeling has returned to me. I'm the only one not bound or unconscious.

Strategy.

Think.

There are eight of them and one of me.

Get Axl free first, since no one is on him.

Then Jax.

The three of us together should be able to—

"Four Legends at once." That same man from earlier speaks. "She's going to promote us. We'll get our pick of rooms in the palace." He approaches with heavy steps, then crouches and tilts his head as he pushes a blade against my cheek. He hesitates, no doubt for dramatic effect, before slicing with quick, decisive precision. I clench my jaw, refusing to react to the hot, sharp sting. He turns to look at his comrades. "They bleed the same as we do." With a satisfied grunt, he hovers over me, then cuts my face again—deeper this time, the bastard.

I hiss but hold my position. I need surprise on my side to finish this.

"Not so fucking special without your powers, are you? Amazing what a little nullifier can do." He brandishes the bloody blade, leveling it over my eyes this time.

Focusing through the pain and fear, I ready my muscles, envisioning my strike.

Going on three. One . . . two . . .

But before I can act, the Fader grunts, and the knife drops to the ground with a clatter. His eyes are wide with terror as familiar emerald bands of energy tighten around his torso, then yank him back so fast, he doesn't even have time to scream.

For a split second, I think my father has come to bail us out of this mess . . .

"Butterfly," Jax huffs before the Fader holding him down hits him in the back of the head with the butt of a blaster.

Rylee.

She's here. Looking murderous and gorgeous as ever, dressed in Jax's black jacket and . . . Is that a nightgown fluttering around her legs? I let out a ragged breath. She's awake—and she's saving our asses.

Hope and relief slam into my chest so hard, it feels like a physical blow. And then something else drives into me, a force that strikes like a lightning bolt, shattering me from the inside out. My mind clears as my body floods with my power. Bit by bit, it snaps together like the pieces of a puzzle, settling in all those empty spaces created when I gave it to Rylee.

I laugh as I grip it, taking over where she started.

I'm on my feet, shoving the Faders back while tearing through Axl's ropes with my energy bands.

The Faders holding Jax release him, whimpering and grabbing their heads as he slowly climbs to his feet.

The Nightmare's power is restored, too, judging from their cries of terror.

And Kal's, as well, because he's up and moving, his focus on Rylee, who is heading toward us with that glittering determination I love so much in her blue eyes. A roll of her wrist, and the last remaining Fader claws at their throat like they can't breathe.

I've seen her do this before—stop someone's air supply. It's her own special power.

A whistle pierces the air, and the Faders scatter in all directions, their confident bravado gone.

We should chase after them, but I can't make myself move.

My friends must feel the same, because they come to stand on either side of me, the four of us staring at our mate.

Her long blond hair is wild, hanging over her shoulders as she stares back, breathing heavily. She looks terrifyingly adorable, her skin a little pallid, as she finally closes the distance between us. We stand silently as she studies each of us in turn, shaking her head.

"Which one of you wants to explain why I woke up with *Baydel* sitting on my bed?" She cocks a brow at us.

"Uh-oh," Axl says. "We're so fucked."

CHAPTER 7

Rylee

A laugh rips from my lips at Axl's declaration, the levity spearing through the panic.

Panic at waking up with Baydel right there.

Panic when I heard they were in a battle, powerless.

Panic when I arrived and they were . . . overrun.

My incredible, half-god mates were *overrun*.

Because of me.

Because they'd sacrificed their powers to bring me back.

Guilt threatens to steal the joy of seeing them alive.

Pierce gasps, his reflexes reaching out like he's trying to catch something. Jax, Kal, and Axl flinch, too—

White-hot lightning splinters my mind, stealing the breath from my lungs. The powers I'd somehow sent back to them return in a painful rush like I've lassoed them in and yanked them back.

I topple forward. Pierce catches me, scooping me into his arms and holding me against his chest. "Rylee?"

Ocean and sun, endless thoughts and energy. Emotions. So many variations. They swarm through me, slamming into my body with such force, it's like I've hit a rock wall at full speed on a velomage.

"Sorry." My head is swimming. "I don't know how to stop them from coming back to me."

"Yet," Pierce says. "You don't know how to do it yet, my darling. We'll figure it out."

I reach up, gently touching his cheek where the Fader cut him. The wounds are partially healed.

"Your healing abilities," I say, each word difficult to get out. Damn, their power weighs a fuckton. "They're attached to your power? Not your goddess-given immortality?"

Kal comes into view, then Axl and Jax, creating a little protective circle around me that I want to live in forever.

"Not entirely," Pierce explains. "Our powers accelerate our naturally quick healing abilities. Without them . . ." He glances at the other three before looking down at me. "We'll still heal. It'll just be slower."

"I'm sorry," I say again. "We need to figure this out."

"We will," Axl says.

"We have time, love," Kal adds.

Pierce shifts me tighter against him. "The important thing is that you're back now."

Tears fill my eyes, emotion catching up to me. So much has happened.

"You're alive," Jax says, finally speaking. I meet those indigo eyes, relief uncoiling inside me. "That's all that matters."

I take a deep breath, allowing their words of assurance to soothe my sense of urgency.

"Take me home?" I practically beg. "Not to the palace," I hurry to add. "From the way Baydel spoke to me before, he'll have a whole slew of questions. I'm not ready. I need . . ." I bite my lip, trying to articulate what I can feel stretching awake inside me. "I need to be with you," I continue. "Just the five of us."

"My place is closest," Jax says, glancing around at the Faders' destruction.

I shift against Pierce, silently indicating for him to put me down.

He does, and I manage to hold myself up, despite it feeling like I have a mountain sitting between my shoulder blades. "Your powers . . ." I sigh. "Are *heavy*."

A small cry sounds from behind us and down the road, effectively stopping all plans to leave so quickly.

"The *people*," I say, coming back to reality. "Of course, we'll go home after we've seen to their needs."

Jax locks gazes with me, intense emotion and pride radiating there. He steps into my space, dragging a knuckle down my cheek. "I can stay," he says, his voice softer than the Nightmare's ever is. "They can take you home and then—"

"No," I cut him off. "These are *my* people, too." I do my best to hush their powers roaring inside me. It's as if being right next to their original owners makes them struggle and tug and fight to return to them.

I get it.

I just need a minute to figure this all out.

I try to convince the powers of that, as if they're sentient creatures roaming beneath my skin and along the four mating bonds I have with the Legends.

"I want to help the people," I continue. "I'm fine, I promise. If I feel like I'm going to pass out again, I'll tell you."

Jax seems keen to argue, so I turn to Kal. "Let's take the left side of the block," I say, then glance to Axl. "You and Pierce take the right." I look up at Jax. "You take the middle. We'll work our way down, helping where we can. When we're done, we'll go home."

Jax dips down, kissing me quick and hard and branding. I melt at the touch. My connection with him flares to life in a way I've never felt before. Pride and love and undiluted passion pulse down that bond, his emotions mixing with mine until I'm not sure how to decipher which is which.

"I missed you, butterfly," he whispers against my lips, then pulls back and holds my gaze for a moment before stepping away. "You heard our mate," he says to the group. "Let's get to work."

Anger and exhaustion settle heavily in my bones as we reach Jax's home after several hours of helping shopkeepers and injured citizens. The familiar smell of leather and smoke hits me the minute we step inside. It's welcoming in a way that clogs my throat with emotion. I feel like I've been away for a very long time.

I'm the first to head down Jax's staircase, wanting nothing more than a good soak in his massive tub.

She's alive.

Kal's voice flits through my mind, quick and soft as a welcoming breeze. It stops me short on the last stair.

Are you listening to us? Pierce's voice is direct and clearer somehow, as if his power knows who its true wielder is.

I take the last step, turning to face them as they follow in behind me. We linger in Jax's living room, and I close my eyes, focusing on the connection to Pierce that sears inside me right now.

Yes. I visualize my voice skittering along that connection of ours, pushing that word into his mind.

A smile stretches his full lips, his eyes lighting up as he steps closer to me. Goddess, he's so handsome. I can't help but reach up and touch him, sliding my fingers over the smooth brown skin of his cheek and into his curly black hair. "Well done," he says. "Are you able to shut us out?"

"I'll try." I draw my hand back, focusing. He told me once before it's like mentally closing doors on all the voices in your mind, but since there are only four of them, I don't have as many doors.

My fucking beautiful kitten. I'm so glad she's back. I don't know what I would've done without her. Axl.

My fault. Jax's voice is jaded, cold. *I should've checked the elixir. I should've known. She's struggling with our powers, and it's because I couldn't live without her.*

I cringe against the emotions that storm my senses—grief and anger, relief and love. Each is stronger than the next. I stumble back, just a step, as if the physical distance will give me some breathing room.

Oh no.

What's wrong?

Please don't break.

Fuck.

I can no longer separate their thoughts. I hold up a hand, silently signaling I need a minute, as they each come for me.

I concentrate on my breathing. Focusing on the rise and fall of my chest, the way the air feels cool as I inhale and warm as I exhale. In and out. Over and over.

I don't know how long I do this.

I only know that in doing so, I manage to close those heavy doors on their thoughts, shoving their emotions behind them, too. Though a small fraction of the emotion seems to slip through—a soft tingle against my skin that I'm not sure how to fully subdue.

Maybe I can't.

Pierce told me even Jax has a hard time completely shutting it out.

I have so much to learn.

Thankfully, Kal and Axl's powers are different. Easier to shift and maneuver. I can feel the air around us, from my own power, and I have this sense of the sky, like a whisper begging me to come play. And then I can pinpoint every amount of water in this house—the liquid flowing through hidden pipes, the moisture beading on the roof in the cool midnight.

It's incredible, the vastness of their powers.

Terrifying, for sure, but incredible.

"I'm okay," I say, finally opening my eyes.

They haven't moved, and each of them sighs, as if they'd been doing the breath work with me.

I smile at them, feeling clearheaded for the first time since I woke up. I know that I won't be able to pause and do a breathing session every time I get overwhelmed. I know we need to figure out a better plan on how to manage this, but right now? I'm just happy to be with them.

And now that the powers are coaxed to sleep, I *feel.*

Their bonds—each of them is connected to me in a way that's so much more significant than they were before. The Choosing ceremony, the Athanry, the process of becoming immortal—they strengthened the mating bonds in ways I've yet to understand.

But they're there, each of them, like golden beacons that flow freely between us, strengthening and connecting us in a way that feels *significant*.

And demanding.

There's a silent need pulsing along each of these golden bonds.

And it grows stronger by the minute.

"I'm okay," I say again when none of them look convinced. Anticipation trembles down my spine as desire ramps up, overtaking all other thought.

I'm immortal. I survived. But I was taken from them and them from me before we could fully celebrate this accomplishment. Despite everything else, I'm *here*. With them. And we get to spend forever together. The significance of that settles along our mating bonds, and I can't stop the burst of excitement that makes my heart skip.

"I'd like a bath," I say, my voice feeling so much more my own now. It's almost intoxicating to come back to myself in this way. Because that hasn't changed—my need for them, my love for them.

"Of course," Kal answers first. "We'll be here when you're done."

I arch an eyebrow at him. "What part of that statement did you interpret as me wanting to be alone?" I smile at him suggestively, crossing the space to run my fingers over his broad chest.

It's wonderful to have the powers sleeping. It gives me a sense of control I've been desperate for.

"Rylee," Kal chides softly, stroking my hand. "You've been unconscious for seven days—"

"I'm fine."

"We don't want to push you too far," Axl says, but he's grinning down at me in challenge.

"I won't break," I fire back. "You know I won't."

"But you did," Jax says, and it's all I can do not to flinch. "You did break. Because of us. Because of our power."

"I know. I can't begin to dissect everything that happened. And I don't want to."

"Darling," Pierce says. "We need to."

"I know we need to, but you don't understand . . ." I touch my throat, then slide my fingertips down my sternum and outward across my breasts, lingering there as I look directly at each of them. "I need you more." And I do. Like I need air to breathe.

Kal flashes a grin before leading me toward the bathing chamber. Warmth radiates in my heart as I lean against the doorframe and watch him start the water. His blue eyes meet mine, comforting and caring as ever, and my body tightens at the flash of desire in them.

I glance over my shoulder at my other mates. Axl's long black hair is wild over his bronze shoulders, and his muscles are on full display, his Legend jacket already shed and tossed over one of Jax's sofas.

Jax's jacket is still on, his hands shoved in his pockets, his moonlight skin making his indigo eyes more stark. He's contemplative as he watches me as if I might crumble any second.

"Can't you feel it?" I ask, suddenly worried they *can't* feel it. That they don't feel the bonds like I do. That I'll always need them more than they need me because I'm a Chosen, not a half-god prince—

"You mean that undeniable instinct to claim you right here and now?" Axl asks, his raspy voice cutting through my thoughts. "Fuck yeah, we can feel that."

His words silence my doubt.

"We just don't want to overwhelm you," Pierce adds.

"You won't." I sound confident, but I have no way of knowing beyond this instinct driving me. "I know everything didn't go as planned, but I'm here, and I love you. All of you. For now, can't that be enough?"

"That's more than enough," Kal says.

"Good. I can't hide it from you. And I won't waste time pretending that I don't want all of you. I do. Right now. No waiting." I turn to enter the bathing chamber, but I stop, realizing how that sounds. I glance over my shoulder apologetically. "But only if you want me. Don't follow me in here if you're truly not comfortable. I'll never force any of you to be with me."

Axl rolls his eyes, already hauling his shirt over his head and tossing it to the side. "That's the most ridiculous shit you've ever said."

Pierce slides his jacket off and lays it neatly over the back of one of Jax's couches. "Honestly, it's like you don't know us at all," he teases, brushing by me as he enters the bathing chamber, his passing touch sending chills over my flesh.

Kal smiles softly at me from where he's near the bath.

And of course, it's Jax I'm holding my breath over. We had so little time together before the Athanry. And his emotions before . . . He was so angry.

"Reckless little butterfly," he says, stopping in front of me. He gently grips my chin, his long, lithe fingers tipping my head back. "So eager to put your life at risk again?"

I shiver at the intensity in his gaze. "It's my life to risk," I counter, giving him the same energy. "And last time I checked, I have each of your powers on top of mine. Maybe it's you four who will be at risk from me losing control."

The reality of that statement catches up with me, a sliver of doubt creeping over the insatiable need to be with them.

Jax's grip on my chin tightens, a slick smile shaping his lips. "Now that's something I can't wait to see."

Warmth floods beneath my skin, adding to the ache in my core. Still, I don't look away. "You haven't said it."

He tilts his head in question.

"That you want me." I swallow hard. He hasn't said it. And I don't know why, but I need to hear it from him.

Jax's eyes slide along my face, tracing the curve of my jaw still in his grip, before he moves that hand down and around my throat. My pulse skitters as he strokes his thumb over my skin. He holds me there, anticipation squeezing my lungs tighter with each second he doesn't answer.

Push and pull. That's me and the Nightmare. Fight and flee and fight some more. I half expect him to kiss me instead of answering, but then he parts his lips.

"That's one thing you'll never have to worry about," he says. "I want you more than I want my next breath. And that's *before* the primal mating bond instincts."

I whimper at the declaration, at the kiss he seals it with. And I damn near drop to my knees when he smiles at me—*my* smile. Not the Nightmare's terrifying signature, just Jax's.

He passes me and enters the bathing chamber. Butterflies take flight in my stomach as I close my eyes for a moment, then follow a breath later.

The chamber is dark, save for a few candles that I'm guessing Kal lit, the golden light flickering against the black stone that makes up the room.

The soaking tub is laid into the floor, more a small pool than a tub, really. Axl, Pierce, and Kal are already in the water, steam wafting around them. They've each taken up a corner of the space, and I'm struck with the memory of the Athanry—them moving to the corners as I stepped through a liquid starlight door . . .

And *died*.

My chest tightens, my breath quickening. I focus on the purring bonds inside me. Listen to the needy demands of connection.

My mates.

I need to touch, kiss, and love my mates. Strengthen and solidify those bonds to whatever end.

Everything else will sort itself out later.

Still, my fingers shake as I rid myself of Jax's jacket, then the nightgown I woke up in, letting them pool in a pile at my feet as Jax gets into the tub, taking up the free corner.

I step in, sighing with pleasure at the hot water against my skin.

I walk until I'm in the middle and bend my knees slightly to dip my shoulders, leaning back to soak my hair, too. When I tip my head up, I glance at each of them.

"Why so distant?" I ask, worry creeping into the anticipation flaring in my core.

"Your choice," Kal says. "It's always your choice with us." He nods to his friends. "Whoever you want first."

My heart expands in my chest, bringing a smile to my lips. "And if I want all of you?"

"Don't tease us." Axl groans.

"I'm not."

"Are you sure, darling?"

"Yes," I answer without a hint of hesitation. "I told you, these connections, these new bonds inside me are almost painful with need."

That word—*painful*—has them all moving toward me, as if pulled by the very bonds I mentioned.

"Say it again," Jax demands, always needing clarification before he allows himself to let go.

"I want all of you." The words come out on a rushed breath.

"Who wants to make our mate come first?" Jax poses the question to the group, and I swear I melt.

"Me," Axl says faster than anyone else, gliding through the water until he can reach me.

I gasp as he draws me toward him, his powerful arms wrapping around me the same time his mouth crashes against mine. It's a homecoming, this kiss. Filled with passion and love and his playful energy I can never get enough of.

"Axl," I say against his lips as his hands roam over my body, the warm water making his touch slick.

"Missed you." He dips his hand between my thighs. His fingers brush over my heat, teasing that sensitive bundle of nerves that's desperate for attention.

"Yes." I breathe the word, rocking into his dominant touch as he strokes and circles my aching center.

"So close already, kitten?" he asks, drawing back enough to look down at me. "Wait till you feel her," he says to the group. "So slick and hot for us. Needy little mate."

I can't argue. Can't respond. Not when he's sliding two fingers inside me, stretching me in all the right ways. I rock against his hand, driven on pure need as I chase the release building inside me.

"Stop toying with her," Jax demands. "Let her come."

"Says the king of edging?" Axl fires back, a teasing grin on his lips.

"Play nice," Kal adds. "She has a long night ahead of her."

I tremble, from their words, from the way their eyes are on me as Axl pumps his fingers, the heel of his palm teasing me. His other hand comes up to cup the back of my neck, tilting my head. "Impatient bastards," Axl says before he slants his mouth over mine at the same time he increases the pressure between my thighs, plucking the last string that sends me right over the edge.

"Axl!" I gasp against his kiss, waves of pleasure rippling down my spine as my orgasm rips through me. I've barely caught my breath before he gently pulls his hand away, grinning down at me with a prideful look in his eyes.

"I love watching you come like that," Kal says from beside me.

"Quite riveting," Pierce agrees.

"My turn." Jax draws me in close, claiming my mouth with a searing kiss. His hands are possessive as they roam down my back, dipping to cup my ass as he lifts me.

Immediately, I wrap my legs around his hips, trembling when his hard length strokes my oversensitive flesh.

This. I've needed this. Their touch, their support, all of it.

Pierce joins us, and his lips find my back, kissing across my shoulder and neck as his hands shift my hair out of the way. He plants a kiss on the cloud mark at the base of my skull, and my heart stutters. Thought empties out of my head as he positions himself behind me, rubbing himself through my wetness, then teasing my ass with his slippery, hard length.

Sandwiched between the two, it would be easy to lose myself entirely, especially after what Axl just did to me, but I manage to draw my lips away from Jax, reaching for Kal, who's right there, ready to kiss me.

I moan against the feel of him, his bond flickering to life inside me. His power races down that invisible thread and back again without my permission, the sensation like a giant wave rushing toward the shore.

"Rylee," Kal groans against my mouth.

"I—" My words cut into a gasp as Jax spears himself inside me, no more teasing. I tremble at the way he fills me, my breaths switching to a moan as Pierce does the same seconds later. "*Yes.*" I breathe the word, their connections inside me sparking in a way that feels like I'm incinerating from the inside out.

I turn my head, my eyes lust-hazed, my mind swimming with the powers I can't keep dormant when they're touching me like this.

"Axl," I say, smiling as he kisses me. "Do you like this?" I reach my hand through the warm water, finding him hard and aching as I wrap my fingers around him. I concentrate on the feel of him pumping into my hand, center myself on that bond between us, so playful, so adventurous, and grip the power radiating there. The water, controlled by his magic I hold, yields to me, swirling around his cock in time with my strokes.

"Fuck," he growls. "Yes. That feels so good."

His words make my already warm skin even hotter, or that could be the way Jax and Pierce are fucking me at the same time at a perfect pace, one thrusting as the other pulls back.

I'm a well of sensation and power and bonds, all melting together to create something I may never survive.

I don't care. It feels too right, too good, too *everything*.

"Kal," I whimper, my core clenching around Jax as he pumps into me, keeping rhythm with Pierce. "Please," I say, parting my lips and flicking my eyes down to where his body disappears beneath the water.

He shudders, moving to the other side of us, his cock brushing my jaw as he climbs onto the shallow ledge.

"You sure?" he asks.

I suck him into my mouth in answer. His groan is everything, sending tingles down my spine.

My thighs clench around Jax's hips, Pierce holding me up from behind as I stroke Axl and suck on Kal. The four of them consuming me in this way, all at once, our bonds blazing with passion, sends me nearly into madness. My Legends of Chaos, indeed.

I could die here—*again*—and be happy.

But where's the fun in that?

I want to live.

I want to live with them forever.

The certainty of that snaps through me, a welcome conviction that makes me feel stronger, more powerful than ever before.

I moan around Kal's length, relaxing my jaw as much as possible as he pumps into my mouth.

"Fucking look at you," Kal groans. "Taking all of us at once. Our mate."

"Perfection," Pierce adds, his word short and tense as he pumps into that tight space, driving me right up to the edge again.

"Made for us," Axl says, thrusting into my strokes, trembling as I keep that water swirling around him.

"You love this, don't you?" Jax asks, his tone demanding. "Love us ruining you. All at once."

All I can do is moan my answer, each of them consuming me in a way that feels like an obliteration. We work so well together. We fit so well together. It's no wonder I was picked for them and them for me.

Their powers bounce and shift, radiating down the bonds with more ferocity the closer they bring me to the edge. The longer they keep me dancing on it.

I don't know how much more I can take.

It's all too much and not enough.

Kal's thrusts increase in speed, his need driving mine, all of ours. Everything speeds up, my head spinning from the pleasure building like a storm beneath my skin.

"I'm coming," Kal warns, and I shiver as he spills into my mouth. I swallow him down, then gasp for breath as he gently pulls out.

"Fuck, that was hot," Axl growls, spilling into my hand, his warmth quickly washed away by the water.

"Oh my *goddess*," I say, my head falling back against Pierce's chest as he and Jax unleash themselves on me, their pace quickening.

I can do nothing but hang on as they splinter my being with pleasure that comes in waves. I clench around them both, moaning with release as they both find theirs inside me. It's an undoing, an unraveling.

Power soars down the bonds, slamming into them so hard, Kal and Axl stumble back a few feet. Jax and Pierce hold on to me but flinch at the onslaught. Their powers are returned, the act feeling like a release of its own, a deep breath after being underwater for too long.

Immediately, I feel lighter, like the mountain on my chest has lifted. I can breathe fully. Those golden bonds inside me purr with satisfaction.

"I'm . . . sorry," I say through my heaved breaths as Pierce and Jax gently slip out of me.

"It's all right," Pierce says, softly kissing my neck. *You've done nothing wrong.* He speaks the latter directly into my mind.

Axl coaxes the water around us to swirl in gentle waves, flicking his fingers with a smile on his lips.

Kal levitates out of the water, soars to the other side of the room, and wraps a towel around his hips. Watching him fly, the joyful look on his face, is *everything*.

And then there's a wave of warmth that radiates inside my soul, a pulsing of contentment washing over my entire being. Jax's power. The other side of it. No nightmares or terrors, just happiness. Safety. All the things he knows I need to feel right now.

"I—"

I'm crushed by a weight that steals my words. Their powers snap back to me like a string stretched too tightly. I grit my teeth but manage to hold on to my senses this time.

Am I getting used to it? This uncontrollable back-and-forth?

I shake my head, noting the pool of water around us has gone still without Axl playing with it. I can no longer feel Pierce in my mind or Jax's calm washing over me. And Kal, he's rooted to the floor, but a supportive smile still shapes his lips.

"Tomorrow," I say, looking at each of them, their sated, loving expressions doing everything to keep reality at bay. "I promise, I'll be ready to focus on everything tomorrow." I catch my breath, slipping into my best *please* face. "Can we just have the rest of tonight?"

"That's not fair," Axl says as he hauls me against him, hugging me like he never wants to let me go. "You can't use that look. I'm helpless against it."

"Good to know," I tease, resting my head against his chest.

"Tomorrow," Pierce says.

"Thank you," I whisper, exhaustion encircling me as they take turns washing me—my hair, my arms, legs, body. It's almost ritualistic, with the silence settling around us, filled with everything we're not discussing.

And by the time I'm clean and rinsed, dried off, and we're all settling into Jax's bed, I know there's really only one thing I can say right now with any sort of certainty.

"I love you," I whisper into the dark. "All of you."

They echo the sentiment, and I hold fast to the assurance as I allow sleep to take me, hoping with everything in me that I don't wake up tomorrow on that endless staircase to find this has all been a dream.

CHAPTER 8

Jax

I've never known happiness like this—genuine, soul-filling joy.

It's foreign to me.

And yet, I know what it feels like to lose it, to lose *her*.

I never want that to happen again.

The thought keeps me from sleep. Propels me out of bed and up to my top-floor balcony. Rylee holds my power again, so I can't feel the stars like I used to—their energy fueling my power, like the sun does for Kal, or the ocean for Axl, or knowledge for Pierce—but something about looking up at the midnight blanket calms me.

A warm sensation slides down my spine, and I can't stop my smile.

"You should be asleep, butterfly," I say, turning to find Rylee padding barefoot across the balcony toward me. She's wearing one of my black shirts and nothing else, looking like temptation personified.

Except for her eyes, which are filled with fear and shadowed by dark circles.

I hurry to set my drink on the table near the couches lining the balcony and immediately cup her cheeks between my hands.

"What's wrong?" I ask, hating that I don't know. Hating that I can't even begin to understand what she's been through.

She shakes her head. "I'm okay. Just a nightmare."

I shift my hold on her, gently dragging her backward and into my lap as we settle on the nearest couch. "Tell me?"

She doesn't have to. I don't know if she trusts me enough with certain parts of herself. Everything has happened so fast between us, and she's kept secrets before, understandably. And yes, she keeps choosing me, choosing all of us, but there are so many pieces of us left unexplored. *Untested.*

A rope wraps around my chest and squeezes tighter the longer she remains silent.

She trembles in my lap, and I draw her closer. I can't tell if she's cold or if the nightmare still has hold of her.

"Why should I tell you?" she finally asks, her voice light as she shifts to look me in the eyes. She rubs her hand along my chest. "So the real Nightmare can chase away the others?" Her smile is gentle, almost sad.

I capture her hand against my chest, holding it there. "I will gladly destroy anything that brings you pain."

She blows out a breath, blinking back tears as she wraps her arms around me and lays her head against my shoulder.

I lean my cheek against hers, holding her tight.

"When I was asleep . . ." she starts, not moving from her position. "Not just now, but this whole time . . ."

"Seven days." I fill the space for her.

"During that time, everything *felt* real." She flinches, and adrenaline courses through my veins, sharpening my instinct to protect her. "I was trapped in Evaluna's temple. Stairs with no end. I couldn't get to you and the others. I spoke with your mother." She shrugs. "At the time, I thought it was a continuation of the Athanry."

"And now?"

"Now I don't know. It had to be just a nightmare, right? Maybe what Evaluna told me was all in my head, too."

I swallow hard. "What did she tell you?"

Her features grow severe. "That war is coming."

That adrenaline in my blood prickles. I smooth my hand along her cheek. "A nightmare. I hate that you endured that while asleep."

She huffs. "I would've much preferred to dream about you and the others the entire time."

I grin at her, brushing a soft kiss against her lips before pulling back. "What about tonight? Did you dream of the temple?"

She swallows hard. "No," she admits, tucking closer. "Tonight, I dreamed of my sister. She had a knife. Sank it into my back."

I flinch at the visual painted in my mind—it was *my* blades that hurt her, not her sister's.

"I never should've thrown those blades."

"I would've," she says, not taking her eyes off me. "If any one of you was threatened. I would do anything to stop it."

She's releasing me of blame, but I don't accept it. Her mercy is undeserved.

"Are you ready to talk about her?" I ask.

Her eyes gauge mine, studying.

"I don't know." She tilts her head. "You're not angry with me." It's a statement, not a question.

I gently tug some of her long blond hair with my free hand. "Reading my emotions, butterfly?"

"Yes. I think? It's confusing."

"No one expects you to immediately understand and control our powers," I assure her. "We've had our whole lives to explore the depths of them, to connect with them, partner with them. You . . . you're on a much quicker learning curve."

She laughs, and I swear I fall for her a little more in that moment. "I've been on a steep learning curve since you called my number at the Choosing ceremony."

"Do you regret it?" The vulnerable question slips out before I can stop it.

A crease forms between her eyebrows. "Not for a second," she says. "How can you ask me that?"

I shrug, looking away from her to the stars blanketing the sky. "You died." The words choke out of me. "And I don't believe I'm worth all the pain I've brought to your world." The admission stings, but it's difficult to hide things from her anymore.

"Don't you dare say that," she says, gripping my chin and forcing me to look at her. "You're worth *everything*. You and the others make me feel alive. You Choosing me is the first time in my entire life that I've felt complete. Like I'm finally where I'm meant to be. And I would do all of it . . . the trials, the Athanry, dying . . . I would do it a hundred times over if being with all of you was the end result."

A knot forms in my throat. I feel my power spiral around the bond connecting us, a feverish sort of pursuit that has my gut clenching. Shit, she's angry and hurt and loves me so fucking much. I can feel it all for a split second before the power snaps back to her.

"I love you," I say, smoothing my hands up and down her back, trying to calm the storm of emotions inside her.

She sucks in a sharp breath, visibly swallowing as she nods. "I love you, Jax. I'm sorry about the power . . . I can't . . . I don't know why that happens."

"I have a guess," I say. "It seems to snap back to us when you're angry or when you think we're in danger." Like at the battle right after she woke up the first time or earlier tonight, when she found those Faders surrounding us. "Or," I continue, "when you're out of control, completely letting go." Like when we were all with her tonight in my bathing chamber.

A subtle flush rakes over her cheeks, and I've never wished for my power back so badly, if only to feed off that desire churning in her eyes.

She dips down, kissing me. Slowly, softly, no urgency in it.

I hold her tighter against me, savoring the safety in this kiss.

She's alive.

She's with us.

Despite the shit show waiting for us when we crash back to reality. Nothing else matters. Whatever we have to deal with, we will.

And the goddesses themselves will have to deal with my wrath if they try to take her from me again.

CHAPTER 9

Rylee

"Now look to the left, please." Dalfon Faras, the top Occuli healer employed by the kings, gently turns my head in the direction he wants.

I shift my focus to a wardrobe on the left wall, but it takes everything inside me not to keep looking at him.

When we first entered Jax's rooms in the palace after we returned this afternoon—at the kings' beckoning—to find this guy waiting for us, I thought I might crawl out of my skin. The idea of letting one of the ancient conjurors touch me with those green flames was as appealing as undergoing the Athanry again.

But when Dalfon manifested the flames from his palms, they weren't green. His are a cerulean blue and glittering silver. When he drags them against my skin, they don't burn like the green ones did when I was cornered by one of the kings' Occuli in the Ruby Aire library. These feel cool, tingling, like the flow of blood after circulation has been cut off.

Dalfon has solid black eyes, the signature of an Occuli, and wears the customary purple robes, but his face is soft. Approachable, even. I don't know how to explain it, but his disposition is less harsh than the other Occuli I've encountered, though he's the first healing Occuli I've met.

"No offense," I say, careful to keep looking to the left as he manipulates his blue flames to narrow and focus the light toward my eyes. "But I didn't know Occuli knew that word."

"Which word?" he asks, his tone flat, as if he only has access to some of his more basic emotions. There's still a trace of the gravelly otherworldliness in his voice, but it's not as imposing as the kings' Occuli.

"Please," I answer, hoping I'm not offending the conjuror, especially since his focus is on me. He could easily command his magic to put me to sleep in seconds.

A shiver races down my spine at the thought, and the sleeping mate bonds awaken inside me, along with the collective power attached to them.

I breathe, turning inward as I coax the powers to calm. I've started visualizing my mates' powers as synonymous with their mating bonds inside me. It's the only way I can keep them in control, so I'm running with it, even though I'm not certain that's how it works.

Dalfon drops his palm, extinguishing the blue flame. I shift where I sit on the edge of Jax's bed. "You have not had much exposure to the whole of Occuli, yet you make a sweeping assumption about my kind?" There's no malice in his tone, no tension in his body language, and of course, I can't read his eyes because they're pools of black.

"I'm sorry," I hurry to say, guilt an oily grime beneath my skin.

How many times have I wanted to rip someone's head off for making assumptions about the Ashlanders? And here I am, doing the same thing because a few of the ancient conjurers *scared* me during the Choosing months.

"I meant no disrespect—"

"Of course you did," he cuts me off, his tone more casual. "There are many Occuli across the realms, most in Silvac, but many here in Lumathyst," he says, his long purple robes billowing about him as he shifts some things he'd placed on the bed next to me—small glass vials, herbs, and tonics. "And your first interaction with them wasn't a good one. I can respect that. But don't fault us all."

"I won't," I say, my stomach twisting. "I apologize. Genuinely."

"You don't have to apologize for anything," Kal grumbles from where he waits impatiently in one of the armchairs across the room. Pierce and Axl sit on a small sofa next to it, and Jax lingers against the wall near the door, his eyes never far from me.

"Yes, I do," I fire back, fastening him with a stern look. "I do," I repeat, then shake my head as Dalfon finishes gathering his effects, slipping the items into the deep pockets of his robes. "I need to do better," I say, more to myself than them.

"You're doing wonderfully," Pierce argues.

"Yeah." Axl nods his agreement. "Don't feel bad because the healer got his feelings hurt."

"My feelings are not hurt," Dalfon says. "It's quite difficult to do that, actually."

"I don't want to be the sort of person who assumes things about our people based on a few bad experiences."

"And that's the key, isn't it?" Dalfon asks.

"What is?"

"Figuring out what type of queen you want to be."

I swallow what feels like a rock lodged in my throat. The realization of just how big this world is, and how little I actually know about it, hits me in the chest. I somehow feel heavier, even though the powers inside me are already sinking me like a stone.

Queen.

I'm going to be queen.

"She'll be the perfect queen for Lumathyst," Kal says without hesitation.

My eyes soften at him, then at the others nodding their agreement.

"I won't be," I say as I stand. "Unless I work at it." I turn to Dalfon. "I will do better, and I hope you accept my apology for the assumption. The Legends told me how you cared for me while I slept. I can't thank you enough for that."

"I do accept it." Dalfon dips his head. "And it's my turn to apologize to you, your highness, for in the time I cared for you, I couldn't rouse you."

I smile and shake my head. "That wasn't your fault."

He returns my smile—sort of. His expressions are as flat as his voice. "Your vitals are operating at regular levels. If you get headaches, which are common after being unconscious for so long, take the herbs I've left you."

I nod my thanks to him.

"And send word for me if you encounter anything strange." He heads toward the hallway. "It has been so long since a new immortal was made," he continues as he opens the door. "We must be open to all possibilities."

I'm about to respond, but he bows deeply and leaves. For a moment, we stand in silence, staring at the closed door. Then, an overwhelming wave of exhaustion hits me, and I slump down on the bed, feeling the full, overbearing weight of not only my mates' powers but the daunting prospect of what it will mean to be queen.

"Are you okay?" Pierce crosses the room to take my hands in his.

"I'm just . . . I'm overwhelmed."

"We know," Kal offers from where he sits.

"And out of control," I add. "I have no idea how to deal with your powers or even use them properly."

Jax slides his hand down my back before shifting away, giving Pierce space.

"We have time to sort it out," Pierce assures me. "It's a problem, but one we can solve."

I smile up at him. The Mind, ever excited about a challenge.

"Do we have time, though?" I ask, hope building inside me. "With the attack yesterday . . ."

"We have time," he says. "The Faders haven't increased in their numbers. Haven't shown a motive other than destruction and a general hate for all things royal."

I blow out a breath. I still need to tell them about Erin. But we're in the palace, and it doesn't feel safe to talk about anything here.

"Are we done here? Can we go someplace . . ." I lower my voice to a whisper. "Soundproof."

"We—"

A knock on the door sounds, startling me. Pierce's power alerts, weaving inside me in one quick blink.

She's been awake for two days and hasn't sought us out? I'm going to kill her.

Happy tears spring to my eyes as I squeal. I drop Pierce's hands, his power settling deeper at the loss of touch as I race to the door.

"Rylee." Kal says my name cautiously, rising from the chair as if he can stop me. "You don't know who that is."

I make it to the door in a blink, faster than I've ever moved before, and throw it open.

"You have *some* nerve not sending for us the second you woke up!" Ivy chides immediately.

She stomps into the room, her long black hair falling in waves over her shoulders, her dark eyes pinned on me. I throw my arms around her.

She embraces me back. "I could kill you for scaring me like that," she whispers.

I draw away, releasing her to grab hold of Layce. She looks equally concerned and relieved, her mouth trembling as she holds back tears.

"You had us worried," Layce says before letting me go. "But we never gave up on you."

"I almost did," Mirren says, her tone filled with ice as Ivy and Layce move to give her room. "One more day. That's all I was giving you before I smothered you with one of those pillows." She nods to Jax's made bed, but there is genuine relief in her eyes.

"I missed you, too, Mirren," I say, hugging her.

She awkwardly pats my back before shoving away from me. "No embracing," she says, straightening her shirt.

I laugh, my heart filled with so much love and joy now that my family is all together in one room.

Well, almost my entire family.

My shoulders drop.

"We need to talk," I say to all of them.

"You're damn right we do," Ivy says.

"For one," Layce says, a tease in her tone, "you held out on us for *months*. The clothes you have access to now." She shakes her head. "I've already lifted six dresses, and no one has even batted an eye."

I laugh, Kal doing the same at my side.

"We already told you both," Kal says. "As the future queen's ladies-in-waiting, you're welcome to whatever you want."

"All you have to do is ask," Pierce adds.

"You made them my ladies-in-waiting?"

"We requested the positions," Ivy answers instead.

I swallow hard. Of course I want them with me, need my friends by my side on this journey, but . . .

If our enemies see how much they mean to me, they'll be at risk. They already were, just from their association with me, but now? There's so much more to lose.

"I feel like dinner in the Ruby Aire is called for?" Kal offers.

I nod, thankful for him keeping me on track.

We need to talk. All of us, including Layce and Ivy.

"Please—"

Another knock on the door cuts me off, and foreboding skitters through me at the wall of power I detect on the other side of the door—unstable, heavy, and sharp. It's so much more distinguishable to me now that I've been awake a while and have grown more accustomed to bearing my mates' gifts.

"Baydel," I whisper.

The powers inside me lurch to life all at once, causing me to gasp and stumble back a bit, as if someone has lassoed an invisible rope around my hips and yanked.

Jax is behind me, steadying me, before nodding to Axl.

Shhh. I mentally hush the powers, doing my best to stroke them, calm them. The bonds and their assigned powers feel like four ever-moving rivers of energy, thick, powerful, and with no bottom in sight.

"Ahh," Baydel says as Axl opens the door. "Having a reunion, are we, little bug?"

Ugh, I hate that nickname.

I bow to him as my friends do, lower than the princes.

"We need to see you and our sons," Baydel says, not bothering to step inside. "My study," he continues. "Now." He turns without another word.

Such a power move.

I resist the urge to scoop up buckets from the powerful rivers inside me, in case I need to drown Baydel with their contents.

I clench my fists in an effort to get a grip.

He's not threatening me or them.

He may have detested me in the beginning, done everything he could to get me to not choose them in the end, but he failed. I'm theirs now. Immortal and slated to be queen.

He'll have to respect that now.

Then why do I feel chilled to the bone as we silently say goodbye to my friends and head up to Baydel's study? The sensation is so much, it's hard to put the powers to sleep. They're begging to rise, to consume, to fill me so much there won't be room for fear.

But I stop it, slam door after door closed inside me.

I can't let the kings know I house their sons' powers.

Not until we have a plan.

So, I remain quiet, chin held high as we find the four kings in Baydel's study.

"What's going on?" Kal asks his father, Jullian, the most approachable of all the kings.

We all naturally gravitate to the side of the study Jullian is on. Baydel and Lucas, Axl's father, are near Baydel's desk. Pierce's father, Brooks, lounges in an armchair across the room.

Baydel grins expectantly. Renewed dread trickles down my spine. He's up to something.

"Now that your Chosen is awake and able, we're here to explain the terms of the Kings' List," Baydel says, his smile stretching.

"The what?" Jax snaps.

Baydel takes a seat in the massive throne-like chair behind his desk.

"Honestly, son," Baydel says. "Do you think the Choosing ceremony and the Athanry are all that is required for ascension?"

My blood runs cold.

"What are you talking about?" Jax asks.

Baydel brings his hands together in a point, drawing out the moment because he can. Because he loves to be the center of attention. Loves being the one with all the information. "The goddesses made their Choosing list, their requirements. Did you honestly believe we would abdicate our thrones to you without making a list of our own?" He shuffles through the contents of an opened drawer, pulling out a Choosing invitation and flipping it over to the back.

I glance at it, eyes wide at the shimmering golden script etched into the black cardstock. Writing that most certainly hadn't been on Ivy's real invitation, so definitely not on my forged one.

The world shifts under my feet. My head swims, the bonds crackling to life inside me, the powers pounding on the flimsy wooden doors I've constructed to keep them contained.

Pierce points at the writing on the back of the invitation. "This wasn't here before."

"Because it didn't need to be," Baydel explains. "We magically imbued these terms, ensuring they only appear if the Athanry is successfully completed by a Chosen." He huffs a laugh. "We were starting to wonder if it ever *would* occur."

I swallow hard.

"You're joking," Axl practically snarls, snatching up the invitation. He squints, reading the lines there. "Another list?"

"Gotta be done, son," Lucas says to Axl, his tone casual like he's chatting about tonight's dinner menu.

Brooks nods slowly from where he sits.

"Of course, we want to give you the thrones," Jullian adds. "The list is more a formality. You deserve the roles of kings, and we've done this a long, long time." He huffs an exhausted sigh. "Too long."

"Truly," Baydel adds, shocking me. "You four will make great kings. Like Jullian said, it's more a precaution than anything. A few tasks to ensure you're ready. Unless, of course, the four of you would like to challenge us for the thrones right now?" He cocks a brow, excitement flitting in his eyes as if that's exactly what he wants. A fight between father and son, a battle for the thrones only won through death.

That would make us ruthless rulers and more than untrustworthy. Not to mention, none of my mates could pose such a challenge. Not when *I* have their powers.

"Let me see the list," Kal says, reaching out for the invitation. Axl drops it into his hand, a muscle in his jaw flexing.

"Wonderful," Baydel says with a clap of his hands. "Don't look so worried, little bug," he says as Kal hands me the invitation. "This will be fun."

The Kings' List

In the event a mate is Chosen and survives the Athanry, becoming immortal and unlocking full powers within the princes of Lumathyst, there will henceforth be a season of the Kings' List wherein tasks must be completed to secure the princes' ascension.

These tasks are created to prove to the Royal Authority Council, beyond any doubt, that the princes and their Chosen are fit to rule. Tasks will include but are not limited to: Winning the people's approval through common meetings, training the Chosen in a variety of defensive techniques of historical importance to prepare her to rule at their sides, and more.

The Royal Authority Council shall determine over the season if tasks have been met and will cast their votes on Voting Day. Should the princes and their mate not earn the majority vote, a hold will be placed on their ascension, and the current kings will continue to rule Lumathyst until the kings abdicate or are deemed unfit to rule.

Tiny black dots sparkle in the corners of my vision, the entire room feeling unstable as I finish reading. My breath comes in too-short bursts.

Pierce's hand smooths over mine, a casual caress that keeps me from spiraling out of control.

I thought the trials were over when I survived the Athanry.

But they've only just begun.

CHAPTER 10

Rylee

Fucking Baydel. Such a prick.

Our mothers' terms, I understood. The kings'? It doesn't make sense.

I hate them.

Darling, breathe for me.

Pierce's voice cuts through all the others swarming my mind, as they have been since we left the palace, retreating to the safety of Kal's home in the Ruby Aire.

Axl and Kal stand in the corner of Kal's study, talking in hushed tones. Ivy and Layce watch me with worried eyes from where they sit on one of the few couches while Mirren stands behind them, arms folded over her chest, eyes narrowed as she silently waits for me to explain why I dragged them all here in a hurry.

From where I sit on the opposite sofa between Pierce and Jax, I do as Pierce silently commanded.

I *breathe*.

In for four, holding it for just as long before releasing it.

I do my best to shut those mental doors on the powers rippling inside me—the ones connected to the gilded mating bonds.

A Kings' List.

I barely survived the stipulations of the Choosing. How will I fare against anything Baydel and the other kings devised?

I allow myself a moment to wallow. A moment to mourn what I thought would be a centrally focused future—find the Faders, stop them, figure out what my sister is doing with them, and learn how to give my mates their power back.

Now . . .

Who knows what we'll have to endure?

Another breath.

I'm not the same girl who snuck into the Choosing event. Being with the Legends has made me stronger than even the powers roiling in my blood right now. They make me feel complete in a way I never knew possible.

As long as we're together, there's nothing we can't handle.

I cling to this notion as I do my best to solidify those doors inside my mind, pushing the powers behind the wood crafted specifically for each one.

Kal's door has the sun carved into it, Axl's an ocean wave.

Pierce's has a spiderweb, as intricate and vast as his power.

Jax's has his mark, a full moon with five stars around it.

The carvings help me find the doors easier, drawing them up faster than I did yesterday.

I shut them, and it takes an effort to shove all that power behind them, but I manage.

Once Jax's door is closed, the weight of worry, panic, anger . . . all my mates' and friends' emotions, lift from my chest.

The voices in my head fall quiet as Pierce's door closes.

And I can no longer feel the draw of the sky or the rush of water in my blood as I shut the other two.

I breathe again.

"Sorry," I finally say. "Are we sure it's safe to talk here?" I'm not naive enough to think nothing changed since I was unconscious.

"Yes," Kal answers.

Jax shifts next to me, fiddling with one of his blades. His indigo eyes are searing, and I don't need his power to feel the emotions rippling off him.

Maybe I should've kept his door open a little longer, siphoned some of his anger. But doing that might be a violation of his trust. None of us have had that conversation . . . what is and isn't allowed when it comes to me controlling their powers.

Shit. There's so much to learn.

And I don't have enough time to figure it all out before the first of the Kings' List tasks, the one Baydel told us about before we left the palace.

"Good," I say, nodding. "Again, sorry about earlier. It takes me a while to come back to myself when all your powers wake up and demand attention."

Ivy sits up a bit straighter. Layce gasps.

"The Legends' powers?" Mirren says, gripping the back of the sofa tighter.

I give another nod. "I don't want to keep secrets from any of you. You are my family."

A ghost of Erin flashes in my mind, but I shove it away.

"I'm done with that," I emphasize, eyeing each of them. "You're on this journey with me now, whether I like it or not."

"Offended," Ivy says, but she's grinning.

I shrug. "If I could've kept you out of this new life until I knew it was safe, I would've."

"But it'll never be safe," Layce says, and her eyes flare when all focus snaps to her. "What?" she asks. "You're going to be queen of Lumathyst. Even now, you're considered a princess, right? And a Legend. Those titles hold weight. Stakes. Risks. Not just power."

"Right," I say.

"So you wouldn't be able to keep us safe from those risks regardless," Ivy adds.

"I don't want anything to happen to you," I say, swallowing hard. "Any of you."

"We're with you," Layce says.

"No matter what," Ivy agrees.

My heart expands in my chest so much it's hard to breathe around.

"I'm with you as long as you don't do anything stupid," Mirren says. "Like getting yourself killed or one of the princes hurt."

A soft laugh leaves my lips. "I'll do my best."

"Do *better* than your best," Mirren counters, but there is love in her eyes, hard-earned and hard-fought.

"Okay," I say, taking another breath. "I need to fill you all in." I glance to Jax, then Pierce, then Axl, then Kal. "I'm sure you've all suspected, given my actions the last moments of the Athanry," I start, the memory slicing through me so hard it hurts. It's hard to speak this truth. I close my eyes. "But I found Erin."

"What?" Ivy.

"Where?" Layce.

"Called it." Axl.

I open my eyes, swallowing the lump in my throat. "You know the Athanry was attacked by Faders. I saw several of them refer to one Fader in particular as their leader. I chased after them."

Layce's hand shoots to her mouth.

"No fucking way," Ivy snaps.

I nod, my heart clenching at the admission. "I didn't recognize her at first. You know those uniforms they wear cover everything." I tilt my head, remembering the bloodred emblem on the left cheek of every Fader mask—a circle with a dagger speared through it. I clear my throat. "It was her defensive moves that gave her away. But then, when they came after us . . ." I flash my mates an apologetic look. "When Jax's blades were aimed for her throat, I stepped in front of her."

"Oh, Rylee," Layce says empathetically.

"And I took the knives meant for her," I continue, reaching down to graze my hand over Jax's. "Erin caught me. Stopped me from cracking my skull wide open on Evaluna's marble stairs." I shiver at the mere thought of the never-ending stairs from my dreams. "And then she showed me her face. Asked me to *forgive her* and ran."

Ivy's mouth is parted, but no words come out.

Layce immediately gets up to hug me.

I hug her back, choking out a small sob at the gesture.

Ivy crosses the space, and the three of us fall into a little pile on the rug between the couches, taking a moment to silently grieve.

"Erin is the leader of the Faders," Ivy says as we wipe our cheeks and sit back down.

Pierce immediately takes my hand in his.

Jax smooths his up and down my spine.

"They called her *boss*," I say.

"But . . . why?" Ivy shakes her head. "It doesn't make any sense."

"We all have our breaking points. If she met someone with connections at last year's Choosing event? Someone who offered her a chance at change?" I eye my friends. "What would any one of us have done?"

Layce's brow furrows. "No," she says adamantly. "I don't buy it."

"I didn't hallucinate her being there—"

"I'm not saying you didn't see her," Layce amends. "I just . . . It doesn't make sense."

"All of us have wanted change for a while," Ivy continues. "But the Faders aren't making moves for change. They're creating chaos. Hurting people."

"That doesn't sound like Erin," Layce says.

"I know," I say on a released breath, thankful for their council. "It doesn't." I glance to where Kal now sits in the armchair next to my couch. Axl leans against it. "Nothing makes sense. The Faders, their motivations, the substance they possess."

"Thank you for telling us," Kal says. "I know that wasn't easy."

I breathe in his gratitude. "It is, though," I counter. "It hurts, for sure. But telling you? Being honest with each of you? It's not hard. Not anymore." I shake my head. "Erin is my sister. I love her. I will *always* love her. But if she's truly fueling such hate and destruction, she's lost her way. I'm not saying I don't want to help her find it again, but . . ." I can't choose her over my mates.

I won't.

"Tell us about the powers," Ivy says, likely noting my rising panic.

"Right," I say, then launch into everything that happened. Dying. Coming back. My mates' sacrifice.

"Shit," Layce says when I'm finished.

"Are you reading our minds right now?" Ivy asks, curious.

"No," I reply, but even her mentioning that power has it slamming against Pierce's door, begging to come out and play. "It's difficult to contain them," I continue. "But I'm trying. I've only had two days to come to terms with this. I made . . . doors." It sounds as pathetic outside as inside. "It helps a little, but they don't hold forever."

"Especially if you're worked up," Jax says, and my eyes find his, heat flooding my cheeks.

Our conversation last night plays in my mind. The way he held me beneath the moonlight. The moment all five of us shared before that. It felt like coming home.

"And what did the kings want with you?" Mirren asks. "Baydel came to collect you himself."

Axl growls, shifting off Kal's armchair. "The kings have their own requirements for ascension," he says.

Mirren's eyes go wide, then narrow.

Jax's fist clenches harder on his knee, and I reach over to smooth my free hand across it.

Kal rises from his chair, heads to his desk, and digs in a drawer. He pulls a Choosing invitation out and hands it to Mirren, back side up. She studies it, and her mouth draws into a thin line.

"Magically imbued to only show up if our Chosen completed the Athanry," Kal says, pointing to the script on the back of the invitation. "The Kings' List."

"Another damned list?" Ivy snaps as Mirren passes her the invitation. "Aren't there enough of those?"

I smile softly at her, admiring her instant acceptance of this new life. She's not holding her tongue around the princes of Lumathyst.

"Quite," Pierce says. "Too many, in our opinion."

"Then why haven't you done anything about it?" Layce asks, more curious than malicious.

Right. They don't know.

"We would if we could." Kal is the first to answer. "Our search for a mate wasn't just because we wanted to secure the throne and appease our mothers' wishes. Our powers were depleting with our offerings to the goddesses in order to keep their protection. Only finding a true mate would unlock the full force of our powers, tilt the balance, and allow us to ascend the thrones."

"Wait." Ivy tilts her head, looking at Jax. "You said you gave your powers to Rylee."

"We did," Jax answers. "It was the only way to save her."

"Aren't they going to hurt her?" Layce asks. "The full force of your powers? Isn't that meant for part-gods?"

"She's immortal now," Kal argues.

"Still . . ." Ivy shakes her head. "It seems dangerous."

"It feels dangerous," I admit. Even now, I can feel the weight of all four of those powers threatening to crush me. "But there wasn't any other way."

"Okay," Layce says. "So, the goddesses told you the elixir wasn't meant to harm you. Let's pretend that was the case and you didn't die—"

"Which, by the way, who the fuck tried to kill you?" Ivy cuts her off.

"We're working on that," Pierce answers.

"Let's pretend," Layce continues, "that everything went according to plan. They get their full powers unlocked. You become immortal. You have the ability to balance them out like the goddesses intended. The Kings' List would still occur?" She taps the invitation.

"They've had this planned since our mothers set forth the Choosing rules," Pierce says. "Now that they've brought it to light, it makes sense. They have no insight into what actually occurred at the Athanry, and we need to keep it that way. If they knew we were vulnerable . . ." His voice trails off, and it's all I can do to stop the racing thoughts at the possibilities. "Had everything gone to plan, they still would've made us earn the Royal Authority Council's vote before we ascended the thrones."

"If everything had gone to plan"—Jax's voice is icy—"we'd challenge them and kill them all to take the thrones."

"You don't mean that," I say softly, leaning into his shoulder.

"That's an option?" Layce asks.

"It's always an option," Axl answers.

"But we wouldn't," Kal says. "Regardless."

Ivy tilts her head, a silent question of *why not*.

"Beyond the fact that I'm not keen to murder my father, what trust would that instill in our people, if we start our rule of Lumathyst in a puddle of prior rulers' blood?" Kal asks.

I shiver.

"Okay, fair," Ivy says, taking the invitation from Layce and tapping it. "This section about the tasks needed to earn the thrones is incredibly vague."

"No doubt intentionally so," Pierce says.

"Whoever this Royal Authority Council is could ask you to do anything," Layce says. "This magically binding contract is not written in your favor."

I swallow hard.

"And a season is six months, right?" Ivy asks.

Kal nods.

"What about the ascension? What does that entail?" Layce asks.

Pierce nods. "The ascension consists of a ceremony of sorts. One where the kings pass the crowns to us. They'd retire to their chosen city or travel but would take up the annual donations of power to the goddesses so ours, as kings, wouldn't be depleted."

"Does anyone else's brain hurt?" Layce asks, rubbing at her temples.

I laugh. "Yes."

"Good, I'm not alone." She chuckles, and I revel in the levity.

Ivy brings us back to reality. "But you don't have your full powers. Rylee does. And so, every test meant to prove you four are worthy will now be that much harder because you don't have any."

"Most likely."

A weight sinks in my stomach.

"I have to find a way to give them back to you," I say.

"We'll figure it out," Pierce assures me.

"But while also dealing with all this royal task stuff, you're still expected to be the Legends. You're still expected to handle the Faders." Ivy is stating these things, not asking.

"Yep," I say.

She leans back against the couch. "I'm only a bystander, and I need a nap."

We both laugh at that.

"Now you know everything," I say after the room has gone contemplative and quiet.

"Not exactly," Layce says, eyeing Ivy.

They share a silent conversation, and I swallow hard when I understand. I nod, giving them a look that says, *it's up to you two.*

"It's quite uncomfortable not understanding that." Pierce motions to the three of us. There's wonder in his eyes. The Mind is so accustomed to knowing everyone's thoughts, should he wish it.

"Since we're all in this together," Ivy says, shifting off the couch and heading toward a potted red chrysanthemum sitting on one of Kal's bookshelves. "And we're not keeping secrets . . ." She blows out a breath. "If they throw me in the dungeons for this, I'll *never* forgive you."

I laugh at the audacity of that statement, then remember she doesn't know the princes like I do.

She curls her fingers, and the crimson petals stretch and flutter, a new pod spiraling out of the potted soil to join its fully bloomed brother.

"Holy shit," Axl says.

"Fascinating," Pierce adds.

Layce snaps her fingers. A spark of lightning dances on the tip.

"Goddess, girl," Mirren says after my friends silence their powers. "Do you collect demis?"

I shrug. "I guess you could say we collect each other."

She sucks her teeth. "We've had them in the palace for an entire week. What if someone discovers them?"

"No one will," Ivy says. "We've been in hiding our whole lives, thanks to their fathers." She motions toward my mates.

Mirren holds Ivy's gaze, and I'm not sure whose stubbornness will outlast the other's.

In the end, it's Layce who breaks their stare-down. "When is the first task on the Kings' List?"

"Tonight," Jax answers, his tone cold and low.

"Tonight," I repeat, nerves tangling beneath my skin.

"It's a royal ball," Kal offers. "We're all invited, though 'obligated' sounds a bit more like it. They told us they'd announce the events to the nobles, and the season will officially begin."

"Shit," Layce says.

Shit is right.

CHAPTER 11

Rylee

I clutch the small wooden box in my hand, butterflies flapping in my stomach. We're due at the ball in a few hours, but I've had this planned since before the Athanry.

"What's up, kitten?" Axl asks from where he lounges in a chair in my palace chambers.

Kal is next to him, Pierce and Jax on the sofa across from them. Each one is looking up at me with expectant, curious gazes.

"This feels a little silly now, in light of everything," I say, suddenly questioning my timing.

"Nonsense," Pierce chides. "Nothing you need to tell us or show us is silly."

I smile at him. He's right. With the Kings' List upon us, I may not have a better time to do this.

I stand before them, shifting my weight. "I had Mirren help me secure these before the Athanry. I'd planned on asking you all if you wanted to wear them once I came back, but then everything happened. I wanted it to be more . . . romantic?" I pop the box open to show them the contents. "But I'm afraid the timing of everything doesn't really allow for such luxuries."

I pluck out a ring made from platinum and sapphires and hand it to Axl. Then I hand identical rings—except for their stones, ruby and emerald—to Kal and Pierce.

They grin up at me before examining them. Pierce looks at the interior of the ring. "Thirteen." He reads the number stamped there. "Your badge number at the Choosing."

"The number I once thought was unlucky, but it turns out, it's the number that changed my life for the better," I say, glancing to Jax, showing him the remaining contents of the box.

Jax smirks at the ink and needles there. "You want to tattoo me, butterfly?"

"I didn't think you'd want a ring," I say. "Tokens," I continue, glancing at each of them. "From me to you. And just like you said to me, you don't have to wear them if—"

Kal, Pierce, and Axl slide theirs onto their left hands quickly.

"I'll never take it off," Kal vows.

"So thoughtful," Pierce says.

"I love it," Axl adds, admiring it.

"Where do you want to mark me?" Jax asks, the question sending heat straight to my core.

I kneel before him as I take his left hand in mine. I stroke my thumb over his ring finger in the same place the other Legends now wear my tokens. "Here?"

He grins. "You can mark me wherever and however you want."

I hurry to grab the ink and cleaned needles before I can lose my nerve. "I've never done this before," I say. "But I've watched you enough times, I think I can manage a small one."

"I know you can."

I nod, hurrying to position his hand the way I need it, and get to work. It only takes a few minutes. Jax looks down at the small outline of a butterfly I drew just below his knuckle, a number thirteen within the wings. He dips down to kiss me.

"I love it," he says. "It's my favorite tattoo."

"Really?" I ask, pride swelling inside me. "You have so many."

He hauls me up, perching me in his lap. He cups my cheek, smiling for me. "Really," he says. "Besides you, it'll be my favorite thing to look at every day."

I kiss him, quickly, then look at the rest of my mates.

"I suppose we should get ready," I say, dread leeching into my previously light tone.

"Another ball," Axl grumbles. "Thought we'd be done with them for a while."

I nod but try to appear positive. "You all look *so* good in suits."

Laughter fills the room, and we get lost in it, if only to distract us from the unknown.

"And think of how much fun we'll have," Kal adds. "When we can bring you back here and peel off your dress."

CHAPTER 12

Rylee

A sharp clinking sounds throughout the crowded palace ballroom—the same event hall where I had my first kings' dinner months ago. I glance toward the floor-to-ceiling windows I've been avoiding all night and do my best to shut out the memory of Baydel forcing a demi to dance to his death out of them.

"Thank you." Baydel's voice rings from his and the other kings' table, which is a long rectangle of mahogany positioned on a dais at the head of the room.

Other tables line the walls, piled with the finest food and drink Lumathyst has to offer, and despite being somewhat accustomed to the luxury here, it still stings how quickly they can throw an event together like this. Why can't this much food be sent to the Ashlands just as fast?

"Thank you all for coming," Baydel continues, a wide smile stretching his lips. He looks regal, draped in gold, and *almost* approachable. His demeanor is different than the previous times I've seen him—calmer, as if a weight has been lifted from his shoulders. Just like he'd been when I woke up with him sitting next to me.

Is that because I've officially been Chosen, and he believes his son now holds unlimited power? Or is it another game?

Exhaustion sticks to me like a second skin, only adding to the weight of my mates' powers. It's hard to breathe around everything swirling inside me—their power, confusion, worry. A maelstrom of emotion threatening to take me under.

"The Choosing season has ended," Baydel announces, twirling the crystal wineglass in his hands as he stands behind that table, looking down at the crowd of nobles spread throughout the room before him. Some had been dancing moments before he drew their attention. Even the musicians from the Ruby Aire, positioned in the farthest corner of the room, are silent now. "But *our* festivities are only just beginning." He grins wider, sparing a glance at the other kings seated at the table.

Jullian is watching him with a careful expression, not touching the plate of food before him. Brooks looks calculative and bored, while Lucas is tearing into a hunk of fine bread like it's the most interesting thing in the room. And I can't help it; it makes me laugh. I do my best to hide the sound, but my mates, who stand two on each side of me, flash me curious smiles.

The idea that *bread* is more interesting than whatever Baydel is saying is humorous. I can't help it.

Baydel clears his throat, and the sound draws my attention. My skin tightens when I find his gaze on me, even if it doesn't hold the same hatred it did before the Athanry. It's unnerving, to say the least, and I do my best to re-check the mental doors I shoved each of my mates' powers behind, praying the kings can't sense them in me.

"Since we've never made it this far," he continues, then laughs harshly, which beckons the crowd to do the same. "I'm sure you're wondering what's next in this grand process and how it will affect Lumathyst. I'm happy to say the season of *the Kings' List* will commence tonight."

Whispers ripple through the crowd of nobles. Lumathyst has never gotten this far. The princes have never chosen a mate, who then turned immortal . . . until now.

We're all in uncharted territory.

"Let me explain," he says, quieting the curious conversations. "This will not only be a celebration season, packed with entertainment our possible future queen and kings will provide, but also an opportunity for the Royal Authority Council to stipulate and decide whether the princes and princess are worthy of ascension."

My blood runs cold at the idea of a group of people holding our future in their hands. *Who are they?* I wonder as I take in the glittering crowd.

"The Royal Authority Council, along with myself and my fellow kings, will make a collective vote after the princess and princes have completed the tasks of the Kings' List. And, if they've proven themselves worthy and win the majority vote, the four kings of Lumathyst will abdicate our thrones with confidence that we can finally rest, knowing our kingdom and its people are in good hands."

Interested gasps work their way around us, but I feel like I can't draw a breath.

Royalty, nobility, they've always turned their noses up at me—except the Legends. And now . . . the only way the kings will pass the crowns to the princes is if we *all* pass a vote. How am I going to earn that when I still feel like such an outsider when it comes to the noble and royal classes?

"And don't feel left out," he continues. "You will also have sway with the vote. You can take your opinions and suggestions to the noble families who are on the Council." He turns, gesturing with his free hand now. "Please, come up here so I can introduce you."

"I've never seen him act like this. He almost seems . . . kind?" I whisper to Jax.

"Kindness isn't one of his qualities. Don't trust it," Jax says under his breath.

I smooth my hand down his arm, feeling the tension in his corded muscle.

Five families climb the raised dais, all dressed in gorgeous suits and gowns of every color. Each is a family with a mother, father, and daughter. And then there's Baydel's personal Occuli, the one whose name I finally learned is Frenrick Coolis. My misstep with Dalfon yesterday urged me to find out the names of all the kings' Occuli. I never had before because I'd been terrified of them. It's harder to be scared of something with a name.

"I'm sure you'll recognize these lovely young ladies," Baydel says to the crowd while motioning to the women on the stage.

My stomach plummets.

Mirren showed me pictures from the royal post when I asked about them before.

The previous potentials.

They're all there, except for one. The Ari. No doubt, her lower-class family wasn't welcome at this event, let alone a seat on the Royal Authority Council created to decide my mates' and my future.

Shit.

"They were our sons' previous potentials, of course," Baydel explains, and a soft applause rolls through the crowd. The women bow politely, smiling where they stand next to their fathers—the heads of household. "These families are some of the oldest and most noble of all the lines in Lumathyst and have dutifully performed their roles on the Royal Authority Council for decades. They, alongside Frenrick, will ensure a fair, unbiased vote as we go through the Kings' List and proceedings."

Yeah right. These are my mates' *exes.*

A sharp, jealous *thing* twists in my chest so painfully, I gasp. The thought brings up pictures in my mind. These women's hands all over the Legends . . . my *mates*—

Anger replaces the jealousy so quickly, I feel dizzy. Power floods my veins, a territorial claim demanding vindication.

Fuck.

I suck in a sharp breath, spinning to Pierce, who is closest to me, doing my best to make it look like a loving embrace.

"Breathe for me," he whispers into my ear. "Just breathe. Feel my chest against yours. Match that rhythm. Yes, good."

I focus on his words, his instructions, to block out every other emotion, every instinct demanding I break any hands that touched them before me.

Goddess, this isn't *me.*

"Fuck," Jax grumbles next to me, shifting closer to me and Pierce.

Jax's door inside my soul is wide open, my emotions slicing down our bond, his power pulsing as it slams into him.

It's a relief to be rid of even *one* of the consuming weights.

"Butterfly," he whispers in my other ear.

I clench my eyes shut, not hearing whatever else Baydel is prattling on about. This isn't me. How could I possibly be jealous of women I've never met before? And more than that, I wasn't even in the picture when they were. I was with people before the Legends. This is madness.

This isn't me.

"It's not you," Pierce answers the thought, and I breathe even deeper. His power has returned to him, and the lack of weight is so freeing, it's almost dizzying. "It's the mating bonds," he explains as I turn to look up at him.

"How am I doing this?" I ignore the declaration, wanting to hang on to this sense of freedom. I look to Jax, too.

"I don't know," Jax answers. "I just feel it returned."

"Same," Pierce adds. Kal and Axl stay focused on the crowd and Baydel even though they're listening to us. "Can you sense anything?" he whispers. "Did you do it on purpose?"

I shake my head, shame coating my skin. "I got jealous."

"The bonds," Pierce assures me with a comforting smile. "We feel it, too. It's a natural part of the process. From my research, I'm not sure the territorial instincts ever entirely go away. But it will get easier over time. These next few months will be the hardest."

"I might drown someone if they say they've been with you before," Axl says, arching a brow at me.

Shit.

Kal nods his agreement, but it's Jax I turn to. The most ruthless of all my mates.

His eyes are searing as they meet mine, and he shrugs. "I would've done worse before you were officially mine, butterfly. I have myself under control." His voice dips. "For now."

Heat streaks up my spine like a lick of flame. Jax must feel it, because he laughs—not his terrifying laugh, but *my* laugh. He drags a knuckle down my cheek. "Always surprising."

I loose a breath, finally feeling more like myself again, and nod to them before turning out of Pierce's embrace.

Baydel wraps up his speech, dismissing the Royal Authority Council. Frenrick grins right at me, his black eyes illuminated by a burst of green flame as he joins the party, he and his fellow Occuli likely noting everything to put in tomorrow's royal posts.

A shiver kills all the heat inside me.

That ancient conjurer will *never* vote for me. He's the same one who attacked me in the Ruby Aire library.

Dalfon, the Occuli healer, may have surprised me. There might even be a new friendship forming between us. And maybe I've misjudged the kings' Occuli, but there's something about Frenrick that chills me to my bones. I suppose anyone who had worked so closely with Baydel for so many years would cause the same reaction. My eyes flit to One, Baydel's elite enforcer, standing guard and shadowing the king's every move.

Yep. Just as chilling, even if I've never seen his face thanks to the diamond-encrusted helmet the elites constantly wear.

The Kings' List is meant to hurt or ridicule me. That much is clear when I find Baydel's eyes on me again, a curious sort of look at my lack of response to seeing my mates' exes paraded around onstage.

I smile at him. What did he expect? That I'd cause a scene?

I almost did.

He always underestimates me.

"To the princes," Baydel says, raising his glass. "And to our new princess."

Kal passes me a glass of sparkling white wine, and I raise it along with the rest of the crowd.

"To Lumathyst," I say, loud and clear, my eyes scanning over the crowd of nobles before I stop on Baydel.

Shock flits over his features for a moment before he corrects it. "To Lumathyst," he echoes, dipping his head to me in a gesture that *should* feel kind but somehow only confuses me more.

He's not acting like himself, at least not toward me. I don't understand it. And I certainly don't like it. More games, most likely, and I already have so many to play.

The crowd murmurs their cheers before taking sips, and the event segues into mingling and eating, then dancing. The wide space fills with melodic strings and piano, the mood shifting from strained during Baydel's speech to more casual.

At least for the nobles enjoying the event.

For us?

I feel like a trap will spring any minute. Beyond the Royal Authority Council now holding our future in their hands, what other challenges will be on this list?

"Tonight's introduction of the list and the Council," I say softly as I eye the previous potentials making their rounds in the crowd. "A test for me, I gather?"

"And perhaps us," Pierce offers.

"Baydel thinks I'll be cruel to these women," I say. "Women who are directly tied to the decision now hanging over our heads."

"For certain," Pierce answers, pride gleaming in his eyes. "With the bonds, we would all understand that reaction."

"Completely," Kal adds.

I take a deep breath, happy to find the bonds to Pierce and Jax are still light, their powers on the other end where they belong. What will I need to do to make this last forever? I shut the doors, hoping if I keep them closed with them on the other side, they won't come back to me.

"We can go," Axl says.

I smile up at him, then the others. "No," I say, shaking my head as I turn back to the crowd. "We won't be going anywhere yet. It's a party, after all." I gather the skirts of my dress, made of layers of red silk and tulle. "And you all know how much I love to play."

Pierce coughs over his laugh.

Kal shakes his head with a smile.

Axl gives me an approving nod.

And Jax looks to the ceiling as if he might find assistance there.

It fills my heart that none of them argue, none of them try to sway me to go somewhere safer. They believe in me. After everything, they don't doubt me. I hold on to that confidence as I plunge into the crowd of nobles.

CHAPTER 13

Rylee

Baydel wants me to make a scene? Well, fuck him.

I make a beeline toward the first potential I see. She's gowned in an elegant dress of dark-blue silk that molds to her curves in the most flattering way. Axl's color. I spare a glance over my shoulder, meeting Axl's gaze. It's encouraging yet apologetic.

He has nothing to apologize for. When he selected this potential, I hated the Legends. I hated the kings. I hated all things royal.

So much has changed.

I focus ahead again, finally making my way to the potential, who stands next to a table laden with fruit and chocolates. She plucks a chocolate from a silver tray and pops it in her mouth. She looks bored or timid—I'm not sure which.

I stop before her, fastening what I desperately hope is a genuine-looking smile on my face. I'm learning mating bonds can be a feral bitch, but that doesn't mean I have to be.

"Hello," I finally manage.

The woman straightens when she looks at me, then immediately bows. "Your highness."

I try not to cringe. "*Rylee*, please. And forgive me, I'm not sure of your name."

She rises. "Charlotte Arden." Her voice is soft, and her movements are as delicate as the silk she wears. She motions toward a fashionably dressed man and woman standing before the dais, speaking with Lucas. "My father is Earl Gregor Arden, and my mother is Countess Constance Arden."

"I'm happy to meet you, Charlotte," I say, the words feeling more truthful by the minute. I half expected her to sneer at me when I approached. So far, so good.

"You as well, princess—"

"Just Rylee," I cut her off with a wave.

"But your title. You're mated to the princes."

"I've been Rylee far longer than I've been a princess."

A small smile shapes her cupid lips. "All right, Rylee." She says my name like it's a struggle to drop the formalities. "Is there something I can do for you this evening?"

I tilt my head.

"Not that I'm not pleased to meet you," she says. "But I'm not sought out by high royalty often."

"I doubt that," I counter. "Being an earl's daughter and a previous potential."

She visibly swallows, sparing a glance to where Axl is chatting with Kal across the room.

Fire slices my stomach at the simple, innocent look, and it's all I can do to hush the powers inside me. I suck in a breath, doing my best to hold a casual smile as I settle the powers, relieved that Jax's and Pierce's are still with them.

"Are you all right, princess?" Charlotte asks, genuine concern in her features.

"Yes, of course." I count the number of strawberries on the table beside me to ground myself. "I'm fine."

"I admire you," she says after I've taken a sip of sparkling wine to cool my nerves.

"You do?" I ask.

"Yes." She glances toward my mates again, and I have to practically beat the rebellious mating bonds back down—not easy when I'm trying to focus on her words as she continues. "I must admit, after my own Choosing experience, I wasn't sure if they'd ever find a mate." She focuses back on me, her brown eyes sincere. "Though I certainly hoped."

"Why did you think that?" I ask, ravenous for information. Speaking to the previous potentials won't just be a common courtesy for me. I'm genuinely curious about their experiences.

Charlotte's eyes widen, and she vehemently shakes her head. "I promise, I mean no disrespect." The girl looks downright terrified as she glances around the crowded room where people are dancing and drinking, as if I might call over an elite enforcer and send her to the dungeons for stating her true thoughts.

I remember a time when I felt the same way.

I need to change this fear.

"You have nothing to be afraid of," I assure her. "You can speak freely with me. I'm from—" I almost say *the Ashlands* but quickly correct. "Cedar and Silk. I wasn't raised with these formalities, so you don't need to stand on them. I'm curious about you, that's all. And I wanted to meet you."

She blows out a breath but still looks cautious as she speaks. "Again, I mean no disrespect. The princes are fine men, but after spending one month with Axl, watching him rush off to attend to Legend issues, and the way he was with that ocean of his, it was . . ."

"Overwhelming?" I fill in for her when she goes quiet.

"Yes." She breathes the word. "To say the least. I knew within a few days that I wasn't the fit for any of them. I'm not built for that sort of life. The constant movement, the threats, the brutality in what they do." A shiver racks her. "I hoped someone would be, though. Plus, it was too tempting to leave after the month was up when the king—" She abruptly cuts herself off, immediately taking a sip of her wine.

I step closer to her, a sense of urgency coiling in my chest. "When the king what?"

She blinks rapidly, glancing across the room at where her mother and father still speak with Lucas. "I can't. I didn't mean to say that."

"It's okay," I say, gently smoothing my hand over her arm. "I mean what I say. You have nothing to fear from me." I shrug. "Unless you're still interested in vying for my mates' hearts. *That* would make things complicated."

She laughs, tension loosening from her shoulders. For half a second, I worry my touch has unleashed Jax's power without my knowing—soothed her emotions so I can get her to open up—but I check, and it's still with him.

"No, I have no interest in them beyond their happiness with you," she says. "Happy princes will certainly make happy kings, and we definitely need that."

"Tell me about the king," I say. "What made it easier to leave after a month beyond you realizing you weren't built for Legend life?"

She fiddles with her glass, contemplative.

An itch creeps up inside me at her hesitance. I could take Pierce's power back. Somehow, I *know* I could. All I'd have to do is call it back to me, direct it toward her mind, and no thought of hers would be hidden from me—

No.

I won't violate her like that. Or Pierce.

Charlotte steps closer, lowering her voice. "My mother," she says. "Looks healthy and vibrant tonight, doesn't she?"

"She certainly does," I say, glancing at the countess dressed in a soft blue long-sleeved gown. "She's practically glowing."

"It wasn't like that six years ago. She was very ill," she says, her mouth dipping at the corners as if the memory is still fresh. "Father and I were certain we'd lose her. He'd spent half of his fortune trying to find a healer who could help her condition, but none of the Occuli we could afford were able to fully rid her of the disease."

I swallow hard, a lump suddenly in my throat.

"When the king came to me toward the end of my first month of the Choosing and offered me a way to save my mother . . ." Her voice cracks, and tears fill her eyes. "I'm sorry. I had to take it. I knew I wouldn't be good for them. I knew I wouldn't survive them, let alone the Athanry. And I wanted to help my mother. When he offered, I took my chance and never looked back."

A similar offer to me from Brooks rings in my memory. "Which king was it?" I ask.

Charlotte wets her lips. "King Baydel," she answers.

I nod, not surprised. "You did nothing wrong," I assure her, and she breathes a little easier. "I'm sure anyone would've done the same in your situation." Though I'd been offered my sister and a new life on a silver platter, and I didn't take the deal. My princes were worth more to me than that. Worth everything.

I look at my mates, who are lingering on the other side of the room. Kal and Axl chat with anyone who dares approach them. Pierce and Jax remain quiet, watchful.

My heart fills my chest so much it almost hurts. The bonds inside me are yanking and tugging on the other ends.

All four of them look at me at once, and it steals my breath. We're connected in ways beyond the powers, beyond whatever magic the Athanry gave us.

I couldn't leave them. Not for any offer in the world.

"And now you have your mother," I say, managing to look back at her. "Healthy as ever, it seems."

"She is," she says, a wistful smile on her lips. "I would do it all again. Endure that fear, just to have her this way. My father . . . I don't think he'd survive it if he lost her so suddenly. These extra years have definitely made the two of us not take a second for granted."

"I understand," I say. I wouldn't survive without the Legends. I know that in the depths of my soul.

"May I have this dance?" Baydel's question shocks me as much as his silent approach. My own power, air and wind, swirls inside me, and a buried instinct to fly or fight bursts beneath my skin.

Charlotte bows deeply. "Your highness," she says before backing away a few steps to make room for him.

"Of course, King Baydel." I grind out my answer. "It was lovely to meet you, Charlotte," I say to her. "We'll talk again soon."

I turn to the king, hesitantly slipping my hand into his outstretched one, wondering if he'll use his power, immediately ensnaring my physical motions to make me do his bidding. A flash of our first meeting, when he held me immobile and tried to *touch* me, makes my blood boil.

I force myself to breathe. To stay present. To bury my own power, and the two remaining with me from Axl and Kal.

Thankfully, my movements are my own as he guides me to the dance floor, the crowd parting for him as if they can sense his presence.

He sweeps us into the dance, one hand holding mine and the other lightly touching my hip. His power radiates from him, much like his son's does, a low vibration I can't ignore, but he's not using it against me as we sway back and forth to the light, airy melody of strings and piano.

My heart races so hard against my chest, I struggle to breathe properly, though his touch is light, innocent, with no sign of the previous intention to control or threaten me in sight.

"You look absolutely regal tonight, little bug." His voice is even, calm.

I clear my throat. "Thank you," I say, feeling so unsure in my own skin.

Baydel smiles at me, his gaze casting left and right as we spin around. "I see you were making friends with Earl Arden's daughter."

I dip my head, doing my best to focus and calm the adrenaline crackling in my veins. "I intend to befriend them all."

"So eager to swap stories with the ex-potentials?" He gently pushes me out, spinning me before bringing me back in, not too close, keeping a respectable distance.

"I'm excited to meet as many people as I can," I say truthfully. "I have much to learn."

"That you do," he says, looking at me with a curious gaze. "I must admit, I was worried about you after the Athanry."

I choke on a laugh. "Why do I doubt that?"

He rolls his eyes, spinning us again to the sweep of the music. "I know I was hard on you, little bug. But that's because I want the best for my son. For all of them. I also want what's best for Lumathyst. I've ruled this realm for so long . . ." His voice trails off, his eyes going somewhere else altogether.

That itch perks up again. The urge to draw Pierce's power back. I could do it. Baydel certainly never cared before about *my* consent when it came to his power.

"I won't leave it in incapable hands," he continues.

The reality of that statement stops all thoughts of trying to break into his mind. It would be a fool's attempt. I barely understand these powers, and Pierce told me the kings have some of the best mental shields he's ever seen.

Still . . . *tempting*.

"I want what's best for Lumathyst, too," I hedge. Maybe I can appeal to some sense of royal duty? "So does your son."

"Time will tell," he says.

"The Kings' List will tell," I say, but it sounds more like a question.

Baydel grins, shaking his head. "I will not give you any hints, little bug. You and the princes will have to manage on your own. Even if I'm trying to come to some sort of common ground with you."

Is that what he's doing? Is that what this nice-guy persona is all about? "Common ground?"

He shrugs. "I'd much like it if you could look at me like you don't want to lop off my head at any moment."

My lips part, and I almost stumble in our dance. "I don't—"

"You do," he counters. "I'm quite used to it. Honestly, I find fear a far more powerful motivator than hope. Evaluna always tried to lead with love." He shrugs.

My senses alert at the mention of his mate. The memories of her while I was asleep, everything that happened at the Athanry . . . it all floods in with her name. "Do you miss her?" I can't stop myself from asking.

The smile melts off his face. In the span of a breath, Jax's power hurtles back into me, blazing through the locked door I'd hoped would hold forever. A flash of anger bites me so hard it *stings*. I flinch from the pain but cover it with a cough, grateful it gets easier each time.

"Every day," he says, and something prickles on the back of my neck. Something unnerving. Unnatural. His hand tightens in mine before he loosens it and continues the dance. "Now, we don't like each other. That much is apparent," he says casually. "But you are the Chosen. They've selected you as their mate. You've unlocked their power and will now act as the grounding unit for the Legends. I will respect the goddesses' decision. And I hope, in time, you and I will become friends."

The notion is too shocking to respond to, so I don't.

"I'm a good friend to have, little bug," he says. "And a terrible enemy."

"I don't want any enemies," I admit, the truth of the statement twisting my chest.

The Faders flash in my mind, which directly leads to thoughts of my sister.

"That's naive," he says, swaying us. "You're a princess now. You're mated to the Legends of Chaos. You have a bigger target on you than ever before. Every enemy of Lumathyst is now your enemy. Which makes us as close to friends as I think we'll ever be."

My head is spinning. The game I've been playing has become more complex than I ever imagined. In difficult times in the past—with schemes of robbing the wealthy to help aid the people of the Ashlands—I'd talk it out with Erin. I'd run to her with anything that stood in my way. Any problem I couldn't solve on my own, my sister and I would solve together. Pain throbs in my heart, a signature sensation that I now associate directly with missing her.

"Like I said before." I force out the words, coming back to myself. "I have much to learn."

"How about I give you your first lesson?" he offers, his tone practically chummy.

I like it better when he's sneering at me. That, I know. That, I expect. This? I don't know what to do with this.

I *hate* this man.

I hate what he's done to the Ashlands. Hate how he's treated his son his entire life. Hate his malicious indifference to those in need. Hate the way he takes and takes and *takes*.

There's no room in my heart for forgiveness.

But . . . *strategy*? Yeah, there's room for that. I'm a royal now. I need to start acting like one.

"It would be an honor." The lie flows so easily from my tongue. Jax would be proud.

Baydel's smile deepens as he spins us, the motion giving us a clear view of my mates. They're all watching me with a hawklike precision that's downright intimidating.

"Make them happy," he continues. I snap my gaze back to his. "*Keep* them happy. Whatever they want, whatever they need, provide it."

I part my lips. "Of course I want to make them happy—"

"You must," he cuts me off, his tone grave. "If they make a choice, you support it. You are *theirs*. There is no other choice for you now. If you don't . . ."

"What?" I ask when he doesn't continue.

He slows our dance, giving me a pitying look. "They'll end you."

I shake my head. He doesn't know them like I do. He's just trying to scare me.

He laughs, the boisterous sound rattling me. "You're looking at me like I don't know what I'm speaking on," he says. I try to smooth my features so he can't read me. "But I do, little bug." He grins at the Legends across the room. "I've known them infinitely longer than you have. Heed my advice. You cross those four, and they'll tear you to pieces."

CHAPTER 14

Axl

I hate this suit.

It's too tight, and I'm pretty sure the blue tie is slowly strangling me.

I understand the reasoning behind these events, but after learning about this list, all I want to do is get the fuck out of these clothes and be with Rylee.

Scratch that. I want to *hide* her.

Want to prep my ship and sail with her so far across the ocean, the kings, the Faders, her sister, and whoever else means her harm can never lay eyes on her again. We could seclude ourselves on some unexplored island, spend the rest of our existence living in bliss as we shut out the world.

I laugh at the fantasy. She'd never allow it. Not my kitten.

"Your highness?" Earl Arden approaches. His wife is still speaking with my father across the banquet hall. "May I have a moment?"

I dip my head, flashing a parting glance at the Legends, who are doing exactly what I've been doing—watching Rylee dance with Baydel like our lives depend on it.

Makes my skin crawl, seeing her in his arms, but he's kept a respectful distance, which is something. Plus, she'd rip his head off if he did anything she didn't allow. He may not know it, but she's more powerful than him now. She just doesn't understand the full depth yet.

None of us do.

Fuck, we need to sort out our shit.

"Thank you," Earl Arden says as we head over to a clear space next to the kings' dais.

"What can I do for you?" I ask, hating the tension in my gut. His daughter, Charlotte, was my pick six years ago. It never would've worked between us. I knew that on day one. She did, too. Still, it's awkward.

"I wanted to bring to your attention a slight mishap our ships encountered a few days ago."

I cock a brow at him.

"I can't be certain, but our trade shipment from Cardrayton wasn't complete. It's the third one in the past month that has come up short. The first time, I thought it an honest mistake. The second made me wary. The third?"

"Why wasn't I made aware of this sooner?" I ask.

"Apologies, your highness," he says, bowing his head slightly. "I dared not disturb you after the Athanry."

I breathe deeply, eyes flitting to Rylee for a second before returning to him. Rumors spread quickly through Lumathyst. The gossipmongers practically live off the Occuli's reports in the royal posts, but no one knows the full truth of what happened to Rylee after the Athanry, besides us, Mirren, and her friends.

I want to keep it that way.

"Understood," I say. "I'll dive into it. Which ship?"

"The *Constance*, your highness," he says.

"Take what you need from my stores to make up for the difference while I get in contact with Cardrayton to figure out what's going on."

The earl bows deeper. "Thank you, your highness."

"I appreciate you coming to me," I say, meaning it. I want my people to come to me, unlike my father, who would rather ignore the problem than solve it. He wasn't always that way.

"I wish you luck," he says, a bit quieter. "In this new endeavor." He flashes me an encouraging, hopeful look before bowing again and heading off to rejoin his wife.

I tilt my head, wondering if he truly means that. He's on the Royal Authority Council. His vote will count *for* us or *against* us at the end of this fucking mess. Does he think that's the only reason I'm so eager to help him? Because it isn't. I would've done the same for anyone who came to me with the same issue.

I blow out a breath, shifting on my feet. I'm itching for the water. A good dive would help clear the restlessness from my body. A swim with Rylee would do me even better.

I find her on the dance floor easily. She's stunning, and it hits me all over again that we almost lost her. The pain of that reality is one I never want to experience again.

Fucking Baydel is still twirling her around. I hate that I don't know what he's saying to her. I wonder if Pierce has his power back. Rylee has accidentally given them back to all of us now, only to have them snap back to her unexpectedly. Once she gets ahold of it all, she'll be unstoppable.

She's always been unstoppable. I fucking love this woman.

Her features are smooth, and she looks intrigued and cautious as she dances with Baydel. I make to return to the Legends, wanting to poke Pierce to listen in if he can. He never likes to, but in this case? I think it would be merited.

"Axl."

I straighten and stop cold at the sound of my father's voice.

There was a time when I *loved* hearing his voice. Looked forward to his playful jokes and bets and teachings of the sea.

That joy died a long time ago. I never had it as bad as Jax. My father never beat me. Never tested me within an inch of my life. He just . . . checked out. Stopped caring.

"Lucas," I say. I haven't called him *father* since my mother went to sleep decades ago.

"Earl Arden told you about the trade issues?" He comes to stand next to me.

"Yep," I say, not bothering to give him much attention, some muscle memory kicking in. I'll never be that little boy again, begging him to get out of bed to spend time with me. Never. Again.

"You gonna handle it?" he asks, his tone aloof.

"Yep," I repeat, my eyes trained on Rylee as she moves on the dance floor. Even in Baydel's arms, she's something to marvel at.

"Glad she woke up," Lucas says before taking a sip of his drink.

I look at him then. "Do you actually mean that?"

"Of course I do." He squints like he's shocked I asked the question. "She's your mate."

I tip my chin, not fully buying his answer. I stopped trying to sort truth from lie from him years ago.

I look at Rylee again, the bond between us stretching tight. Fuck, it coils tighter the longer I look at her. I don't know if losing her made the bond stronger or if it's just my innate need for her, but it's intense.

"She's something," Lucas says, following my gaze. "Honestly, son. She reminds me . . ." His words choke off, and he quickly takes a drink.

I study him. Shit. He looks . . . sad?

"Reminds you of what?" I ask before I can stop myself. I know better. Usually, probing questions are met with aloofness and dismissal. In the beginning, I understood. It hurt to talk about Mom, but after losing her, he never went back to being the father I used to know.

Lucas clears his throat, his eyes distant in a nostalgic kind of way. Then, he smiles. "Your mother used to make me crazy."

I freeze, like if I move, he'll stop talking. After Mom went to sleep, I begged him to tell me stories about her, terrified I'd forget her. He refused.

"She could bring me to my knees with a look, and it had nothing to do with the fact she was a goddess." He shakes his head. "It was just her. She was fire and energy, and I never knew which version of her I'd wake up to."

I can't stop my smile. "I remember that part of her," I say, warmth spreading in that cold place in my chest where grief constantly lives. "Do you miss her?"

I've always wanted to know, but now, after Rylee? I miss her right now, and she's in the same damn room.

"Every day."

The answer shocks the fuck out of me. Evidently it shocks him, too, because he blinks several times, clears his throat, and assumes his typical, emotionless mask. I move to face him, giving him more of my focus, and his gaze meets mine, growing uncharacteristically intense and serious.

"You need to be careful, son," he says, barely a whisper. He reaches out, gripping my shoulder. "Very careful."

Adrenaline snaps beneath my skin, instinct reaching for a power that isn't there.

"With what?" I ask. "This list? If it's so dangerous, do something about it."

"I can't." He shakes his head, looking toward Rylee. "With her," he continues. "You need to be careful with her."

My hackles rise. "Is that a threat?" I push his hand off my shoulder, mine curling to fists at my sides. We're eye to eye in height, but I have at least thirty pounds of muscle on him. I might be sans power, but I can still lay him out clean.

"It's a fact," Lucas says, his tone more serious than I've heard it in years. "She's yours now. A princess. The Legends' mate. That comes with risks. Everyone will be watching her. Everyone who wants to hurt you . . ." He glances at her, shaking his head. "Will go after her."

Does that include him? Baydel? The other kings? Or is he talking about the Faders or Erithmore?

"You *all* need to keep an eye on her," he says.

"Like we aren't already?" I'm baffled. Where is this coming from?

His eyes are grave, but in a blink, they're back to the cocky, distant version I'm used to. "Look at her," he says, his tone at a normal level again. "She's fucking gorgeous. Why wouldn't you want to watch her?"

I'm practically gaping at my father as he winks at me and walks away, rejoining the party as if our little conversation never happened. As if he didn't bring up my mother for the first time in decades. As if he didn't just either threaten my mate or give me a fair warning.

Fuck. Me.

I stomp over to my friends, folding my arms over my chest as we watch

Baydel continue to sweep Rylee along the dance floor despite the music shifting to a new melody.

"Any wise counsel from your father?" Pierce asks.

"Honestly?" My mind is still whirling. "I don't know."

Pierce tilts his head at me, but I shrug. I really don't know what to make of it.

"What do you think will be on this list?" I ask, needing anything else for my mind to work on.

"I'll speak to my father," Kal says, patting me on the back before heading to where Jullian is near the dais. If any one of us has a chance at getting answers out of one of our fathers, it's him.

"If Baydel has his way," Jax says, his eyes never once leaving Rylee, "it's a trial meant to kill."

"Fuck," I grumble.

I need the water. Need to clear my head.

And I need my mate even more.

CHAPTER 15

Rylee

Baydel chuckles, the sound making my jaw lock up. It's not a friendly laugh, nor an intimidating one. It's just *wrong*.

A restless energy prowls beneath my skin, and I feel Pierce's power return like a roaring waterfall. I hurry to shove it behind his signature door. Each of my mates' powers pound against theirs to be set free. It's like an itch begging to be scratched. A building yawn with no completion. It would be so much easier to let them out. Let the powers take over my entire being.

Tempting. *So* damn tempting.

I quash the urge to lose myself in the abyss. I need to stay present now more than ever.

Calming my nerves with mental assurances that I'm here, I'm alive, and people are counting on me, I soothe the powers' insistence, just a little. Damn, they want out. Bad.

Is it a response to how close Baydel is? How, despite his *truce* approach, I still view him as a threat?

Breathe.

Just breathe.

The instructions come in the form of Pierce's voice, radiating down our bond despite the fact that I hold his power.

"It's my turn," Pierce says, suddenly at our side in the midst of the dancers.

Baydel pauses for a moment, studying me before he releases me. "I suppose I've held on to our new princess long enough," he says in a sugary sweet tone. He grins, arching a brow at me as if to silently convey his warning one more time.

I swallow the lump in my throat and immediately fall into Pierce's open arms. He draws me close, one strong arm around my lower back, holding me against his body, the other hand taking mine as he leads me around the dance floor.

Every tense thing in me uncoils in his embrace, the ever-sharp edge soothed into submission.

"Did you hear me begging for help?" I ask, half teasing.

Pierce shakes his head. "You don't need to be the Mind to realize that dance was long enough."

I smile up at him, breathing him in. He smells so good. Somehow, his signature scent of amber and violets is more potent right now, as if it loops around the bond and strokes me from the inside out.

My attention to the bond has it perking up, the recently returned power pulsing. I hold on to that feeling, the sensation of connection with Pierce so close, and wrap my mental fingers lovingly around the connection.

"Darling," Pierce whispers, his breath a rush.

Can you feel me? Hear me? I silently push my thought down that bond, following the words all the way to the other end—

Suddenly, I'm not only looking into Pierce's refined features, not only admiring his deep brown eyes, but also seeing . . .

Me.

From his point of view.

I stumble slightly, but he holds me close, practically lifting me off my feet as we continue to dance.

It's jarring, seeing two versions of our present, but Pierce's mind is beautiful.

He softly grins down at me, his eyes wide and curious.

I can hear you. His words slip into my mind just as they would when he spoke to me this way before, only I'm the one in control now. Sort of.

This is okay? I ask. *You've let me in, right? I didn't force this, did I?* I have no clue what I'm doing, and I know if I give this too much attention, allow myself to really feel the extent of the power I hold, I'll crumble under its weight.

You're always welcome in here whenever you want, he says, holding me tighter against him. *I'm yours.*

Warmth radiates down the connection between us, filling me so much it aches.

I wet my lips, doing my best to sort my thoughts from his. I follow that connection between us, allowing the door holding his power to crack open, just another fraction, and grip it tighter. I hold the power, pushing myself a bit farther into Pierce's mind.

Amber and violets. The richest greens.

I close my eyes to focus, knowing he won't let me slip.

Love. Pride. Worry.

Pierce's mind is multifaceted and seemingly unending. Waves of his emerald energy flicker and waft between the spaces of his mind like beautiful, winged wraiths slipping through the open spaces of a spider web.

Go deeper, he encourages me.

I feel his presence everywhere at once. With difficulty, I open the door another inch, his power curling around me at the slow release instead of drowning me. I test it, breathing as I wait for it to overcome me. It doesn't, so I move deeper into Pierce's mind like he asked.

A clearer image appears—hundreds, maybe thousands of sprawling green trees stretch before me, so much like his beloved Emerald Wood. Yet, here, there are no homes or buildings or roads. It's a never-ending forest, and every giant, thriving tree is another piece of him. A thought, a fact, a worry, a need.

It's incredible.

And I'm right in the middle of it, walking barefoot through his mind forest, gently touching trees with my fingertips. Each graze is a story, peeling back another layer of my mate.

Delight fills me so completely, I forget about everything else. I'm safe here. There are no worries, no pressing issues. I want to stay forever. I want to spend eons unraveling every aspect that shapes Pierce's soul.

I touch the rough bark of another tree, then gasp, anguish stealing every happy feeling in an instant. A vision overtakes everything else. It's *me*—lying unconscious on the marble floor of Evaluna's temple. Then in Jax's bed. Dalfon's blue light spiraling around my body as he shakes his head.

Broken. Pierce feels broken here. But there's a tiny ray of hope.

I open my eyes, the deliberate act shooting me back into my own mind and body so fast my head spins.

Pierce looks down at me apologetically.

"You never gave up on me," I say.

"Never." He moves our joined hands, wrapping mine around his neck as he fully envelops me. Proprieties be damned, we're no longer dancing to the melody. He dips down, leaning his forehead against mine. "I will never give up on you."

The declaration chokes me. "I won't, either," I say. "I wasn't going to stop until I returned to all of you." I blow out a breath, sparing a glance at the nobles dancing around us. We're garnering a few looks, and I know I should care about my image, but I just don't. How can I, when I need Pierce to hold me together? "What are we going to do?" I whisper.

I just want to give you your powers back. I push the words down the bond, the act so much easier when he's holding me like this. When he's opening his mind and letting me come and go as I please. *And figure out the Fader situation. My sister. But adding this from the kings?*

All in good time. His words ripple in my mind. *You have returned. There is nothing we cannot face now.* He sounds so certain. *You are exquisite. You will learn and master these powers. And we will handle any threat—be it royal or Fader or other—together. As we should.*

I close my eyes again, embracing him as we swirl and spin. "I love you," I say aloud.

Pierce shifts against me, and I open my eyes as he slides a warm hand to cup my cheek. "As I love you," he says, and the words rebuild some fractured thing inside me. Some flimsy piece on the verge of crumbling.

The music fades, and he dips me as the song ends, his powerful hands moving my body like it belongs to him. I arch my head back with the move, delight radiating along every inch of my bones as his lips graze the column of my neck.

That quickly, I need him. "Take me home?" I ask.

He nods, fire churning in his eyes. "Of course." He holds my hand as he weaves in and out of the dancers, nodding politely as he guides us to the others.

"Our mate is tired," he says to Jax and Axl.

I search the space for Kal. Something loosens in my chest when I find him near the dais, speaking to Jullian.

"Thank fuck," Axl says. "We've been here an hour too long."

I laugh softly at his relief, then glance at Jax.

His indigo eyes are distant—cold, even—as he looks past me to where Baydel is speaking with one of the others on the Royal Authority Council. Baydel introduced him as Duke Loredana.

I've seen that look before, a mixture of worry and fear. I reach for him with my free hand. "Jax," I whisper, and his eyes meet mine.

He holds me in his gaze a moment, that iciness softening a fraction. He dips his head, a silent assurance he's okay. We can't speak mind to mind like I can with Pierce, not unless I learn how to master Pierce's power. But I don't need it or Jax's words to know what he's saying. I can feel him down our bond, and beneath all the anxiousness holding him hostage, there's love. *Need.*

"Kal!" Axl barks his name, not bothering to stand on royal decorum.

I laugh again, especially at the way Kal rolls his eyes as he bids his father goodbye and heads over to our group.

"Draw enough attention?" Kal chides him.

"You were taking too long. Rylee wants to leave."

"You don't have to leave," I assure Kal. "If you're not ready. Not just because I want to."

"You leave, I leave," Kal says, and the other three nod their agreement.

That's enough to make a girl melt. How do they always manage to turn me into a puddle? I know there's so much to worry about, so much to fear, but when they're all looking at me like that, when nothing but love and desire surges down our bonds, it's really hard to give a fuck.

And I'm grateful for that. If I didn't have them, have their support, I would lose myself in the current of unknown threatening to drown me.

You cross those four, and they'll tear you to pieces.

Baydel's warning cuts through my mind, turning my insides cold.

He doesn't know them like he says he does. He *can't*. They would never hurt me. And fuck him for putting that in my mind.

"Where would you like to retire for the evening, love?" Kal asks.

"Are we obligated to stay in the palace?" I ask. "Is that part of the rules?"

"They didn't say as much," Kal answers. "And until they do, we're free to go wherever we like."

Part of me wants to stay at the palace if only because it's closer, but a bigger part of me doesn't feel safe here.

"Jax." I say his name again. "Your home is closest."

"*Our* home, butterfly," he says, pushing off the wall he's been leaning against. "Ours."

I press my lips together to hold back my smile.

Jax exits first, then Kal, then Axl, and finally Pierce, who guides me ahead of him, ensuring he stays behind me. I can't help but feel like the Legends are forming a protective barrier on purpose, which is slightly humorous, since I'm the one holding all their power.

Not like I can use it effectively, but *still*.

Luckily, no one says a word to stop us, too busy enjoying the ball to bother looking our way, and we're heading down the palace steps in no time.

I slide easily onto the back of Pierce's velomage, wrapping my arms around his abdomen and leaning my head against his back. I close my eyes as we take off, already dreaming of Jax's comfortable bed. Today has been exhausting to say the least, and since I regained consciousness, sleep hasn't been consistent. I need proper sleep to sort all this out—

Jax slams to a halt a few blocks outside the palace, causing the others to stop so quickly, Pierce and I almost crash into Axl ahead of us.

"Faders," Axl growls.

CHAPTER 16

Rylee

A wall of ten Faders comes down the main road of the royal city. Their white uniforms look stark under the golden torches lighting the road, the red emblem like painted blood on the full-face masks.

They've never attacked the royal city before that I know of. What's drawing them here? Or are they just growing bolder? The roads are empty save for enforcers trying to block the invaders' path, the small handful going down in a heap after a few cracks of those magical blasters some of the Faders carry. Others are armed with swords or chains, others weaponless.

Erin. She could be among them. This might be my chance.

I'm off the velomage in a second, racing toward the fray, not stopping for a moment to *think*.

The closed doors inside me fly wide open, beckoned by my panic or my anger, I'm not sure which, and I don't care. I let it flood me, feed off the intoxication of it all until I'm numb against the betrayal threatening to end me.

"Rylee!" Kal shouts, but I can't stop.

One second, I'm near them; the next, I'm far ahead, zooming so quickly I barely feel it, stopping just a few feet away from the enemy.

Erin, are you here? I scan the line of Faders but can't distinguish one from another. I need to see them move.

All right, then. I'll make them move.

"Rylee!" Pierce yells my name, but it's like he's far away. There's a pulsing, pounding thrum rushing in my ears that matches the racing beat of my heart.

"If you came here to talk, let's talk," I say, but my voice sounds wrong. Laced with power and a grit that must come from the hurt inside me. "If you came here to harm, you've seriously misjudged my patience."

"Rylee, get back!" Axl this time, and I don't see them, but I *feel* my mates racing after me.

I glance behind me, noting how far away they are.

Shit. I used Kal's power of flight without knowing.

I focus in front of me again, waiting for a response.

The Faders don't move.

"I will hear you," I hedge. Maybe if I can get them to talk to me, we can come to some sort of peace. Especially if it's my sister. "Tell your leader," I say, hoping it will cause one to move. It doesn't. "I'm open to negotiations for peace."

My voice is laced with all the power inside me fighting for dominance. It coils and thrashes in my soul, through the opened doors and along the bonds and around them. I do my best to hold on to some sense of *self* before I become something else entirely.

Tension mounts in the silence, every second feeling like an hour while I wait.

Footsteps sound behind me, cracking the thick moment as the Legends reach my side.

The farthest Fader on the left is the first to move. He reaches behind him, pulling out a sword caked in a familiar white substance.

"No peace," a masculine voice calls from the middle of the Faders. "You have your orders!" he yells to his group. They all shift into a defensive position. "Capture them if you can. Kill them if you can't!"

All at once, the rest of the Faders draw their weapons and rush toward me. One pulls a blaster, then another, cracking off shots of blazing magic that soar right past me.

I whirl around, watching as Kal and Pierce barely dodge the deadly magic.

They're not after me.

They're after the princes.

Capture or kill.

Everything hones to that certainty, slowing my vision as four more shots light the night sky, aimed right for my mates—

I *explode.*

CHAPTER 17

Rylee

Earth and water and emerald energy.

Wind and nightmares and endless strength flood my body, erupting from the very depths of my soul.

Protect them. My instincts react on a breath. There's no situation where I don't keep them safe.

A wave of power greater than anything I've ever felt—deeper than Axl's Sapphire Sea, wider than Kal's beloved sky—pulses out of me. A scream rips my throat raw at the release, my vision a whiteout. I see nothing but that white-hot light for a few seconds.

I smell it first.

The raw power, a sort of scorched earth scent. Then smoke. There's so much of it as my eyes clear.

I fall to my knees. A sharp pain ripples up my bones from the impact, and tears fill my eyes at the scene before me.

Bloody strips of white canvas strewn along the cobblestones.

Ash and soot and broken bodies.

"Oh my goddess," I gasp, my heart threatening to pound out of my chest. "*No.*"

Erin.

Arms scoop me up. Indigo eyes fill my vision.

"Look at me," Jax demands, his voice primal.

I submit. Look at him and not the gruesome scene before me.

"They tried to kill you," I say through gasps of breath. My face crumples in his hands as the severity of what happened strangles my heart. "Did I just kill my sister?" I cry, unable to stop the wobble in my voice.

"No, Rylee." Jax shakes his head. "You didn't. She's not here. She's *not* here."

I'm trembling as he pulls me close. My teeth chatter as panic threatens to consume me. How does he know she isn't here? She could be. And I . . . I . . .

I feel empty. Their powers are far away on the other ends of the bonds, returned to them.

What have I done? Erin . . . She could be among the bodies.

My eyes fly past Jax, to the dead Faders. So much blood.

Some of it might be Erin's. Jax has no way of knowing.

Flashes of my sister, dead because of my lack of control, rip through me. My heart breaks, grief filling my soul. I'll never see her again, never get to fix what's broken between us.

"Jax," I whisper, fisting his shirt. "Please. Make it stop."

He pulls me to my feet, and a calming wave washes over me like soft, warm smoke. My trembling eases. Each pulse of emotion whispers, *it's okay, everything will be okay*. My mind clears enough for me to think.

"This one is alive!" Kal calls.

Jax and I immediately race over to where he kneels next to a Fader, pulling off their mask.

I blow out a breath. Not Erin.

"Men," Axl says, drawing my attention from where he's scanning the bodies. "Rylee, they're all men."

Relief hits me, then couples with guilt so thick it threatens to choke me. There should be no relief in this.

"I didn't . . . I don't know what happened." Such a pathetic excuse for this slaughter.

"You defended us," Pierce says firmly. "You did what any one of us would do in the face of such danger."

I hear him, but his words don't absolve me.

What have I become?

More calm presses into me, and I squeeze Jax's hand tighter.

Later. I'll fall apart later. Right now?

"We need to take him to the dungeons," I say. "We need to heal him so he can speak to us. Give us information."

Axl nods to Kal, some silent conversation as Kal turns to me.

"I'll take him," he says. "Can you hold it?"

His power. All their powers are *theirs* right now. Blown right out of me and returned to their rightful owners.

"I'll try." It's the only answer I can give, but as Kal bends to scoop up the unconscious Fader, throwing him over his shoulder before launching into the sky, I feel spent. Weak. Like I wouldn't be able to call their powers back to me if I tried.

I feel like *me*.

When before . . .

"Look at me," Jax demands. I turn, looking up into his searing eyes. "You did nothing wrong. They threatened us. You had no choice."

Tears spill over my lashes as he brings me to his chest.

I don't argue. I can't. We need to get to the palace.

But he's wrong.

There's always a choice . . .

And I'm *terrified* of the one I made.

CHAPTER 18

Rylee

I wipe the tears from my cheeks as we make our way back to the palace. I don't dare look in a mirror because I'm sure I look like death. Luckily, we don't run into any of the ball guests, and instead head straight for the dungeons below the palace.

Pierce, Jax, and Axl cast me concerned glances as we make our way down a set of spiral stone steps, golden torchlight illuminating the smooth rock as we descend.

My heart beats hard in my chest, my head pounding with the rhythm.

I'm still free of my mates' powers, which is the only solace I can take from the night's events. I halt on the steps, my chest tightening.

Pierce slides his hand along my back, patient. Quiet. All three of them know better than to ask me to sit this one out. I'm with them. Now and always.

Even if I'm out of control.

Fear prickles the back of my neck, and I tell myself it has everything to do with the dungeons and not whatever happened back there.

Bodies. There were *so* many bodies.

I cringe, forcing the thoughts away.

Another smooth wave of calm washes over me, and I flash Jax a grateful look. If not for him filling me with the emotion, I don't know if I'd be standing right now.

The air feels thick as we clear the last step, infused with the smells of wet stone, packed dirt, and something putrid.

I pause as the dungeons stretch out before me. "I've been trying to avoid this place my entire life," I whisper, an icy shiver skating over my skin.

It's cold down here, the stone walls leeching any warmth the torches create.

And the space goes on forever. Paths are chiseled from rock with evenly spaced bars for doors among them.

Cells.

My stomach turns.

Pierce takes my hand, gently tugging me down a path to the right. "Kal and the prisoner are this way."

Axl presses in on my opposite side, Jax at my back. Their support gives the illusion of safety, but the farther we twist and turn, the worse I feel. We pass prisoners in their cells, some sleeping, others watching us quietly from the dark corners. One snarls at us as we walk by, and another hums while rocking near their bars.

I wonder which prisoners are demis.

How many innocent people are wasting away in the dark? People who crossed borders they weren't supposed to? Wore clothes they weren't allowed to? Stole food to avoid starvation? Used a power they were born with?

Acid fills my stomach. Another item to add to my ever-growing list of responsibilities once the Legends ascend the thrones. I'll need to research the history of the prisoners here and ensure they're where they belong.

What will I say to them if they're innocent? How can we possibly mend what's been done to them?

As we turn a corner, relief pools in my chest at the sight of Kal, but it quickly ebbs once we're close enough for me to see the stern lines of his face.

"Has he said anything?" Axl asks, peering into the cell.

I follow his line of sight, spotting the Fader lying unconscious on the dirt floor.

"Occuli healer just left," Kal says, arms folded over his chest. "He should wake soon."

I take a step closer, then pause as power slams into me. "Damn it," I groan as Jax's ability returns to my body. Emotions flood from each of them, and it's all I can do to not buckle under the weight. "I didn't mean to take it," I explain to Jax.

"It's all right—"

A loud gasp cuts Jax off and snaps all of our attention to the Fader, who is no longer asleep.

The Fader scrambles around on the dirt, hands splaying and searching for something before he reaches for his head. Fingers spear into his hair, and his eyes widen as he looks up at us. He drags his nails down his face hard enough to draw blood.

"Goddess," I whisper, taking a step back.

Axl bangs on the bars. "Knock it off."

The Fader goes still at his command, then bursts out laughing.

"You are under the control of the Legends of Chaos," Kal says, his voice nothing like the soft, sweet tone he uses with me. *This* is the Legend rumors spread about. The one who steals dreams. He pries open the barred door and closes it with a clang behind him. "Cooperating with us will be very beneficial for you."

Tension coils in my stomach at how close Kal is to the Fader, but I hush that anxiety with the knowledge that Kal is fully in control of his power. I can feel it on the other end of the bond—strong and unflinching.

I hope I don't take it by accident.

The Fader leaps to his feet, and the rest of us instinctively move toward the cell.

But he doesn't go for Kal.

He slams himself into the stone wall on his left, then races to the one on his right to do the same.

"Fuck is wrong with this guy?" Axl asks.

"Stop," Kal commands, but the Fader isn't listening. I'm not even sure he can understand Kal in this state. *"Stop,"* he says again.

The Fader doesn't stop. Each leap he takes into the wall is more intense than the last.

Stone cracks beneath the force of his hit before he speeds into the next wall, his movements abnormally powerful.

Kal snatches him up by his uniform, preventing him from crashing into the stone again.

"Is he a demi?" I gasp, adrenaline crackling in my veins.

Kal holds the Fader aloft. The man goes limp, drool pooling from the corner of his lip. "We don't know," Kal answers. "The Occuli checked him for marks, but he has too many scars to truly know." He dips his head, studying the Fader's eyes more intently. "Shit," he hisses.

"Enhancements?" Pierce asks from my right.

"Eyes dilated. Incoherence." Kal glances at the massive crack in the stone wall. "Abnormal strength."

"Shit," Axl says.

Kal does his best to gently set the Fader down on a small hewn bench attached to the farthest cell wall. He crouches when the Fader makes no move to jump again. "What is your name?"

A small laugh. The Fader's eyes loll back and forth like he's following a trail of something we can't see.

"Pierce," I whisper, glancing up at him. "Can you hear him?"

Pierce dips his head, brown eyes focused.

I go quiet, not wanting to interrupt his focus. He interlocks our hands, our bond going taut. I gasp as he propels the power down it, swirling past my mental door and around the golden thread of our connection—

Capture them . . . any means necessary. Capture . . . Legends. Win . . . freedom. More. Need more.

The Fader's thoughts are fragmented and hard to follow, but the intent is clear, and the emotion behind it is chaotic and malicious.

I grip Pierce's hand harder, doing my best to not let my instincts sweep me away again. Because if they did? This Fader would be added to my already too-large body count.

Fuck, that's sobering enough to hush the protective mating bond instincts inside me.

"Kal," I say through clenched teeth, barely holding on to myself. "I need you to get out of that cell."

Kal flashes me a questioning look but immediately backs away from the Fader and exits the cell.

"You got something?" he asks Pierce and me.

"His mind is cracked," Pierce says, his voice so much calmer than mine. I know they're used to death threats, but I'm not. "The effects are unlike any enhancement I've encountered."

"So we were right," Axl says. "Their strength and abilities are from enhancements."

"This one's, at least," Pierce answers.

Kal looks back at the Fader's cell. "What does he want? Can you hear that?"

"More of whatever he's hooked on," Pierce says.

"And to capture you all," I snap, watching the Fader twitch on the bench.

Jax brushes his shoulder against mine, grounding me.

I lean into that touch, into his emotions, which are drenched in curiosity, not fear.

"Can you push deeper?" I ask Pierce. "Maybe find something we can use to uncover where they're hiding?"

Pierce tightens his grip on my hand. "Close your eyes and look with me."

My heart expands at his immediate inclusion. He wants me to see. Wants me to *learn*.

He believes I'm strong enough, despite what I've just done. The carnage I caused.

I don't deserve him. Any of them. But I do as I'm told.

Closing my eyes, I follow the coiling, spiraling power around Pierce's and my bond, letting him take the reins and doing my best to focus on the way he does it.

It's so damn natural for him, almost like breathing. I can sense it in the way he merely forms a thought, and his power does as he commands. He spears that power deeper into the Fader's mind—

We're no longer in the palace dungeons. No longer outside a dank cell.

Though there's stone *everywhere*. And Faders. All masked yet walking around with no sense of urgency. The vision goes in and out, as if the Fader's mind is missing pieces of memory.

Cold, empty, fearful, vengeful. The emotions splinter from the Fader, skittering down Jax's power that I hold. It's hard to concentrate on one power, let alone two.

A crevice in a slice of rock. The Fader wedging himself in it to be out of sight. A bright white powder fills the palm of his hand. It tastes like dragon fruit on his tongue. Relief consumes him once he's swallowed. Then a surge of energy.

The scene disintegrates into another. He's looking down at a . . . body.

I swallow hard. The person's lifeless eyes are glassy and cold, his skin drained of color, splotchy and almost gray. What could've killed him to make him look like that?

He nudges the corpse with his boot.

The vision pops to another. He's looking up at a Fader who stands on a slab of stone, illuminated by flames contained by iron lanterns positioned haphazardly throughout the space.

"Do you understand?" A familiar feminine voice radiates from above the crowd. "We must find a solution. That's more important than *any* other order given. We're running out of time." The woman raises her arms. "Go. Don't let me down."

Submission and loyalty fill the Fader's mind at her orders.

I gasp, flinching back to the present. *Erin*. What solution? What other orders?

There was no one else next to her. No one visibly pulling her strings. She's their leader. She's truly behind the atrocities they've committed.

My *sister*.

Pierce releases my hand, eyes still closed.

"Are you all right, love?" Kal asks, hands on my shoulders as he draws me to him.

I shake my head against his chest. "No," I whisper. "No, I'm really fucking not."

CHAPTER 19

Rylee

"You have mistaken me for someone else," I say on a tight breath as I take a step backward toward an alleyway in Cedar and Silk. Three enforcers are herding me toward the wall of a local market building.

Shit. How did they spot me?

Three weeks of dipping in and out of Cedar and Silk to visit Layce while also lifting the occasional valuable from a duke or two. They'd never miss the baubles I took, but the family of Ashlanders who need food and medicine would certainly appreciate the coin the items fetch.

"Duke Featheroy mentioned a blond girl," one of the enforcers says, practically sneering as he looks me up and down.

I don't look like an Ashlander today. I look like an Ari, thanks to the dress Layce loaned me.

"I assure you, there are a lot of blond girls in Cedar and Silk," I say, doing my best to keep my tone sweet instead of sharp. "I've just finished my shift at the dyer." I pray to the goddess Neph that they believe me and don't go check at the local shop where Layce works. She'd cover for me, but her boss? Mistress Mardone won't tolerate lies. "You have the wrong girl."

They don't, but fuck them.

The heavy coin purse hidden in the deep pockets of my dress practically pulses. The duke probably doesn't even know I lifted it from him. He's pissed I rejected his advances and sent the enforcers after me. Easier to accuse me of a crime than deal with the fact that someone could reject a wealthy man like him.

Ugh, the rich. They're all the same. Entitled, naive, out of touch. I hate them all.

The three enforcers share a look, hands poised on the hilts of their blades. Are they going to cut me down right here in the streets?

I've worried the same more than a few times. I'm no stranger to close calls. In fact, I live *for them. Live for the feeling slicing through my blood now—adrenaline and danger. It makes me feel alive when the Ashlands threaten to snuff it out of me.*

"She's right," a familiar voice calls from behind the enforcers. It's all I can do not to smirk. They're so fucked. "You've got the wrong blonde."

The enforcers spin around, the motion revealing my sister a few feet away. She's admiring a very expensive golden figurine as she holds it aloft. We lifted the pretty piece from the duke's home, too.

"Don't move!" one of the enforcers yells, as if she was poised to run.

Erin doesn't need to be poised to run. She moves swifter than a feline made of smoke.

She winks at me before tossing the figurine in the air above the enforcers' heads, and we bolt as they scramble to catch it.

My booted feet pound against the road. I'm much louder than my near-silent sister, who runs ahead of me. A wild laugh rips from my lips as I hear the enforcers curse behind us, but we cut around a corner too fast for them to follow.

Erin looks like a damn gazelle, smiling over her shoulder as she effortlessly weaves through the back alleyways behind taverns and restaurants and shops. "Keep up," she taunts, the challenge propelling my speed.

Wind calls to me as it rushes past my cheeks, the power in my blood begging for release. I hush it, knowing it's not needed to outrun these three fools. I only use it in dire circumstances. This little run-in? It's a regular Wednesday for Erin and me.

A blink and I lose sight of her, the quick loss enough to slow my steps for a few precious seconds. I skid to a stop at a fork in the pathway, looking left and right and then ahead. The breath in my lungs comes sharp and quick, my skin flushed from the chase.

Shit. Erin, where did you go?

Grunts and curses sound down the path behind me, and I hustle forward, instinct propelling me. I glance over my shoulder just in time to see the first enforcer make it into the alleyway—

I'm jerked to the left, into a darkened room that goes nearly pitch as Erin shuts the door. Our chests are heaving, and she holds a finger to her lips to ensure my silence.

I control my breathing, the effort painful as shadows block out the slivers of light slipping through the cracks in the closed door.

The smells of sawdust and freshly cut wood fill the small space, and as Erin quietly reaches for me, shifting me behind her, I realize she's yanked us into a woodcarver's supply closet. There are plenty of saws and hammers in here if we're caught and have to defend ourselves, but I'm seriously hoping it doesn't come to that.

The last thing we need to be hauled in for is robbing three enforcers of their masculinity.

"They probably went this way!" one of the enforcers hollers right outside the door. Then, after a few moments in which both of us hold our breaths, I heave out a relieved sigh at the sound of them rushing off in the opposite direction.

I wait for Erin to move from her position in front of me, a protective stance she's never let up on, even after I came of age.

"Erin," I whisper, gently poking her shoulder to get her to move.

"Wait," she says on a soft breath.

I go absolutely still.

"Listen," she demands just as quietly.

I do, straining my ears.

Shit.

A low, heavy breathing remains in the alleyway. I hadn't heard three sets of footsteps, just two. Goddess damn it, she'll never let me hear the end of this.

After a few more tense moments, the final enforcer heads off in the direction of the others, and Erin finally shifts from in front of me, arching an eyebrow.

"That was a trap," she says, adopting that motherly tone. The same one she's used since our parents were forced on a Never List mission years ago. "And you almost fell for it."

Shame pricks my chest. "We weren't caught."

"Because of me," she says, shaking her head. "Rylee, you need to be more careful."

"We were fine." I wave her off, despite knowing she's right.

"Today," she snaps. "What about tomorrow? Or the day after? What about the next time you decide a shot of adrenaline is worth your life, and I'm not here to bail you out?"

I roll my eyes. "You couldn't get rid of me if you tried. And besides," I continue, "you're one to talk. Who was it that ran away for three months last year? All because you fell for a man from Oak and Iron?"

Erin's lips part, then close, her shoulders dropping as a smile smooths away the lecture. "Fair enough," she says. "And I didn't fall for him. He was just a fun distraction."

"Yeah, right," I say. "And that fun distraction made it where I was taking care of that ridiculous cat of yours for a few months too long. I almost killed him a time or two."

Erin gasps, faux shock written all over her features. Her blue eyes, same as mine, widen. "You wouldn't dare!"

"Disappear on me like that again and see what happens," I tease.

"I didn't disappear," she argues. "You knew where I was the entire time. I sent you letters."

"Pictures," *I counter. "You sent me scribbles of paint. Made me interpret them like some ridiculous puzzle."*

"And you loved each one," she says, playfully nudging me in the small space.

I did. Challenges, life-or-death situations—I live for those things. Anything to keep my mind sharp and my passion high, especially when it's so easily stolen in the still moments in the Ashlands. Movement, distraction, it's all that keeps us going.

"Still," I say. "We're lucky the post allowed them through."

"Even if they hadn't," she says, her eyes shifting to something more serious. "You know I'd never leave without letting you know."

"I know. And you know I'd never want to hold you back."

"Oh, not this again."

"I'm just saying," I argue. "Your power allows you to go undetected. Escape the stickiest situations. If either of us could make a go of it out there without catching attention, it's you." Even if it would break me, I wouldn't fault her for wanting that life.

"You underestimate yourself," she says. "One day, you're going to realize you were meant for so much more."

Something thick clogs my throat, an emotion I don't acknowledge if I can help it.

Hope.

I lost all hope for a better life a long time ago.

"Anyway," Erin says, her smile catlike as she reaches behind her. "How much do you think we can get for this?" She pulls out the small golden figurine, blue eyes twinkling.

A laugh escapes my lips, unfiltered and free. "The one you threw was a decoy?"

She nods, tossing me the statue. I catch it against my chest, huffing at the slight weight to it. "You didn't think I'd part with the real one, did you?"

I examine the treasure in the dim light filtering through the cracks in the door. "To save your sister?" I tease. "Figured you'd sacrifice it."

"Who says I can't save you and get the prize, too?" She shrugs. "Let's take that to the market in Oak and Iron. Krev always gives us an extra ten percent."

I hand the statue back to her, thinking of the coin purse in my pocket. "Only because you supply him with endless amounts of those cacao beans Ivy grows. Plus, I think he has a thing for you."

"A win is a win." She peeks out the door for a few seconds before giving the all clear.

"A win is a win," I repeat, following her onto the path as if nothing had happened. "We can grab some medicine from the apothecary there, too, after we see Krev," I say as we walk, thinking of what a win today actually is.

A fever outbreak has struck the Ashlands these past weeks, and the lone, secretly run store that offers basic goods has long since run out of medicine. With our haul today, we can replenish it for a month.

Pride fills my chest, right next to the anger that's a constant from the restrictions placed on Ashlanders. It shouldn't cost us five times the amount the nobles pay just to heal ourselves. Let alone eat or dress or, goddess forbid, indulge.

I try to ignore the injustice of it all, letting it slide into that cold hate for all things wealthy and royal that's a permanent fixture in my heart, and focus instead on the win.

And that's all we can hope for.

Erin throws her arm around my shoulders, tugging me in for a hug as we make our way down the paths, navigating the roads that will lead us to Oak and Iron.

"You did good today, despite me having to save you," she teases.

"I'm getting better," I agree. "One day, I won't need you to save me."

"I eagerly await the day to be rid of such a pain," she jokes.

"Love you too, sis." I laugh, knowing how much harder it is for her to say those words. But I feel them. And that's what matters most.

"Darling." Pierce's voice cuts through the memory.

I blink. Once. Twice. Reorient myself.

I lean my head against Pierce's chest, shifting to look up at him where we're cozied together on one of the chaise longues in his rooms in the palace. He'd been reading to me, and my mind had wandered.

"I'm sorry," I say, meeting his gaze.

He sets the book he was reading on the end table next to him, then wraps his arms around me to draw me closer. "You showed me," he says. "I don't think you meant to, but I saw where you were."

"That's okay," I say. "I have nothing to hide from you anymore."

Nothing to hide from any of them. Secrets are a game we used to play, and while this future is uncertain, at least I can rest easy, knowing that's in the past.

I glance around at the empty chairs and sofas.

"Kal went to speak with Jullian." Pierce answers my silent question. "Axl is grabbing food. And Jax . . ."

I sit up straighter.

"He's gone to see Baydel in the hopes of baiting him into revealing more information about the Kings' List."

Apprehension claws at my stomach. "He shouldn't have gone alone."

Pierce rubs his hand up and down my back, a prideful smile shaping his lips. "You know, we have dealt with the kings on our own for quite some time."

I blow out a breath, a soft laugh escaping me. Of course I know that. "It doesn't stop me from worrying."

"Just as we know you're the strongest woman we've ever met, and yet, we will always worry about you."

Leaning in, I brush my lips over his, breathing deeply at the contact.

"I love you," I say, just because I can. Just because I know every day is not guaranteed.

I love you. He speaks the words in my mind, and I follow that connection down our bond, marveling at the way his power is still linked there, easily sharable. It's been that way for hours, with no regression or snapping back. I don't know how we're maintaining this equal connection, but I'm grateful for it.

Your sister is lovely, he continues, a flicker of the memory flashing behind my eyes. *And your hate for royalty and the wealthy . . .* His grin deepens as he kisses me again. *We're lucky you gave us a chance when you did instead of slitting our throats in our sleep.*

There's a joviality to his thoughts, but it still stings.

I would never, I argue. *Even when I hated you all, I didn't. You're different. You all are. And sometime soon, Lumathyst will know that.*

Pierce shrugs. *As long as you and my people are safe, I don't care what anyone thinks of us.*

I sigh, reality sweeping in to rob me of this small comforting moment.

Do you want to talk about her?

Erin. The memory still squeezes the life out of my heart.

Your bond is strong. Apparent in that lone memory. I'm sure you have countless others.

Tears bite the backs of my eyes. I have hundreds of memories like that one. My sister, her laugh, her support, her protectiveness of me. And yet . . .

Another memory takes shape in my mind, one that isn't mine. The vision of her through the Fader's eyes, giving orders, commands to a group determined to capture or kill my mates and harm the people of Lumathyst.

"It doesn't make sense," I say out loud, knowing he saw the train of thought. "Even with our hatred of the royals," I whisper. "Erin cared for the people. Not just Ashlanders. I would understand somewhat if the Faders were only attacking the wealthy earls and dukes, but they're not. They're attacking innocent shop owners and lower-class citizens. That doesn't fit."

Pierce is quiet, holding me, listening intently. I don't feel one ounce of judgment or doubt from him. Don't hear an errant thought about how people change, despite the fact that *I* can't help but think those things.

People *do* change. I know that.

I've changed immensely. But at my core? I'm still an Ashlander who wants to set right the wrongs we've endured for far too long. I know that will take time, and many small steps are required before a greater whole can be realized.

I sink against Pierce's chest again, exhaustion wrapping around me.

Pierce drags a hand up my back before running his fingers through my hair, gently massaging my scalp.

It feels so good, sitting here in the quiet with him, and it eases the pain storming me, the never-ending odds stacked against us.

"We will figure this out," he says after some time. "I promise you."

CHAPTER 20

Rylee

Sunbeams illuminate the ballroom floor in an array of colors glittering from the stained-glass windows decorating the east wall of the space hosting the next Kings' List event. The scents of fresh fruit, sparkling wine, and baked bread float in the air in a way that makes my stomach growl.

Ivy, Layce, and Mirren accompany us as we join the two dozen or so people gathered in the vast space, something Kal assured me would be acceptable to the kings, seeing as they're my ladies-in-waiting now. Even though I would never call them that. They're my friends, my *family*. Still, if they need a formal title to have an excuse to stay with me, then so be it.

Ivy and Layce follow Mirren's lead with a reserved elegance that causes the slightest hint of irrational jealousy to prick my insides. They look the part, their silver tops and pants matching Mirren's as a staple of those who attend the nobles and royals. Their demeanors shift, the calm, non-attention-drawing smiles, the dips of their heads, the hands placed casually behind their backs as they blend into the corners of the room.

They play their parts so well. All of them. And yet . . . I don't like it. My friends and Mirren are vibrant, brilliant, outspoken women. But here? They have to be quiet.

It's not fair.

But we have to play the game.

Change as drastic as I want can't come overnight.

I survey the room, noting the same noble families from the last event. The dukes and earls are positioned at a long table next to the kings' raised one—a position of power above the table designated for me and my mates.

I stifle a smile. If they only knew how outmatched they truly are now.

Then I spot the Occuli Frenrick Coolis at the nobles' table, and chills erupt on my skin. Why couldn't Dalfon be the Occuli appointed to the Royal Authority Council? At least he's civil with me. Conversative, even.

If we have any shot at earning Frenrick's vote, I need to let go of the fear, the anger, and make things as right as I can between us. Maybe, despite his magical outburst against me, we can come to some kind of understanding of each other.

I take a deep breath, flashing my mates a forced parting smile as I leave them at the table, heading straight to the Occuli sitting eerily still on the end, not even touching the plate of food before him. The second I'm within reach, he slides out of his chair preternaturally, bowing deeply, which stops me in my tracks.

I'll never get used to that.

I dip my head as he straightens to standing. "Forgive me," I say, though my voice cracks. "We've never officially been introduced," I continue, doing my best to ignore the fact that the previous chatter has stopped and all eyes are on me. "I now know you're Frenrick Coolis," I say. "And I'm Rylee Gray."

The Occuli tilts his head to the side, the move shifting the luscious purple robe he wears. The fabric is thick, covering his body as it drapes to the floor. I can't tell if he's wearing boots or slippers or walking around barefoot. He's bald, his head and face clean-shaven.

"You can call me Frenrick," the Occuli says, the otherworldly voice no longer holding the ichor it did when he caught me in the library in Ruby Aire. He bows slightly again before focusing those pitch-black eyes on me.

I don't know if I'm growing more accustomed to his presence, or if it's because of the increased power now collected in my soul, but I'm not as wary of him as I once was. Maybe it's because he's not wielding those green flames toward me and scrutinizing my every move. Or perhaps it's because I'm immortal now and there's nothing truly to fear—other than failing the Kings' List, which is why I've approached this creepy man in the first place.

"Frenrick," I say, dipping my head. "I'm glad to officially meet you. Our encounters prior to the Athanry, especially the incident in the library, were unfortunate, and I hope for more positive interaction in the future."

The Occuli nods but offers no further conversation. I hold steady for a few moments, feeling all the eyes on me—the kings, the nobles, and the elite enforcers, who are positioned, as usual, behind and near the kings.

"Hope you enjoy the feast," I say a bit awkwardly, hoping I've done more good than harm by engaging him. Then I retreat to my designated seat on the left of Kal, with Axl, Pierce, and Jax all to his right. Jax took the farthest seat away, the one closest to Baydel's table.

After a few moments, Baydel raises his voice above the resumed chatter.

"The kings and the Royal Authority Council and families are here to discuss your intentions," he says.

I remain silent, doing my best to appear much calmer than I feel. What intentions? Does he want to know how we'll take care of the people of Lumathyst? Protection strategies? He's brutally vague, taxing as ever.

"We'd love to explain," Kal offers.

"If you gave us more specifics," Jax adds.

"The Fader situation," Jullian clarifies, and Baydel sends him a sharp look.

"Yes," Baydel says, returning his attention to us. "While I wanted to start this meeting off with giving the Royal Authority Council time to offer ideas on how you can earn their votes for ascension, we must discuss the most pressing matters first."

The nobles nod their agreement. Each of the previous potentials sits near her father, no mothers in sight. All except for the Ari family, of course. They didn't earn a seat on the RAC, which doesn't seem fair to me, but not much does in royal decorum.

Charlotte Arden flashes me an encouraging look, and I smile softly at her.

Margreet Loredana, on the other hand, Pierce's previous choice, looks at me like a bug she'd like to crush.

"The prisoner you captured," Baydel continues, "exhibits signs of an illness the dukes have noted in their cities." He motions to Duke Windsor, who sits next to his daughter, Beatrice, from the Ruby Aire, and then to Earl Arden from Sapphire Cove.

That gets my attention, and I drop the berry I was about to eat.

Kal looks to Duke Windsor. "Why are we just learning this?" he asks calmly.

"Forgive me, your highness," Duke Windsor says from his seat at the opposite table. "Some of the other Ruby Aire nobles and I have just been made aware of the situation. The enforcers only brought it to our attention when the effects reached the more prosperous portions of the city."

Anger gnaws beneath my skin. "You're saying it's been happening in the Ari neighborhoods in the Ruby Aire, and the enforcers didn't feel the need to report it?"

Duke Windsor dips his head.

Kal smooths a hand over my leg beneath the table, the touch supportive.

"There weren't that many cases," the duke continues. "The number of people seeking out the Ruby Healers tripled in the last week."

Goddess.

"And they're all showing signs of confusion, abnormal strength, and agitation?" Kal asks. "Like the Fader we detained?"

"Yes, your highness," the duke answers.

My blood runs cold. So, the enhancement drug isn't contained to mere Fader activity. It's accessible to common citizens of Lumathyst.

"Clearly," Baydel cuts in, "we have the makings of an epidemic on our hands."

I blow out a breath.

"You remember the last one," Brooks says, looking more to his son than anyone else. Pierce nods, the line of his jaw taut.

"We imprisoned the person behind the previous enhancement epidemic," Pierce offers. "He died in the dungeons years ago."

"Whatever this new one is, it isn't like what we've dealt with in the past," Lucas says. "It's not even like the lower enhancements. Those, we can handle. This . . ."

Shit. I don't think I've ever seen Lucas look concerned about anything other than how much food is on his plate or if his wineglass is empty.

Foreboding swirls in my stomach like a cold wave. It was one thing when we thought the Faders were concocting the enhancement to be a match for my mates' powers, but if it's widespread, that could mean . . .

"Have there been any deaths?" I ask.

"Three," Earl Arden answers, expression grim. "One in Sapphire Cove, and two in Ruby Aire. Well, we're assuming they're caused by the enhancement."

Did we miss this because of *me*? Because of what happened in the Athanry and my state after? I shift uneasily in my seat.

"What do you mean you're *assuming*?" Kal asks.

"The bodies . . ." The duke cringes. "They're not like any the healers have seen. When some Ruby Aire enforcers found them in the streets, they assumed Faders had gotten to them."

I swallow hard.

"But," he continues, "upon further inspection, we're not sure. There were no visible marks. Blade or blasters or otherwise."

Pierce casts me a curious look. I'm just as confused.

"So you think they took too much of this new enhancement?" I ask.

"Possibly," the duke answers. "The bodies looked odd."

"In what way?" Jax snaps.

"Almost like they were drained of life," the duke says. "Those in the healers' quarters look similar. It's easy enough to assume that those who died took too much of the enhancement."

Something pricks the back of my mind, the memories from the Fader we captured flitting to the forefront. He nudged a body with his boot. It looked drained of all life. My stomach churns.

"How many enforcers have you deployed to look into the matter?" I pose the question to the kings. I know all too well the investigation tactics of the enforcers, have seen them search for enhancements more times than I can count back in the Ashlands.

Every week, they'd turn over our small hovels—the tiny shacks made of warped wood and rusty nails we called home—looking for all sorts of contraband. Not just enhancements, but basic things like wine, chocolate, or books. Possession of those luxuries was a crime for Ashlanders, while considered mere entertainment for Aris and up. And yet, they'd sent *teams* to search our places regularly. Surely they were doing the same now.

"None," Baydel says, a shocked laugh accompanying his tone.

"What?" I ask, stunned.

"Why not?" Kal echoes my sentiment.

"We're in the season of the Kings' List," Baydel says matter-of-factly. "This situation has only just been brought to our attention, and as set forth by our list, this situation falls directly under the definition of proving yourselves and your intentions for the good of Lumathyst. *You* are the ones who must take care of it. How you do so will reflect on your ability to rule Lumathyst."

A weight sinks atop my shoulders, as if the entirety of Lumathyst settles there.

Of course, I didn't think the kings would simply hand over their thrones, but I didn't think they'd need so much proof that their sons can rule. They're their *sons*. Where's the trust? The pride? Has their power gifted to them by the goddesses corrupted them to the point they no longer hold faith in their own children?

Or is this about me? About their lack of faith in the mate they chose? Each of the kings, save for Jullian, expressed their disapproval of me. And yet . . . I'm here. I survived, somehow. Isn't that enough?

I take a steadying breath, the four powers inside me surging against the doors I've shoved them behind. My own power slips through, a cool wind swirling in the vast room, too soft for anyone other than me to notice.

Goddess damn them. We should be working *together*. Our combined resources would be vastly more advantageous than turning this into a ridiculous test.

"The Faders were an issue long before the Kings' List," I blurt out, unable to stop myself.

Lucas presses his lips together like he's holding back a laugh. Brooks looks slightly amused. Jullian, proud. Baydel looks pissed—that flash of anger the first sign that his previous nice-guy act has been just that. An act.

"They haven't been a true threat until now," Baydel counters. "The recent attack is the first time they've made it past the royal borders."

"Ah, so because they finally made it into *your* city, you're now treating it like a real threat? The way we've been asking this entire time—"

"You may be the new princess," Baydel cuts me off, his tone firm, "but do not forget your place. You are speaking to the kings of Lumathyst."

"And it's *for* Lumathyst I speak," I fire back, not deterred. I probably should be. I should hold my tongue and quell my fire, but whatever survival instinct I had is gone.

I feel unstoppable.

All it would take is one more burst of power and they'd be bowing.

Stop.

I kill the thought, squeezing my eyes shut as if that will help me silence the unwelcome voice in my head. It sounds like me, but . . . that *can't* be me. I don't want to kill anyone. Well, maybe Baydel, but not right now. Not because he's *stern* with me. I have more emotional regulation than that. Right?

"Rylee speaks the truth," Kal says, his touch on my leg gentle and reassuring. "With this many lives at stake, we should share our resources—"

"No," Baydel cuts in. *The prick.* "You will handle this matter. The result of which will go toward the vote. We and the Royal Authority Council will determine at the end of this season whether you've done enough or not. That's final."

He may as well have rung a death knell for how quiet the room falls.

I want to look behind me, to find Ivy and Layce and give them a *can you believe this asshole* look. But I don't. I can't draw unnecessary attention to my friends.

"We'll take care of it," Pierce says, nothing but confidence in his tone.

I wish I had the same level of certainty, but after months of not being able to track the Faders' leader down to try to negotiate or put an end to them, it seems hopeless.

Their leader. Erin.

Every single time, that reality burns like a white-hot knife. I always thought betrayal would feel like ice in my veins, but it doesn't. It *sears*.

And with that burning, I find clarity.

I know what I need to do.

I need to stop looking for the leader of the Faders.

I need to continue the search for my *sister*.

Now that I know she's here, not off on some adventure, I'll find her. Draw her out if I have to.

And in that, I'll settle this.

Put an end to it.

And my mates will ascend the thrones as they deserve.

That notion gives me hope enough to school my features and scoop up my wineglass, taking a fast sip. "Now that this matter is settled," I say with a calm that rivals Kal's, "what other tests does the noble Royal Authority Council have in store for us?"

Shock rolls over their faces, though the Occuli is reactionless. I hear a small huff of a laugh behind me. Ivy. I can practically feel her pride.

No, I *can* feel it. Pride and a sharp anger that matches mine. Jax's power is potent, slipping like smoke beneath the cracks of the mental locked door.

I breathe in her pride, noticing Layce's worry and Mirren's unflinching stubbornness.

My girls are certainly with me.

My mates' emotions are too complex to sort one from the other.

I don't bother trying to sense the kings.

"So eager," Baydel finally responds. "Don't worry, little bug," he says, adopting that kinder tone he's been using since I awoke.

Back to playing games. Wonderful.

"They've each given their wise insight," he continues. "Expressing the most important qualities of a future queen." He motions to Margreet. "And I dare say she's come up with the best one."

CHAPTER 21

Pierce

Damn.

I knew the stipulations stated the Royal Authority Council would suggest certain tasks for the Kings' List, but seeing it in real time is the ultimate test to my patience.

Margreet may look kind enough, sitting next to her parents with a soft smile, her hands folded demurely before her, but underneath that facade is a vicious mind and twisted soul.

Regret rakes along my brain. She was my choice four years ago. She'd been lovely at the Choosing—there hadn't been that instant connection I felt with Rylee, but Margreet knew what she was doing. She engaged in conversation that piqued my curiosity and seemed genuinely interested in the four of us, so I selected her number.

I knew she wasn't the one before I even went into her mind. When I did, it was by accident. A slip in my power as my nerves grew tense. And in that brief slip, I saw an endless well of greed—a desire for more wealth, more power, more status. That's all she wanted. And that would be fair, I suppose, had she stated that up front.

She hadn't.

And the more I got to know her, the more I couldn't stand her. She enjoys stepping on those she views beneath her, which to her is everyone. Margreet is the type of woman who lives to bring others down—it inflates her ego, makes her feel big. That would never sit right with me, and we did our best that first month to ensure, in the politest way possible, that she would not elect to continue in the Choosing process.

She couldn't argue with our own vehement rejection and left after the first month, taking her earnings and newfound connections with her.

And now she'd suggested a test for my Rylee?

This wouldn't end well, regardless of what the challenge held.

"Margreet Loredana," Rylee says, giving the previous potential all her attention. "Lovely to officially meet you."

Margreet's thin lips curl. Her dark-blond hair is slicked back so tightly, it pulls at her skin, making her cheekbones look like they might burst through at the slightest smile. She narrows her brown eyes at Rylee, the look a mixture of intrigue and jealousy.

"I've been dying to meet you since the last Choosing," Margreet replies, her tone sugary sweet. "And I'm honored the kings took my suggestion to heart, to ensure you truly deserve the crown."

I cast my gaze down the table at my mate, silently supporting her, wishing I could slip into her mind. I can't. She holds my power. I can feel it like a weight on the other end of our bond. Still, I send love down our connection, hoping she can feel it.

Rylee sits up a bit straighter, giving the kings a once-over before returning her full attention to Margreet. "I'm grateful the kings care so deeply about Lumathyst and wish to ensure it's in good hands."

Margreet tips her chin a bit.

"Your test?" Rylee asks, her tone soft, kind, no hint of the irritation that mine would surely hold if I spoke.

This is taxing, to say the least. Rylee endured the Athanry. The goddesses made her immortal. She is our Chosen. These tests are unnecessary.

I cut a cold glare at my father, silently demanding that we speak more on this matter privately. As it is, there's nothing I can do to stop this now.

Not with the vote being up to the kings and the Royal Authority Council combined.

"Should be simple for you, really," Margreet says almost casually. "Important, though."

Rylee raises her eyebrows.

"History is the best place for any future ruler to start," Margreet says, glancing toward Baydel, almost like she's seeking his approval. He gives a slight dip of his head that wouldn't have been noticeable had I not been looking.

Interesting.

"History," Rylee repeats, visibly swallowing.

Shit.

We haven't had enough time to properly go over what she does and doesn't know about Lumathyst, our allies, our enemies. Ashlanders aren't given the same education as higher-class citizens—something we will remedy immediately upon ascending the thrones. If I had my power, I could feed her the answers. I reach for it, desperate to take it back, but I hit the door Rylee's constructed, not to keep me out, but to keep it from slipping out of her at the wrong time and overwhelming her. She's so damn strong.

"Understanding the realm you're trying to rule is vital," Margreet continues. "And since you're from one of the lower cities"—she scrunches her nose—"we're left wondering how qualified you truly are to wear a crown."

"Careful." Jax's voice is like sharp glass. He parts his lips, baring his teeth, about to say more when Rylee raises a hand in his direction, effectively stopping him.

"It's all right, Jax," she says.

It's an effort not to move closer to her, to shield her from whatever will happen because she chided the Nightmare—old instincts die hard, even as I know Jax would never harm her.

"Margreet wants what's best for Lumathyst," Rylee says, flashing Jax an assuring look. She's wonderful. After all she's been through, she still has the fortitude to play this new game laid out for her. "It's what we all want," she continues, glancing at the kings.

Margreet nods. "Who is Lumathyst's biggest trade resource?"

"Biggest?" Rylee tilts her head.

Margreet smirks, as if she's won some battle. "Yes. You do understand what trade is, do you not?"

Fuck.

Jax pushes his chair back an inch like he might scoop Rylee up and take her out of such an unnecessary character assassination attempt. I shake my head, deterring the idea even though I'd be right behind him. Rylee doesn't need us to fight her battles for her, no matter how much we want to.

Rylee's grin is effortless. "I do," she says. "For clarity, I'm inquiring about which trade you're referring to? If it's steel and wine and spirits, then Cardrayton would be the answer. If it's agriculture products, like citrus, seeds, and grains, then it's Vleyica."

Margreet's features shift to something more bitter.

"And if it's for the minerals, jewels, and other properties the royal cities depend on, it's the Ashlands. Minus what is carted in from other realms like Silvac," she continues. "Though, I suppose you can't call that trade, since the Ashlands aren't given much in return."

Margreet's mouth pops open.

Baydel rests his hands on the table, locking in on Rylee so intensely, I'm terrified he's about to snap her with his power.

When a few seconds of weighted silence go by without her flinching, I relax.

Margreet clears her throat. "And our relationship with Silvac?"

Rylee immediately looks to the Occuli at the end of their table. Frenrick seems bored, and quite honestly, I can't blame him. This is ridiculous. Rylee knowing or not knowing our history will not dictate her ability to rule. This information can and *will* come later. Margreet wants to make her look ignorant in front of the RAC. Diabolical.

"Silvac and Lumathyst have a peace agreement," Rylee answers, though the confidence in her tone wavers a bit. We've only spoken about Silvac once, and that was after her first encounter with Dalfon. There are a great many things we need to catch her up on where it comes to royal history, customs, allies, and more. We thought we'd be able to in a more relaxed setting, not one riddled with trials and lists and prodding opposition at every turn. "One that holds as long as no official missions from Lumathyst are launched in an attempt to steal from their Source."

Fuck yes. Brilliant. She remembers the discussion with Dalfon where he told her about the magical element from his homeland.

Margreet flashes a worried look at Baydel, and I tilt my head. Shouldn't she be seeking the approval of her duke father over Baydel, who is a stranger to her beyond his position as king?

Curious.

Kal breaks the silence. "Is this truly the test? Honestly, this is not indicative of her ability to rule."

"She will continue," Baydel says with a warning look. "If it's such a ridiculous test, Kal, you should have no issue with your beloved completing it."

A muscle in Kal's jaw ticks, but Rylee lays her hand over his beneath the table in assurance. She dips her head toward Margreet to continue.

"And speaking on those missions," Margreet says. "Can you tell me, on average, how many people make the Never List each year?"

Shit.

Rylee's lips part, the slightest hesitation there.

Margreet's smile twists in delight at Rylee's pause. "Come now," she says. "This should be an easy one. Knowing the number of traitors to the crowns among Lumathyst is incredibly important." She shrugs. "Or would be, to someone who actually knows how to rule a kingdom."

Rylee is silent.

"Well, for goddesses' sake," Margreet says, waving her hand toward Rylee. "*Do* say something."

Rylee's fists clench beneath the table. "Fifty?"

I close my eyes, my disappointment not in her guess but in Margreet and the kings' tests. There was no reason for us to discuss anything like this beforehand. She'd have no way of knowing the number.

"Wrong." Margreet shares another glance with Baydel before looking at Rylee with pure delight. "Closer to five hundred," she explains. "Growing marginally each year. I daresay the enforcers are getting better about spotting the traitors. Better for us, to ship them off in service of the kingdom rather than let them stay here and risk the kings."

Rylee's lips press into a firm line before she finally speaks. "I was unaware."

"Obviously." Margreet rolls her eyes. "You need to catch up." She shakes her head. "One final question. Though after your last, I'm quite certain you won't be able to manage it."

Damn, this woman is sour. Foreboding gnaws at the back of my mind—it's too quiet in here without my powers.

Margreet snaps her fingers, and a couple of enforcers cross the room like they've been instructed to do her bidding. She's of nobility, but this is absurd.

The enforcers get to work unrolling a large piece of parchment, the size of a small dining room table, hanging it from two golden rods for all to see.

"This is a blank map of Lumathyst," she says, pointing to the illustration. "And the surrounding realms across the seas. Fill it in."

Oh, no.

No one—other than a few of the *oldest* and most privileged bloodlines in history—know the true placement of the realms. The kings have kept any real map from the lower cities, under the guise of keeping the knowledge of how and where to ally with enemies across the seas out of potential rebel hands. Even sailors facilitating trade only know of specific routes and are sworn to secrecy on that knowledge.

Margreet's laid a trap.

And there's nothing we can do but watch as Rylee falls into it.

CHAPTER 22

Rylee

"That's out of line!" Kal pushes back from the table, standing up so quick you'd think he had his powers back. "Only a few families know the correct configuration—"

"And they're in this room," Baydel cuts him off. "If your Chosen doesn't know the answer to this question, then the fault lies with you for not educating her properly."

"We haven't had time since the Athanry!" he snaps. "You can't possibly mark this against her."

"Kal." Jullian says his son's name with an affectionate plea, flashing him a look I can't interpret.

Kal takes a breath, softening his tone. "The question is unfair."

"Ruling a realm is hardly fair," Baydel counters. "Sit down."

Kal hesitates.

I reach up, smoothing my hand over his arm, urging him back into his seat next to me.

The tension in the room mounts, causing the powers inside me to press against the locked doors so hard, I feel like it may crack my bones.

I grit my teeth and keep the doors shut. I can't attempt to use Pierce's mind-reading abilities so he can show me the correct places on the map. Not now, after Kal's reaction. They *know* I don't have the answers.

And besides, the last thing I want is to use their powers in the presence of the kings. If they felt it, sensed it was in a place it didn't belong? We'd really be done for.

Though, failing Margreet's test doesn't feel all that great, either.

I scoot my chair back before crossing the room. I do my best not to glare at the enforcer who hands me a quill and glass bottle of ink.

My skin tightens as I feel all eyes on me. I'm lost, totally unaware of how to properly complete this task. I dip the sharpened quill into the ink, my fingers trembling as I study the blank outlines on the map.

Maybe I can get lucky and guess. I've seen a map before, despite them being forbidden in the lower cities. Dukes love to display them on the walls of their studies, a place I equally love to steal from. But, after Kal's reaction, I'm wondering if even *they* have a correct one.

I've traveled all over Lumathyst since the Choosing, so the cities are easy enough for me to decipher. I start there, if only to look busy while everyone watches, most of them waiting for me to fail.

It's the unlabeled expanses of land across the seas that hit the hardest. The realms I've only heard of, never seen. Swallowing hard, I scribble *Cardrayton* over the spot closest to the Sapphire Cove. Axl told me a few stories from his travels there in the past.

I study the blank map. I can't guess beyond this. That would make me look as foolish as I feel. I sigh, letting the quill drop to my side.

"Like most of us in the lower realms, I've never been given access to a comprehensive map. I cannot continue." I hate that I'm admitting defeat, but better that than randomly placing names of realms I know little to nothing about.

Anger rises up like a flame brought to life in my chest. Another restriction against the lower classes, and for what? To keep us dependent on the kings. On those placed above us.

Margreet laughs so sharply, it echoes in the vast room. She pretends to hastily cover her outburst, but I can see the victory in her eyes. "Poor thing." She delivers a haughty smile. "So many spaces left blank." She eyes the rest of the RAC. "How can we expect her to rule if she can't even get our basic geography correct?"

I clench my teeth so hard it hurts.

"You've got me there," I finally answer. "As you know, I wasn't raised like those of you in this room. I'm from a lower city, and my education was limited. If that's the point you're trying to prove, then you've certainly achieved it." I shrug. "Education can be remedied," I continue, letting them all see the severity of that statement written in my features. "And I intend to do that immediately. Unless you'd like to enlighten me now." I glance at Margreet, then wave to the map.

"It's not our job to bring you up to speed," Margreet practically hisses. "The princes should've ensured you understood the intricacies of the realm before they chose you. Or, perhaps, they should've chosen someone who wouldn't need such coddling."

My adrenaline slices through my veins. Oh, this one *hates* me. She doesn't know a true thing about me, other than the princes chose me and I'm from a lower class, and she despises me for it.

I swallow the knot in my throat. "Are there any further questions on your history test, Margreet? Or are we free to go?"

Margreet gapes at me for a moment before looking to Baydel for guidance.

He dips his head. "You're free to go. The Royal Authority Council will make note of your lack of knowledge. In the meantime, get a handle on the enhancements. And maybe think about trusting your Chosen with the secrets you've kept from her."

Those words hit like a knife in a target, flooding me with questions. Why *didn't* they tell me about the maps? Do they doubt me?

They are your mates, I remind myself. Kal gestures to the door, and I lead the Legends out of the room, Mirren, Ivy, and Layce following behind us.

They chose you.

I belong here.

I repeat the last phrase a few times to ground myself as we make our way into Jax's room in the palace. I know we need to get out of the royal city to start digging into the enhancement issue, but right now, I need a second to think.

"Rylee," Kal says the moment Jax's door is closed and we're all inside. "We haven't had time. You just woke up, and then they dropped the list on us."

"We didn't intentionally *not* tell you," Axl adds.

I take a deep, steadying breath before nodding to them. "I know," I say and feel really good that I believe that. "I get it."

"If we thought it pertinent to the circumstances of this damned list, we would've gone over geography," Pierce says. "I should've known Margreet would pull some superiority-complex type of test."

"She's a fun one," I say with enough sarcasm that Ivy and Layce laugh.

"She's definitely not your biggest fan," Layce says, taking a seat on one of the couches. Ivy settles next to her.

"Can't really blame her, can we?" I smile at my friends.

"Sure, we can," Ivy says with a smirk.

"She lost out on the chance of happiness with these four," I say, motioning to my mates. "I'd be cross, too."

"She wanted a crown," Pierce says. "Not *us*."

I scrunch my nose up at that. "Who wants a crown when I can have the four of you instead?"

"In addition to, not instead of," Kal corrects. "You can have it all."

"Pompous royals," Ivy says, then shrugs. "No offense," she adds, glancing at the Legends, who've spread throughout Jax's room.

I'm still standing in the middle of them all, shaking my head.

"There's so much to do. So, before you *educate* me"—I say the word with emphasis and roll my eyes—"on all the things I apparently need to know, starting with a proper map, I need to figure out some other things, too."

Pierce's eyebrows rise, intrigue radiating from his eyes.

Jax is silent and calm where he leans against the wall.

Axl and Kal settle in a couple of chairs near him.

"Like what?" Kal asks.

"A lot of things," I say. "Practicing the powers with you four, definitely.

Digging deeper into the strange deaths and the enhancement issue is a given. That needs to be cut off. But . . ." I sigh. "I need to get back to the Ashlands, too. Not just because I want to check on the people there, but because of the terms of the Kings' List. The new enhancement was likely tested in the Ashlands first, though I doubt any mysterious deaths have been investigated. Plus, maybe there's some clue I missed about Erin there." I doubt it. I searched for her for an entire year before I got Chosen, but it's worth a shot. "And if there is," I continue, "that will help us with the Fader issue."

"I was wondering when you'd want to go," Jax says. "But I thought it would be under different circumstances."

"Me too," I admit. "I'd hoped to be returning in order to start elevating them. We're not there yet, and I know we have to be strategic about it. We can't do everything all at once. I get that. Searching for information there will be a good reason to go back. One that won't raise questions from the kings. Plus, it feels wrong to have been gone so long without checking on those I left behind."

"You did have other important things going on," Ivy says.

"I know. You told me to make them fall for me." I smile at the memory of her demands after I was Chosen.

"You rarely listen," Ivy teases. "At least for once you did."

"And then the whole Athanry incident." I shake my head. "More issues to solve. Poison and Faders."

Axl glances around at the company in the room, then sits up straighter. "Do you want us to make you a list? No one is taking notes."

I laugh, the reaction drowning some of the heaviness. I love him for his ability to always bring light to a situation. "No," I answer. "I need us all to be on the same page."

"We're with you," Pierce says, the others nodding. "Always."

I nod back. "Thank you."

"We'll figure it all out," Kal assures me.

Mirren doesn't voice her support, instead electing to pour a round of drinks. She hands them out, a sense of solidarity filling the room as she hands me a small crystal glass of amber liquid.

"One impossible situation at a time." Ivy repeats the encouraging words she spoke to me at the Choosing, the ones that stopped me from spiraling, holding up her glass toward mine.

I clink my glass against hers, then Layce's, before gesturing the cheers to the rest of the room. "One impossible situation at a time."

CHAPTER 23
Rylee

Erin sits atop her thin mattress, her back pressed against the wood-planked wall of our hovel, slivers of the setting sun slipping through the various cracks. Her brow is furrowed, her blue eyes on the paper in the small leather notebook perched against her legs, a piece of broken charcoal pinched between her fingers.

My heart warms at the sight. I'd found that leather sketchbook in an earl's garbage barrel while sneaking around borders with Ivy and Layce. There's a split in the leather on the front of the binding that makes it look less pristine—likely the reason the earl had tossed it in the first place—but it was perfectly usable; beautiful, even. Especially now, after Erin started filling it with her drawings.

I rarely got the chance to give my sister gifts, but this had been a special treat.

"Staring is considered impolite," Erin says without looking up from her work.

I laugh as I sink onto the bed, careful not to mess her up. "Since when have you ever been concerned with what is and isn't polite?"

"I care," she says, then laughs as she pauses her work to look at me. "Sometimes."

"Sure," I say, then nod to her sketchbook. "Can I see?"

Erin quickly closes the book. "It's not ready yet."

She never likes to show me her work until it's finished, and sometimes her pieces take weeks. They're always stunning, though. Her paintings should be hung in the palace for how good they are. No, scratch that. The pompous royal dictators don't deserve her work.

"Find anything interesting today?" she asks, shifting off the bed. I follow her lead, crossing the small space to settle on my identical mattress, watching as she lifts hers. She wiggles a loose piece of wood from the floor and tucks her sketchbook safely into the hiding space before sitting on her bed again.

"A few minerals," I say, resisting the urge to wipe at the layer of grime coating my skin. I'd been forced to work a double shift today after one of the enforcers caught me trying to take an extra ration of water on my break. It hadn't been for me. A boy had almost passed out right next to me.

"Did they force you to work with those imported stones again?" Erin asks.

"No, they didn't," I answer, thinking about the stones. I only worked with them once when the enforcers ordered me to break them down. They made me so nauseous, I could barely stand. I swiped one and took it to Ivy, hoping she could figure out why it made me sick, but before she did, they switched me to the mines. The mines didn't make me ill, just exhausted.

"You look tired, Rylee."

I lean my head back against the wall. "I'm always tired."

"Do you ever think about taking me up on my offer?"

A mixture of anticipation and fear swirls together. "Sometimes," I say, looking at her. She's not covered in grime, but she wasn't assigned to the mines like me. I'm pretty sure they kept her in the sorting stables to keep us apart as much as possible. We tend to get into trouble whenever we're allowed to work together.

"It would be easy," she says.

"For you, it is," I counter. "A snap of your fingers and poof, you're gone."

Erin laughs, flickering in and out of sight on the mattress to show off.

"Not all of us were blessed with such a gift," I continue. I curl my fingers, conjuring a soft breeze that brings relief from the stifling heat inside our little home.

"You don't need the gift of blending into shadows to escape."

Erin can basically evaporate. The enforcers don't even notice when she's gone.

But I notice. She deserves her adventures. If I had her ability, I'd probably run off any chance I got.

"Where did you go last time?" I ask, referencing her adventure a few months ago. She'd been gone for a week.

"The Emerald Wood," she says. "I wish you could've seen it, Ry." Her eyes light up. "Everything is so green there. And the main city? It's stunning. People sit in tea shops for hours just reading and eating."

"Sounds like a dream," I say a little bitterly. I'm happy she gets to experience such things. I really am.

Erin's shoulders drop. "Please come with me." She hops up, crossing the small space to my bed and plopping down next to me. She grabs my hand. "We're going to the Choosing next week. You have *to come this time.* Please?"

"I'd sooner visit one of the goddesses' temples and curse them than spend one minute *among the nobles and royals."*

"Ugh," Erin groans. "Come on. It's worth it. The food and the jewels. You need to go at least once."

"Bring me back a treat like you always do," I say.

Erin shakes her head. "You really won't come with us?"

"There are very few places I won't *follow you, sister," I say, arching a brow. "But into the royal palace of Lumathyst, among the kings and the Legends of Chaos, is most certainly one of them. You'll be fine with Ivy and Layce."*

"I know I will be," she says, rolling her eyes. "But you miss out on all the fun."

"Your idea of fun and mine are vastly different." They always have been. Erin is a feather drifting on the wind, going wherever her instincts take her. I'm a mountain of stone, doing my best to stay grounded and not crumble after every storm.

Erin releases my hand, accepting my refusal. "I'll make sure to bring you back something extra special this time," she says, returning to her bed.

A soft mewing sounds outside the door, and she's up and swinging it open before I can move.

A black cat slinks inside. He's rail thin, weaving between her legs as she shuts the door.

"Hello, Ash," she coos. "No food today," she continues as they head back to her bed. The thing settles in her lap as she strokes its wild fur.

"I'll see Layce tomorrow," I say, looking down at the stray that has somehow become another mouth for us to feed. "I'll grab something for him then."

"Thanks," Erin says. "He looks skinnier than the last time he turned up."

"Nothing will kill that cat," I say, eyeing the numerous scars inlaid in his black fur. He's missing half his left ear, too. "Certainly not starvation."

Erin laughs, nodding. "He's as stubborn as you are."

I shrug. She's not wrong. Even if it's a jab about not going to the upcoming Choosing with her.

I should go.

I should go with her.

Because when I don't, she'll never come back—

A throbbing ache pierces my mind . . .

"Rylee?" Erin asks, her hand slowing on the cat's back. "Rylee?"

I look around the room, suddenly feeling as if I'm seeing everything in slow motion. My heart races in my chest.

This is wrong.

Am I dreaming?

Footsteps echo to my left, toward the back of the home that has no entry.

"Pierce," I say, relief uncoiling my tight chest at the sight of him standing there, his hands tucked into the pockets of his emerald green dress pants. His matching suit coat is unbuttoned, his brown eyes on me.

"Rylee." His tone is so soft, so understanding.

"I did it again." I motion toward my sister, who is now frozen on her bed, one hand on the cat's back, eyes open and unblinking.

"It takes practice. It takes time."

I shove off the bed. "We don't have time," I say, stopping next to him.

He looks at my sister. "I know you didn't mean for me to venture into this memory with you," he says, returning his focus to me. "But I'm honored to have seen it. The bond you two have . . ."

"It's not . . ." I cut him off, a pain like a knife in my chest. "It doesn't matter anymore."

Pierce slides his hand over my cheek, calm and comforting.

I look up at him, unable to resist.

"You can still love the pieces of the sister you knew while having questions about the ones you don't understand."

Tears well in my eyes. Unwelcome tears, but I can't stop them. Not when he's offering such support when he has grounds to hate my sister for what she is. What she represents.

"I'm sorry I got sidetracked," I say, sliding my arms around him.

"Don't be." He embraces me and tucks his chin atop my head. "You're doing marvelously. When I first came into my power, I slipped into everyone's mind constantly and could barely hold myself in one place for long. Then other times, I'd trip up and create different realities for people. Once, I made Jax believe he was stranded atop a snowy mountain for a full hour. I didn't mean to. It was just part of the learning process. It almost drove me mad."

"I bet it drove Jax more mad." I smile, looking up at him.

Pierce laughs. "He rather enjoyed it, I think. Took it as a break from feeling everything at once." He sighs. "We all struggled back then."

"I don't believe that."

"Do you want me to show you?" he asks. "Or would you like to take a break and return home?"

Exhaustion weighs me down. Before I fell into this memory, we'd been training for hours. Working on my ability to shift in and out of his mind, to block out his thoughts, to manipulate his reality.

I glance at the image of Erin and the cat on the bed. What if she's returned home or left clues as to where she is?

"He looks friendly," Pierce teases.

"He's anything but, I assure you," I say, happy to slip into an easier space.

Pierce chuckles, squeezing me tighter. "Home?"

I nod. "Home."

"Close your eyes," he whispers.

I do as I'm told, the action effectively blotting out the scene around us. Something tugs at me through my middle, a force that drags me up from the deepest well.

"Open," he says.

I part my lids, blinking a few times to reorient myself in the real world.

Pierce sits across from me, mimicking my seated position—legs crossed, arms resting gently on our knees, back straight. The emerald floor beneath us is cool and grounding, the sound of trickling water from a stream soothing through the open windows. The smell of pine drifts on the wind, and the rustling of the trees provides a calming backdrop to our training.

We haven't moved for hours, but my muscles feel as if we've battled. Before I slipped into the memory with him, I'd been marveling at the many facets of his power. A world of possibilities, and I'd do anything just to return it to him.

I'm never going to be able to learn it all, am I? I can't speak the words aloud.

You will, in time, he answers. "And we don't expect you to know everything."

"I know." I flash him an apologetic look. "But the kings and RAC clearly expect me to. *I* expect me to."

"That's unfair to you."

I shrug. "Life is rarely fair, is it?"

Pierce purses his lips, and it's an effort not to smile at the pouty look he's giving me. "Have we reached the pessimistic portion of our training?" he asks, his tone slipping into that low, seductive lilt that sends warm shivers dancing over my skin. He shifts to his knees, crawling across the small space toward me.

The sight alone is an undoing, but I hold my position. "I think a bit of pessimism is earned," I say, but I'm already breathless as he reaches me.

"Is that right?" he whispers, sliding his cheek along mine, his lips teasing the shell of my ear.

"Yes." I breathe the word, arching my neck to give him better access. "The circumstances—"

"—are dire," he finishes, pressing kisses down my neck that set me ablaze. "For certain." He lingers on my collarbone, and everything inside me tenses, our bond tightening, pulsing with need. "And yet," he continues, drawing back to meet my gaze, "I can only see you." His brown eyes trail over the curves of my face. "You're here. My mate."

The words send tendrils of heat spiraling beneath my skin.

"I'm here," he continues, dragging his lips lightly over mine. "*Your* mate."

I *break.*

I lift my hands, cupping his face. "I love you." I'm unable to hold the words back.

Pierce visibly swallows, shifting before me, sliding his arms behind my back and adjusting us until my spine kisses the cool floor and he's settled between my thighs.

There's no race to tear off our clothes.

No greedy intensity. Not when he's looking down at me like this.

"I love you," he says, trailing one hand along my jaw. "That's the reason I can't be pessimistic. Even with the Kings' List and the Faders and the Royal Authority Council . . . even with all of that . . . I can feel nothing but love. You're here. And to me, to *all* of us, that's all that matters."

Because there were moments when they thought I wouldn't be. When *I* thought I wouldn't be.

That reality hits me like a stone.

I shake my head. "I shouldn't let these things distract me from the good that brought us together."

Pierce dips his head, his mouth slanting over mine in a searing kiss. "You're allowed to feel however you want. And just know . . ." His words slow as his hand moves down, lazy and explorative over the thin cotton shirt I wear. Lower, over the satin pants that cover me. "I'll be right here to remind you of the good when you get lost in the bad."

I gasp as he touches me. Brazen and possessive. The bond between us is so strong, it's like it's been hewn from the emeralds surrounding us. It blazes and burns right down the center of me as he moves above me, his hands everywhere at once, his mouth on mine.

He's got his power back. I gave it to him? *How?*

"Sharing," he groans against my mouth before slipping his tongue between my lips.

I dig my nails into his back as he holds me tight, using his mental gifts on me. I feel that mental touch everywhere—a soft caress on my inner thigh, a hot brush against that sensitive bundle of nerves that makes me tremble, a long, demanding stroke down my back.

"Pierce," I moan.

The weight of his power has lifted, allowing my soul to breathe, since his power isn't pounding against that locked door inside me. Not with the bond like it is now . . . that door wide open. It's so damn freeing. My head spins with the loss of control, with the assurance that Pierce has me and won't let me fall.

"That's right," he says, shifting between my thighs. "I've got you. I've always got you."

I catch his gaze, feeling the sincerity of those words down our bond. I reach up, kissing him, pouring every ounce of love and need and connection I can into that motion, sending it all radiating down our bond.

He doesn't take it slow after that.

One second, I'm fully dressed; the next, I'm as bare to him as he is to me, spun around with my back against his chest, both of us on our knees.

"I love it when you have your power back." I gasp, reaching up and behind me to lay my palm against his cheek. "You're so much better with it than me."

His hands glide around me from behind, one palming my breast while the other slides between my thighs.

"You're my match," he says. "You will exceed my talents in due time."

I don't argue, can't even form words when he's stroking me like he is. I'm wrapped up in him, body and mind, and I can't get enough. He pushes me right to the edge of pleasure until I'm a tight string about to snap. Every touch, kiss, *word* has me throbbing, aching.

"Pierce." I arch against him. "Please."

Please, what? He speaks the question into my mind.

You know what. Even my mental voice is breathless.

Ah, ah, he says. *Show me what you want me to do to you.*

Fire licks my spine at the challenge, the demand. I smile, pressing back against him while conjuring the images, then draw them up in his mind—him positioned behind me like he is now, slicking his length through my wetness, generously coating himself before circling backward, teasing me there before slowly, gently inching his way in.

Darling. Let me make that a reality for you.

He fists his cock, dragging it up and down my heat, immediately reenacting the fantasy I showed him. He's wet as he guides his thick head to that tight hole, circling it. I gasp, a thrill shocking me as he slowly slips in an inch. The space is so snug as he gently pushes in, but he's so slick he almost glides, the sensation spinning my mind in the best way. This angle allows him access to the deepest parts of me, and he's holding us there in delicious anticipation.

Pierce draws out of me and does it again just as slowly.

I do my best to match the pace, relishing the feeling while also aching for more.

"You're perfect," he says, his voice strained as his hands tighten on my hips. The grip intensifies as I push back when he thrusts, the two of us finding a rhythm that works us both into knots. The bond between us is solid and *burning*, only adding to the tension pushing me right up to the edge.

His hands roam over my body that's on full display for him, massaging my heavy breasts, plucking my nipples until they're pert for him. Then lower, rolling his fingers over my clit and dipping two into my heat in time with his thrusts. In this position, there's only so much I can do beyond hang on—

The thought leads right to another one, and before I know what I'm doing, I'm taking back his power. Using it like he's used on me so many times. A mental caress over every nerve ending he has, sparking them with pleasure.

"Fuck," he groans, the word sounding refined from his lips. "Rylee."

Pride flows through me, right next to the aching pleasure as he slides in and out of my body until I see stars.

I see everything good and perfect stretching out in front of me.

"You're handling the power like it was *made* for you," he groans, his lips on my neck before he drags his teeth gently down it, causing pleasure to coil beneath my skin.

Everywhere he touches feels hot and needy.

Everywhere we connect feels all at once too much and not enough.

And when he thrusts into me again while pressing down on that sensitive spot between my thighs . . .

I *fly*.

"Pierce!" I gasp his name as my orgasm rips through me, sharp and blinding and beautiful, traveling from the crown of my head to the tips of my toes.

"Rylee," he groans, spilling into me, sending one end of pleasure right into another until my breaths are ragged and my body is limp, only held up by his arms wrapped around me.

We catch our breath slowly, holding each other as the bond settles between us, the needs of it sated for now. Relief fills the very dregs of my soul. And I can feel his power flowing freely between the two of us, intricately working together like the silk threads of a spiderweb—

The connection severs, and it all slams back into me. The full force of it nearly drowns me before I shove it back behind his door and lock it.

"Too much," he says. "We did too much today."

I shake my head, trying to find my voice as he carefully pulls out of me, quickly scooping me into his arms and carrying me to his bathing chamber. He draws a bath, and we sink into the warm water, soaking our tired muscles. I relish his soft, caring touch as we wash. Revel in the comfortable, content silence that wraps around us.

And after we've dried off, we retire to his luxurious bed. He draws the covers over us, dragging the tip of his finger down the line of my jaw.

"Tomorrow, we'll take more breaks between training," he assures me.

"I'm fine."

"Rylee," he chides me, eyeing the pillow I can't raise my head from.

"I'm fine," I assure him. "You did this to me. Not your power."

He opens his mouth to argue but stops at my silent look. He settles next to me, holding me.

"Don't let me sleep too long," I whisper. "I need to get back to training."

"All right," he agrees reluctantly.

Because he has to.

Because he's only the beginning.

I need to master all four of their powers if I want any shot at giving them back. But with everything going on, I'm not sure we have the time.

"And after," I continue, sleep threatening to take me entirely, "I need to go to the Ashlands." My eyes are heavy. Closing. "Will you take me, Pierce?"

"Wherever you want to go," he says, but he sounds very far away. "Always."

CHAPTER 24
Rylee

I eye the line of carriages waiting outside the gates of Pierce's home and smooth my hand over one of the horses.

"When did you manage this?" I ask Pierce, who is dressed casually this morning in a pair of cotton trousers and a green shirt.

I opted to forgo any finery this morning, too. Something felt inherently wrong about wearing a formal gown for a trip to the Ashlands. Pierce anticipated this, laying out a sturdy pair of leggings and a simple white shirt for me.

"Before dawn," he answers, reaching over me to stroke the horse as well.

My heart expands in my chest. Whenever I think I can't fall for him any more, he does something like this.

Ivy and Layce pop out of one of the carriages, Mirren from the one behind them.

"There's enough food stashed in these to feed the Ashlands for a week," Ivy says, dipping her head toward Pierce.

I think it's the first time I've seen her look at one of my mates without suspicion.

"And medicine," Layce says, motioning toward Mirren's carriage.

"I know we're going in an official capacity to make inquiries about the enhancement and the deaths connected to it." Pierce adjusts a piece of hair off my face. "But I figured we could bring some much-needed wares to the people, too."

I swallow the lump of emotion in my throat, wrapping my arms around him in a quick embrace.

"I don't know how to thank you for this," I whisper, trying to hold back tears.

He hauls me against him, bending down to envelop me completely. "You never need to," he assures me, pulling back enough to look down at me. There's confusion in his refined features. "When are you going to understand that we're in this with you? What's ours is yours now. And while we can't immediately elevate the Ashlands, we can give them relief while we work on it."

"And the kings?" I ask, nodding toward the line of carriages. "If they question us, they'll believe our efforts to investigate?"

"I've sent a detailed explanation of our efforts to uncover all we can about the enhancement, including venturing into several different cities, and insisted we start in the Ashlands. They can't deny us. Not when we're performing in direct correlation to their list's demands."

"I'm so glad you're on top of things," I admit. "I wouldn't have thought of that."

"You never give yourself enough credit." He sighs. "You did think of this. You're the one who said the enhancement was likely tested on Ashlanders first. You *will* be an incredible queen."

I glance down, unable to meet his adoring gaze. Part of me still doesn't feel worthy of his praise or their love. Especially with the way things started—me lying to them to survive. And now, with my sister and what she's doing, plus my complete lack of knowledge on how to rule anything, let alone an entire realm.

Pierce's power slams on the door I've locked it behind, jerking me out of my thoughts. The punch behind it is *incessant.* I close my eyes, willing it to hush, sending my own power over the door to soothe it into submission.

"Are you ready?" Pierce asks after a few moments.

I nod, and he holds open the door to the nearest carriage, helping me in after I've waved to my friends, who climb into the ones behind us.

Soon the sounds of hooves clop on the road out of the Emerald Wood, the cadence a soothing kind of lull that fills our cabin.

Pierce is quiet and content next to me, our hands interlaced as we ride in silence. I don't have the words to explain the emotions storming me—the anticipation of bringing these supplies to the Ashlands or the fear that we'll cross that border and it'll never let me go again.

I *want* to go back.

Want to search for clues, information, anything to help us.

Want to help my people, even if I can't do it as much as I would like.

But I also don't feel like the girl I was when I left. And then there's the more ridiculous curiosity, the idea that I'll return and find Erin there as if she'd never left. Never organized in a radical group focused on destroying my mates' cities. Never abandoned me for a cause she finds justified.

The pungent smell of earth and mineral and dust slips into the carriage, ripping me from my thoughts.

"We're here," I whisper, almost like a warning as I move the silk curtain covering the small window.

My heart leaps into my throat at the line of enforcers guarding the entrance to my homeland, their uniforms gilded and glistening under the early-morning sun, steam wafting from their mouths as they halt our party.

One approaches our carriage, and every instinct in my body has me scooting as far away from that door as possible as it swings open.

I'm mated to the Legends. They cannot arrest me. They cannot hurt me.

"What's the meaning—" The enforcer's words immediately stop when he recognizes Pierce, and he dips into a low bow. "Your highness," he says, his tone shifting from irritated to formal in a second flat. "How can I assist you?"

"You can move your men and let us pass," Pierce says in a voice I rarely hear him use—the Legend's voice, the unshakeable tone of a future king of Lumathyst. There was a time I would've cowered under such a tone, but now? It only makes that bond between us perk up and ask to be played with.

"Right away, your highness," the enforcer says, bowing again as he waves to the six other enforcers lining the entryway to the Ashlands, standing in the middle of the open wrought iron gates with bars three times their size jutting into the air.

No one gets by those gates. Not unless you know how.

Not unless you're stupid enough to think crossing the border is worth the risk.

"All of your carriages are permitted entry?" the enforcer asks.

"Naturally. We have royal business here, and beyond that, my mate is feeling charitable," Pierce says, motioning to me.

I do my best to look relaxed and graceful, like a real princess as opposed to the scared Ashlander I truly am.

"She's brought food and medicine," he continues. "We'll need more enforcers to help distribute it through the proper channels while we conduct our business." He turns to me. "Anywhere in particular you'd like to set up?"

I clear my throat, hoping to find my voice again. "The center square," I say, hating that my voice cracks. "We should call the quadrants in groups, one at a time, to get their stipends."

Pierce nods, then cocks a brow at the enforcer, who doesn't move. "Did you not just hear her deliver an order, enforcer?"

He shuffles on his feet before bowing. "Apologies, highness," he stammers. "Right away." He closes the door, barking orders at the other enforcers as we're waved beyond the gates.

I watch as we cross over the line, unable to tear my gaze off those bars attempting to reach the sky. My throat threatens to close, the sensation not unlike when Baydel used his power against me.

"We will tear down those gates together." Pierce squeezes my hand. "Piece by piece."

"I can't wait for that day to come." I smile at him.

Once we've reached the center square, Pierce holds open the carriage door for me, helping me step out of it and onto the sodden ash ground. I go oddly numb as I survey the area—it's exactly as I left it, though a chill hangs in the air today, rather than the goddess-forsaken heat when I left. Spring is approaching, but winter seems reluctant to let go.

I eye the highest mountain in the north portion, the one to thank for our name—Ashlands. It's consistently erupted in a storm of fire every decade or so, leaving our air and land covered in the white ash in its aftermath. The ground is soft and slightly wet, my flat boots immediately caked in the gray sludge. Overcrowded hovels line the center square, some brave Ashlanders peeking out through the cracks in the silver-soaked wood to view the commotion.

Beyond the crammed wooden shacks are jagged pathways with ruts carved into the dirt from handcart wheels rolling over them so many times—people carting their findings from the other mountains that stand like foreboding giants in the distance.

I swallow hard. Everything is drained of color here. Of life. And it makes my heart break all over again. It was one thing growing up here and crossing borders to see my friends and lift trinkets from the wealthy, but now? After living as a royal for so many months? The differences between the two lands are insurmountable.

Unfair.

Wholly, unjustifiably unfair.

Rage licks beneath my skin. The kings and their rules. The suffering they inflict.

My mates' powers respond to that inner hate, rising in a fast wave, begging for release.

I draw in a breath. These people are innocent. The power will do them no good here. But the food? The medicine? That will. And that's enough to ground me.

After a full two hours, I've finally gotten used to enforcers asking me for further orders and barely flinch as they approach me. Another two hours, and we've fully unloaded the carriages and have arranged individual stipends for the people.

Ivy and Layce take charge of the food distribution while Mirren covers the medicine and clothes. Pierce oversees everything, ensuring there's not one disrespectful remark from the enforcers as the first quadrant is called to collect.

It's hard to watch. Hard to stand next to Pierce when I feel like *I* should be in the line of people looking at us suspiciously. Like this is some trap concocted by the Legends to trick them into doing something wrong.

I would've believed that, had this happened before the Choosing. Before my life changed entirely.

I see people I recognize, but they don't recognize me, or if they do, they don't dare say so. I nod and smile, but I feel like a fraud.

And after the second quadrant is called and things are still running smoothly, Pierce and I share a knowing look. It's time for us to search for answers.

"Shall we?" he asks, extending his arm.

I loop my arm through his, allowing him to lead me away from the crowd. I'm so grateful Pierce instructed the enforcers to treat Mirren, Ivy, and Layce as an extension of us, obeying their requests as if we made them ourselves. Without them, I'd fear one of us would need to stay behind to ensure the enforcers didn't interfere with people retrieving their goods.

"The head Ashlander enforcer is this way," Pierce explains as we turn down a few worn pathways.

"I remember," I say softly, my grip tightening on his arm. Every Ashlander knows where the head enforcer's offices are kept, which is why I've always avoided this section of the center square.

Pierce leans down to whisper in my ear. "I'll start the questioning, then you can dismiss yourself whenever you feel ready."

I nod, my nerves tangling in my throat. Anticipation and hope dare to bloom deep in my chest, making it hard to speak. I try to reason with the emotions, hitting them with logic—the last time I was here, I found nothing to lead me to Erin.

Maybe Pierce will fare better with his endeavors with the head enforcer.

The enforcer's office is kept in a simple wooden building, but it's more well-kept than the others lining the square. There are less holes in the wood from hungry insects, and a fresh coat of stain makes it appear newly built. The main door is open. No doubt one of the enforcers told him we were coming.

"Your highness." The head enforcer, a man named Ned, bows to Pierce before gesturing him inside.

Pierce hesitates outside the open doorway, arching a brow as he looks from Ned to me.

"Your highness," Ned hurries to add, bowing to me in a panicked hurry. It's almost comical. "Forgive me," he rushes to say. "I'm so unused to visits from the royal family and have yet to adjust to your new mateship."

Pierce tips his chin up, studying the enforcer before finally leading us inside. The office consists of a small desk, a grouping of mismatched chairs, and an ancient-looking cabinet pressed against the farthest wall.

Funny. I used to fear this place and this man, and now? He, along with his quarters, seems so small.

"We intend to remedy the lack of visits." Pierce opens the discussion. We each take a seat in the chairs, the enforcer settling behind his desk.

"My man told me you're looking into some recent deaths?" Ned asks.

"Yes. Mysterious in nature. Have you had any in the Ashlands recently?"

I hold my breath.

Ned considers for a long moment. "Nothing I would concern your highnesses with," he answers. "Ashlanders die from all sorts of things." He says it so casually. It sets my teeth on edge. "Malnutrition is one of the most common. Right ahead of mining accidents." He shrugs. "Circumstance of their position."

I scoff, unable to hold back my reaction. "Such a flippant way to dismiss Lumathyst deaths."

Ned sits up straighter in his seat, eyeing Pierce as if he expects him to scold me.

He doesn't, of course.

"Ashlander deaths, your highness."

"The Ashlands are part of Lumathyst, are they not?" I snap.

He opens and closes his mouth a few times. "Yes," he says, but it sounds like a question.

I take a breath. His confusion is a direct result of how the Ashlands have been treated by the royals in the past, but I can't play that role. I can't pretend it doesn't matter. It does. And maybe it's time everyone knows I will not behave the same way the kings do.

"Then perhaps take care in how you speak about the deaths of these people," I say. "No life is worth more than another, regardless of where they reside."

Ned looks to Pierce again.

"You do agree," Pierce urges. "Don't you?"

Ned clears his throat. "My sincerest apologies, highness."

"Now, I'd like you to think again." Pierce leans forward on his seat at bit. "Have you noticed anything that would make you believe something else was the cause of a death recently? Something other than starvation or mining? An illness?"

"There was one just last night," Ned answers. "I didn't think to mention it because . . ." He hesitates.

"Because why?" Pierce prompts.

"We determined it was a common overdose." His eyes flash to mine. "A sadness, for sure, but unavoidable to those who seek out enhancements from the peddlers who smuggle them across our borders. Most likely from the *Droguedens* or similar suppliers."

"What was common about it?" I ask.

"The way we found him, your highness. He was in a state of unrest in the streets, mumbling incoherently before he erupted in screams. These enhancements, they prey on the weak and crack the mind. This one took so much he started ramming his head against one of the buildings. We tried to stop him, but we weren't fast enough."

Goddess, the picture he paints. It sounds like the Fader in the palace dungeon.

"Is the body still with the mortuary?" Pierce asks.

"Yes. It's procedure to bring in an Ari from Cedar and Silk to try to identify which enhancement he took, so we know what to watch for in the other workers . . . the other Ashlanders."

Pierce and I share a look, then both stand together. "Take me to him," he says.

"Of course, your highness." Ned is around his desk in seconds, leading the way out of his office.

"Would you please go speak to the people on my behalf, Rylee?" Pierce asks. "Inquire if anyone saw anything or has heard about a new enhancement?" He turns to Ned. "The man's name and residence?"

Ned hurries to answer. I'm relieved it isn't a name I recognize, but I'm saddened all the same. Had we stopped this new enhancement before . . . many lives could've been spared.

"I will right away," I answer Pierce. We'd already planned on separating, but his verbal permission will stop any questions regarding why I'm wandering the Ashlands alone.

"After you," Pierce says to Ned, who dips his head and leads them away.

I take a moment to breathe before getting to work.

After an hour of trying to speak to people, ensuring it's no one I knew from before, it's evident no one trusts me enough to give me any real answers. I can't fault them. What reason would they have to tell me the truth? And the few who did deign to speak with me had nothing concrete to tell me. They knew as much as I did—that enhancements, while rare, occasionally made their way into the Ashlands because there were plenty of desperate souls searching for an escape. Sometimes, that escape cost them their life.

Defeat settles heavily in my chest as I relent, giving up on my endeavors and switching to a different, easier objective. I turn down a familiar path, my heart thudding rapidly once I see it.

The third home on this forsaken road. The cracked door, rotting in the corners and hanging slightly off the hinge. The small stone paver just before it, soaked in ash and wet earth.

I linger outside the door, glancing around for any watching eyes. There are none. This quadrant has cleared out for their stipend, and there are no enforcers in sight.

I'm alone.

And I feel that notion in my bones as I quickly unlock the door, thankful it's still locked. With the diminishing population, I doubted they'd put anyone else in our home, especially when it's lowlier than most, but I wasn't certain.

I head inside, leaving the door slightly cracked behind me. Our home remains untouched. My absence hasn't been noted, likely because the only way they'd realize I was gone is if the Ashlands' head enforcer had a direct need of me. Thank goddess, he never has.

The space is narrow, so much I can almost touch the walls with both hands outstretched. Two thin mattresses with lone sheets sit atop the board floors, one tucked up against each wall. There's just enough room to walk down the middle toward the back, where a simple rusted bucket acted as our bathing chamber. Restrooms are communal in the Ashlands, as well as kitchens. We'd never be permitted to cook our own food, if we had any, or prepare tea. Little things that the nobles take for granted every day. Dust coats every inch of the space, including the paintings on the walls near our beds.

Empty.

Frozen in time.

When I left here for Ivy's the night of the Choosing, I thought I'd return right away. I didn't even make my bed before leaving.

I shake my head, feeling like that life is a world away as I sink to my knees atop the thin mattress, wiping my palm along the wood wall it's pressed against. The motion uncovers the moon and stars Erin painted there ages ago. Emotion threatens to break me, but I do my best to breathe. I glance down at Jax's tattoo beneath my collarbone, then at the painting Erin did, and wonder if the goddesses knew all along that I would end up with the Legends or if it's some massive coincidence.

The goddesses told me there were other things at play, beings, *Fates* that they couldn't risk angering. My mates told me more about them, too. They're the beings who sit above the goddesses, with most realms, like Silvac, only worshipping them because no goddesses ever came to their lands. Maybe it's those Fates playing this game and using me as a piece in it. Maybe none of it is real. Maybe I hallucinated every experience with Evaluna.

It felt real.

The time that I slept. The time I spent in Evaluna's temple. Her warnings felt real.

And there's shit all I've been able to do about it. Hopefully Pierce is gleaning more than I am today.

I sigh, slumping onto the bed, wondering if I'll ever find the strength to get up.

I gaze at Erin's side of the room, hating the disappointment that sinks in my stomach. She hadn't been here for a year before I left, and she's the leader of the Faders. Why would she have come back here and left something for me to find? Some clue to absolve her of her recent actions.

A sister's foolish dreams.

I roll my eyes before closing them, content to sit in the silence for a while longer.

After a few moments, I *feel* the presence more than hear it.

"You're still as sneaky as ever," I say, opening my eyes to find Ash sitting on Erin's bed.

He blinks as if to say *you're incredibly late* and then flicks his tail back and forth.

"I know," I respond. "I'm sorry. But before you write me off . . ." I reach into my pocket, draw out the small bundle of dried meat I brought with me, unwrap it, and show it to him.

He cautiously stalks over, eyeing me, then the meat, then me again, before he snatches it up, mewing softly as he devours it. I stroke his fur, relishing the feel of soft and scarred.

He's stayed relatively healthy, from the look of him, since I've been gone. He's always been a terror for vermin in the area, and there's an endless supply.

Once Ash finishes the treat, he leans into my touch a bit more but keeps looking back at Erin's bed.

"I know. I miss her, too."

Miss the sister I knew.

This other sister, the leader of the Faders . . . I don't know how to feel about her. Betrayal burns like a wasp sting.

"Look, I know you've always been on the fence about being domesticated, but I'm going to take you home with me," I explain after he's settled in my lap. I scoop him up, surprised when he lets me. Usually, he's cross with me at best, hostile at worst. I suppose without Erin around, beggars can't be choosers. "You'll have a meal every day," I say, as if he understands. "It's hard to get used to." I stand up, giving my old home one last look, unsure of how to feel about leaving it.

Ash wiggles out of my arms, landing on the floor on near-silent paws. He pads over to Erin's bed and rubs against the edge of the mattress, looking up at me as if he's trying to tell me something, which is ridiculous, of course.

"Let's go." I motion to the door.

The cat doesn't budge.

I stare the creature down. "You'd rather stay here and starve?"

Another blink.

I sigh as he resumes rubbing the edge of the mattress, and I can't shake the thought that I should check her secret spot beneath the bed, even though I checked it every day after she went missing. With another sigh, I shift the mattress.

"You were there," I say to the cat. "You saw me. It was always empty."

I shift the loose plank of wood, reaching down into the small, hollow space.

My fingers hit something. I grip it and draw it out with a gasp.

"Her sketchbook?" Tears spring to my eyes. I awkwardly turn it over in my free hand, glancing down at Ash. She's been here! "Did you see her put this here?"

Ash yawns, as if he's bored with my line of questioning, which is absurd, of course. I scoop him up in one arm, not wanting him to get any ideas about running off. He's my responsibility now, and for some reason, I feel like keeping Erin's cat with me will cause her to come to me. Ridiculous, sure, but it's something.

I stare at the sketchbook for a few moments, wondering when she returned it. Was it right after I left for the Choosing? Later? Why did she bring it back? Have the Faders outlawed art in their ranks, too? But if she's their leader, why would she have the need to hide anything?

Questions fly through me more rapidly than my beating heart. I pocket the book, instinct urging me to hide it, as if an enforcer will try to take it from me any second.

Hurrying out of my old home, I clutch Ash with both hands, more than ready to rejoin Pierce and my friends, and, if I'm being honest, return *home*. To any of them. I'm not unaware of the privilege I now hold—four homes to choose from, four incredible mates, and more power than I know what to do with. But it's at home where I'll be able to freely study Erin's sketchbook.

And the sooner we solve the Fader issue, the sooner we earn the Royal Authority Council's vote by completing the Kings' List, the sooner I'll be able to help the Ashlands beyond a basic stipend.

I find Pierce near the center square, saying goodbye to Ned, who stalks back to his offices. Ivy, Layce, and Mirren are giving out the last of the stipends.

"Anything?" I ask once I reach him.

"I'm afraid so." He sighs. "The body looked as we've seen before."

In the Fader's mind.

"Could you tell what he'd taken? Did he have any left in his pockets?"

"No. I will send Dalfon to come inspect him, though, as soon as we return to the palace. Maybe he can ascertain what he took or where it's coming from. I know you said the enforcers here do weekly inspections for all contraband, but I'll send some enforcers we actually trust to do that from now on. They'll be briefed on what to look for and what to ignore and will only report on enhancement findings."

My shoulders drop. I wish there was more that we could do, but this is a start. I try to hold on to the notion that we're trying. And I found Erin's sketchbook. That's something. Plus, her cat.

"I see you found what you were looking for," Pierce says, shifting the heavy subject as he reaches out to pet Ash.

He hisses at him, scrambling away from Pierce's outstretched hand.

"He's like that with everyone," I explain.

"I'm glad you found him." He quickly draws his hand back.

"Me too," I say, observing the last line of people collecting their goods. There's a little levity on the faces of those who linger beyond the center square, clutching the bundles of goods to their chests and looking at my friends with gratitude. That brings joy to my heart, allowing me to breathe a bit easier.

I glance at Pierce. "Can we order the enforcers to shorten working hours? Or is that too much change?"

"I fear that would draw the kings' suspicion and might compromise the vote. But if it's what you wish, I will make it happen."

I stroke the cat in my arms to calm my anger at being so trapped, despite all the power I now hold. "If we lose that vote, we lose the chance to truly help here. Help everywhere that needs it."

He nods.

"It can wait," I say reluctantly. More than ever, I want to earn that vote. Want my mates on the throne not only because they deserve it, but because I know we'll have the full power to do so much for Lumathyst. So much good can happen, if we can only get there.

And if we don't earn the vote?

It'll be a challenge against the kings for their thrones. A battle easily won if my mates' powers are their own.

But because of me, they're not.

Which means we have to play the game.

I sigh, feeling defeated but hopeful as the last of the food, medicine, and clothes are handed out.

It's something.

It's a *start.*

And with how shitty things have been? It's all I can ask for.

CHAPTER 25

Rylee

I crash into the pool so hard it stings.

Axl's power bangs on the door, playful and restless, as the warm water surrounds me.

Frustration rattles my very core as I kick toward the surface, sucking in a deep breath as I clear the water. I wipe the hair from my face, turning as I hear a deep laugh behind me.

"It's not funny," I say, but I can't stop a laugh from slipping out.

Kal flashes me an apologetic look, waving me off.

"It's not," he says, barely containing his amusement from where he stands at the edge of the pool. He folds his arms over his chest, his red sweater sticking to his muscles.

Ash lounges on a cushioned chair at the opposite end of the pool, his tail flicking back and forth. He eyes me in a very judgmental way, but at least he's stopped skittering off when Kal takes a step too close to him. He still tries to claw at him any time Kal tries to pet him, but I think the all-you-can-eat fish dinners have stanched any permanent escape attempt. He's still prone to nightly explorations beyond the princes' houses, but he's come back every morning.

Though it's midday, the sun shining brightly above us, early spring still brings with it a bite in the air. Luckily, the ruby stone pool deep in Kal's grounds is heated by some Occuli-powered magic. It's a goddess-send, especially today.

Kal shifts to kneeling as I swim toward the edge. He reaches for me and tips my chin up to meet his eyes. "You would've laughed at me when I first learned to fly, too."

"You were a child. Not an adult. I highly doubt it was funny."

Kal gives a casual shrug. "Axl certainly laughed."

"I managed to hold myself aloft for ten minutes that time," I say, blowing out a breath.

"You're incredible."

"It *feels* incredible when I get it right. It's all the times I get it wrong that bother me. We don't have time for mistakes like this." I motion to the water, miming my splash earlier.

"There's nothing else we can do *but* this," Kal counters. "Rylee, you mastering these powers is crucial for your mental, physical, and emotional health. Nothing else matters."

So much else matters, but I'm not in the mood to argue those points with him again.

I think he can see it on my face, though, because he gives me a faux pout and backs away from the edge of the pool. He gathers the hem of his sweater, pulling it over his head in one smooth motion.

I swim back a little, heart racing at the sight of him. It doesn't matter that I've spent countless hours studying the curves of his muscles, the blue of his eyes. I'm always stunned.

"Let's try again," he says, unbuckling his trousers and letting them fall to the ground. He steps out of them, leaving him in nothing but tight red shorts, his massive thighs on full display before he slides into the water and slowly stalks toward me.

"What?" I blink out of my haze. "Were we training? I've suddenly forgotten everything from before you took off your clothes."

Kal laughs, the sound full and rewarding. "You think you don't torture me in that bathing suit?" He eyes the emerald green two-piece I wear. "But I know you'll feel so much better once you've gotten the hang of this. And you're already doing so well. Let's try again."

He's not wrong. If I can give myself any credit, it's for the amount of information I've learned over the last month, the first half with Pierce, the second here with Kal. From the history of Lumathyst to the goddesses, the kings, and the realms across the sea. History lessons are a reprieve from playing with powers all day and night. Though, when I left the Emerald Wood, I felt all the more confident about Pierce's power.

"Okay," I say, slightly pouty. "I'll pretend I'm not hurt you didn't come in here to ravish me," I tease.

Kal's smile deepens. "Think of this as foreplay."

I laugh. I can try to blame my insatiable need for him on the mating bond that crackles between us, but I know a lot of it's just me. I've always had an appetite when it comes to the Legends, and no matter how much I'm with them, I always want more.

Kal shifts in the warm water, gliding behind me. My bare toes are on the smooth stone as we stand there, his chest grazing against my back. He slides his hands over my shoulders, down my arms, and to my fingertips, gently lifting them out of the water. He stretches my arms to either side of me.

"Close your eyes," he whispers, his lips at the shell of my ear where he dips down to speak to me. "Concentrate, like we've practiced."

I take a deep breath, doing as I'm told. We've done this a hundred times now, and it's always easier when he's touching me. Just like it was easier when Pierce was *in* my mind with me. Their powers are more bendable when they're close, but Kal had given me space moments ago to test my limits, and that's when I crash-landed into the pool.

"Feel the sun on your face," Kal continues, his voice a soothing balm for my tangled nerves. "Feel the wind kiss your cheeks." He drags his lips over my cheek for emphasis, and warm sparks ignite down my spine.

I hold my focus, miraculously, and concentrate on the elements he refers to. The ones his goddess mother, Neph, blessed him with. Blessed my ancestral line with.

The sun is warm on my skin despite the crisp chill on the wind, and the contrast with the heated pool creates all sorts of sensations.

"There's a thread," he continues. "Or at least, I've always pictured it as a thread. A line of energy I can draw from. The sun and sky have always replenished my power, fueled it as I believe my mother intended."

"I thought your power was endless," I say, keeping my eyes closed as I search inwardly for the thread he speaks of. "At least it's supposed to be, now that you're mated."

"It feels like that now," he says. "When you return them to us. Where before we found you, they were so much less."

I can't imagine *less*. Not when I can feel the full strength of his power inside me now. The door I lock it behind is wide open, the other three tightly secured while I work with Kal's power. His feels like the sun—warm and consuming, strong and healing. It radiates beneath every inch of my skin, filling me with hope and strength and dreams of soaring the skies. I can practically taste the clouds on my tongue. His power wants to fly so badly . . .

There.

I gasp, mentally gripping the thread he speaks of. "I . . . I found it," I whisper, terrified that if I speak too loudly, I'll lose the thread. It's like a string of clouds and sunlight braided together.

"Good," Kal says, pride radiating from his voice. His hands drift off my skin, but I can still feel him behind me. "For me, it was easier once I found it. As long as I held on to it, I never faltered. Hold on to it enough, and it becomes second nature."

I focus harder, mentally gripping the thread in one hand and the well of his power in another. I smile. "This is incredible," I say. "Kal, your power, the way the air and sun feed into it, back and forth like a never-ending stream. It's amazing. It's endless. It's—"

I open my eyes, turning to look up at him, but he's not behind me.

He's below me.

I gasp, jolting in the air where I hover a good four feet above him. I didn't realize I'd flown. I almost lose the thread, but I hold on to it like my life depends on it.

Kal smiles up at me. "Look at you," he says, eyes full of pride. "Stunning."

I wet my lips, a blush creeping over me. I'm certain I look awkward, floating here with no sense of direction, but the longer I do it, the easier it feels.

Remembering our earlier exercises, I move to the left, then to the right, flying short distances and keeping the pace slow, the speed controlled by how much power I draw from the well inside me. The one that flows freely around the bond between us now that I'm not forcing it one way or another.

"Good," Kal says, never taking his eyes off me. "You're doing so well."

I press my lips together to hold my focus. When he says things like that, it *does* things to me. Probably because he praises me so much in the bedroom, it's hard to take it any other way.

"Want to test your limits?" he asks.

I halt, tilting my head. "Should I?"

He grins up at me. "I think you should."

I slowly return to him, dipping back into the water enough to get eye to eye with him. "You trust me?"

"With my life," he answers immediately.

The instant declaration fills me with a reckless sort of confidence.

I take a deep breath, nodding as I embrace him. He wraps his arms around me, holding me close, and then I draw a little more power from his well inside me—

We shoot into the sky so fast my heart drops to my stomach.

"Shit!" I gasp, trying my best to slow us, to push some of the power back behind the door.

"It's okay," Kal says in a calm tone. "You're okay. You're in control."

"I'm so not," I say, feeling his power rush through me, as if touching Kal has given it some release it's been dying for.

We rush higher, the wind cold against our wet skin as the pool grows smaller and smaller beneath us. My body trembles, my mind whirling. I'm nothing but a vessel for the power to fill, to use when it wants. I'm nothing—

"Rylee." Kal's voice is demanding but gentle, drawing my focus. I meet his gaze, clinging to him.

What if I drop him? What if I lose control? I didn't mean to go this high.

"Rylee, love," he says again, holding me tighter against him. "You are in control."

"I'm not." I shake my head. "It's too much, Kal. Your power—"

"*Our* power," he cuts over me. "Breathe. We're not in danger. You have the ability to take us wherever you want. I trust you."

I'm shaking now, and he is, too. If I don't get us back to the heated water, we may freeze to death. Or I'll lose control and we'll plummet to our deaths. That would be such a horrible way for Kal to die. An incompetent mate *drops* him. How tragic.

I can't let that happen.

I yank at the power, at the thread, hauling them inside me like the reins on a wild horse. That quickly, we halt. The sky is quiet, bright and blue. Peaceful. It's hard to be afraid of power when it comes from such a source of light.

"Good girl," Kal says.

A laugh rips out of me.

I glance down at the pool far below us and take a deep breath. "Hold on to me," I say, even though he already is.

I tilt to the left, and he moves with me instinctually.

"This is so much easier when you're in control," I grumble, doing my best to only draw a little amount so we don't soar into the water at a speed that would break us.

"Give it time," he says. "I wouldn't have given you anything I thought you couldn't handle. None of us would've. We made the choice knowing you'd be brilliant with them. Even if we never got them back, we knew they were meant for you, like we all are."

Emotion threatens to steal my focus as I look at him, carefully keeping our slow descent. "But I am able to give them back," I say. "That's something. I want to. Your powers belong to you."

"Rylee." Kal sighs, his eyes loving as he trails them over my face. "They belong to *you*, to *us*. We're connected in more ways than we ever imagined, and that's a good thing."

Warmth fills my chest. He's so open, so optimistic. Never once threatened by my hold on powers he was born with.

"Besides," he continues, "you're making this look easy."

I shake my head. "You're too good to me."

"Never," he says. "You've got this."

I control our speed the entire way down, the feat a victory in itself. I stop and turn us upright a foot above the water, prepared to slowly let us slide in.

Kal captures my lips with his. His kiss is soft yet searing, and my eyes close automatically at the feel of him against me. He slides his tongue between my lips, flicking it against mine as we hold each other.

Water crashes all around us as we drop unexpectedly into the pool.

We pop back up to the surface with gasps. Kal laughs, and I join him.

"We'll have to work on distraction," he says through his laughter.

I catch my breath. "Apparently."

"We can take it slow." He smooths his hand over my cheek as he studies my face, then dips down and kisses me again. "You're doing incredible," he says against my mouth. "You know that?"

In reply, I kiss him harder, longer, losing myself in the joyous feeling of his embrace.

"Let's try again," I say, pulling back and gripping his power once more.

"Again." He nods.

And we take to the skies.

Over and over.

Him kissing me, touching me, distracting me each time.

Enough times that I learn to split my focus. Learn to put my desire in one area of my mind and the power control in another.

Enough times that I feel more confident and freer with every sweeping pass.

Enough times that when we hit the water on my terms, I can think of little else but finishing what he keeps starting.

"Enough flying." I meet his eyes, getting lost in their blue depths. He's so patient with me, so understanding as we train. "I don't want to play with your power anymore."

A small smile shapes his lips, and he pushes back some of my wet hair that sticks to me. "Tell me what you want to do, and we'll do it."

Warmth flutters beneath my skin, only making me all the hotter in the pool we stand in.

I slowly draw my fingers up his bare chest, exploring the muscles there, relishing the way he feels beneath my touch. I dip my head, brushing my lips over his chest, up his neck, reaching up on my tiptoes to kiss along his jaw.

His hands flex on my hips, drawing me against him as he captures my mouth with his. I gasp against the contact, throwing my arms around his neck as his hands slip around my ass, hefting me up and spinning me to place me on the edge of the pool.

"Rylee," he groans against my kiss as I part my legs, urging him to step between them.

He hooks his fingers in my bikini bottom, slowly dragging the fabric down my thighs and laying it to the side.

"Beautiful," he says, gliding his powerful hands over my thighs as he leans in to kiss down my neck. I arch into his touch, anticipation curling in my core. His hands travel upward, slow and torturous as he unhooks my top, freeing my breasts.

"Kal," I whimper when he cups my breasts. I dig my fingers into his hair, my breath hitching as he explores my body, bare to him. There's no urgency right now, despite being outside. This is his home, and while I know he'd enjoy it, we have no fear of being caught here.

It's just him and me and the growing need between us.

"Kal," I gasp as he bends, sucking one of my nipples, the contrast of his hot mouth against my now-chilled skin sending sparks along the curves of my body. "*Yes.*"

He grins, wrapping a strong arm around my lower back, urging me closer to the edge of the pool. Kissing his way down my body, he sinks in the pool a little, aligning his mouth perfectly with my heat. His blue eyes flicker up to mine.

"You're going to come on my tongue," he demands. "And then I'm going to fuck you senseless."

I shiver at the words, the promise in them. A gasp tears through me as he sets his mouth on me, his tongue sliding through my heat with confident laps. My hand flies to his hair, my fingers gripping the strands as he eats at me.

"Kal, yes." I breathe the words. "Just like that."

He groans against my oversensitive flesh, his muscled arm behind me hauling me forward, holding me tighter against his face.

Energy zaps and surges with each lick, each tease over that sensitive bundle of nerves. My heart races, the powers inside me stretching and sizzling. Pleasure builds like a storm, and I'm driven to pure instinct as Kal slides his tongue inside me over and over again. I grip his shoulders, holding on to him when I feel like I might fly apart.

More. I need to touch more of him. Feel more of him.

"Rylee." He says my name like a plea, and I snap my eyes open. "I can feel you." He laps at me again, sucking harder on my flesh. "Everywhere."

I gasp, my mind splintered between the pleasure, which is building with every sure stroke of his tongue, and the power unleashed from me. Pierce's power, spearing straight into Kal with my wish to touch more of him. Now that I realize it, I feel it, too. With Pierce's power, I'm in Kal's mind, brushing and teasing every nerve he has. Making him feel every ounce of desire he's creating in me.

"Fuck," he groans, holding me tight as he ups his pace.

"Kal." I moan his name, everything narrowing to the sweet edge pulsing inside me. *"Yes."*

He sucks me into his mouth, hard and deliberate. I arch off the edge of the pool, gasping as my orgasm tears through me in a glittering burst. Waves of pleasure roll over me and into him.

"You taste so good," he says, his voice lust-drenched as he releases me just enough to remove his underwear, the effort quick and easy in the water. He tosses them where mine lie, then stands up to his full height in this shallow end of the pool, the angle aligning him perfectly with my trembling heat.

He kisses me, and I whimper at the taste of me on his tongue.

"Is it . . ." I can barely get the words out. "Is what I'm doing okay?" I have enough clarity to ask now that I'm not in the throes of it.

"Fuck yes, love," he says. "Keep doing what you're doing." His words send licks of flame over my skin, our connection blazing and solid between us. The trust is unshakeable, and I'm intoxicated with the way he gives open access to his mind, to the way he feels about me, which is more than I could've ever dreamed.

I send it all right back to him with Pierce's power—love and trust and pleasure and need. It crashes into him in waves, returns to me, and goes back. An open door of energy and sensation that I can't get enough of.

Kal drags his hard cock through my sensitive flesh. "Feel so good."

I rake my fingers through his hair, kissing him harder as I rock against his length, groaning as he intentionally keeps himself from moving inside me. The tease winds me ever tighter, white-hot knots flickering in my core.

"Kal," I beg. "Please."

He smiles against my desperate kiss, stilling between my thighs. He holds my gaze as he gently grabs my wrists, maneuvering my hands to wrap around his neck. "Hold on to me."

A thrill rocks through my chest at his demand, at the way he moves those hands to my thighs, urging me to lock my ankles behind his back.

I do as I'm told, anticipation shooting through my veins.

And then we're out of the pool, Kal effortlessly climbing up the stairs, kissing me frantically as he walks me to the closest available surface—the exterior wall of the pool house.

I gasp as the bare skin of my back meets the chilled wall, my grip on him tightening. But I only feel the chill for a moment.

The next, he draws out of our kiss, holding my gaze as he sinks inside me inch by inch. My eyes flutter as he fills me in the best possible way.

This. I've needed this all day. And as he pulls out to thrust in again, the bond between us glistens.

He pumps into me, fast and hard and perfect, each connection stroking that spot deep inside me that has me gasping for breath.

Kal curves his mouth over mine, like he wants to drink my whimpers of pleasure. I grip his shoulders, my thighs clenching around his hips as he alternates between thrusting and grinding himself against my slick heat. It's a killer combination, one that has me seeing stars as my pleasure builds in my core again.

Power ripples along the bonds, all doors wide open. I can't keep them shut. Not when he's unraveling me like this. He smiles against my mouth, breaking our kiss as his eyes meet mine.

"Brilliant," he says. "Our powerful little mate." Another hard kiss. "I can feel you in my mind." Another thrust. "I can feel you in my heart."

I'm shaking, my body on the cusp of another release.

"You consume me," he groans. "You understand that?"

"I'm yours," I say, wanting him to know we're on the same exact page.

"You ready to come for me again?" he asks, his voice low and demanding.

"Yes." I tighten around him. *"Yes."*

He smirks, kissing me, curling his tongue along the roof of my mouth as he pumps hard and fast, shoving me over the edge in a blissful fall.

I flutter around him, my orgasm cresting as he finds his release inside me, too. The two of us come down slowly as he holds me there. When my senses clear enough, I draw the other powers back, shoving them behind their doors with an effort.

"And that . . ." Kal kisses me again, lazily this time. "Concludes today's lesson."

CHAPTER 26

Rylee

Axl's power thrums hot and wild through my veins. If I had any tangible way of *measuring* their specific powers, I would say his is the hardest to contain.

Ocean waves crash against my stomach where Axl and I stand waist-deep in the water in his Sapphire Cove, the icy liquid only bearable thanks to the special suits made to maintain optimum temperature. My cheeks are freezing, and I tremble as a crisp breeze blows by. The sun is setting on the horizon, casting the empty beach in an orange-and-purple glow.

I tried to coax Ash to come to the beach with us this evening, but the cat adamantly refused, content to stretch out in front of Axl's crackling fireplace, as long as Axl wasn't in the room. I swear, at the rate the cat is going, he'll demand his own house one of these days.

"Rylee," Axl says, drawing my attention to where he stands an arm's length away from me. "We're not calling it quits yet."

"I didn't ask to."

He cocks a thick brow at me, nothing but pure mischief and challenge in his eyes. "You don't need to. And I don't need Pierce's mind-reading abilities to know you were staring at that beach like it's calling your name."

It's hard to bite back my smile, but I make an effort. "I'm exhausted," I admit. We've been out here for hours, and I've only managed to control the ocean in small bursts. His power is unruly, unlike Pierce's or even Kal's. They're all so different, and each one is unique in how I have to shove it behind the locked door so it doesn't overcome me, and how I must call it to me when I need it.

"I know you are." He scoots closer to me. "But you need to control this. It's the only way you'll be able to use it, if you need to."

He doesn't say the rest—that I need to control their powers in case a Kings' List task is dangerous or we're attacked by Faders again.

"Want to try something new?" he asks after a few moments.

My heart rate kicks up as I note the look in his eye. Trouble—*fun* trouble—usually follows. "I'm listening."

Axl spans the distance between us, towering over me. The specialty suit he wears is a rich blue, covering his body in a confining way I know he's desperate to be rid of. His long hair is tied back, his neatly trimmed beard accentuating the sharp line of his jaw. "It's going to require a lot of trust," he continues.

The bond between us goes taut as he skirts a hand down my shoulder.

"If you're not there," he says, "I'll understand."

"That's the most ridiculous thing I've heard you say today, and that says something, since earlier, you told me to *talk* to the ocean to get it to comply."

He laughs roughly, then shrugs. "Just because the Fates mated us doesn't mean you have to fully trust me."

I swallow hard, my heart twinging. So many people have struggled to trust him in the past—family, friends—because of his power. They've all dealt with it, but his power is an all-consuming, intimidating thing, not unlike his personality. Kal and I needed to have similar conversations when we worked with his power. Pierce, too. Trust is everything.

I reach up and place my hand over the center of his chest. His power surges beneath my skin, reacting to the contact and fighting my efforts to shove it down. It's like trying to shut a door against a tsunami.

"I trust you, Axl," I assure him, never breaking our gaze. He lays his hand over mine. "I wouldn't have gone blindly into the ether and met the goddesses if I didn't."

Emotion fills his eyes for a few seconds before pure challenge coats them. "You know I'm not like Kal or Pierce, right?"

"Really?" I laugh at that. "I hadn't noticed you're all completely different. When it comes down to it, you're just hot men who deliver orgasms at my beck and call," I tease, giving him a chiding look.

He puts his tongue in his cheek, nodding. "You're going to wish you hadn't said that."

"What do you have in mind?" Apprehension dances through me.

He tilts his head, wrapping one strong arm around my back to draw us closer together. "Like I said . . ." He grins. "You're going to have to trust me."

"The more you say that, the more nervous I get."

"Take a deep breath, kitten." He grips me tighter, the bond between us surging, pulling, tugging.

My eyes go wide as I do what he says. Then panic bursts in my chest as he dunks us beneath the ocean surface, drawing power down our bond like he's drinking it in.

I blink, adjusting to the salty sting against my eyes, doing my best to hold my breath as my heart races. We soar now, cutting through the water as he takes control of his power. It's incredible and slightly awkward. I hold the well, but he's drawing from it like it's the easiest thing in the world. And his power is *ecstatic* to be back with him. I can practically feel the giddy bubbles bursting inside me.

We draw to a stop in the deep, just above the seafloor, with what seems like twenty feet of ocean above us. Pressure pushes against my skull because of the depth, the sensation igniting my survival instincts.

Axl holds me tight, looking calm and at home as ever floating in the dark water, only small beams of light hitting the seafloor from the setting sun.

I lock eyes with him, raising my eyebrows in a *what now* question. If he wanted to prove to me that he can draw his power from me at will now, then he's most certainly done that, and it gets easier each time we practice. My stopping it from snapping back unexpectedly is the hard part—almost impossible.

A punch hits me in the chest, his power careening back to me as if the mere thought makes it happen. I release a bit of my precious oxygen in a yelp from the shock of it, propelling my legs to head back to the surface. There's no way I'm leaving Axl down here too long without his power.

His grip on me holds, and he tugs me back down, not allowing either of us to surface.

I tilt my head, eyes flaring as I yank on him.

He shakes his head.

My throat tightens, and my lungs burn. His have to be, too. I shove against him, trying to get us to surface.

Again, he stops me.

Goddess, this man is immovable. I want to claw at him.

Axl's power thrashes inside me, searing with a sharp sting beneath my skin. The bond between us quakes as Axl twitches.

He didn't take enough *air*.

He's going to drown down here because he's a stubborn ass who won't let us go up for air. The idea of losing him, failing him in this way, sends me into a chaotic spiral. I'm going to make him regret this, the stubborn ass.

But first, I have to save him.

He twitches again, and I swear on the goddesses I'm going to lose my mind.

I dig my mental hands into his power. He does not die down here. And where Kal's power is like holding a thread, Axl's is a partnership, a submissive release into the waves. The sea won't be controlled so much as convinced.

Once I submit to it, it's all too easy to see I can't get us to the surface fast enough, so in the span of one thought, I whirl my hand in a giant circle around us, creating a spherical pocket as I spear my own power toward the surface, yanking air back down and into the sphere to fill it.

We drop to the seafloor in a heap, the two of us gasping for breath as I struggle to meld the two powers together. It's like braiding my hair, only with our bond and our powers, and my brain feels like it might melt from the effort.

Axl laughs as he climbs to his feet.

He *laughs.*

I catch my breath as I rush to him and slam my hands against his hard, massive chest, barely budging the giant an inch. "You stubborn *asshole*!"

"Maybe," he says, not doing a thing to block me as I shove him again. "But look at how well you're doing." He eyes the bubble of safety I've created. "I can't do this."

I spare one second to look, to marvel at the constant motion of the sphere, the feel of whirling wind against my skin, the soft sandy floor beneath my bare feet. Maybe I could appreciate it more if I wasn't so pissed off.

"You were dying from asphyxiation, Axl!" I hurl at him again.

"And you stopped that," he fires back. "You're *still* stopping it."

I glare up at him. "You want me to master these powers that badly? At the cost of your life?"

"If it protects you? Helps you? *Fuck yes.*"

I shove him again, but this time, he stops me. His large, powerful hands capture my wrists, drawing me against him. I fight, but only for a second.

"I'm furious with you," I say as he tugs me closer, the bond between us flaring.

"You can be mad at me all you want." He dips his head. "But you're still maintaining these powers, and with enough steam left to roar at me." He drags his lips over mine in a teasing graze that melts me. "When are you going to realize you weren't just made for us? You were made for *this.*" With his chin, he gestures to the space around us, emphasizing the amount of power I'm wielding.

Damn this man.

I want to throttle him.

I want to kiss him.

It varies from second to second.

"I've known it from the start," he says, laying searing kisses along my jawline. "You're most in control when your emotions are high. You require higher stakes. Who better to take those odds with than the Player?" He smirks down at me.

"I could claw at you right now," I say, but the sting has left my voice.

He shrugs. "Then claw at me." He releases my wrists, fully aware I'm not moving a muscle away from him. "I'm not Kal," he says. "I'm not going to hold your hand and give you time we don't have. I'm not Pierce," he continues, dragging his fingers down my neck. "I won't mentally walk you through things. I'm rough and to the point. I'm hard on you because I know you can handle it, even when you think you can't."

I'm trembling now, my muscles contracting against the weight of our combined powers. With each breath, I'm fascinated by the way they meld together, creating something infinite.

"You were reckless," I say, arching an eyebrow at him.

"And you love it," he says.

I laugh, shaking my head.

"Now," he says, planting a kiss beneath my jaw. "I'm going to keep testing you."

"How?"

He slowly walks behind me, his fingers on the zipper at the nape of my neck. He drags it down, bending to graze his lips over my bare skin. He works his way back up to the shell of my ear. "How long do you think you can control this much power while I fuck you?"

A bolt of heat sears straight down my middle, turning me liquid.

"Axl," I gasp as he pulls the rest of my suit down, urging me to step out of it.

I do.

Goddess damn me, I *do*.

He's out of his just as quickly, and I can't help but eye him. He looks like the god he is down here, the ocean whirling behind him, bronze skin taut over eons of muscle.

"Focus," he demands, a low growl to his tone as he spins me around so my back is against his chest. He presses his cheek to mine, bending to run his hands over me.

A warm shiver skates down the center of me. I can feel every hard inch of him pressed against every soft part of me. Our bodies are slick from the ocean, and I tremble from his touch.

One hand palms my breast, which is heavy and aching. The other glides down my stomach, then between my thighs. He slides his fingers through my heat, all the while holding me so damn tight.

"Axl." I shiver at the dominant, claiming touch. I lean my head back against his chest enough to look up at him, reaching up to grip his neck from behind.

His eyes are liquid fire as they lock with mine, owning me with every confident graze of his fingers through my slick flesh. Droplets of icy water splash down on my oversensitive skin. I glance up at the whirling ocean around us, seeing it shift slightly.

"Hold it," Axl demands, the authoritative tone of his voice sending a bolt of pure pleasure down our bond.

I tighten my focus around his power, feeling the constant motion of the vast ocean all around us.

Axl pumps his fingers inside me, causing lightning to crackle through my veins.

I draw in a shaky breath as he claims my mouth, making my heart flip in my chest. I can feel him hard behind me, and I instinctively rock back against his length, shifting so he slides between my thighs, right where his hand is.

"Fuck," he growls against my mouth. More droplets of water break through, crashing against us as I lose another fraction of my control. "Hold it," he demands again. "I'm nowhere near done with you."

I shiver at those words. At the promise in them. At the game we're playing. High stakes is right. If I can't keep this water at bay, can't keep my air power filling this bubble we're in, we will easily drown.

The danger only plucks every pleasure string in my body, my mind whirling with adrenaline and a power rush I worry will sweep me away if

I allow it. If I give in. Because it would be so damn easy to do so. To let his power consume me, have its way with me.

Our bond tightens, a long string of heat pulling straight down the center of it and into Axl . . .

"Axl!" I gasp as he takes control of some of his power, the cool splash of water swirling around my swollen clit as he continues to pump his fingers in and out of me. *"Yes,"* I cry as the motion stretches me tight, snapping as he takes my mouth in a scorching kiss that has me seeing stars.

I clench around his fingers, my orgasm tearing through me in a sharp burst of pleasure that has a rain of ocean trickling against our skin. I catch the slip in power, yanking it back to me as fast as possible, solidifying the sphere around us.

"So fucking strong," Axl groans as he draws his fingers from me, immediately rewarding me with his cock. "You were made for this," he says again, accentuating each word with a long, slow thrust that has me dancing on the edge in seconds.

I grip him harder, pushing back against him with every thrust he makes, the two of us falling into this incredible rhythm that I never want to end.

His hands roam everywhere, this position giving him full access to any part of me he wants. He grazes and teases me as he pumps inside me, turning me into a panting mess as I flit between pure ecstasy and terror of losing my hold on the power I wield.

He's testing every limit I have, and somehow, I'm passing with flying colors.

The notion grips my heart. He *sees* me. And here, with him, I'm safe, regardless of the precarious situation we're in. Each of my mates makes me feel seen in different ways, and I honestly have no idea how I got so lucky.

"Axl." I keen his name, pleasure buzzing along my veins. I flutter around his cock, and he pumps into me harder, faster. "Yes," I gasp as he unleashes himself on me.

Sparks erupt as I fly over the edge once more, this orgasm more powerful than the last. The explosion makes my hold on the power slip, a wave of ocean crashing against us as Axl spills himself inside me.

I grab his power again, quicker and easier than before. It yields to me, sated and satisfied as I draw that air bubble around us tighter, giving us just enough space to breathe as the ocean churns a few inches from us.

Axl holds me, kissing the back of my neck as we catch our breaths. "That was close. Lucky we didn't die."

I burst into laughter, shaking my head. "Stubborn ass." I turn in his arms to look up at him. "Trust me?"

He dips down, leaning his forehead against mine. "With all that I am."

I smile, shifting against him to grab our abandoned suits. We hurry, and with considerable effort, we get back into them. Facing him, I wrap my arms around him and meet his gaze. "Then hold your breath."

He makes a show of taking a huge breath, and I mimic him, my heart hiccupping slightly as I shift the powers, letting the ocean crash all around us before I propel us higher and higher.

It's effortless, easy in a way it never has been. I don't question it. Not as we clear the surface. Not as we make the swim back to shore. And certainly not as we walk hand and hand back to his villa, the bond between us glowing bright and feeling damn near unbreakable.

Ash hisses a greeting at Axl, one that he returns with dramatic flair. It's hilarious to watch the giant ocean god of a man argue with a cat, but I'm glad Ash hasn't run off. Pretty sure the creature is using me for safe sleeping spots and good food, but I can't really blame him. I just wish my ridiculous fantasy of him being my good luck charm and somehow drawing my sister out of hiding would've worked by now.

After a quick bath, Axl fixes a simple dinner of baked fish, roasted root vegetables, and rice, insisting I eat two helpings to restore my energy levels. It's not a hard sell, especially when he's a fantastic cook that rivals the royal chefs in the palace. Between bites, I study my sister's art journal, going over the pictures for the hundredth time since I found it. All the paintings are familiar. I love them, of course, but there is nothing new. No hint of where I might find her. I shut it, finishing my food as Axl pores through some Sapphire Cove requests his chancellor dropped off this morning.

After our stomachs settle, we take a quick bath before we crash into bed.

"Love you." Axl nuzzles my neck as he draws me against his chest, sleep coating his voice.

"Love you," I whisper, the sounds of his deep breathing a soothing lull beneath my cheek as I rest against his chest. I can't help but wonder if Axl is onto something. He's not wrong about Kal and Pierce holding my hand through the training process, never pushing me. But not Axl. He'll always be the one to push me when I need it.

And Jax . . .

I'll go to my lesson with him in a couple of days. Anticipation curls through me at the thought of how *his* teaching approach will be. Because my Nightmare likes to play with all sorts of toys.

Much like Axl, he'll never be the soft landing that Kal and Pierce are. And that's one of the reasons why I love them so damn much. Either way, I'll need my rest if I'm to survive it, so I do my best to sleep, dreaming of ocean depths and water gods.

CHAPTER 27

Rylee

"Are we going to Tareena's temple again?" I ask Axl, my hand in his as he guides us through Sapphire Cove.

We've spent the morning shopping, supporting the local businesses, and sampling from the markets along the way. Ash trails behind us, following us from a safe distance that's almost comical. I've tossed him some fish, but he followed us long before I ever tempted him with food.

Axl woke up and demanded we have a few hours where we weren't training, and instead just enjoy his city. I didn't realize how much I needed it until now. There's a hopeful contentment brewing in my chest. It's been gone too long, with everything going on. I'm sure Axl knew that.

"No," he says, taking a path near his mother's temple. Instead of leading to the steps, it goes past it and to the right, splitting a hunter green hedge that stands twice my height. "I wanted to show you my mother's gardens."

The two enforcers standing guard at the entrance bow as Axl leads us through the hedge.

"Oh, Axl," I say as the space opens up before us. The giant hedge stands as a beautiful, natural border, masking all the treasures inside. There are rows and rows of different types of flowers and plants, all broken into sections, split by the marble pathways around them. "This is stunning."

He takes a deep breath, his hair down and blowing a little in the breeze. "I love it here."

"I can see why," I say as he squeezes my hand, taking us down the closest path.

"My mother started these gardens shortly after she met my dad," he says as we walk. "They worked on them together."

It's hard to envision Lucas working with Tareena to build something like this, but there's a glint in Axl's eyes that keeps me from saying as much. He looks so happy here, breathing in the floral scent coating the air.

"He almost let them die," he says, pausing in front of a patch of cylinder-shaped flowers. Rows of tiny sapphire petals spiral around the tubular green base, looking like little spikes.

"Why?" I ask.

Axl strokes one of the flowers, then continues to guide me down the winding paths. "After she went to sleep," he answers, "my father just stopped coming. I didn't know. When I finally returned here on my own when I was older, there were barely any flowers left."

I look around, noting the lush and vibrant garden that stretches for what seems like forever. "You brought it back to life." It's not a question. I know him. Know his love for his mother. And this garden, it's evident what a labor of love it is.

"Not bad," he says, huffing a laugh. "Right?"

I tug him closer, hugging his arm as we walk. "It's incredible. Ivy would lose herself in here."

"Let her know she can come here whenever she wants," he says. "I'll make sure the guards know."

"You're the best," I say, smiling up at him. "Do you know that?"

"Course I do." He winks at me.

I chuckle. "This really is stunning," I say as we walk. "What you've done here."

"It's mostly my mom," he says. "She left the seeds for me. There are hundreds of plants in here that the Occuli healers use for their tonics."

"That's amazing," I say, gasping when we round a corner and spot a patch of golden flowers. "Wow, these are . . . I've never seen anything like these."

The soil is midnight rich, multiple sections of flowers stretching from thick stems in full bloom. Their petals are a burnished gold, the silk-like structures glistening.

"They remind me of your eyes," I say, kneeling to get a better look. "And they smell like honey and cinnamon." Even their leaves are a dark golden color. "Definitely the flower of a goddess."

Axl kneels by me. "One of my favorites, too. They—" He cuts off abruptly. "Hey!" he yells at Ash, who prances between the flowers, plopping down and stretching out like the space is his own personal bed. "You can't hiss at me every chance you get and then take a nap in *my* garden," he grumbles.

"I think it means he likes you." I chuckle, shaking my head at the cat. "He hasn't left to explore on his own once. It's funny, I didn't think he'd domesticate for anyone other than Erin. And even with her, Ash opted for independence." I nod to him. "And lounging like that? Pretty sure that means he's no longer afraid of you."

Axl arches an eyebrow at me as we stand back up.

"Really?" He wraps an arm around my shoulders, and we keep exploring the gardens. "It's about time. I haven't had to work that hard to get anyone to like me since you came into my life."

I playfully swat at his chest. "You didn't have to work *that* hard."

He draws me in closer, kissing the top of my head. "Sure I did."

"You're insufferably likeable," I argue.

"You're only saying that because you're my mate."

"Please." I roll my eyes. "I was a goner long before I knew you were my mate."

He glances down at me, looks like he's considering arguing, then shrugs. "Okay. I'll agree with that. I hooked you pretty quick." He dips down, slanting his mouth over mine. "Still hooked?"

I melt into him. "Always."

CHAPTER 28

Rylee

There's no escaping the Nightmare's playroom . . .

Not that I want to.

Gentle fleece-lined cuffs secure my wrists and ankles to the corners of a cushioned table. My body is tense and hot, tight with anticipation.

"Try again," Jax demands in an icy tone that gives little relief to the yearning I feel in every nerve in my body.

I blow out a breath, particularly dizzy from the past . . . how many hours is it now? Ten? Eleven? I lost track so long ago. The lesson started off exciting enough—a touch and tease for every time I successfully controlled Jax's power—but now? I'm a coiled spring of need, exhausted and aching for release.

A beautiful form of torture.

Jax glides his fingers over my bare leg as he stalks around the table, my body fully on display for him. I'm at his hip height, and he looks all the more ruthless towering over my bound body. His indigo eyes catch the muted silver light in the room, and shivers burst across my oversensitive skin.

"Butterfly," he warns, stopping at the head of the table, looking down at me from above. He traces the lines of the tattoo he gave me beneath my collarbone, lingering on the moon and stars. Sparks flicker to life with every graze of his fingertips, my entire being coiling tightly.

He draws his hand back, and I snap myself into focus.

The door I keep Jax's power behind is open, the others straining against their locks. They want to play, too. I do my best to ignore and separate. The shadow-smoke-like essence of Jax's power swirls around our bond, teasing and coaxing as much as my mate. As elusive and jaded as him, too.

I've tried forcing it to work for me, *demanding* it bend to my will. That may have worked for Kal and Pierce's gifts, but not Jax's. It's like the power needs to trust me as its new owner, something I've learned from the others. But I'm not sure if it ever will. I try my best not to wonder if Jax fully trusts me, too. We're mates, yes, but everything is still new. Maybe his power is so much like him, I'll have to fight to the last dregs of my energy to even marginally control it.

It certainly feels like that now.

My body is peppered with a sheen of sweat that glistens over my bare skin, both from the exertion of lassoing Jax's power and the constant teasing and toying Jax has done with me.

"Focus," he demands.

"I'm *trying*." The words slip out before I can think better of them. I gasp, biting my lower lip as if that will somehow erase my slipup.

Jax's lips shape into a smirk that has chills erupting everywhere.

I'm so fucked.

Silently, he moves out of my sight line. I carefully lift my head from the table to track his predatory prowl to the other side of the room, where he keeps his toys.

My heart races as he ponders the tools, taking his sweet time to select one. Finally, he plucks out a smooth glass figurine that seems to be a perfect replica of his cock, then stalks back over to me.

Everything inside me tightens as he drags the cool glass up the inside of my leg, stopping at my inner thigh.

"That's the second time you've snapped at me," he says in an even tone. He moves the smooth, rounded glass between my thighs in a too-light touch. "Looks like I'll have to keep you here longer."

Goddesses save me.

I don't know how much more I can take.

Heat thrums through my veins at the way he's teasing my slick, aching heat with the new toy. At the way his eyes lock on mine while he does it, such dominance in them.

This is the Nightmare. He can do whatever he wants to me, and I can't stop him. It's a thrilling feeling, especially when I've given myself to him entirely.

"Try," he says, sliding that smooth, cool piece inside me just an inch. I gasp at the contact, at the way he gauges my reaction, at the intensity of it all. *"Again."*

He pulls the glass out, rubbing the solid piece against my sensitive clit. I tremble, my eyes fluttering closed at the contact I'm desperate for. Instinctively, I arch my hips, seeking out more of the delicious friction.

Jax takes it away, arching an eyebrow at me.

I blow out a frustrated breath.

He smiles.

The bastard *smiles.*

I shake my head, my body clenching with need as I draw myself inward. Jax's power is vibrating against our bond, delighted with Jax's edging.

I take a deep breath. Then another one. Doing my best to drown out the need pulsing through my veins. Doing my best to shove the images of Jax finally giving me what I want out of my head.

I sharpen my mind to his power, electing to stroke that smoke-shadow essence.

Please, I beg. *Play with me.*

There's a moment where I think it'll be as before, quiet, uninterested. Without a threat—like Axl orchestrated—or being completely immersed in all of them at once, I haven't been able to control Jax's power at will.

But it bends, just a fraction, snaking up and coiling around my soul like a serpent's caress. A whimper escapes me at the sensation—at the way it opens to me.

Jax's desire is as sharp as his blades. I can taste it on my tongue, crisp and heady. Can feel it in my bones. It's everywhere at once, his power detecting the emotion in the span of a breath.

How does he live like this? Feeling everyone's emotions all the time? If we weren't secluded in his playroom, I'd be bombarded with the emotions of everyone in Lust—his club in Obsidian City and home to his playroom—just like I was with thoughts while using Pierce's power.

I don't know how they bear it.

I latch onto that sharp desire of Jax's, grip it with the power now flooding my entire being. It's like being engulfed by smoke the second I have it in my control, the second I feel his emotional state become *mine.*

"Good," he whispers, like he's afraid if he speaks too loudly, he'll ruin my focus.

I'm in too deep for that now. Drenched in the power, in the rush I get from knowing I can sway him to feel anything I want, if I merely *wish* it.

I could make him cry, make him laugh, make him so angry he'd break his teeth. There's a certain exhilaration in all the possibilities and uses for this power on other people—enemies in particular. The things I'd love to make Baydel feel after all he's done to me.

But he's the last person I want to think of.

I want nothing but Jax.

My mate.

My Nightmare.

So instead of forcing him to feel anything, I focus harder. Where Pierce's is a multifaceted silk web I have to weave, and Kal's a sun-and-cloud thread, and Axl's a compliance with the depth of water, Jax's is a push and pull. A give and take.

And right now, I want to give him something. He's on the other end of our bond, just waiting for me to manage this power . . . this river of smoke that glides between the two of us. Gathering as much smoke as I can, I direct that river toward the other end of our mating bond. Pump it full of offerings—my gratitude, my love, my desire.

"Fuck," Jax gasps as the power returns to him and he's flooded with everything I'm feeling. "That's it, little liar. That's *it.*"

He moves the smooth glass piece against my aching heat, rubbing the rounded tip over that throbbing bundle of nerves before sliding it inside me, inch by glorious inch.

Jax bends, his lips slanting over mine, swallowing my gasp of pleasure as he pumps that piece in and out of me.

"Jax." My mind whirls, my muscles clenching.

He's relentless, not pulling back an inch from my mouth as he fucks me with that toy. As he unravels my very being with his tongue and lips and tools. I'm at his mercy, unable to move much in my restraints. I want to dig my nails into his back. Want to draw him as close as possible. Want him covering every inch of my body.

Pleasure builds beneath my skin, a lightning storm that makes me see stars as he ups his pace.

"Fuck," he groans against my mouth. "Your desire . . . it's *flooding* me." His kiss is bruising, sending bolts of pleasure to every fired-up nerve ending I possess. "I love it. I want to drown in it."

"I'll be the one drowning if you don't let me come," I snap.

He draws back an inch, something churning in those indigo eyes as he looks down at me. It's gone in a blink, replaced by the unflinching dominance I've seen all night. He slows the pace to a torturous level, holding me on the cusp of release like he's done for hours.

The power slips a fraction, threatening to fly back to me. I halt it with the will of my mind, drawing on my own wind power inside me to keep that smoke drifting his way.

Jax smiles. "So impressive."

I shudder beneath him, my breathing hitching as he holds me on a knife's edge.

"Deserves a reward." The second he says the words, my body floods with warmth and love and desire and pleasure. The emotions hit me all at once, drenched in moonlight and stars and all things that are never-ending and all-encompassing, just like my Nightmare.

Jax pumps the toy into me, his eyes falling to where he maneuvers it. I go brazen with the sight of him watching himself fuck me with it. My entire being tries to separate from my body as he drives me closer and closer to that sweet edge.

"Jax," I gasp as my pleasure builds. "Jax, yes. *Please.*"

His eyes find mine again before he kisses me with a possessiveness I wholly submit to. It's exhilarating, the way he takes control of my body. The way he knows just how to push, touch, and tease me into madness.

Jax ups his pace, shifting so his thumb strokes over my throbbing clit with each pump—

"Jax!" I cry out against his mouth as my body trembles, my orgasm a flood of pleasure that washes over me. It peaks in a crescendo that sends me straight to the moon, letting me hover there for endless blissful moments before I slowly come back down to reality.

He kisses me softer, gently pulling out the glass before he gets to work on unbinding my ankles.

"Don't look too satisfied," he warns as he moves to my wrists. "We're just getting started."

I don't have time to respond before he's undressed and climbing atop the table, settling between my thighs in a hurry. He pauses only to meet my gaze, a silent question.

"*Yes,*" I say on a ragged breath.

The answer is always yes.

He smirks, watching my face as he slides his hard length through my oversensitive heat. "I can't let my toys have all the fun," he says, gliding in an inch.

I gasp at the contrast between seconds ago—smooth and cold—and Jax's searing heat. It splinters my mind in the sweetest way.

"Can I touch you now?" I ask, but it sounds more like a plea. I've played in this room enough to know that just because he released me doesn't mean I'm free to do as I please. Not here. Not in his playroom. It's his rules. And they're my undoing.

"Only because you asked so nicely, butterfly." He glides inside me.

My arms fly around his neck as I wrap my legs around his hips.

"Fuck," he groans, thrusting into me without preamble. He's prepped me for hours and just delivered a mind-bending orgasm. I don't need any more foreplay. I just need him. All of him. "You're so perfect."

I scrape my nails along his back in the way I know he loves before dragging one hand to his jawline. I grip it enough to draw his focus, enough to position his mouth just a breath away from mine.

"Perfect for you," I say before taking control of the kiss now that he's lifted the rules. I claim his mouth in the way I've wanted to all night—just as possessive and punishing as he's been. I nip at his bottom lip enough that he pumps into me harder, faster.

I'm completely lost in the moment with him.

The power, his and mine, swirls together. Wind and emotion—desire racing back and forth between us like endless sways of smoke. He doesn't chide me for the back-and-forth, for the way the power seems to belong to both of us now, instead of one or the other. He can't, not when he's claiming my body, not when our bond has fully awakened and demands satisfaction.

My skin is on fire. I can't touch enough of him. Kiss enough of him.

He rises up, using a free hand to push my knee farther back as he pounds into me. The sounds of our sex fill the playroom, the desire flowing between us ramping up so much, I can't tell whose is whose. There's no differentiating from the power. And I don't care.

This is me and him.

Consuming. Jagged. Endless.

Mates.

Matched on every level.

I feel him riding the edge through our bond and meet his thrusts with lifts of my hips. The two of us are on a collision course, ready to break.

"Jax." I breathe his name as everything in me narrows to the way he's making me feel—loved and cherished and taken care of in every way a person can be. It's scary how much I care for him and how much he cares for me. I can feel that through the bond and power and everywhere we connect. It's dangerous and never-ending, and I'm drowning in it, just like he said.

I kiss him again, softer this time as we crash together over and over again.

"Jax. I . . ." I can barely speak as my pleasure builds. "I love you." I breathe the words, unable to hold them back as I soar, my release bursting in a million sparks beneath my skin.

Jax groans, spilling inside me with his own release, dropping down to cover my body with his, his forehead pressed against mine as he catches his breath.

He draws back after a few moments, eyes softer than usual. He smooths back some of my hair, kissing me gently. "I love you, Rylee Gray."

He rarely says my name, so I always feel it in my bones when he does. If I could melt any more for this man, I would. As it is, I'm practically a puddle beneath him.

"So fucking much." He kisses me again, slow and lazy, like we have all the time in the world.

Power careens into me so hard I gasp.

"Goddess damn it," I snap as the onslaught of Jax's power steals my breath.

Jax laughs, the motion doing things to our connected bodies.

"You're getting there," he says.

"Not fast enough."

Seriousness shapes his features. "You're getting there," he says with more conviction.

I swallow hard. "I held it longer that time."

"You did," he says. "Soon, you'll be able to send it or keep it at will."

It's hard to picture that kind of control.

Jax smiles down at me, shifting gently off me. He disappears for a moment, then is back quickly to clean me. He helps me sit up, immediately stepping between my thighs to draw me close.

"Let's get you taken care of," he says. "Water first. Then food. You can eat while I attend to some business." He scoops me up, carrying me across the playroom and through the bedroom door at the back of the room. He perches me on the bed as he heads to the small bar cart in the corner. I eye my sister's art journal where I left it on the nightstand, ignoring the urge to pick it up and thumb through it again.

"What business?" I ask when he hands me a large crystal glass of water, then sets a plate of bread and fruits beside me on the bed.

"List business," he says with a shrug.

I arch an eyebrow. "You need to say more words."

He heads to the wardrobe near the bar cart and pulls out pieces of black clothing before sliding into them. Damn, what is it about him buttoning up his shirt that's so sexy?

"Jax," I warn.

He sighs, finishing the last button. "I have a contact," he says. "He's meeting me at a club across the city."

"Contact for what?"

Jax eyes the untouched plate of food next to me.

I immediately grab a strawberry and bite into it.

"He might have information for us on the new enhancement strain that's tearing through our cities."

I almost choke on my second bite. "Really?"

Jax nods.

"And you're just now telling me about this?"

"You have more important things to worry about," he says. "If you haven't noticed."

"Nothing is more important to me than getting this list done and putting you, Axl, Kal, and Pierce on the thrones where you belong," I argue. "You're what Lumathyst needs. You can make real change. Nothing is more important than that—"

"*You* are more important than that," he cuts over me, his tone sharp and rushed.

The grief hits me like a boulder to the chest. Not mine . . . *his*.

The loss is a bottomless well of fear and worry and darkness.

My loss.

Tears immediately fill my eyes.

Jax growls, raking his fingers through his blue-black hair. He takes a steadying breath, closing his eyes for a few moments.

The grief ebbs, shifting to a cool sort of contentment. It's not my doing; it's his. His ability to regulate himself is incredible. I wish I had that sort of control, but I suppose having the power to influence other people's emotions taught him a lot about controlling his own.

"I don't want anything to happen to you," he whispers.

I rise from the bed, grabbing a white button-down discarded over one of the chairs and quickly slipping into it before I reach him. His sentiment is appreciated, much like Kal's when he expressed the same worry, but it's pointless.

"You picked me, Jax. First as a potential, then as a Legend, and finally as your mate."

"And all of those decisions . . . *my* decisions led you straight to your *death*," he says.

I flinch at the prick of guilt that stings my chest and slide my hand over the center of his.

"You're wrong," I say. "I chose to sneak into the Choosing. I accepted the pin. I played the game. I fell in love with each of you. I chose you and Axl and Kal and Pierce. I took the Athanry elixir knowing the risks. Each of you told me not to. And even after it killed me . . . after all of it, I still came back to you. *I* made those choices. And I would do it again. I would Choose you a thousand times—"

He cups my cheek, his gaze steady on mine, covering my mouth with his seconds later. His other arm snakes around my lower back, hauling me against him in an embrace that feels otherworldly. Like if he can hold me close enough, he won't lose me again.

I understand it. The idea of losing them sent me over the edge in an explosion of power I still think about. But there's nothing we can do about it now. Nothing except work together to make things right.

"You've always let me make my own choices, so *keep* letting me," I say as he draws back an inch. "Don't let fear change that."

The growl from his chest is low, but I smile because it means he knows I'm right.

"You have to eat first," he says, relenting. I clap and hurry back to the bed. "And drink two more glasses of water."

"Yes, Nightmare," I say, already biting into the bread.

CHAPTER 29

Rylee

"Remember when Kal told you that you may not always like what you see?" Jax asks me an hour later as we linger on the darkened road outside the southern portion of the Obsidian City.

"Yes," I say. "And you all made me a Legend anyway."

"We're not just being Legends tonight," he counters. "This is something I'd normally do on my own. Even the guys understood that." He stares down the road. "The person I am in these establishments . . ." He places a hand on the seat of the velomage we stand next to, returning focus to me. "The Legend I am."

"The Nightmare," I say in understanding.

"You've only heard stories."

"I've seen you in action a time or two," I counter. "I'm not afraid of the Nightmare," I say, stepping closer. "Or you. I love every part of you, Jax. The sharp pieces, the dark ones, the ones you never show anyone but me."

"And if I have to treat you as the Nightmare would?"

"You know how much I love to play games," I say, smiling up at him. "Do you think something like that could sway me from you?" I focus inward, on his power, on the way it's free and circling around our bond. Content. I push my unflinching love down the bond, and he trembles when he feels it.

"I don't deserve you," he says under his breath.

And I hate how much he believes that.

"We deserve each other," I say. "I'm not perfect, either. I've done things I'm not proud of . . ." My voice trails off, the image of destroyed Faders, bloody bits along royal roads, flashing in my eyes. Guilt threatens to swallow me whole. And the fear that follows chills my bones.

That was a mistake. A slipup. An instinctive reaction to a threat to my mates. I had no control. They were a threat, sure, but what if they hadn't been? What if someone innocent had been caught in the fire? What if—

"You need to follow my lead in there," he says, drawing my attention.

"I understand."

"The way I have to act." He struggles again. "I might have to speak to you like I did before. The people who frequent these kinds of places, the contacts here, they only know one version of me. They only respond and offer information to one version of me."

"I got it," I say with a shrug. "I can be your little liar again." Can be the subject of such contempt from him again. Only this time, I know what's on the other side of it. Know where it comes from.

He smooths his hand gently over my throat, his thumb stroking the center. "Okay," he says. "Are you ready?"

I nod, and we remount the velomage, driving the short distance to the club. He pauses outside the entrance of the nondescript building, waiting for me to hop off. I do, examining the exterior as he heads off to park.

The building is smashed between two others, this one sitting lower, only two stories, where the others are at least five higher. It looks lopsided despite being made of the slick black rock that dominates the Obsidian City. There are small, faded carvings all along the solid exteriors—patterns of shapes and swirls that are almost completely worn away. I check for a sign, for a name for the place, but there's only a small symbol over the lone steel door: thick lines creating what looks like a jagged *R* with two lines striking off the back of it. Jax explained before we came that there are a few of these in every city, even the lower ones. *Drogueden* is the common name, a place where royal law is ignored, experimentation is encouraged, and enhancements flow as freely as whiskey in the legal nightclubs like Lust.

I've heard of them before but never dared venture into one. I'd seen the consequences of some of the stronger enhancements too many times to take such a risk.

A guard sits atop a stool near the door, his eyes focused on a book illuminated by a lone sconce over his shoulder.

"You're lost," he says without looking up from his book. "Lust is on the north end."

I tilt my head. "What makes you think I want to go to Lust?"

The guard draws his gaze from his book, looking me up and down. His eyes linger over my black attire—tight black pants shoved into sturdy black boots, a sheer black top revealing the dark-green lace covering me beneath. "You look like a Lust girl."

I laugh. He's not wrong.

"I'm *the* Lust girl," I say, stepping closer to him. He's twice my size and intimidating enough, but his primary emotion is boredom. "But I'm not lost."

"The only way you can come in here is if you accept the terms."

"And those are?"

He pulls a card from a shirt pocket and hands it to me.

I read it aloud. "'By accepting this card and passing through these doors, you're agreeing that this establishment can't be held responsible for any visions, hallucinations, or lost time you may experience while present, including but not limited to any losses or injuries experienced herein.'"

The terms remind me of another magically binding contract I accepted not long ago.

"It's no joke," the guard says. "It's Occuli bound."

I raise my eyebrows. "I didn't realize Occuli could be contracted for this sort of magic."

The guard looks surprised, and once again, I feel ridiculous for how buried I kept my head for so damn long. Of course Occuli can be bought. Just like anyone in need of money.

"I hope your book isn't as dry as this contract," I say, lightening the exchange.

He laughs, glancing down at it. "It isn't. Now, are you going to accept the terms or head back to Lust where you belong—"

"She's with me." Jax's voice cuts over the guard's, and it's a marvel to watch how quickly the casual mood shifts.

"Your highness," he says, immediately standing and bowing while placing his book on the stool behind him. He hurries to pull the door open for us as Jax stands next to me, hands in his jacket pockets, his harness with knives on either side peeking through, looking ever the picture of the Nightmare. "Should I tell Caro to clear out your usual booth? I saw earlier that someone had rented it."

"No need," Jax says, his tone icy. "I'll be joining that person."

"And . . . her?" The guard studies me.

Jax narrows his eyes, a predatory move. "She accepts the terms." He looks down at me. "Don't you?"

Shivers dance down my spine. "Yes."

The guard bows deeply, waiting for us to head inside.

We do, and the door closes immediately behind us.

The smell hits me first—a sharp, almost medicinal scent mixed with earth, herbs, and alcohol. It's overwhelming and tickles the back of my throat. Music thrums, slow and hypnotic, from a source I can't pinpoint. There's no stage here, but some people are dancing near the bar. Everything is bathed in silver from the iron candelabras with silver flames hanging from the low ceiling. Even the small bar seems to glow with the otherworldly light.

"Occuli?" I ask Jax.

He nods. "Not all of them live to serve the kings," he explains. "Some, like the ones who build and power our velomages, like to dabble in creation for a cost." He motions to the silver flames, then motions to the room as a whole. "The music is demi-powered."

I nod, doing my best to breathe as this new world I'm adjusting to keeps growing. I knew the kings forced most known demis to work for them throughout the cities, using their unique powers for any tasks or desires they required, but seeing it happening feels heavy.

"And those?" I ask, nodding to the random private rooms with leather couches and chairs lining the left side of the space. Each one is sectioned off and framed with thick velvet curtains that offer privacy if closed. Some are open, the people inside not a bit concerned with the fact that we can see into the room, watching them inhaling or sniffing whatever enhancement they've bought tonight.

"They're for aesthetics," Jax says, and I can't help but huff a laugh.

Now the strange, overpowering smell makes sense. There are any number of enhancements floating in the air here. It's a marvel I don't feel the effects from simply breathing. It makes sense that Jax would meet his contact here. This is a semi-safe, controlled environment to buy and use the stuff. Naturally, a new supplier would be here, or someone who knows of a new supplier, because the customer base is active and willing to pay. But the enhancements that are legal here aren't hurting anyone. The new one? It's killing people.

Two men exit a booth and walk by us with metal contraptions in their hands that look like silver straws. One brings the thing to his lips, then shortly blows out a dark, blue smoke. His eyes glaze over as he passes us, and Jax guides me forward and toward the bar.

"Your highness," the female bartender says as we reach it. "I didn't expect you tonight." She effortlessly slides tumblers of whiskey or small packets with colorful powders to the other patrons while doing her best not to make eye contact with Jax. Fear and respect ripple off her, fear being the dominant emotion.

"Caro," he says with familiarity. "He's already in my booth?"

Caro nods toward a private section in the corner. The number *one* is emblazoned in silver on the black velvet curtains, which are closed. It's only then that I notice all the booths are numbered.

"What do the numbers mean?" I ask.

"Tracking," Caro answers me. "I have to know who goes where and with what, or it's chaos." She offers me a timid smile, then dips her head to Jax. "You looking for something in particular tonight for the two of you, your highness?"

He smiles at her—the Nightmare's smile. "I'll take the purple tonight," he says. "Need something to entertain us while talking to him."

"Atlas is a real piece of work," she says, reaching behind the bar. She slides two small packets of purple powder toward Jax.

"Caused trouble already?" Jax asks. "It's so early."

"When does he *not* cause trouble?" She seems to think better of her question and shakes her head.

"Understood." Jax scoops up the packets, pocketing them before heading toward booth number one. I can feel Caro's relief grow the farther we get away from her. We navigate our way through dancers, all of whom give Jax a wide berth once they recognize him.

His power reaches from beyond the door I've locked most of it behind, little whisps of that shadow-smoke slipping through the cracks, enough for me to get hit with other people's emotions—fear, intrigue, and a heavy dose of numb bliss. There are so many people enhanced out of their minds right now, and I have to say, sensing that emotion isn't half bad. It's almost tempting. To *not* feel for a moment.

Jax draws back the curtain, holding it open for me. "Get in," he demands.

I awkwardly step inside, noting the man with his arms stretched along the back of a black leather couch. The space is small, and not exactly in the cozy way, at least not with the stranger sitting there, studying me with a curious gaze. There's another small sofa right next to his, and on the opposite side is a wooden platform—more of a box, really—with a pole rising from the center, up to the ceiling. It's a more basic version of the dancing booths at Lust, but it's clearly for the same use.

"You're late," the man says as Jax steps in behind me.

I expect a heavy dose of this man's fear to slice through me, because surely he's scared to death after accusing the Nightmare of being late.

No fear comes. Just a heavy dose of . . . resentment? Anger? Boredom? It shifts so quickly from one to the next, I suspect he's doing it on purpose. And maybe he is. Maybe he does it any time he's around Jax to keep him guessing?

It's unnerving. I do my best to ignore it.

"I'm never late, Atlas," Jax says in that icy tone of his. He takes a seat on the opposite sofa, yanking me down next to him. "Some things are more important than listening to you."

Atlas leans forward a bit, the low light illuminating his features clearly.

He has one of those silver contraptions in one hand, drawing it to his lips and blowing out a puff of red smoke a few seconds later as he studies me. I study him right back.

His eyes are gray, the same muted shade as the stick he holds. He takes another drag off the device, the pencil-thin contraption positioned between two fingers. The smoke is sweet and hazy as it curls around his lips on his exhale.

His left arm, which I can now see is entirely made of metal, rests on his thigh. It's not the first limb replacement I've seen—there are countless people who've lost an arm or leg in the mines in the Ashlands—but it *is* the fanciest. The metal is flawless, looking like it's made of the same material as the bracelet Axl gifted me. And it hums with power, no doubt with Occuli magic as he moves his metal fingers. He doesn't try to hide the piece, either, wearing a suit tailored to showcase it, leaving one sleeve long and the other cut off.

I wonder how he lost it. He's got muscles for days packed beneath his silver suit, almost like strength training is his literal job. The only soft thing about this man is his hair, which is a cool blond that hangs just so over his forehead.

"I guess I'd be late, too," he says, and I blink out of my study at the faint sliver of desire slipping through the man's boredom, only for it to disappear as quickly as it came. He motions to me with the fingers holding the device. "If I had that to play with."

Jax possessively grabs my thigh. "Time means nothing when I'm between these legs."

I shiver at the words, at the spike of Jax's emotion that bursts on the back of my tongue, a growly sort of possessiveness that makes me go hot all over. I push as much of Jax's power as I can manage behind the door, not needing the distraction right now.

"You're the one who asked for this meeting, Jax," Atlas says, his tone annoyed. How long have they known each other for him to speak so casually to him? "What do you need from me now?"

Jax is silent as he settles deeper into the sofa, leaning back, fiddling with his jacket, not so subtly showing off his blades while he does it.

"Don't posture," Atlas says, rolling his eyes. "You know how difficult it is for me to get away to meet you like this."

My lips part, shock rolling through me for a moment before I lock it down. I'm supposed to be the submissive mate at the Nightmare's side, not an opinionated one, wondering who the fuck this Atlas guy thinks he is.

"Such sacrifices you make," Jax says.

Atlas's eyes snap to Jax's, the device poised just near his lips, halted there by Jax's comment. There is *something* in those gray eyes that has apprehension trickling down the back of my neck—a cold depth that screams *shark-infested waters*.

"Don't," Atlas warns. *Warns*. Who the fuck *is* this guy?

Power rattles inside me, begging to be set free again.

I shove it down once Jax releases that slow, sardonic laugh. "You're right, Atlas. We can play the greater sacrifice game another time. Tonight, I need information."

Atlas takes another drag off the device. I wonder what the red smoke does, because he doesn't seem intoxicated. He seems eerily calm. Especially considering who's in here with him.

"I *live* to give you information."

Jax laughs again, this one laced with a hint of his real one, which sets me at ease.

"There's a new enhancement," Jax says. "One that's breaking the minds of everyday Lumathyst citizens. Quite possibly killing them, too. Four bodies have been found."

And one from the Fader's memory, too, though we'll never be able to tell if that's included in the ones already found or not. The memory was too distorted for me to see much.

"I've seen its effects." Atlas takes another drag off the device. "I call it *Tox*, because of how toxic it can be depending on who takes it."

"You've seen it here?" Jax asks, casually stroking my thigh.

"No. Caro would never stand for that."

Jax shrugs. "Had to ask."

Atlas sets the device down on a little side table near him. "It's nasty stuff," he says, folding his arms over his lap, the metal one gleaming in the low light. "I've started my own inquiry into whoever's baking it."

"Why would you spend your precious, *limited* time looking for a baker?" Jax asks.

Atlas grins. "I have my reasons."

What reasons? I want to ask so badly.

Jax stiffens next to me, straightening his spine as he leans forward a bit. "I never like your reasons."

Atlas shrugs him off. "Once you demanded this meeting, I had a hunch what you were looking for."

"It's spreading."

"An infectious spread," he says. "Without care for class. Tox ensnares royal and lower equally. More instances in Oak and Iron recently. Have you visited the healers there?"

My heart drops into my stomach.

No. No, we haven't. Because we've been training. Trying to prepare me for what's to come.

"Of course not," Atlas says. "Too busy playing with your new toy."

"No need for the games," Jax says, pulling out a blade and fiddling with the sharp edge. "We've done this too many times, Atlas. As much as we hate each other, we work well together."

Atlas returns his eyes to me. "I've heard things about this new enhancement," he says, studying me, sizing me up. Almost like I'm a riddle to solve.

"And?" Jax presses.

"It affects people differently."

"You're saying not everyone's mind is broken when they take it too much?"

"That's exactly what I'm saying." Atlas gives his attention to Jax. "Some take it and are rewarded with a quick hit of power. More refined than anything we've ever seen on the market before. The power lasts longer and packs a bigger punch before it fades. Definitely makes it more addictive to those types."

I remember the Fader in the cell. The one who could barely string his thoughts together.

"What differentiates these reactions in people?" Jax asks, almost to himself.

"Blood," Atlas answers, looking to Jax now. "I haven't tested the theory for myself. I don't have time for that. But I've heard whispers that it acts differently for people with power. Occuli, demis." He looks right at me when he says it, those gray eyes meeting mine in a curious way before he looks back to Jax. "Maybe even Legends."

"How does it affect those people?" Jax asks, but his tone says he already knows.

The nullifier. The one the Faders used against them before. Tox and the nullifier are the same thing.

"Takes the power. Possibly to the user's demise."

The deaths. The drained-looking bodies. Could the duke have been right in assuming it was connected? And if that's the case, then those three deaths in the Ruby Aire and the Sapphire Cove were people with power? Demis, most likely, since the duke didn't mention them being Occuli, who are easily identifiable by their eyes. You'd have to look for a specific mark that could be anywhere on the body in order to identify a demi.

"Probably why the kings haven't really cared much about it until now," Atlas continues, drawing my attention. "Who cares about a few dead demis? With only a handful, they can manage the loss. But widespread? They need those loyal demis and their powers to do their bidding, don't they? And even worse, if the remaining demis felt they were being targeted? They might just rise up. Might take that enhancement for their own and try to use it against the kings."

"Fuck," Jax groans.

"Yeah," Atlas says.

I'm lost in the whirl of thoughts storming my head. If what he says is correct, it means what I've worried about all along is true.

Faders, at least in part, are made up of demis. And my sister is leading them.

It makes sense.

But I *hate* that it makes sense.

"Can you get your hands on some of this . . . *Tox*?" Jax asks. I stare over at him, stomach churning.

"Working on it," Atlas says. "Are we done here?"

Jax nods. Atlas rises from the couch, studying me again while he picks up the slim device and hits it one more time. He blows out the red smoke, eyes locked on me as he stands so still, it makes apprehension bloom on the back of my neck.

"Until next time," he says, dipping his head to me before turning to Jax. "I'll reach out if I find anything."

"Make it quick, Atlas." There's no room for argument in Jax's tone, so Atlas doesn't respond. He bows, then backs out of the room, disappearing behind the closed curtain.

"Fuck." I echo Jax's earlier sentiment.

"Yeah," he says, reaching for me.

I tuck into his side. "Why would someone make a drug that enhances regular citizens but breaks demis and powerful beings? Quite possibly killing them?"

"The stuff they've thrown at us has always been bad," Jax says. "We knew it, because it was enough to nullify our powers and injure us in the process. But for those with *less* power? It has to be so much worse."

"So either it's the Faders baking it, or they're getting it from someone who is also selling it to regular citizens," I say. "There are too many questions around it all. I don't like this."

"I don't, either," Jax agrees. "Atlas, prick that he is, will bring it to us if he can track it down. Once we have it, we can figure out what it is. Hopefully make an antidote."

"Ivy can help," I say. "She's brilliant with medicines."

"I'll make sure she's on it once we have it."

"And in the meantime?"

"We wait."

"The worst."

"Lucky for us, we have a lot to do."

CHAPTER 30

Rylee

"We've been summoned," Axl says in dramatic fashion as he swings open the door of Jax's bedroom.

I squint against the sudden onslaught of light, the golden beams drenching Axl like it can't help but kiss his bare skin. He's shirtless, of course, the way he prefers to be, his ink on full display.

Jax shifts beneath me, my head jostling against his chest. Something silver flies through the air, and one of his blades snicks into the woodgrain right next to Axl's head.

"And it's formal," Axl grumbles, not remotely fazed by Jax's outburst. "We have an hour." He stalks in the opposite direction, and I hear his footsteps on the stairs leading up to his rooms in Jax's home.

A heavy sigh rushes from my lungs as I stretch my limbs, my body arching against Jax's. He tightens his hold on me as I stretch, rolling us until he's on top of me.

"I don't want to," he whisper-growls into my ear, as if *I've* delivered the message. He shifts again, and I gasp as he settles between my thighs. "I want to stay here and keep playing with you."

Heat sweeps through me like a wave of lava. "Not tired of me yet?" I tease.

"Never." He shakes his head, the tip of his nose grazing along the line of my jaw as he inhales. "An eternity with you won't be enough."

Goddesses save me, this man.

I swallow hard, emotion clogging my throat as he draws back enough to look down at me again. He's brutally beautiful, the sharp angles of his face, the fierce indigo shade of his eyes, the powerful intent behind them.

It's been almost three weeks of nothing but practicing with their powers, hopping from city to city, sometimes with all of us present, other times not. I'm starting to learn that despite my wildest fantasies, there may never be a time when we can all be together *constantly*. There's always business to attend to, whether that be Legend or prince issues. And that's okay; we've found a way to make it work. We've had extensive conversations about Tox, the enhancement that gives non-powerful beings a boost in power, while nullifying or killing those who do have powers. We haven't heard back from Atlas yet, but we're hopeful he'll find something more solid for us soon.

And despite nightmares plaguing my sleep, I still wake up every day, wondering how I got so lucky to be mated to such incredible men. I know something new and dangerous is knocking on our doors every second of every day. I know my sister is still out there, acting as the leader of a rebel group that goes against everything I thought we stood for, but . . .

I'm happy.

I'm happier than I've ever been.

And it scares the shit out of me.

This kind of love, this amount of understanding and connection, is something I never thought I'd experience.

My mates have only ever made me feel treasured, loved, even when this one has me in chains and at his mercy.

I smile up at him, calling on the practice I've almost perfected after days and days of nonstop training. I open the door to Jax's power, urging it to wash down our bond, swirling it around the connection, allowing him to feel every ounce of love and desire and happiness I feel in the moment.

Jax gasps as the power and emotions hit him, his eyes widening as he looks down at me in wonder. He smooths some of my hair back, kissing me quickly. "I don't deserve that." He shakes his head. "I don't deserve you."

I reach up, cupping his cheeks. "The Fates beg to differ," I counter, focusing internally on that bond between us. I curl his power around it again, tighter this time, sharpening on that love between us. The one that is all-consuming, dangerous. "You feel that?"

Jax groans, moving against me in a devious way. "I do."

"Then stop with the self-deprecation," I demand. "Unless we're playing a game, I don't want to hear you say such things."

He cocks an eyebrow at me. "Giving me orders now, butterfly?"

I shiver at the timbre of his voice, at the chaos in it.

"Only when I have to," I answer, a little breathless. I move my hand from his cheek to his hair, threading my fingers into his blue-black strands. "Are you going to obey?" I tighten my grip on his hair at the roots, tugging just enough to emphasize my point.

He smiles—not my smile; the one of the Nightmare. Icy chills dust my skin, my heart racing as our bond trembles and he takes hold of his power. It's a relief for all of three seconds before he's sending it toward me, a prickle of fear piercing the back of my neck.

I close my eyes. Practice again. The *prick*.

It's a small dose of fear that slides through my system, sweeping into those hollow, doubtful fractures in my soul. He's doing it on purpose. He's always warned me, from day one, that I should fly away.

He doesn't think he's worthy of the love I have for him. I've felt that more times than I can count since he gave his powers to me to save my life.

It doesn't matter how many times we've had the argument, how many times I've countered it with how much I adore him, how I'm not afraid of him, how I'm not going anywhere . . . he doesn't fully believe it. He thinks I'd be better off not attached to him, that I'd somehow be safer.

I know some of this comes from his past, losing his mom so young and being raised by Baydel. Goddess, it's a wonder he has any love in him at all.

Still, he wants me to fly away. Wants me to be strong enough to make that choice for us both.

He's going to have to get used to disappointment—

Fear grips my heart, a razor-sharp terror shooting through my veins.

I tremble in the Nightmare's grasp. There's no escaping this kind of dread. It's endless. It's . . .

Not real.

All the other powers inside me awaken, alerting at the threat now swimming around us. It's an effort to push through the cold, dead fear, but with the help of the other powers, I manage to clear my mind enough to get *angry*.

"Cheater," I accuse through chattering teeth. "We were talking, not practicing." I can barely get the words out.

Jax's grin deepens into that terrifying smile that usually draws me in. He shifts atop me, his free hand going to my throat.

I gasp as he gently grips it, his thumb stroking over the middle. "You think when you're out there, facing our enemies, that you'll get a warning?"

Another wave of fear crashes into me, but it's met with a wave of frustration. He's right. He's always fucking right.

Internally, I'm scrambling, floundering in my own mind and soul as I reach for any power I can get ahold of. On the outside, I'm as still as a statue, frozen in the fear he's creating.

His grip on me tightens, just a fraction.

I focus. Of course, *my* power, the one I've lived and breathed for years, is the closest.

A deep breath fills my lungs when I grip it, when the wind and air fill me so much they push back the terror.

I *keep* pushing it. Harder. All the way into Jax.

He wants to play hard? Fine. We'll play hard.

I take hold of his breath. *Stop* him from taking his next.

His eyes go wide, the hand on my throat faltering.

"You feel that, Nightmare?" I ask, my head rushing with the way the fear drains from my body, replaced by nothing but *power*—way more than I should possess—as I hold the Nightmare's life in my hands.

I grab hold of Pierce's power, the other doors wide open in response to Jax's sneak attack. I spear it toward Jax's mind, filling it with a visual I want him to see.

Him.

How *I* see him.

I want him to see himself through my eyes—this beautiful, terrifying, increasingly irritating love of my life. My mate. My match in every way.

I show it all to him and send the emotions, too, all while I hold his very breath in my possession.

"Do you see?" I demand. "Do you understand?"

He nods. Just one slight dip of his head. That's all the submission this man will give me, and I lap it up.

I restore his air and retreat from his mind.

He takes a gasping breath but barely finishes before his lips are on mine. A punishing kiss that I return with equal passion.

"Fucking love you," he growls, his hands roaming everywhere they can reach. "You don't understand how *much*."

"I do," I whisper, nipping at his bottom lip. "I assure you, I do."

Another growl as he drags his hand down my thigh—

"If we're going to be late and risk whatever punishment the kings will see fit for such a crime, then I'm at least joining you two." Pierce's voice is like liquid velvet from where he stands in the open doorway.

Jax groans, shifting to look back at him, his free hand moving quicker than I can follow.

A blade hurtles straight for Pierce, who doesn't flinch.

I do. Immediately. Instinctually. A band of glittering green energy springs from my fingertips to stop the blade a hair's breadth from Pierce's shoulder, the tip almost touching his immaculate emerald suit.

"Thank you," he says, taking a step away from the blade and brushing a hand casually down his suit jacket. "This is one of my favorites."

Jax is grinning down at me in an innocent way that makes me laugh.

"Enough with the knife throwing," I playfully demand, nudging at his bare chest. "We need to get dressed."

I earn a growl for that.

"Please," I say, meaning it. "The tasks on this damned list are hard enough. Baydel is waiting for me to fail. Lucas and Brooks probably are, too. The only king I think we have in my corner is Jullian, and I'm not sure if any of the RAC likes me at all. Even after all the work we've done in the cities with the people. We can't afford to test them."

Jax relents, rolling off me.

"Thank you," I say, sliding out of his bed.

Pierce's eyebrows draw upward as he looks me up and down. Heat pools low in my core at that look. It doesn't matter how many times my mates have seen me fully bare to them, they still look at me like it's the first time.

My heart is so damn full, it almost eclipses the growing anxiety at being summoned for the next task on the Kings' List.

Almost.

But it comes full force after we've all dressed in our finest, my mates in their signature colors and me in a mixture of ruby and sapphire today—a tight pair of red leggings that are buttery soft beneath the long-sleeved dress of blue, the fabric around my waist split on either leg to show the pop of red.

Ash is atop an onyx table in Jax's entryway, lounging in a sunbeam, his limbs half hanging over the edge as we approach the front door. He hisses as Kal and Axl head out first, then downright growls at Pierce when he pauses to try to make small talk with him.

"I won't give up," he says to the cat, like it can understand him, before turning and winking at me and heading out.

Jax grins at Ash, stopping to stroke his fingers over his scarred head. The feline purrs under his touch, leaning into it and demanding more.

I know how he feels.

I laugh, drawing Jax's attention, but he doesn't dare stop petting.

"What?" he asks.

I shrug. "It's . . ." A strange and satisfying thing to see. The Nightmare's companion. I shake my head. "I'm glad he likes at least one of us," I say. "He barely tolerates me, and he clearly doesn't like the others."

Jax tilts his head, and Ash lies back down, clearly finished with him. "I've never had anything prefer me over my friends," he says, almost to himself. He blinks a few times, that hardened edge to his features returning as he faces me. "Not that it's ever been a competition between us."

My heart aches for him, for how little he thinks of himself.

"I love you all equally," I say.

"I know," he says, sliding his hands into his jacket pockets. "And I'm still shocked by that."

I part my lips to argue, but he stops me. "I'm trying," he says. "I really am. I'm working on it. I just . . . I'm going to need time. This is all new to me."

I nod, fully understanding.

"Are you ready for this?" he asks.

"I'm starting to dread that question," I tease. "But when have I ever been ready for any of this?"

He laughs, low and rough. "When have any of us?"

"At least we're in this together," I say.

"And you're in control of everything," he adds.

"Mostly," I say, knowing that I'm not perfect at wielding their powers, but I'm in a more stable place for sure. Of course, it hasn't truly been tested. If a Fader attack happened and they were threatened, I wouldn't trust myself with their powers. All the more reason for my practices at locking them up or forcing them back to their rightful owners.

"There's nothing you can't face," Jax says, stepping closer. "You died." His voice cracks over the words. "And here you stand. More powerful than all the kings combined."

I choke on that. "I'm only here because of what each of you sacrificed," I say. "And as for being more powerful than the kings?" I shrug. "I'm not consistent. Sometimes I can hold the powers for what feels like forever. Other times, it's mere minutes."

"It's more than you could do when you first awoke," he says. "With more time? You'll be unstoppable."

I don't know what to say to that, especially when all I want to do is give them their powers back. I don't want them. It's too much. It's all too much.

"Let's go," I say instead of voicing that sentiment. "We can't be late."

Jax nods, gesturing to the open door.

I walk out, smiling at the Legends already mounted on their velomages. Jax mimics them, and I climb on behind him. The five of us ride toward the palace like a deadly unit intent on earning our place in this realm.

CHAPTER 31

Kal

I can't remember the last time I walked into the palace without a sense of dread filling my gut.

Maybe as a child, when my mother was still alive, but even those memories are hazy.

I have pieces, flashes of her that come and go as quickly as clouds pass over the sun. I remember her warmth the most. She had this calming, unconditional love that poured out of her naturally, and she was always patient with me, even when my powers surfaced and I couldn't control them.

I always felt safe in her presence.

I still trust my father, but not fully. Not when he rules alongside the others. I hate this feeling. Hate walking up these palace steps, entering through the grand doors, feeling like I might have to face an attack any second.

Enforcers line the walls as we walk down the grand hallway on the main level, guided by my father's elite enforcer, Three.

He's silent, as usual, but I can't shake this feeling. I glance at Jax instinctually. If this was a normal situation, he'd give us a silent gesture for the vibes of the room, something that would give us an edge. But this isn't a normal situation. It never will be again.

We contemplated Rylee trying to return our powers and hold them before coming to this event but ultimately decided against it. While she's been successful in the past, it's unpredictable how long our powers would stay returned to us. And the last thing we want is for our powers to snap back to her in front of the kings, revealing our sacrifice and losing our shot at the thrones.

I look at Rylee, who is on my left, Axl and Pierce on her other side, Jax to my right, the four of us forming a protective and supportive unit around our mate. She stares straight ahead, chin held high, slipping into that mask I always see her put on right before she walks in here. She holds all of our powers, not that anyone else knows that beyond the trusted circle, but damn what I wouldn't give to know what's happening inside her right now. Does she feel the tension in the enforcers with Jax's powers, or am I being paranoid? Can she feel my energy down our bond? I don't want to shake her up.

I try to calm myself, stroking that bond between us in a soothing way in an attempt to hide my nerves. This place shouldn't feel like a trap waiting to spring—it should be a safe haven for us. Maybe someday. If we can finish this and take the thrones.

If not?

I can't allow myself to think that way.

"Right on time," my father says as we're led into the main ballroom. The kings are sitting on a raised dais, as per usual. Three takes his spot next to my father, the other elites next to their assigned king. They're standing at attention, which gives me pause. Are they prepared for an outburst? A scene? Fuck me, what are they about to drop on us? On Rylee?

Things have been too quiet lately. Our time with Rylee, training her, being with her, it's all felt like a glimpse at a future I've only dreamed of. I knew the kings wouldn't offer us that peace for long.

Out of habit, I reach for a power that's not mine anymore, finding the bond between my mate and me instead. It fills a different spot inside my soul, and I know if I follow it, I'll find my power on the other end. It doesn't mean I can take it, especially not long enough to risk Rylee. Even knowing this, all I want to do is grab her and fly out of here.

"Indeed," Brooks says from where he sits, nodding to his son.

Pierce nods back, then dips in a gracious bow to the Royal Authority Council, who sit just below the dais, all eyes on us. I don't like the way Margreet is positioned in front of Baydel, who is in the middle, a smirk on her face that looks like she's just won some competition she's been vying for. She knows something, and whatever it is, it doesn't bode well for us.

"Your highnesses," Rylee says in a soft, sweet voice that doesn't match her true energy at all. I hate it. Hate that she feels like she needs to perform, but I also admire her for it. She plays the game so well, it's a marvel she hasn't been doing it her entire life. She does it better than any of us.

Baydel smiles down as she bows, and we follow suit and half bow as well.

"Thank you for coming," Baydel says. "Today's matters are quite urgent."

I spare a look to my friends, practically holding my breath. Each of us is tense and trying not to show it. It's in moments like this that I wish we'd taken Baydel up on his previous offer, challenged them all and been done with it. Of course, we couldn't have done that, not without our powers, but at least we wouldn't have to deal with this incessant bullshit.

"The Royal Authority Council and I have come up with a critical task," Baydel says, grinning down at us. "It will be crucial in our decision process."

I draw in a breath, doing my best to control my pounding heart.

Baydel rises, jerking his head in a beckoning motion. "We need a word," he says, eyeing Jax. The other kings rise as well, my father nodding to me.

Rylee moves to follow us as the kings head toward the double doors, but Baydel stops her with a raised hand. "Just the princes for now, little bug."

I cringe at the demeaning pet name he's given my mate and grind my teeth against the instinct to snap.

Rylee tilts her head, concern flashing in her blue eyes.

I scan the room, breathing a sigh of relief when I spot Mirren, Ivy, and Layce lingering in the back, almost hidden near the dining tables. They slowly make their way to Rylee, and it's a small comfort to leave her behind with people we trust.

Not that she needs protection or that I think the RAC is going to launch some sort of attack on her, but right now, everything seems like a threat.

Rylee dips her head, moving toward the nearest open table and taking a seat, Ivy and Layce flanking either side, Mirren hovering behind the three like a concerned mother hen.

"Kal," my father says, drawing my attention as he stands in the open doorway. The others are already gone.

I quicken my pace after one last assuring look at Rylee and follow my father down the hallway and into one of the smaller gathering rooms near the ballroom.

This one has walls lined with thick tapestries, the woven fabric glistening in our signature colors with depictions of our mothers' statues. A fire crackles in the wide hearth on the focal wall, casting the thick rug of gold and red in warmth. Rich brown leather chairs are arranged in a way that begs casual conversation, but it's the four vials sitting on the center of the end table that send ice through my veins.

The vials are basic enough—cylindrical glass capped with a small cork—but it's the murky green liquid inside giving off the foreboding vibes.

"The fuck is that?" Axl says without preamble, jabbing a finger toward the table as our fathers urge us to sit next to them.

"Sit down," Lucas demands, having already selected a seat around the table.

Axl looks like he'll argue, but I give him a silent warning. We're in no position, not without our powers. And more than that? Whatever we do in opposition will always come back to Rylee. We have to protect her at all costs, even if it kills our pride to do so.

So, we sit.

"This next test requires a bit of Occuli magic," my father explains, motioning toward the vials.

Jax has a blade out, fiddling with it like he couldn't be more bored. Pierce's eyes are calculating as he stares at his father, and Axl is shaking his head like he won't be swayed.

"What is the next test?" I ask to move the conversation along. I'm usually the one who can keep my tone level enough to do so, and I'm happy to perform that role for our group.

Baydel grins, his hands coming together in a point. "It will accomplish two things, but really, it's a test for your mate. The RAC insisted."

I arch a brow. They insisted or he *forced* them to insist? I can never tell with him.

"Again," Axl growls. "What the fuck is that?"

Lucas grabs a vial from the table. "Drink it."

Axl takes the vial but doesn't uncork it. His eyes meet mine.

I nod, fully understanding him. The last time we drank from a vial, we met our mothers after Rylee died in the Athanry. That sort of thing leaves a lasting impression. This is triggering as fuck.

Not that the kings know that. They weren't there when it all happened, thanks to Jax's explosion of power driving everyone away. And when we came to, after the incident with the Faders and Rylee, we replaced the remaining Athanry vials with a fake liquid so the kings wouldn't be any the wiser. The last thing we need is for them to know we drank every last drop of what our mothers left behind for us.

"It's a binding tonic," Baydel says with an air of excitement to his tone. "To ensure you won't access your powers."

"Why?" I ask as my father hands me a vial, a look of regret on his face.

"So you won't interfere with the next task," my father explains.

I glance to Pierce, who takes his, leaving it corked. This is usually the moment he'd speak to us mind-to-mind, giving us an edge. That won't be happening today.

Shit, if this stuff will deny us access to our powers, what will it do to us *without* any?

My eyes go to Jax, who holds his own vial in his free hand.

The risk of asking such a question will give away too much.

Jax pops the cork out with the edge of his knife, sniffing at the mixture. His lip curls. "Your Occuli's doing?" he asks Baydel.

"Naturally," Baydel says, clearly pleased. "Frenrick is the best, and you remember how much I used to love to dabble in potions and tonics. We've worked on this one for a while yet. For this exact task."

"You still haven't told us what it consists of," I say.

"And we won't," Baydel says, his look cutting to me. "Drink, and we'll begin."

Fuck me. The amount of trust they're asking for is absolutely something we can't give.

"You know what happens if you refuse," Baydel reminds us. "The Royal Authority Council, along with the four of us, will never grant your ascension to the thrones."

"You can't rule forever," Jax says, cold and low.

"I assure you," Baydel says, eyes on his son, "I can." He clears his throat. "Especially if I think for one second Lumathyst isn't safe in your hands."

I can. Not *we* can.

My heart pounds hard against my ribcage, apprehension clawing up my throat. I look to my father. He's hard to read, but there's hope in his eyes, and something else . . . a plea? He nods to the vial.

"The sooner you take it," he says, "the sooner we can explain things to Rylee and get the task over with."

"You sound like it should be rushed, Jullian," Baydel quips. "Tests of this importance, years in the making, take time."

My father ignores him.

I look to my friends. If we're lucky, we take this and nothing happens. Since we don't have our powers, there's nothing for it to bind. But, since it was designed for someone with powers, what if the reactions will be different for someone who doesn't?

We don't have time to talk, to strategize, and in the kings' eyes, we shouldn't need to.

"How long will the effects last?" Pierce asks.

"A full day," Brooks answers, earning a sour look from Baydel. "Two at most."

It has an ending. That's good to know. As long as the potion doesn't kill us first.

Rylee would lay this palace flat if it did.

I silently pray to the goddesses, to the Fates beyond, that it doesn't come to that.

"Cheers," I say, but it sounds like a question. I uncork the vial and bring it to my lips.

My friends do the same, and silently, we swallow the potion at the same time.

Together. We always do anything important together.

Legends to whatever end.

The empty glass vials clank against the table as we set them down. I cough, clearing my throat of the viscous substance that seems to stick as it slides down my throat. My tongue tingles, almost going numb, and suddenly . . .

It's hard to breathe.

My eyes widen, panic snapping through me.

Black edges my vision, my limbs heavy and thick as I sink deeper into the chair. My head lolls to the side, and it's all I can do to look across the way to Axl, to Jax and Pierce, all of whom are in similar positions . . .

Then everything goes black.

CHAPTER 32

Rylee

"What do you think this is about?" Ivy whispers from where she sits next to me.

"Another task from the list, no doubt." I turn in my seat, looking up to Mirren. "Should I speak with them?" I ask only loud enough for the four of us to hear. The Royal Authority Council is behind us, chatting among themselves and sipping from crystal glasses filled with sparkling wine. Like this is any other entertainment put on by the wealthy.

But this is my life. My mates' lives that are being tested and tried, all for the sake of proving themselves worthy of thrones that should be their birthright.

"Only if you have something to say, girl," Mirren whispers back.

My heart deflates. I have no grand speeches planned. No well-thought-out pleas for their acceptance. That's not me. It'll never be me.

But . . . perhaps I should've prepped for this? Maybe I should've spent less time training, practicing with powers, and poring over my sister's art journal, and instead focused on composing articulate speeches that prove I'll make a good supporter alongside my mates when they become kings?

Too late for that today. If I stand up and speak to them off the cuff, there's no telling what will fly out of my mouth. I certainly don't want to fail this test before it's even begun, whatever it may be.

A sharp gasp tears through me, adrenaline shooting through my veins like someone hit me with a magical blaster. I stand up so fast, I knock my chair over, almost taking Mirren out. She barely dodges it, looking at me like I've lost my mind.

I grip my stomach, trying to catch my breath and stop the roll of nausea that hits me all at once.

"Rylee?" Ivy is next to me, hands on my back.

"What is it?" Layce asks from my other side, trying to catch my gaze.

I clench my eyes shut, hushing the bonds inside me. They're *tensing*, flailing like they're fighting off some invisible force. They demand I get up and do something—

They go quiet.

Cold.

My eyes snap open. "I can't feel them."

"Can't feel what?" Mirren asks, wary.

"My bonds," I say, my voice cracking. "They've gone *numb*."

Mirren gasps, covering her mouth with her hand. "Goddesses save us."

I'll kill the kings.

Eviscerate them.

I take a step toward the open double doors, ignoring the confused looks from the Royal Authority Council.

"Your highness," Charlotte calls toward me. "Are you all right? Do you need—"

"Rylee," Mirren snaps, stepping in front of me. She smiles politely toward the RAC, turning us away from their prying eyes, and navigates me away from the door. "Remember where you are," she whispers.

The panic in her voice makes some of the bloodlust ebb.

"This is a test."

"Mir." I quiet myself. "I can't feel them."

And . . . and I can't feel their powers anymore, either. It's like something has draped over them, heavy and numbing.

"But we don't know why," Mirren says. "You can't assume the worst. You can't explode until you know the facts."

I grit my teeth and breathe. She's right. And the only relief I can take from not feeling their powers anymore is knowing I won't erupt right now.

"What if—"

"All right, little bug." Baydel's voice cuts off my words. He scrunches his brows, noting my closeness to the doors. "Thinking of skittering away?"

"Of course not," I manage to say.

"Good. We've just made all the arrangements."

I swallow hard. Waiting. Gripping Mirren's offered arm like it's a lifeline.

They didn't kill my mates. They wouldn't do that. That wouldn't prove anything.

They're fine. They're fine. They're fine.

Icy terror streaks behind the chant I silently repeat. If they're not fine . . .

That buried, primal well of wrath bubbles inside me. The one that exploded the night the Faders shot at them. I lock down my emotions, doing my best to numb them like the bonds and the powers. I can't afford to lose control. Not now. Not ever.

Jullian looks at me kindly from where he stands behind Baydel, Lucas and Brooks not far behind him. "Rylee, today's task—"

"Now, now, Jullian," Baydel cuts over him. "Don't get ahead of yourself. You'll ruin all the fun."

Jullian's gaze sears Baydel for a moment, before he pushes it away.

I don't respond. Can't.

Every ounce of strength I have is going to sheer willpower to keep from lashing out at the kings for whatever it is they've done. I'm sure I could kill them with my bare hands at this point.

"Come." Baydel gestures to the RAC and the rest of the people lingering in the ballroom. "To the arena." He turns his focus to Mirren. "You will prepare her."

Mirren dips her head, though confusion flits across her face.

"I'll stay behind to assist," Jullian offers.

Baydel studies him for a moment before he rolls his eyes. "If you must," he says. "But don't give away anything. I want to explain everything once we're all seated."

"Understood." Jullian watches them leave, everyone exiting in a flurry of excitement.

Except for Ivy and Layce, who follow the crowd and look back to flash me worried glances. I try to nod my assurance to them, but I'm not entirely sure everything will be fine. I have no clue what I'm about to step into.

Jullian leads us down the hallway and into a small weapons chamber. "Put her in leathers, please, Mirren," he says. "And arm her with some blades. Small ones. Not enough to draw too much attention."

"Arm her?" Mirren gasps, all formality for the king forgotten. "Am I sending her into battle?"

I swallow hard as I look at the array of weapons. I've only practiced with a few during my training with the Legends, and before that, with Erin.

"I've been forbidden to say."

Of course. Mirren beckons me over to a partitioned space in the corner of the room. I hurry over and take the fighting leathers from her. These were made specifically for me after the Athanry and hug my body perfectly. The Legends' crest—a crown with all four princes' gemstones inlaid in the points and a golden gem on the fifth point—is on the back of the long-sleeved jacket.

I use the time it takes to get dressed to *breathe*. Whatever this task is, I'll face it as I have any other. Dressed, I move toward Mirren and Jullian again. Each offers me a pair of blades, and I take them, sliding them into the holsters fitted to my thighs. Jax will be proud when he sees me decorated in knives.

That thought gives me a little courage.

"If you were a betting man, like Axl, what odds would you give me?" I ask Jullian, hoping to get something out of him.

"You've always surprised us, Rylee Gray," he says. "You can do it again. If you want it badly enough."

I glare at him, beyond caring about propriety. "I'm getting really fucking tired of having to prove myself."

"I know," he says. He turns, readying to lead us to the arena. "It isn't fair."

"Can you give me *any* advice?" I ask.

"Yes," he says, lingering for a moment. "Don't die."

CHAPTER 33

Rylee

Jullian leads us through the palace, taking so many twists and turns, I become woefully aware of how many wings I've yet to explore. Mirren stays close to my side, a silent show of support.

"This is where we must leave you," Jullian explains as we stop before a stone wall just off a heavily decorated hallway. He motions to the wall, as if that's supposed to mean something to me. "When this opens, walk straight ahead. Baydel wants to showcase the terms in front of the RAC."

I blow out a breath, nodding.

"Mirren." He gestures to her. "We must join them."

She seems reluctant to go but eventually follows at Jullian's prodding. The two disappear down the hallway and around a bend.

I slide my fingers over the hilts of the blades, wondering what kind of task this will be. Apprehension clouds my every breath. The numbness of the mating bonds ramps up a sense of urgency that makes it hard to think straight. They took them from me. Did something to them. All for a test?

The stone wall shifts upward, some magic propelling it up as it disappears into a hidden chamber, effectively silencing my racing thoughts. A cool, damp breeze touches my cheeks, the smell of stagnant water and damp sand wafting on the wind. Jullian and Brooks's elite enforcers—Three and Two—stand just a few feet away, jerking their heads in unison for me to enter the massive room.

Anxiety immediately replaces every other emotion in my body. I can't help it. Seeing an enforcer, elite or not, always raises my hackles. You can take the girl out of the Ashlands, but not the Ashlands out of the girl.

Longing hooks my chest and tugs at my most recent memory of the Ashlands as I walk toward them. I'm not doing this damned list for fun or just so my mates can sit on the thrones they deserve. I'm also doing this for the people of Lumathyst. Especially those in the lower cities, who starve while the wealthy fill their wastebaskets with unspoiled foods. For those who are sick and have two choices: go in debt to the royals for basic medicine and access to healers or die. For those who are forbidden to read for pleasure while the nobles purchase crates of books because the color of their spines looks pretty in a study they rarely use.

For change.

For a *good*, decent change.

That's why I step into the unknown now. Regardless of how dangerous it is. I've faced death and the goddesses themselves. One of them is haunting my dreams. I can handle whatever damned task the kings concocted for me today.

The weapons strapped to my thighs feel heavy as I follow the elite enforcers. An added, awkward weight I'm not used to, though somehow, I'm adapting. Maybe it's all the training I've done with the Legends, or everything I did with Erin prior to this moment, but I keep my chin held high as we head deeper into the massive space.

The floor is covered in a gray sand, not unlike the powder that coats the streets of my homeland. I swallow hard, ignoring the soft familiarity beneath my boots, instead focusing on the dome-like structure that reaches up farther than I can see.

The space lives up to the promised arena setting, with rows of golden curved benches layered in a wide circle around the sand-covered floor. The kings are in the front row, naturally, which sits at least twenty feet above where I stand. A few rows above them are a scattering of the RAC and their families.

Charlotte dares a small wave of encouragement, while Margreet looks like she's salivating at the very prospect of my impending doom as she sips from a wineglass. Royal staff members are serving food and drinks from silver platters as if they're here to watch the Ruby Aire Players' latest performance. It turns my stomach. This is my *life*. My mates' lives. How can they revel in such spectacles?

"Now that we're all here . . ." Baydel stands from his central position among the seats. "We can begin." He looks down at me, his focus so intent I'm certain a wave of his power will hit me any second.

"The terms of our alliances with neighboring realms are coming to an end," Brooks says before Baydel can continue. "It's time for us to re-sign our peace and trade agreements. Normally it's something *we* would do, but seeing as it's time for our sons' ascensions, this is the perfect opportunity for them to forge their own alliances and terms with the other realms."

"And seeing as there are several neighboring realms, you'll have to split up in order to secure ties in each of them," Lucas interjects.

Split up?

"And what better way to decide who you're *allowed* to accompany than a little experiment?" Baydel asks.

"Experiment?" Panic slashes down my spine.

Baydel grins. "Do you remember our first dinner together, little bug?"

My blood runs cold. The demi. The way Baydel made him dance to his death. I couldn't forget if I tried.

"Yes," I answer.

"Do you remember what you said to me?" Baydel draws his hands together before him. "That you would've *spared* the traitor who made an attempt on my life? Because you didn't relish death or bloodshed? That you'd spare him, putting him in the dungeons instead?"

I press my lips together and nod.

"Your actions made us all wonder if you'd say the same if the princes' lives were in danger." He grins, devious and icy. "Evaluna defended me with the full force of her power. And while you have no power to speak of . . ." He sneers, looking me up and down. "That doesn't exclude you from the duty of protecting and defending your future kings."

My fingers tremble, adrenaline crackling beneath my skin. Wind flickers there, ready and willing to flare. I still have my power. Whatever the kings did to my mates has not affected my own.

"And, after your atrocious display of ignorance with Margreet's test," he continues, "we've decided it's of the utmost importance to try you in this regard. And, to ensure your reactions are true and just, we've ensured the consequences of any misstep of yours will be *dire* for the princes."

I move, unable to digest his words while standing still. I pace in the sand, hairs prickling on the back of my neck as the elite enforcers follow behind within striking distance, way too close for comfort.

"Today, One is the ruler of an enemy realm," Baydel explains. "Treat him and his demands as such."

I tilt my head, utter confusion rippling through me.

Baydel snaps his fingers, and his Occuli, Frenrick, stands. He directs a burst of green flame toward the middle of the arena, and the bright pop of light blots out my vision for a second. I blink the impressions away, my eyes clearing. Where there was once nothing, my mates have materialized.

"No." Shock steals my breath.

Their hands are bound behind their backs, their mouths gagged, each of their necks stretched to capacity by a noose. They stand on thin platforms perched atop a large wooden contraption, their boots barely steady on them.

"No!" I yell this time, racing toward them, only for Two and Three to grab me. I thrash against their hold, but there is no sense to my movements. I can only see *them*. Their eyes, the way they're struggling to breathe.

One leaps down from the platform, his boots thudding against the ground before me.

"I've captured the esteemed princes of Lumathyst," he says, his voice slicing through my panic. It's slightly muffled by the helmet he wears, but I focus all the same. I've never heard him speak this much, but there's something to his voice that nags at me. "They shouldn't have come to my territory." He gestures to Two and Three, and they haul me to my feet.

I shake them off, settling myself as much as I can. "Release them," I demand.

"They broke our peace treaty," he responds. "I'm well within my rights to execute them here and now."

Acid bubbles up my throat. "Release. Them." I hush the wind in my blood. I could steal every person's air in this room. Halt it. Suffocate them with it.

I won't. Not yet.

One tilts his head. "What will you give me to release them?"

That question halts the murderous, panicked thoughts. What would I offer for them, if I were queen? "We can renegotiate the terms of our treaty," I hurry to answer, hope building in my chest. "I know the princes. They wouldn't break the treaty. There must've been a misunderstanding. Let them go, and we can see to righting it in a way that benefits both realms."

One turns his head, the diamonds on his helmet sparkling beneath the torchlight in the arena. I can't see his eyes, of course, but it's easy enough to tell he's looking up at Baydel.

I follow that line of sight, just in time to see Baydel shake his head.

My stomach drops.

"The offer is a good start, but I'll want more."

Of course he will. "We can discuss further terms when you've released the princes."

"I *am* a forgiving ruler." One sounds like he's enjoying the role Baydel has forced him to play, but this feels like anything but a game. "I'll entertain your terms, but you must pick one prince."

The floor shifts beneath my feet.

"Excuse me?"

"Choose." The demand in his voice needles beneath my skin. "Choose one prince to save. The rest will die today as recompense for breaking our treaty."

My heart stops dead at his words.

"Pick one!" Baydel hollers from his seat. "Let's see who you think could rule Lumathyst on his own." He's downright jovial, tearing into a leg of meat like he's watching the most entertaining event.

Based on Baydel's behavior, I'm inclined to believe it's all theater, but Lucas and Jullian and Brooks? They're *terrified.* Their fear is tangible as they focus on their sons, who are struggling on the goddess-forsaken platform. This is real.

I tear my eyes from the kings, looking past One to my mates. They're each silently communicating something different to me.

Kal begs me to sacrifice him, a solidified peace in his expression.

Axl is clearly angry with the situation, muscles bunched, but when I meet his eyes, he winks at me, assuring me he's fine with whoever I choose.

Pierce nods his encouragement, like he has no doubt I'll make the right choice.

And Jax? He's ice-cold, staring at his father with narrowed eyes, body completely still and relaxed as if he's already accepted his demise.

My heart rips into pieces. I can't possibly choose—

"Choose," One snaps, making me jump.

"I can't," I admit on a loosed breath.

"Weak." One stomps back to the platform, climbing it in a few powerful strides. "Pathetic." He kicks the platform beneath Pierce. It sets him off-balance, the noose around his neck tightening so much he groans.

"Stop!" I race toward the platform.

Two and Three dart into my path again, but this time, I'm ready. My muscle memory from avoiding enforcers in the Ashlands kicks in, and I evade their attempts to grab me. Pulling on my training with my mates, I swing, landing a punch to Two's side that makes him double over. A kick knocks Three off his feet.

Fuck choosing. I'll tear through these enforcers and get my mates back myself—

Two wraps his arms around my neck, shoves me to the ground, and pins me down by the throat. I can't breathe for all of five seconds before I wiggle free of his grasp and swipe his legs out from underneath him.

A hit jerks my head to the left, a sting erupting across my cheek from Three's backhand.

The Legends roar from behind their gags. It's fuel to my pursuit.

I'm on my feet again in seconds, drawing two blades from the holsters at my thighs. "I don't want to kill you," I say to the elites. "But I will. Release them."

One laughs. "I like your spirit," he says from where he remains on the platform. "But it's not enough."

The words hit some raw, stinging thing inside my chest.

"Choose one," he says again. "Or they *all* die." He kicks Kal's platform, and he flinches as his noose tightens.

Goddess, they don't have much time. Will the kings really kill their own children for the sake of a task?

From the horrified expressions on Lucas, Jullian, and Brooks's faces, I believe so.

Am I really about to lose them all because I can't choose one to save? What if I do choose one—will that end this horrific test? But I love each of them. There's not one I love more than the others. Not one's life I value more than another. This is an impossible task.

Tears well in my eyes, angry and hot.

One kicks Axl's platform. Then Jax's.

They're all fighting against the ropes, struggling as their faces turn red from the tightening nooses.

My stomach roils. I can't choose. I would sooner cut out my own heart—

"Take me!" The answer rips from my lips. "Take *me*," I say again, breathing heavily.

One goes still where he'd been about to kick Pierce's platform again. "You?"

"Yes. Me." I walk toward the platform, looking up at One. Two and Three follow me but don't attack. "I'm a princess of Lumathyst," I say, doing my best to sound confident. "I'm worth more to you than them."

"What makes you think that?" One asks.

My powers. They don't know about them. But if an enemy realm did? They'd go after me, not the Legends.

"As their mate, I hold more value to the Legends than anyone else in the realm." Their love for me is one of my greatest strengths. I use it, pulling it into every fiber of my being to try to end this.

One turns to look at Baydel again. I do, too.

He shakes his head.

I focus on One again.

"You won't choose?"

"I choose me," I say. "Take me. My life for theirs."

One hesitates, pacing the length of the wooden structure before he stops and nods toward Frenrick, who's sitting near Baydel.

Another burst of green flame, and the last remaining elite enforcer, Four, comes in from the left, dragging something behind him.

No, not something. *Someone.*

The man is cringing against the hold Four has on him, and he yelps as Four tosses him to the ground like he's no more than a doll.

"This Ashlander plotted to kill your beloved princes," Baydel says from where he sits. "He also happens to be a demi." A flick of Baydel's wrist, and the man stands awkwardly enough that I can tell Baydel is using his power to force him to. "Measly power, but enough that it made him bold."

I glance from my mates to the Ashlander and back again.

Four shoves the Ashlander toward me. The man is blubbering, tears streaking his dirt-lined face. He's malnourished and squinting against the golden torches lighting up the arena, as if he's been in the dark for a very long time. Could be from the mines, but more likely, they dragged him from the dungeons for this task.

"You won't choose," Baydel says. "So, I'll offer you a deal to end this. Kill him. Execute him for his crimes, and all four of the princes shall go free." He casts a look to One. "Do you find this fair?"

One dips his head.

Of course he does. He never really held any power in this experiment.

Baydel moves his hand again, and the Ashlander flies to his knees before me.

"Please," he stutters. "I didn't—" His words abruptly cut off, his lips pressed together like some invisible force snaps them closed.

Hatred slices through my veins like ice as I glare up at Baydel.

"Kill him and save our sons," Baydel implores.

I grip the blade in my hand so hard it trembles.

Groans sound behind me as One kicks the platforms out from under the princes one by one. They can barely touch with their toes now, struggling against their restraints as they fight for strength to balance to keep the ropes from tightening fully. They won't be able to maintain this for long before they suffocate.

This can't be real.

I've slipped into a nightmare with no end.

And for what? A list? To prove I'd make the right decision should we find ourselves in this situation?

But we *wouldn't*. The princes would never break a peace treaty or allow themselves to be captured. *I'd* never allow it.

The kings separated us, and our defenses were down because we thought this no more than another task on the Kings' List.

Which it is. A test of how I'd react to such a situation. They've risked their own sons' lives to test me. I don't know why I'm surprised. Their cruelty knows no bounds.

I stare up at my mates on the platform, their faces going purple now as they struggle to balance on their tiptoes, and fire rages in me.

They want to know how I'd act as queen in such a situation?

Then so fucking be it.

I raise the blade, looking down at the Ashlander before me. Bile creeps up my throat.

"This is one of our people," I say, angry tears in my eyes as I hold that blade at the ready. "And I will not condemn him for a crime not yet proven." I spin, flinging the blade, just like Jax taught me. I grab my remaining three, rapidly firing each of them, and hit my targets.

The Legends hit the wooden structure beneath them in a heap, immediately ripping the nooses over their heads.

I'm unarmed as Two, Three, and Four grab me, forcing me to my knees despite all my efforts to throw them off. They're too strong, and without using my power, I'm truly no match for them. I'm not desperate enough to expose myself to the kings just yet.

One jumps off the platform just as my mates get to their feet. He races to me, a blade drawn as he shoves the other enforcers off me, putting that knife to my throat as he hauls me up and in front of him, my back to his chest.

"You want her?" Baydel roars from the stands, clearly agitated by this turn of events. "Then *kill* the Ashlander."

The breath stalls in my lungs. I go entirely still in One's hold, my eyes on the Legends stalking toward us.

I part my lips to speak—

"Don't," One whispers in my ear, like he doesn't want anyone else to hear him. His grip tightens, his left arm so tight around my middle, it feels like a vise threatening to crush my ribs, and that blade is perched against my neck. One wrong move and I'm done. "You can't afford to say or do anything stupid."

"Kill him," Baydel is yelling now, as if that will prompt the Legends to act more quickly. "Or she dies."

"Let her go." Kal speaks directly to One. "This has gone on long enough."

One doesn't budge an inch.

"You know what to do," Baydel says, but the elite doesn't move. *"One."* He says his name with more of a threat.

"Be very still," One whispers before he jerks me backward against him. I yelp, but the blade at my throat somehow doesn't slip.

"He will kill her," Baydel snaps, "if you don't do as you're commanded."

The Legends share a look, that silent form of communication they're all so good at, even without Pierce's powers.

Baydel wants to break us. *That's* what this is about. First with him trying to make me choose, and now with this senseless demand. He knows I won't forgive them if they choose me over an innocent person.

They won't do that, though.

They *won't.*

I know them better than Baydel does.

He can't break us. *Nothing* can break us.

Jax lunges, scooping up the Ashlander in the span of a breath, his hand at his throat.

My heart stutters, and I try to move, to speak, but One holds so firm I can't.

Axl, Kal, and Pierce don't move to stop him.

"Yes." Baydel's grin stretches from ear to ear. "That's right, son. Do it."

I'm not sure I'm breathing. Jax knows Baydel's cruelty better than anyone. He, like me, doesn't doubt his father's desire to kill for sport. Jax knows I can easily become a victim of this madness.

My heart cracks as Jax's indigo eyes meet mine. There's such agony there.

Don't, I silently beg. *Don't let him break you. You're better than him.*

Jax blinks, glaring up at Baydel. "This is one of our people." He lets the Ashlander go. "And I won't condemn him for a crime not proven."

CHAPTER 34

Rylee

Tears stream down my cheeks, pride overtaking every other emotion at Jax's words. My words. Our words. Together. We're all together on this.

Baydel didn't break us.

Jullian, Lucas, and Brooks rise, clapping intensely.

One releases me, and I immediately race to the Legends, falling into their embraces.

"You are quite extraordinary," Lucas calls from where he stands.

Wait, what?

"Marvelous," Brooks says. "I daresay if Eirdis were here, she'd be *over-joyed* at our son's choice."

"I find their lack of action not only a disappointment but a direct threat to our realm," Baydel says. "They couldn't do what it takes to protect the best interest of Lumathyst."

"I agree," Margreet chimes in.

"Come now, Baydel," Jullian says. "Her loyalty to both the princes and Lumathyst's people are uncontested queen behavior. And the princes' response in return. They're a unit. A formidable one that opposing realms will surely note and avoid crossing."

Jullian's words are enough to warm some of the icy confusion freezing my soul. That, and the fact that the Legends are by my side, safe, despite the angry red marks blossoming on their necks.

"There's no question they passed this test," Brooks agrees. "But let's make it official. A show of hands of those who think they've failed?" He eyes the members of the RAC, and my nerves twist. They're voting on our success or failure right in front of us.

Margreet raises her hand. "They failed. They didn't do anything they were told."

Shocker there.

Lucas shakes his head. "And those in favor of a success?"

I hold my breath.

Everyone, except Margreet, raises their hand. Ivy, Layce, and Mirren show their support, too, despite their votes not counting. I nod up to them, silently assuring them I'm okay and I'm grateful for them.

Even Baydel raises his hand, probably not wanting to be seen disagreeing with the masses.

"Fine," Baydel says. "As much as you refused to choose one prince in the experiment, you *must* choose now. You may only accompany one of them to secure allies." He nods, and the elite enforcers hand each of the Legends a roll of parchment.

I snap my gaze to Kal, then Axl, then Pierce, and finally Jax, silently pleading.

"Don't worry." Axl is the first to speak. "We'd never make you choose." He winks at me. "We Legends have a way of deciding such things," he says to the crowd. "A tradition we've had since we were adolescents." He lowers his voice so only I can hear. "We usually only ever use it when a tiebreaker is needed, but today it will work just as well."

"And what is that?" Baydel sounds more irritated than intrigued.

"What's the date, again?" Axl asks.

"The eighteenth," Lucas answers.

"Mine," Pierce declares. "I'm the winner on any date containing a one in an even-numbered month."

My heart swells at the way they've taken the burden from my shoulders.

The impossible weight lifts, but just behind it is the anxiety of being separated at all.

Baydel waves us off. "You have your assignments. The royal ships are being prepared."

We take that as our dismissal and hurry out of the arena before the kings can change their mind.

Kal takes the lead, guiding us through the palace until we reach the safety of his rooms. He shuts and bolts the door behind us, and I feel like I can truly breathe for the first time in hours.

"I can't feel any of you. I thought I lost you." The words tear from my mouth.

"Baydel forced us to drink one of his concoctions," Lucas grumbles. "Almost as bad as that nullifier the Faders use."

"It bound our powers entirely," Pierce adds. "But it should wear off by tomorrow."

"Knocked us out long enough for the elite enforcers to put ropes around our necks, too."

"I couldn't access them, either." Anger bubbles, hot and erratic. "This needs to end." I rub my palms over my face. I've always suspected, but now I know for sure, that our mating bonds and powers are linked. That's why I find focusing on our connection an easier way to access their power. "Where are they sending us?" I ask.

They each unroll their parchment at my question.

"Silvac." Pierce tilts his head. "We're to negotiate terms with Silvac." He poses it like a question.

"Is that bad?" I ask.

"Not necessarily," he answers. "But the last time we attempted to renegotiate terms, we lost half a battalion."

"Vleyica," Kal answers.

"Cardrayton," Axl says.

"Keleshore." Jax.

"They're really separating us," I say, sinking down onto one of the ruby sofas in Kal's lounge area.

"Yeah, kitten, they are."

"And we're just going to go along with it?"

"It's complicated," Pierce offers, coming to sit next to me. "These sorts of trips wouldn't be uncommon were we to take the thrones. There will be times we must separate to carry out one royal need or another."

I open and shut my mouth a couple of times. "It feels calculated more than complicated. Especially after that *experiment*." The image of them hanging, their lives slipping away from them, will not be one I soon forget.

"It does," Pierce agrees. "But if the Royal Authority Council assigned it, then perhaps the intentions are wholly political."

I huff, folding my arms over my chest. "I hate politics."

Kal comes to sit on my other side, smoothing a hand over my back. "You can hate it, but we need to learn to use it to our advantage. So we can make a change for the better."

I soften, just a little. "Okay, Dreamer. Tell me how to be okay with them sending us to different realms? Being separated by that much distance seems like a punishment right now, not to mention it's the kings who are forcing it."

I still can't feel the bonds, but I know once the potion wears off, that connection and need will come back with full force. I'll have one mate with me, but how am I to stand being without the others without any way to check on them?

"Any amount of time away from you is a form of torture," Kal says. "But what kind of rulers will we be if we don't endure that sacrifice for the greater good of our people? Or realm?"

My iciness all but melts. He's right. My optimistic dreamer.

I glance to my Nightmare, who seems lost to his thoughts. I can't help but wonder if he's replaying the way he snatched that Ashlander up by the throat. Can't help but wonder if for a second, he thought about killing him to save me. Can't help but know, deep down, that if it had been a true threat to my life, he would've. Just like I did to those Faders.

"Jax?" I pose his name like a question.

His gaze slowly meets mine, a silent response of *I'm fine*.

I don't think any of us is fine, but I nod.

"What about your cities? Will your chancellors take over matters?"

"Yes," Kal answers. "They'll act in our stead."

"And you trust them," I say, not ask. I know they do, but still. "What if the Faders attack while we're gone? What if . . ." What if there's a battle and Erin is killed?

"I'll give orders to capture, not kill," Axl says.

"We all will," Jax adds.

"And in the interim, we'll have to hope they don't attack. We'll resume our efforts to make contact with them and handle the enhancement issue when we return," Pierce says.

I rub at my temples. "Seems like the worst time to leave. So much is happening."

"I wish there was another way," Pierce says. "But if it gets us any sway with the RAC, we have to try."

"How long does it take to get a diplomatic contract signed, anyway? It can't take that much time." I dare to hope, standing and crossing the room to where Jax is still brooding. I smooth my hand over his cheek, drawing his attention.

"My father was once in Keleshore for two months," he answers. "They are a thoughtful people who take their time on major decisions."

"Of course he assigned you to that realm." I roll my eyes. "Should I just challenge them all?" I ask, not totally joking. "It may be easier at this point."

Jax's laugh is music to my ears as he hauls me closer. "That's my murderous little butterfly," he says. "If you want to kill them all, I'll stand at your side and watch."

Heat streaks through my body at the support.

"The kings have been alive longer than any of us can fathom," Pierce interjects. "There are facets of them that even we don't understand."

"And beyond that," Kal offers, "we don't want that kind of blood on your hands."

I sigh. I know.

"Would I love to watch you tear my father to pieces?" Jax asks. "Yes. Yes, I would. Would I risk your life at the chance of gaining the throne that way? No."

"It's my life to risk," I challenge.

"It is," he says. "But think of how cross I'd be with you if you died again."

A laugh tears from me, free and raw and open. "Jax." I draw closer to him. "I don't want to be away from any of you."

"I don't want you to, either, butterfly."

"None of us do," Pierce agrees.

Axl crosses the room, gliding a finger down my back. The touch makes me arch into Jax, who is still holding me against him. "We should make the most of the time we have."

Fire ignites in my core. He's right. I don't know how long we'll be separated. I don't want to waste the little time we do have whining about our situation.

We proved to the RAC, to the kings, that we're an unbreakable unit. Separating us won't change that, and now, I want to give into the need that always pulses beneath my skin, barely leashed.

Jax spins me so my back is to him. It's almost like he's presenting me as an offering to Axl, and it sends liquid heat through my veins. Axl's lips shape into his effortless grin as he tips my chin up, dipping down to capture my mouth with his.

My eyes flutter closed, the heat from his kiss warming me from the inside out.

"As much as I love seeing the Legend crest on your back, it must go." Jax slides my jacket off from behind, letting it fall to the floor. He draws closer, shifting my hair away from my neck and planting a kiss right where my cloud mark resides.

I moan into Axl's mouth and grip his shirt with one hand, the other reaching up behind me to touch Jax's face.

"Axl, surely there are other things you can do to our mate with your mouth." Kal's voice is low and close, he and Pierce having crossed the room to join us. We're all still huddled near the doorway.

Axl draws back, pure mischief in his eyes. "You're right." He bends, hefting me up and over his shoulder.

I squeal at the sudden move, laughing as he takes me through Kal's quarters, positioning me on the edge of a small breakfast table in a nook in his bedroom.

"Lift that pretty ass for me," he says, hooking his fingers into my pants. I do as I'm told, lifting off the table as he drags them, my undergarments, and my boots off. He grips the back of the chair at the head of the table, pulling it out and plopping into it before me as I hurry out of my shirt. "Now this is my favorite kind of feast."

A flush rakes through me as he scoots the chair forward and spreads my thighs with his powerful hands.

"Lie back," Pierce demands from my left, where he's come to stand on the other side of the table, Jax right next to him. Pierce is unbuttoning his shirt, shedding it. Jax is doing the same. Anticipation flutters in my core.

A gentle nudge, and I lean back until my spine kisses the smooth wood of the table.

Kal is on my right, shirtless as well.

Axl dips down, kissing my inner thigh. My breath hitches at the touch, and Kal leans down, capturing that gasp with his lips.

I whimper into the kiss, the way it sends sparks bursting across my skin. Someone slides their hand over my breasts—Pierce, I can tell from his touch alone. Another set of hands—Jax's—reaches out to touch me, smoothing over my stomach, then lower, closer to where Axl is teasing me.

It's everything, having their focus on me. Unflinching and undeterred.

Axl's mouth travels higher up my thigh, taking his time with me as if we have as much as we need. As if we're not uncertain of the future that lies ahead. It's everything I need to push those chaotic thoughts away. He plants kisses over my skin, drawing higher until he reaches my center.

I'm a coiled spring as his lips hover above my sensitive heat.

"Mmm," he hums as he gently kisses me at the apex of my thighs. The vibrations from his touch have me arching off the table, desperately seeking more. "You want me to fuck you with my mouth, kitten?"

I tear my lips away from Kal's, looking down my body to where Axl is seated and grinning at me. "Yes." I answer like it's a plea. "Axl. Please."

Pierce glides his hand along my side, his touch a brand as he shifts and bends my leg over Axl's broad shoulder. "Do prepare her properly, Axl," he says. "We want her ready for us."

I tremble at the way they work together over me, the way they cherish me.

Axl keeps his eyes on me as he slowly, agonizingly dips his head lower. He licks up my aching slit, one long lap that has my back bowing. Kal reclaims my mouth as my palms smack against the table. Pierce teases my breasts, while Jax bends to kiss along the side of my neck.

I gasp between Kal's lips as Axl unleashes himself on me, licking and sucking me into absolute oblivion. Their combined touches, their constant worship of my body brings me to pleasure so quickly, I'm dizzy.

My hands fly out, gripping Kal and Jax's shoulders as Axl slides his tongue in and out of me.

I draw away from Kal's kiss, unable to contain my ragged breaths as my orgasm builds. "I . . . I . . ."

I can't form words. Not as Kal nibbles my earlobe. Not as Jax nips at my neck. Not as Pierce pinches one of my nipples. Not as Axl sucks that pulsing bundle of nerves into his mouth.

I moan, the sound tearing through me just as hard as my orgasm. The sensation is a crescendo of tingles that travel everywhere at once, unraveling every coiled thing in my body.

"I could watch you do that to her every day," Kal says.

"She's ready for us." Pride gleams in Axl's eyes as he draws back, licking me off his lips.

My heart hiccups as Kal gently lifts me from the table, whisking me quickly to the edge of his bed. He situates me atop his lap, my back pressed against his chest as he slicks his hard cock through my wetness over and over again, making me shiver. He must've finished undressing while Axl finished *me*.

Jax and Pierce, too, apparently, because both are deliciously bare as they follow us to the bed.

Axl is the last to hurry out of his pants, his cock springing free as he steps between my thighs. He kisses me then, quick and hard, my flavor bursting on my tongue. It makes my head spin.

Kal teases my tight hole with the head of his cock, making me gasp into Axl's kiss. Axl grazes my oversensitive flesh with his length, his hands smoothing down my legs and urging me to wrap them around his waist.

I do, my thighs clenching as he pushes into my heat an inch. Kal gently does the same to that tight space behind me. Axl leans back, breaking our kiss as he pumps into me, his timing impeccable with Kal's.

I'm a tangle of connection and sensation. Energy and anticipation. Hunger snaps through me, a need I'm not sure will ever be sated. Even without the pulsing demands of the bonds, I'm starved for them.

Pierce grips my chin, turning my head to the left, where he's climbed onto the bed.

Jax is on the other side, his lips on my neck again.

I wish I had more hands to touch them all, more places for them to consume me. If I had Pierce's power, they'd be at my mercy for all the wicked things I'd do to their minds. But it's just us, just *me*, and I reach out in the only ways I can.

"Pierce," I say, kissing him quickly before I urge him to get on his knees, the height of the bed angling his cock in the perfect position for my mouth. "Please." I part my lips, flicking my tongue over his thick head.

"Darling." He glides into my mouth, and I moan around the way he fills it.

The way Axl and Kal are filling me as they slowly thrust themselves inside me. It's a torturous, delicious pace that sparks every aching nerve.

And then there's Jax, dragging his teeth along my neck as I reach for him with my hand. He shifts at my insistence, laughing roughly as I find his cock and grip him. The connection between each of us snaps in place with that final touch, and it's all I can do to hold on as the Legends of Chaos devour me.

Pierce pumps into my mouth in slow, confident thrusts that have me trembling. I flick my eyes up to his, my heat fluttering around Axl's length as I watch Pierce fuck my mouth. I lean harder into Kal, who holds me steady with his gentle pumps that match Axl's.

Jax groans as I roll my thumb over the head of his cock, playing with a drop of pre-come that's beaded there. I whimper around Pierce, the notion that I've gotten each of them worked up so quickly an intoxicating thing.

We can't feel the bonds between us, but we're still just as connected. Just as bonded. The five of us a complementing, perfect joining. The more we crash together, the stronger we become. Every kiss and touch solidifying our love.

"Fuck, butterfly," Jax growls as I grip him tighter. I can't help it; Axl and Kal have me on the cusp of explosion. He thrusts harder into my hand. "Feels so fucking good when you squeeze me like that."

His words are an undoing. I feel untethered, like I might soar into the sky if they let me go.

"Darling." Pierce's voice is strained. "I'm coming." He pumps harder, once, twice, before spilling into my mouth.

I quickly swallow him down, and he gently pulls out of my mouth, rubbing his thumb over my swollen lips. My heart is racing, my breathing ragged as I turn toward Jax.

"Jax," I demand.

His indigo eyes sear for a moment before he grins. "Naughty, devious little butterfly." He shifts, teasing my lips with his hard cock. "You want to swallow us both tonight?"

I open my mouth in answer, and he takes the space Pierce has just been.

Axl groans. "So fucking hot."

I'm pure liquid as he and Kal match a rhythm, my orgasm on the edge of splintering my entire being. Pierce's lips are on my shoulder, trailing along my collarbone and back, worshipping every inch he can reach.

Jax thrusts into my mouth, his fingers tight in my hair. "Such a perfect mouth."

I reach up, grabbing Axl's shoulders as he grinds against me, shifting his thrusts to ensure every connection hits that sensitive spot between my thighs. Kal tightens his grip around my middle as he slides in and out of that tight space. Pierce's kiss leaves sparks along my back. Jax groans, hardening in my mouth as his pumps become more chaotic. Each of them is on the edge as much as me, and it sends me flying right over it.

I moan around Jax, my orgasm flooding me as he spills into my mouth. Waves of heat crash from the crown of my head to the tips of my toes, the sensation like coming completely undone. I don't exist outside of the pleasure pulsing along my body in waves as one orgasm leads into another when Kal and Axl find their releases inside me.

Jax gently pulls out of my mouth, and I gasp for breath, my eyes watering from taking both him and Pierce this way today. My heart skips at the way they're all looking at me, like I'm the gravity holding them to this realm.

Axl leans his forehead against mine as Kal kisses my shoulder, Pierce and Jax moving off the bed to give us room. Kal gently lifts me, Axl shifting so I can settle on the bed while Pierce comes to clean me up.

"I'll start the bath," Axl says, disappearing into Kal's bathing chamber.

Pierce heads in shortly after, then Jax. Kal is the one to scoop me off the bed and carry me to the bath.

We're a flurry of comfortable movements, and I fall into their care as easily as the rhythm of my heart returns.

"I love you," I say to them as we soak in the deliciously warm water of the bath.

Each returns the sentiment as we take turns washing or massaging each other. It's an ecstasy I don't want to end. These moments are as precious as the rare jewels the wealthy covet. They're a glimpse of what our future could look like, should we survive what's coming. Long days initiating change for Lumathyst followed by passionate nights where nothing comes between us. It's a future worth fighting for, certainly, but it's hard to dream of such things when we're challenged at every turn.

We stay together in the bath until the water turns cool. Axl towels me off, and then there's a silence hanging over us as we get dressed.

A knock sounds at Kal's door as we finish.

"They're ready for you," Mirren calls through the closed door. "I tried to stall for more time."

"Thank you, Mirren," Pierce calls. "We'll be just a moment."

"I wish we had more time," Kal says, reaching to cup my cheek.

"Me too." I lean into his palm. I should've started saying my goodbyes while we soaked, but I didn't want to ruin the moment.

He dips down, kissing me quickly before he heads out the door.

Axl draws me into a hug, holding me tightly. "If Silvac gives you any trouble, show them your claws."

I laugh, hating that the earlier bliss is now replaced by a sadness I can't quite describe. I know this will be normal when they take the thrones, but it hurts to part with them all the same.

He kisses me quickly before leaving, too.

Pierce follows Axl out of the room, knowing we have no goodbyes to say.

Jax comes to me last, a quiet weight between us.

"I don't like this," I admit.

"I don't, either." He leads me toward the closed door. "I love you more than you'll ever know, butterfly." He drags his thumb over my bottom lip, which quivers as I try to hold back tears.

"I love you, too, Jax." Something twists in my chest. The nature of his goodbye is unlike the others'. But he's the Nightmare. Of course he'll always see things differently. I'm about to press him on it, but he opens the door and steps into the hallway.

"Jax?" I ask when he stops to look back at me. "We'll be okay, right?" I need assurance. Need something to soothe the concern in his indigo eyes.

He draws up a cool, calm mask, the worry melting from his face. He replaces it with the Nightmare's smile. "Death couldn't separate us. *Nothing* will ever keep me from you again."

CHAPTER 35

Rylee

"We're approaching Silvac," Pierce says, his tone soft.

I pry myself away from the edge of the boat as I spot land across the water.

"Thank the goddesses," I say, my stomach churning.

It's been this way the entirety of our weeklong journey. I've never been away from Lumathyst, and while I've been on Axl's ship before, it was never in seas this rough. Something I now wonder if he controlled for my benefit.

We've had so many rough days on this journey.

Angry skies and thunderous waves that rocked even a ship as big as one from the royal fleet. The only reason I've been able to function at all is because of Dalfon's remedies and shots of healing magic that help me maintain *some* composure. Try as I might, I couldn't wield Axl's power enough to sway the tides.

I was surprised at seeing Dalfon when Pierce and I boarded the royal ship set for Silvac. A handful of enforcers, staff, and sailors also set sail with us. Dalfon convinced the kings to allow him to accompany us, insisting it was too soon after my recovery from the Athanry to be so far from an experienced healer. And though I felt fine, health wise, I appreciated the sentiment.

Plus, as an unexpected surprise, Dalfon has helped me study the history of Silvac on the journey, generously answering any of my questions to help me prep for our arrival and negotiations. He even taught me a few greeting phrases in their people's language, but he assured me the Occuli speak many languages, including my own.

Pierce hands me a glass of chilled mint tea, and I sip it as I watch the crew rush about the ship, responding to demands from their captain in an effortless flurry of movement.

I take a deep breath. "Here's hoping I don't insult the Gemeni." The twin rulers of Silvac are, from what I've learned, an eccentric pair.

"You've been studying with Dalfon the entire trip," Pierce says. "You're more prepared than I am."

I roll my eyes but smile up at him. He looks regal in a suit of emerald green and black, not a wrinkle in sight.

"I should go change," I say, gesturing down to my simple, blue cotton dress. When feeling the effects of the sea, I wanted free-flowing over tight garments. Plus, spring has shifted to the warmer side, and when nightmares often woke me in a cold sweat, it felt good to have light clothes on. Quickly, I retire to our cabin and change into something more representative of a princess of Lumathyst—an elegant sleeveless gown of soft green to complement Pierce's suit.

The beach we dock on is made up of glistening black sand, the granules sparkling under the blazing midday sun. Soft waves crash against it as Pierce takes my hand, the two of us following a couple of enforcers farther down the beach, where people I can only assume are Silvac guards are waiting for us.

Lining the beach to the north is a luscious array of tropical forestry that steals my breath. Vivid colors burst from the thick vegetation—rich greens, bright oranges, buttery yellows—it's hard to tear my eyes away.

"Your highnesses." A smooth, feminine voice calls for my attention as we reach the welcome party awaiting us.

There are only four of them, which makes our much larger group seem a bit excessive. Dalfon is behind us, with more enforcers and staff behind him, too.

Pierce dips his head to the four, and I quickly follow suit.

"Hello," he says, offering them a respectful smile. "Thank you for allowing us to visit."

The one who spoke nods slowly, her black eyes glistening as she turns to me.

"The Gemeni are most interested in your new princess," the Occuli says. Her voice possesses the same qualities as Dalfon's, a specific lilt I've come to associate with the magical beings. But the four before me are nothing like the conjurers of the kings.

These Occuli are all stunning women with varying appearances—two are tall and lithe with smooth black skin and long braids adorned with glistening jewels shaping their faces, while the other two are shorter and pale, with curves and long, flowing red hair that hangs over their shoulders.

And there are no purple robes here. Instead, they wear thin, see-through silver fabric that looks ultra breathable while also flattering. Long-sleeved tops flow over their hips, and lightweight pants cuff at their ankles; their feet are bare in the sand. Each wears a number of jewelry pieces, varying in material from gold to silver to emeralds and rubies and diamonds and more.

"I'm Altair," she says, motioning to herself, then her next companion with matching braids. "This is my sister, Seraphina. This is Circe and her sister Tatiana." She gestures to the other two. "We'll take you through the great pass and then on to the Sanctuary."

"We appreciate you taking the time to guide us," Pierce says, a hand placed over his chest as he bows again.

I follow suit.

"You've been made aware of our rules with regard to the island?" Altair asks.

Pierce and I nod. Basically, don't touch anything without requesting permission, respect the environment, and don't kill anything. Pretty easy rules to follow. Rules that should be second nature, really.

"We will travel with the utmost respect," Pierce answers. "We're lucky enough to have not only your guidance, but that of our companion"—he points to Dalfon behind us—"as well."

Altair smiles as Dalfon moves to my right side. "Dalfon Faras," she says, opening her arms. "It's been too long."

"It has," he says, embracing her and then the other three.

"I'm glad you were permitted to come," Seraphina says.

"Come," Altair says, pointing toward the luscious jungle awaiting us. "Let us make our journey. The Gemeni are waiting."

CHAPTER 36

Rylee

"Is that the palace?" The question bursts from my lips on a gasp as the path of tall, green palms widens ahead, revealing a structure the likes of which I've never seen.

"We don't call it a palace," Altair answers, but there is no offense in her voice.

"I apologize," I say regardless. "What do you call it again?"

"Sanctuary."

The word clangs through me as I follow them through the quickly clearing path, the tropical oasis giving way to the Occuli-built structures peppering the horizon.

A crystal-clear river winds down the center of the forest, glowing turquoise in some areas, silver in others as it trickles toward what I would've called a palace built right into the mountain the forest hugs.

The stone is covered in green vegetation, orange and red flowers blooming in chaotic rows that make the Sanctuary feel alive. We take the sandy path next to the river, the smells of citrus and spring wafting through the air as we make our way toward the massive structure.

The closer we get, the more stone buildings can be seen on either side of the Sanctuary, though they're hard to spot at first. They, too, are covered in the forest's rich flowers and vines, making these homes look like they were birthed by the land instead of forged by hands.

Along with the citrus smell, there's an almost lightning-like tinge to the atmosphere that grows more intense the closer we get to the Sanctuary. I've felt Occuli magic before, when Frenrick tested me during the Choosing.

This is infinitely more intense than anything I've experienced. It awakens the powers buried inside me, the bonds stretching in curious awareness. A pang of longing hits me, followed quickly by worries over how Axl, Kal, and Jax are faring.

I miss them.

"Come." Altair beckons us up a set of stone steps and through a pair of guarded wooden doors.

A zap of energy slices down my spine the minute I step over the threshold, and with the way Pierce's hand clenches mine, I'm sure he felt it, too. We share a silent, concerned glance but don't say anything.

Such uncharted territory, even with Dalfon's previous help in studying.

"The Gemeni will meet you in the meditation room," Altair says as we're funneled quickly through the Sanctuary.

I do my best to make a mental map as we follow her, but it's difficult. The hallways are more like cave tunnels, decorated with the elements—flowers and trickling glowing water—and are impossible to use as markers. The floor is made of the same soft black sand that coated the beach when we arrived, yet somehow we leave no trace of footprints to indicate a clear direction back.

A small sense of dread blooms in the pit of my stomach, some buried instinct cautioning me to be on alert. Maybe it's all the Occuli guards standing at attention in front of the various tunnels we pass. Maybe it's the magic that floods this space, constantly reaching out and testing my own power, like internal shocks. Maybe it's simply the unknown, my world growing and expanding at such a fast rate I can barely adjust.

Pierce, on the surface, looks calm, poised, like he belongs here. Like he belongs *everywhere*. Internally, I can feel the tension through our bond. He's on alert, too, but his attention feels much more contained than mine.

Altair stops before a wide-open cave tunnel, the rock a smooth, glittering gray and illuminated by floating blue flames spaced evenly down the walls. The scents of damp earth and blistering cold waft from the tunnel, tinted with a hint of spice.

"I'm sure Dalfon did his best to prepare you," she says. "But he has not been home for quite some time, and things change. I would advise you not to argue with the Gemeni."

I arch an eyebrow at her, trying to decipher if that's a friendly warning or a threat. Could be a combination of both, but we're in too deep to turn back now.

"Thank you for the warning," Pierce says. "We're here not to argue but to negotiate."

Altair looks unconvinced but dips her head toward the guards at the tunnel's entrance. They step to the side, and we follow her until light fills the space and it opens into a vast chamber.

There are rich, wooden chairs gathered on either side of a glowing pool of turquoise water with Occuli lounging in them, some with eyes closed in meditation or maybe concentration. A soft breeze floats by us, drawing attention to the holes in the ceiling that let in natural light from the outside, the beams hitting the black sand like beacons in the night. Tranquil music echoes throughout the space, melodic and haunting. There are tables with food and bone pitchers filled with water and other liquids across the room. Some of the glasses the Occuli drink from are glowing, too.

Magic flows everywhere, so natural and raw it's overwhelming. My stomach churns with anxiety.

"Gemeni." Altair stops before a pair of Occuli perched atop two massive, red silk cushions at the focal point of the chamber. They're twins, identical in everything but their hair. One has long black hair that dips over a set of narrow shoulders, the other a short-cropped style of the same color. They have the same brown skin, the same obsidian eyes, the same lithe build—but the short-haired one wears a dress while the other lies shirtless with simple trousers. "The prince and princess of Lumathyst are here to see you."

The shirtless one sits up straighter, his black eyes lingering on me for a long moment before studying Pierce. The one with the short hair tilts her head, not bothering to stop what she's doing—trailing her finger through the small glowing pool she sits next to.

Pierce and I bow respectfully, but my heart is in my throat. The powers inside me are skittish, mine pulsing just beneath the surface, my mates' coiling behind their locked doors.

"We wondered who would come," the one twirling her finger in the water says.

"And we get the Mind," the other says. "How delicious."

I swallow hard, but Pierce simply smiles.

"An honor to meet you both. Please, call me Pierce," he says, then motions to me. "And this is my mate, Rylee."

Warm chills burst on my skin at the claiming title. I'm not sure if I'll ever get used to it.

"Isn't she interesting, Gem?" the shirtless one says, looking to his counterpart.

The one playing with the water finally looks up at me. She stills for a moment. Another head tilt. "Oh yes, Eni," she says, a lilt to her voice. She stands in one fluid motion, appearing before me faster than I can follow. She inhales deeply, blinking slowly as she looks me up and down.

I do my best not to flinch, not wanting to offend if this is a normal introduction behavior.

"She has old magic in her, but it's also new," Gem says.

My eyes flare, and I do my best to bury the air in my blood, my inherent power.

Gem laughs, shaking her head as she backs up, giving me space as her brother stands to join her. "You cannot hide it here, princess," she says, still laughing.

"But you have no need to," Eni adds. "I suppose you have many reasons to hide where you're from."

I look to Pierce, adrenaline coursing through my veins. I've never so openly been exposed before and have no clue how to handle it.

Pierce flashes me a sympathetic look before returning focus to them. "We're grateful you've allowed us this visit," he says. "It's important to us that we reestablish our alliances in these critical times."

Gem leans against her brother, focusing on Pierce.

"These are critical times," Eni says. "The Source has . . ." His voice trails off, his head dipping toward the glowing water. "Told us many things. Shifts are happening. The Fates are restless."

Dalfon told me more about the celestial entities that sit even higher than Lumathyst's goddesses. The same ones Evaluna mentioned in my dreams. The Occuli worship them, believing they blessed their lands with their precious Source—the all-powerful connection that fuels Occuli magic. According to him, there are many people from all realms who have died trying to steal from it.

Pierce's hand tenses in mine.

"We know what you want from us," Gem says. "Another magically binding contract, tying our two powerful realms together."

"Yes," Pierce says. "As we ready to take the thrones, we want to keep our relationship—"

"Relationship." Gem cuts him off with another laugh. "The one where you send spies to our lands in search of the Source? The one where you employ our kind to do biddings you cannot?"

Ice fills my veins.

"The one where you ignore our warnings? Or before, when you brought your armies to our shores."

"We are not our fathers," Pierce counters. "I assure you, no missions were sanctioned by the Legends."

Eni scoffs. "The Legends. All-powerful now, right? After your . . . *mating*?" He studies me, and it's all I can do not to cower from his probing, black stare. "Why haven't you taken the thrones for yourselves, then?"

"I have no need to challenge my father—"

"Because you don't want to or because you can't?" Gem asks, eyeing me.

Do they know? That easily?

"They will take the thrones soon." I finally find my voice. "And they will make a change for the better."

Gem tilts her head. "They. Them. Why not *we*? Are you to sit in the shadows, silent and cold?"

Anger rumbles beneath my skin. "They're meant to rule."

"Enough," Eni says, smiling broadly. "It's too soon in your visit to be so serious."

Whiplash. I basically sputter my next breath.

"We need to come to terms," Pierce implores.

"You two need to rest," Gem drawls. "And enjoy our hospitality while it lasts. It is so rare for those from Lumathyst to be invited here. Relish in this honor. We will discuss terms tomorrow." She snaps her fingers, and Altair returns to usher us away.

I stop, unable to take it for one more second. "Are you even going to be open to reestablishing terms?" I ask. "Because from the way you two are acting, we might be wasting each other's time."

"Do you have somewhere more important to be, princess?" Eni grins widely. "Time is such a trivial concept."

I take a breath. "This is important to me because it's important to the well-being of my home. And no, time isn't trivial to me. There are pressing matters at home that need our attention, but we ranked meeting with *you* above them. If you're toying with us, send us on our way and be done with it."

"I like her," Gem whispers to her brother.

"Such spirit," Eni responds.

They turn to each other, sharing words in a language I can't understand.

Pierce leans into me, a solid show of support. I'm glad he's not upset with my outburst. I can't help it. We've got Faders to worry about, other trade agreements to solidify, and the enhancement still harming our people. I'm not here to speak in riddles and play games.

"I apologize if our behavior has led you to think we're wasting your time, princess," Eni says, his body language relaxing a bit. "We are grateful you made the journey. You must understand, it's rare for us to have visitors. We're out of practice." He motions behind us. "Please, take a night of reprieve, as will we, and then tomorrow, we'll discuss terms."

I dip my head, still wary as we follow Altair out of the room.

"That went well," she says as she leads us down another few tunnels before motioning to a large wooden door in another hole in the rock wall.

"Really?" I blurt.

"Yes," she says. "I don't know if I've ever seen the Gemeni so engaged in a conversation with strangers before. They certainly never spoke as much to the king."

Pierce and I share a look.

"Which king was the last to set the terms?" Pierce asks.

Altair takes a moment to think. "King Baydel Lavine," she finally says. "He spoke much, but the Gemeni responded little. Gem and Eni were younger, though, fresh to take the thrones after their parents met the Fates."

The idea of Baydel making terms with the Gemeni has hope building in my chest. If he can get them to agree, certainly they'll like dealing with us better?

"These are your rooms," Altair explains, opening the wooden door. "You're free to explore the Sanctuary as long as you have a guide. Either Dalfon or I would be best."

"Thank you," Pierce says.

"Besides the Source," she continues, "we're most known for our library, as I'm sure you've heard. It's the oldest and most extensive collection of written history across all the realms."

My lips part at the kernel of information.

Altair smiles at me. "Perhaps you'll explore it before you leave," she says before she heads off in the opposite direction.

CHAPTER 37

Rylee

Before I can rattle off one of the hundreds of questions racing through my mind, I'm stunned into silence by the room we've just entered.

Pierce closes the door behind me, looking just as enamored as we take in the space.

The rock walls are jagged and curved, creating dips and natural slides for the glowing crystal water that cascades freely from an opening in the ceiling above us. A soft waterfall of liquid trickles into a winding pool that flows down the center of the room. A smooth rock pathway offers access to the other side of where we stand, across the mini river, where a flat expanse of rock stretches, a luscious bed perched atop it. Behind the bed, an arch is carved into the rock wall, and the space is filled with old tomes with a variety of colored spines. Warm, golden flames hover in the corner, illuminating the enchanting space.

"Okay, this looks like paradise," I say, stepping along the rock pathway to the other side of the room, glancing up through the opening the water is coming through. I can see the tops of the green palms we walked through earlier, and a soft, indigo sky as the sun sets.

Pierce opens the door behind him, peeking out before closing it again. "No guard, not locked."

"Checking to make sure it's not a pretty prison?" I ask.

"You can never be too careful," he says, bolting the door behind him.

I nod, rubbing my temples. "What are we going to do if they don't agree?"

I didn't expect it to be easy, but I didn't expect to see the disdain I glimpsed earlier, either.

"We will handle that if it comes," Pierce says, crossing the pathway to take me into his arms.

"I don't like not having a plan," I admit.

He smiles down at me. "I know," he says softly. "But what good will a plan do you now? We have no inkling what tomorrow will bring."

"Coming from the man who is always a hundred steps ahead?"

He parts his lips, then closes them.

"You already have a plan, don't you?" I ask.

"I might have considered several outcomes while you were speaking to them."

I huff a laugh. "And here you tell me to not worry."

He shrugs, drawing me closer against him. "Because I'm doing enough of the *what-if* game for the both of us."

His touch has the bond between us yanking taut. We share a silent look, and that's all it takes before his mouth is on mine.

Pierce's kiss is always breathtaking, but there's something more behind it right now. A sense of urgency that has my heart rate soaring. We're in a new place with so much unknown around us, but one certainty we can be sure of is each other. That's a connection and understanding that makes me feel seen on every level.

Slowly, he spins me around so he can help me out of my clothes, and then I do the same for him. I open his door in my mind, letting his power slide along the bond between us.

He groans as I direct an energy band to slip between us and tease his hard cock.

I grin, triumphant as I control the power. Such a power that he's teased me with so many times.

"You love it, don't you?" he asks, kissing along my jawline as his hand slips between my thighs. "The power. The hold you have over me."

I rock into his touch, trembling as he glides his fingers through my slick heat. "I love the way you make me feel."

Pierce dips his fingers inside me, effectively shutting off that line of thought. "And how do I make you feel?" he asks, his voice low between us. He's looking down at me with those rich brown eyes, hanging on my every move, every word.

My lips part, a gasp releasing as he pumps his fingers inside me. Sparks erupt under his touch, a warm tingling that travels feather light over that sensitive bundle of nerves. That sensation lets me know he's taken his power back, and I look down between us.

The energy he controls has replaced his fingers, and his hands are free to roam over my body, teasing and touching every inch he can reach.

"Worthy." I finally breathe the word. "You make me feel worthy." I don't know how else to describe it. The way he handles me, the way all of my mates do, makes me feel like a queen.

"You're my queen," he says, then captures my mouth with his. "Of course you're worthy. All we can hope is to worship you properly for the rest of eternity." He drops to his knees, the energy bands disappearing as I look down at him there, grinning up at me before he dips his head and licks straight through my heat.

I gasp, my hands flying to his shoulders as he does it again.

The bond between us pulses with need, with the demands of more, more, more. Intensifying the longer he eats at me, working me up in tight knots until I'm sure I'll combust.

I reach for the power, *his* power, and slip into his mind, ensuring he feels everything he's doing to me, all the while directing that energy band to wrap around his cock and squeeze him just the way he likes.

Pierce groans against my sensitive flesh.

I smile, doing my best to hold that concentration, to keep filling him with the love and desire and pleasure I feel. To keep teasing him as he's teasing me—

It all slips as he draws away, sweeping me off my feet and carrying me to the bed. The waterfall next to it fills the room with a steady hum, barely covering my gasp of pleasure as he spreads my thighs wide and spears himself inside me.

"Pierce. Yes. *More.*"

He pulls out slowly, dragging himself against all my sensitive spots, only to plunge into me again.

Instinctively, I try to close my thighs around his hips, to take some control of the pace, the angle, but he keeps his hands on my knees.

"You will stay spread for me," he says, eyes flickering from mine down to where he's pumping into me.

A hot shiver streaks down the middle of me at the demand, at the way he's taking control. I reach for him, needing to touch him, and I grip his forearms, moaning as he thrusts into me again and again.

"You feel amazing." He groans the words, emphasizing them with powerful strokes that have me gasping for breath. "Hot and slick."

"Pierce." My heart races as my pleasure builds beneath my skin, curling and twisting toward release. I push against his hold, wanting him to go faster, deeper.

He grins down at me. "Needy little mate."

He releases me, enveloping me until we're chest to chest, my legs wrapping around him as he unleashes himself on me. The power collides between us, emotions and pleasure and love surging from one end of the bond to the other, a free flow that's all-consuming and pushes me right over that edge.

My orgasm rips through me in waves, sparks erupting from the crown of my head, turning me into an absolute puddle. Pierce follows my release, holding me tight as he spills inside me, then dropping his head against my chest as we catch our breath.

The constant waterfall next to us fills the room with a peaceful sound as he shifts to look down at me.

Whatever awaits us, he says into my mind, *I'm happy to face it with you.*

I press my lips together, emotion tangling inside me. I reach up, cupping his face as he dips down to kiss me gently, slowly.

I push the words into his mind. *Whatever awaits us.*

CHAPTER 38

Rylee

"Wow." My astonished whisper echoes through the near-silent expanse, drawing a few dark glances.

I duck my head, trying to hide behind Pierce, who chuckles softly. The thirty or so Occuli working in the massive library go back to their books, some shuffling wooden carts back and forth, others scribbling on rolls of parchment with a variety of tomes open and spread on tables.

I can't help but gawk. There's no other way to react to this library. It's the biggest I've ever seen, and I thought the one in the palace was impressive. You could fit two hundred of the palace libraries in here, maybe more. I can't see it in its entirety.

The rock walls go on for ages, almost like some magic has multiplied the amount of available space the mountain has, and they're so tall, I have to arch my neck to even attempt to look to the top. The walls hold rows upon rows of books, with massive ladders that roll both directions. Several Occuli are on them, grabbing books and propelling them down by magic.

Pierce tugs on my hand, leading me deeper into the space. Stacks of shelves make up a mazelike center of the room, and the smells of parchment, ink, and leather fill my nose as we explore.

"Okay," I whisper, overwhelmed by the possibilities. "This was worth the trip regardless of what Gem and Eni say." Even if it has taken them days to go over our proposed treaty.

Pierce laughs, our bond humming with our shared excitement. I open his door, breathing deeply as his power spirals down the bond and toward him.

He sucks in a sharp breath, then grins down at me. *You're getting so much better at that*, he says directly into my mind.

It helps that you're touching me, I say, indicating our joined hands. *It's not like I could send Axl his power right now.* I wish I could.

You'll be able to soon enough. I have no doubt.

Such confidence.

In you? Always.

We make our way through the stacks, admiring the shelves of books. The deeper we go, the older the books get, until soon there's nothing but rolled parchment stored inside iron canisters to keep them from rotting.

"Vleyica," Pierce reads aloud. "Cardrayton, Silvac . . . *Lumathyst*." He drags his fingers along the inscriptions resting above the rows of iron canisters, then turns to me. "These are the histories of the realms," he says in astonishment as he lingers in front of Lumathyst's. "I thought we possessed the oldest recorded histories," he continues. "But these look much older than the ones the historians keep in the palace."

I tilt my head. "Maybe they're copies? Didn't they do that for all the histories?" I vaguely recall mention of that in my younger days of mandatory school in the Ashlands.

"They did," Pierce says, returning his attention to me. "Though, if I remember correctly, I know some of Lumathyst's were lost in a fire." He reaches for one of the iron scrolls decorated with intricate swirling designs—

"There you two are," Altair calls, drawing our attention. "The Gemeni want to see you."

"Have they finished reading our proposal?" I ask, eager to get out of this lingering *waiting* mess.

"They didn't deign to tell me."

I nod, motioning for her to lead the way.

Pierce looks curiously at the iron again, almost like he's reluctant to leave, but hastens to follow us after a few moments.

We make it back into the meditation room, this time finding it empty save for Gem and Eni. They've elected to sit in a pair of wooden chairs near the glowing pool today, a table resting between them with our proposal atop it.

Pierce and I take the chairs opposite them, and I can't help but look at the luminous liquid with a little wariness. The last time I entered a glowing pool of water, I met the goddesses and a premature death. Of course, it wasn't the Athanry doorway that killed me, but still. It's oddly similar.

"You've swum in the Steorra before," Gem says matter-of-factly.

Pierce looks to me, then back to Gem. "The Athanry," he says.

"Yes," Eni responds. "You didn't think your kings conjured that doorway, did you?" He laughs. "Lumathyst fools. They're constantly making their people believe they're capable of so much more than they are. Why do you think they cling to their Occuli so tightly?"

Gem shakes her head. "What would your kingdom look like without our help?"

"You're not the only ones with magic," I remind them. "Or power." I don't say it maliciously, just factually. I understand their contempt for the kings likely better than anyone, but only someone naive would underestimate them. "There are others who can create magic."

"Demis," Gem says. "Blessed by your goddesses as we are blessed by the gifts from our Fates. Are we so different?"

The question is a pointed one that I dutifully ignore. "What do you think?" I ask, nodding to our parchment on their table.

Gem and Eni share a look before glancing back toward us. "It's a pretty story."

"It's not a story." I take a breath. "It will happen."

"*If* you take the throne," Gem says. "We don't like to deal in *ifs*."

"So, you're rejecting our terms, or do you have something else in mind?"

"We like you," Eni says to me. "You have something that calls to us. But these words, while painting a harmonious, downright generous future, are just words without validity."

I sit back in my chair, a bit defeated. "How do you propose we prove our intentions to you?"

If they give me another damned trial, I may mentally break. I speak the words down the bond, knowing Pierce is listening, still holding control over his power. It moves unhindered between us now, with every moment easier and easier down our shared bond.

They won't, he says.

Are you reading their minds?

I'm trying, but they're not like the people of Lumathyst. Their minds are cloudy and protected—

"It's not kind to have a conversation where others can't hear," Eni says, smirking a little. "Don't look so shocked, Legend. While I can't read minds like you do, I can sense power. You two are dripping in it."

Pierce casually rests his ankle on his knee. "Apologies, Eni," he says smoothly. "You've yet to answer Rylee's question."

Eni leans into his sister, whispering something in her ear.

"Now who's not sharing?" Pierce calls them out.

They both laugh, nodding.

"All right," Eni says, tapping the parchment. "Truly, these are far more generous terms than we expected. After the last set of terms we felt prematurely tricked into, you can understand our hesitance to trust."

Baydel had made the language of the previous terms very vague, ensuring that Occuli who traveled to Lumathyst would be bound to the royal service whether they liked it or not. Dalfon had explained as much during our studies on the way here. Luckily, he's been able to spend most of his time here catching up with old friends and not needing to heal me. I feel stronger every day.

"We are not the kings," I remind them. "We want different things."

"Clearly," Gem says. "But who's to say this isn't all a trick to magically bind us again for fifty years?"

"Again," Pierce says, "you never answered my mate's question."

The twins share a look. "We will sign your terms," Eni says. "On one condition."

I hold my breath, the silence stretching into an eternity.

"That is?" I finally ask.

"You leave collateral," Gem says so plainly I'm sure I've misheard her.

"Explain," I say.

"You can return to Lumathyst with our signed support as allies, but only if one of you stays behind here in Silvac. After a certain amount of time passes, and our lands aren't flooded with Lumathyst enforcers determined to steal from our Source or demand services from our people, we'll conclude you've upheld your end of the terms, and we will let them return."

I gape at the two of them. "Collateral? How long?"

They share another look. "A month."

My chest tightens. It's already agony being away from Axl, Kal, and Jax, and it hasn't been much more than a week. Separating any longer than necessary is going to hurt.

"Is there any other way to prove—"

"No," Gem cuts me off. "We know the price of what we're asking, which is why it will prove your intentions. Sacrifice for the good in the long term."

"And if we don't agree to it?" Pierce asks, deadly calm, those deep brown eyes of his calculating.

Eni shrugs. "Then we don't magically bind ourselves to Lumathyst as allies and we go about our lives separately. We'll be open to ally with anyone we choose."

I blow out a breath, my heart racing.

Pierce visibly swallows, looking at me apologetically.

I can hear the words before he utters them like a haunting melody. "I will stay."

I close my eyes.

What else is this world going to take from me?

CHAPTER 39

Rylee

"I don't want to do this." I pace the soft, sandy beach. "It shouldn't be like this."

Pierce follows me step for step. "We've been over this—"

"I know we have!" I snap. "I'm sorry. I *know* we have. I know it's for the greater good. I know it's only a month. I'm still sick and tired of other people dictating how I can live my life!"

Pierce opens his arms, and I fall into them.

I'm sorry, he says into my mind, nothing but love and support radiating down our bond. *If I could secure the agreement any other way . . .*

I know. It's truly not the worst scenario. After the horrible terms Baydel set upon them last time, they really have no grounds to believe us. They could've said no. They could've treated us horribly. They could've done any number of things.

They didn't.

I'm being a brat, I admit.

Pierce laughs, shifting me out of the embrace far enough to look down at me. He cups my cheeks. "You, Rylee, are a warrior. A queen. Never a brat."

I laugh, shaking my head. "I love you," I say.

The staff and enforcers are behind us, loading our belongings. I hold the signed terms in my satchel slung over my shoulder. Another task complete in order to earn the Royal Authority Council's vote, and yet, I'm forced to leave my mate behind while the others are across the seas, and I have no idea how they're doing.

"Why can't I stay instead of you again?" I ask, even though we've discussed it a thousand times already.

"Because in Lumathyst you have friends, allies." He glances to Dalfon behind me, awaiting my return to the dock. "And here . . . while they're friendly, it's unknown. I won't risk you."

"I don't want to risk *you*."

"The month will go by quickly. We'll secure all terms, ascend the thrones, and start our lives together."

It's a beautiful picture, but he's leaving out all the what-ifs:

What if the others don't secure their terms with the other realms?

What if the Fader attacks get worse?

What if my sister ends up leading us into a great and terrible war Lumathyst can't come back from?

What if my dreams of Evaluna aren't dreams but actual warnings?

What if I return to Lumathyst, alone, and single-handedly turn the Royal Authority Council against us and lose the princes' shot at the thrones?

Pierce strokes the worry lines between my eyebrows. "We cannot face that which hasn't happened. Focus on what you can control and breathe out the rest."

I blow out a deep breath, grounding myself. I can feel his power in a steady beat that keeps the pathways of our bond open and his abilities with him, firmly where they belong.

"How long do you think it will hold?" I ask.

"I think you're capable of anything," he says. "But we won't know until it's tested. I willingly gave the power up in order for you to return. I had no idea if I'd ever possess it again. If you wanted to keep it forever, I would support that."

"I don't want it forever," I admit. "You saw what I did when you four were threatened. I lost control. I keep it behind locked doors due to that failure."

"It's not a failure. My power is your power. It belongs to you like I do."

I shake my head. It's his. He needs it. "I'll keep it with you as long as I can."

"Time to go," Dalfon calls from the base of the ship.

My heart drops to my stomach. "What if something happens?" I whisper the question as I throw my arms around his neck. "What if you don't come home in a month? What if the others—"

"Nothing will stop me from coming back to you," he cuts me off, nothing but determination and pure promise in his words. "Do you understand?" He holds me tighter, drawing me back enough to kiss me. It's a promise and a plea.

I nod, kissing him again, pouring every ounce of love I have down our bond.

"I'll do my best to have your throne waiting for you when you return."

"Our throne," he corrects me. *"Ours."*

I release him.

"See you soon," he says, stepping backward, as if he knows I need the distance to gain the courage to leave him.

I take one step away, then another, my heart growing heavier with each bit of distance gained between us.

Dalfon quietly leads me into the ship, and I go to the bow as we sail away, watching Pierce get smaller and smaller the farther we go.

And after I can no longer see him or any evidence of Silvac, I retreat to my cabin and cry into my pillow.

CHAPTER 40

Rylee

Baydel sits in his cushioned chair atop the dais in the gathering room. I haven't even been able to see to my needs or take a breath privately in my rooms in the palace. The moment we docked in the royal port, Dalfon and I were ushered to the palace by a dozen enforcers.

"This is . . ." Baydel rolls the parchment up and passes it to Lucas, who sits on his left. He read the contract at least three times before addressing me.

"Impressive," Lucas says after a quick glance. He hands it to Brooks.

I tilt my head, swallowing hard. The journey was a long one. I did my best to distract myself by practicing the meditations Pierce taught me, controlling the powers, checking in on my mating bonds, and asking Dalfon more questions than he could probably stand. He was always gracious with me, though, which I appreciate. All the space in between that, I lost myself in my sister's art journal. Gleaning nothing beyond my love of her talent and the grief I feel missing the sister I knew.

Brooks eyes me from where he sits. The calculating look reminds me of Pierce so much it hurts.

A month. That's all we'll be separated. And we're already down one week, thanks to the travel time.

It feels like an eternity. Especially as I stand here before the kings, *alone.*

Mirren and Layce and Ivy are in the back of the room, waiting for me, and Dalfon is a few feet away from them, conversing with Baydel's Occuli. The rest of the Royal Authority Council is scattered about the room, too, sipping hot tea out of fine porcelain cups and nibbling on more snacks than are needed for such a small group.

But despite that, I'm alone.

Mirren, Layce, and Ivy aren't princesses of Lumathyst. The expectations the kings and the RAC are enforcing are placed on my shoulders and mine only.

I feel like an exhibit. A piece of curious entertainment for the RAC to gawk at and study. Some of the previous potentials who I've gotten to know since their announcement, like Charlotte, Beatrice, and Emma, don't look at me so drastically, but they *do* look, all the same.

"Did the Gemeni require a specific task from my son?" Brooks asks, finally passing the parchment to Jullian.

I shake my head, my heart feeling shredded. The bonds inside me are stretched, as if trying to reach across the vast distance that separates me from the Legends. "Only for him to stay," I answer.

Baydel studies me a bit harder, a small, almost imperceptible smile on his lips. After a second, it vanishes as he looks down the row to Brooks. "A hardship," he says. "But one worth the risk, in order to gain that." He points to the scroll in Jullian's hands.

"And if my son doesn't return in the time frame they set, Baydel?" Brooks asks, eyeing his fellow king with a stern look that has me taking a step away from the dais.

"If they do not allow him passage home, it would be an open declaration of war and a clear break in the agreement they signed." Baydel shrugs. "I highly doubt Silvac wants to end the centuries of peace we've had between us."

I keep my lips shut. From the little I saw of Silvac, everyone is *itching* for change.

"Thank you for bringing this to us, Rylee," Jullian says, his voice the most familiar and soft toward me. "I know it must've been hard to leave Pierce behind."

I blow out a breath and nod.

"Queen behavior," he continues, addressing the Royal Authority Council. "To endure such a hardship for the good of our people."

Baydel looks at Jullian as if he said I like to set things on fire for fun.

But I flash a grateful look up to Jullian for the shout-out.

Margreet looks to Baydel like she's incapable of forming a thought of her own without direction from him. I do my best not to roll my eyes.

"Has there been any word from the others?" I finally ask when I can no longer take it.

"Kal is faring well," Jullian answers. "Expects to be home soon."

Relief blazes through me at that.

"Axl too," Lucas adds.

Tears prick the backs of my eyes. I know we anticipated Cardrayton and Vleyica to be easier to reconfirm terms with, but it's great to hear at least two of them will be returning soon.

"And Jax?" I ask when Baydel hasn't readily offered a response.

"I received word he made it to Keleshore."

He doesn't continue, and it makes all that hope and relief turn to ash.

"Nothing on how he's doing?" I push.

Baydel tilts his head. "Do you doubt my son's ability to garner an ally?"

"I don't doubt Jax in any way," I say.

"Then you have nothing to worry over," he says. "You understand the requirements while you're home. Meet with the people, hear them, and do your best to continue work on the enhancement issue. It took one of our own servants just this morning." He says it so emotionlessly, I almost miss it. "It's imperative you keep up the work while the princes are away."

I blink a few times, chest tightening. "Can I see the body?"

"Did you suddenly become an Occuli healer in your time in Silvac?" Baydel snaps. "What need would you have—"

"I want to see it," I demand, so damn tired. "To see if I can find anything to help me stop this madness."

Baydel snorts a laugh. "Because you've been so successful in the past, little bug?" He shakes his head.

"I will take her," Dalfon says from where he stands behind me, near my friends.

"Thank you, Dalfon," Jullian hurries to say before Baydel can respond. "He's in the healing quarters. His family has been summoned."

Dalfon dips his head.

"Fine," Baydel says, then flicks his wrist, dismissing me in a way that makes my hackles rise. "Neither we nor the Royal Authority Council have any other need of you in this moment."

I bow dramatically. "Thank you ever so much for your attention, your highnesses."

They each note the bite in my tone.

I don't care.

It takes all of my willpower to leash the emotion raging inside me. I know violence isn't the answer, but *damn* Baydel likes to test my patience. Sometimes I think there's no other way to communicate with him other than through pain and suffering.

Dalfon leads the way out of the room with Mirren, Layce, Ivy, and me following him.

"You want us with you?" Layce asks, her voice low as we weave through the palace, following Dalfon all the way to the healing quarters.

"Yes," I say. "It's going to take all of us to solve this." And I hope we can. I honestly don't know what seeing the dead will do, but this enhancement has claimed too many people. Hopefully Atlas will reach out to me with some answers now that I'm back, but with Jax gone, he might not. He has no reason to trust me. I'll ask Mirren to look into him, see if she can dig up where he might frequent so we can find him.

Dalfon leads us into a wide room, the space filled with single feather beds, some occupied and blocked off by hanging linen curtains, others empty. The walls are lined with dark wooden shelves packed with herbs and liquids in glittering glass bottles. The pungent odor of burned sage and crisp mint hangs in the air, and there's a charge, too, like Layce's lightning powers, from all the Occuli healers using their blue flames behind those closed curtains.

We walk past all of this, heading to a closed door. Dalfon speaks with another healer, who lets us in.

The minute the door closes behind us, there's a weight in the room I can't describe. It's heavy and thick as we stop before a hip-height marble slab with a thin, sheer cloth laid over what is clearly a body.

The most recent death.

Dalfon picks up a scroll resting on a smaller table near the marble. He reads it quickly before setting it back down. "Found in the palace's reception area," he says. "No traces of the enhancement on his person."

"Baydel says he worked here?" I ask, keeping my voice as gentle as possible. It feels wrong to speak too loudly.

Ivy steps closer to the marble, her brow furrowed.

"Yes," Dalfon answers, eyeing Ivy.

"Can I?" she asks Dalfon, her hand poised over the sheet.

He nods.

She slowly pulls it back, then clenches her eyes shut.

"Ivy?" Layce and I are at her side in seconds.

I can't blame her for the reaction. The person looks . . . wrong. Of course, no dead body looks right, but this . . . His skin is pale and grayish, his cheeks gaunt. Just like the Fader's memory. Just like the duke had described to us before. Like the life has been drained right out of him.

Ivy gently replaces the sheet, leaning into Layce's and my embrace.

"I knew him," she whispers, tears lining her eyes.

"Oh, Ivy, I'm so sorry." I hug her tight. I should have thought of this—she has friends and acquaintances all over Lumathyst. "I wouldn't have asked you to come if I thought there was a chance you'd know him personally." It's hard enough to see this as a stranger.

Ivy takes a deep breath, glancing at Dalfon, who has shifted in front of us so we can no longer see the body as he examines it, his blue flames crackling to life.

"We'll wait outside, Dalfon," Mirren says, urging us through the doors, out of the healing quarters, and into the hallway.

"It's the same as the memory," I whisper.

Ivy takes a breath, then glances around at the empty hallway. "I *knew* him," she says again, her gaze more intently on mine. "Last year, for the Choosing, he gave me a gift," she says with more emphasis.

My blood runs cold. A gift. Last year. The Choosing.

A map of the palace springs to my memory, one I spent countless hours studying. One that cost me half a year's earnings to buy from Ivy's friend who worked in the palace. This friend.

I hug Ivy tightly. "I'm so sorry," I say again.

"Do you think . . . Do you think it's connected?" She whispers the question in my ear. "Do you think it's the reason—"

"No," I hurry to say. "No. If he'd been caught"—I lower my voice to a whisper—"he wouldn't have passed that way. Baydel would've made it public." I release her, and Layce squeezes her hand.

Mirren listens and watches us with a careful eye. I flash her a look that says I'll explain later.

Ivy nods, blowing out a breath.

Dalfon comes through the doors.

"Did you discover anything?" I ask, hopeful. The only thing I confirmed by looking at him was that he looked exactly the same as the memory from the Fader, connecting them and the deaths the duke spoke of.

"It's curious," he says in that otherworldly, even tone of his. "There was no evidence of the enhancement on him. No visible injuries. No trauma to his head."

"Do you think the enhancement could do this to him?" I ask. "Even if he didn't have it on him, maybe he took it all at once. Took too much?"

Dalfon considers. "It's possible. I couldn't pull more from the body."

"Can you normally?" Layce asks.

He dips his head.

"So why not now?" Ivy asks.

"I'm unsure."

Fuck. When an Occuli as powerful as Dalfon can't find the answers, what chance do I have?

"Thank you, Dalfon," Mirren says. "Rylee needs her rest now." She urges us down the hallway, leaving Dalfon to return to the healers' quarters.

Mirren locks the door to my chambers behind us a few minutes later.

"Rylee," Ivy says the second we're in the safety of my room. "He was like us."

My eyes widen. She doesn't need to say the word out loud. *Like us* means he was a demi in hiding. Ice fills my veins. "That means if the enhancement truly did that to him . . ."

"Then with enough, it could hurt you," Mirren finishes for me. "Or the Legends. Badly."

"Shit," Layce breathes. "That means it could *kill* us."

Power snaps through my body at the thought, wind spiraling around the room like a protective barrier.

"I won't let that happen," I vow. "We'll find it."

A silence settles over us, the four of us sinking onto the sofas and chairs in my sitting area.

"We're so glad you're back," Layce says after a few moments, and we all laugh at the broken heavy silence.

"But it's bullshit Silvac made Pierce stay behind," Ivy adds.

Mirren nods to me.

"Trust is thin," I say with a shrug. "I spent the entire journey home crying over it like a pathetic, lovestruck girl."

"Valid," Ivy says, and I laugh, rubbing my palms over my face.

"That's good news about Axl and Kal, though," Layce adds. "From what Jullian and Lucas said earlier."

"Definitely. I can't believe I'll have to be in this palace without them for so long." I can only hope to stay out of the kings' and RAC's attention until my mates return.

Ash mews as he comes out of my closet. He stretches before settling at my feet, glaring up at me. I bend, stroking his fur. He's softer and filling out. At least royal life suits him. After a few ear scratches, he bats my hand away.

"Were there any attacks while I was gone?"

"No," Mirren answers. "There have been other enhancement reports, but no more deaths, beyond the one we just saw."

Guilt twists my insides. "We have to find out how to stop it."

I think about Atlas again. I wonder if I should seek him out on my own. Who knows when Jax will be back, let alone the others? They say it could be soon for Axl and Kal, but who really knows what *soon* means? We certainly didn't anticipate Silvac putting the terms on us as they did. What if the other realms do as well?

My chest tightens, a weight pressing on me from all sides.

"It's spread to the nobility," Ivy says, drawing my attention.

"Really?"

Layce nods. "We made a trip back to Oak and Iron and Cedar and Silk. There were several cases at the apothecaries there. And then we traveled through the Sapphire Cove. The cases there have spread from the Ari districts up into the nobles' province."

I glance to Mirren. "Is that normal?" I ask. "For enhancements to travel so quickly from one place to the next?"

"We've seen it before," she says. "Most of the enhancement runners will test any new product in the lower cities first."

I know this—it's why we investigated the Ashlands—but I've never heard of anything spreading this far across the realm before. I grit my teeth. "Because no one will cause a scene over us."

Mirren nods. "But if the product is good enough, it'll move into the royal cities, but normally if it's a harmful enhancement, they keep it in the lowers. They know the Legends don't tolerate dangerous elixirs. They root out their bakers in a matter of days and punish them accordingly."

An icy chill rakes down my spine. I have nothing to fear from the Legends, but I've seen them in action. Partaken in it. And though it's always justified, it's *terrifying*. "So that leads back to our earlier assumption that the Faders are distributing it. Likely to cause more harm to Lumathyst. Or is it simply to cause chaos?"

"It seems to be pointing that direction," Mirren says.

"If I had sample," Ivy offers, "I could figure out what it's made of and then work on an antidote."

"I know," I say. "If we can study it, maybe we can find out not only how to stop it, but where it's coming from."

"What about the RAC?" Mirren asks. "I know you want to help the people, but you also have to uphold royal duties. All the more so now that the princes aren't here."

I shove off the couch.

"Sit back down, girl," Mirren chides me. "You can't solve it tonight. You just arrived from a long journey and look like death."

"I need to fix this."

"You'll *always* need to fix something," she says, ushering me to sit back down. "You are to be queen. With that will come a plethora of responsibilities that will never be solved overnight. You can't take on the entire weight of this realm. You need rest."

"She's right," Ivy says before I can argue. "One impossible situation at a time."

A dark laugh rips from me. "We should embroider that on a pillow."

"It could be our new slogan," Layce adds. "Oh, what colors should we use?"

My smile deepens, hope warming my heart at the support of my friends. I'm glad they're here, despite the danger it puts them in.

"I love you all," I say, eyeing the three. "You know that, right?"

"Who wouldn't?" Ivy teases.

"Love you, too," Layce says.

Mirren tips her chin, then bends to pet Ash, not making eye contact with me. It makes me laugh again as I shake my head.

"We'll figure this out," Ivy says as she and Layce head toward the doors. "Get some rest. Tomorrow, we'll work on everything."

I nod as they embrace me again before heading to their rooms, which are connected to mine.

Mirren finally stops petting Ash, giving me a once-over. "Take a bath. Then straight to bed."

"Yes, Mirren," I say dutifully.

She straightens her shirt, then heads out the door.

I waste no time retiring to my bathing chamber, sinking into the tub of hot water with a heavy sigh.

We gained a small win with the agreement from Silvac, despite them holding Pierce. But nothing feels like a victory. Not with another mysterious death. Not when so many questions are unanswered. Not when so many things have to happen correctly for us to succeed in the end.

After washing, I slip into a soft black robe and sit in my bed, my sister's art book perched atop my lap. Ash leaps onto my bed, pausing at the foot of it while he eyes me. His torn ear twitches a bit.

"It's a big bed," I say, motioning to it. "You can pick your place."

He blinks at me, like *I wasn't asking permission*, before he settles atop the pillow next to mine. I shake my head at the cat, returning to my sister's journal.

I run my fingers over the familiar pages of art, my sister's work almost imprinted in my mind now, but I don't truly see the paintings.

I'm too busy looking inward, down the four bonds that are woven into my soul. They're faint, but I can feel my mates on the other ends. There's a certain comfort in that. And Pierce's power is still his. I've managed to hold the connection even across the vast sea of space between us. He must be clinging to it as well, for it to be happening in a way that almost feels natural.

A tiny blossom of hope blooms in my chest. If I can do it with his power, maybe I can do it with the others' soon.

I flip through the art journal another time before tossing it to the side. My eyes are heavy as my head hits the pillow. I need to find Erin. I've always wanted to find her, but now I *need* to. So many lives depend on it.

The battles between Faders and Lumathyst need to end. The spread of this toxic enhancement needs to end. And by some stroke of madness, we stand on either side of the internal war.

Her with the Faders.

Me with the princes of Lumathyst.

And everything between us is at risk.

CHAPTER 41

Rylee

"Butterfly." Jax's voice calls to me from the dark recesses of my mind, echoing like he's far away.

I reach toward the sound, feeling the bond between us stretch awake. "Jax?"

"I'm sorry."

I'm instantly alert.

"For what? Jax?" I sit up in bed, blinking as I orient myself. I'm in my rooms in the palace, alone. The night sky stretches in a glittering sea of stars just outside my open balcony doors.

"Jax?" I send the plea down our bond.

Silence.

I must've been dreaming.

Throwing the covers off, I pad barefoot to the balcony, stepping outside and inhaling the crisp midnight air.

The reality of how lonely I am without them hits me like a ton of bricks. I used to be fine on my own. We lost our parents to a Never List mission decades ago, and Erin would go off on her adventures whenever the mood struck. Ivy and Layce could only keep me company so much, with me being from the Ashlands. So, I'd always been fine solo.

But after the Legends . . .

I smooth my hand over my chest, trying to soothe the longing ache I feel there.

I miss them.

I miss Kal's unflinching optimism. His dreams and warmth.

I miss Axl's playfulness. His ability to make me laugh even when I feel like I'm drowning.

I miss Pierce's calm understanding. His intimate care of my mind.

I miss Jax's sharp edges. His consuming, all-in mentality when it came to the two of us.

I swallow hard, looking up at the stars, wondering if they might be looking at the same sky from wherever they are.

The fierce ache turns into a restless energy that has me itching to move.

"You need to wake up." Evaluna's voice is soft, a whisper against my ear.

A blink and she's there, standing on the balcony next to me, looking ethereal in a gown of starlight, her blue-black hair shimmering in waves over her bare shoulders.

I bow.

I'm definitely dreaming. But it feels real. I feel the cool stone beneath my bare feet. The kiss of wind against my cheeks. I feel awake.

"You need to wake . . ." Evaluna presses her lips together, a flinch racking her body.

"Are you okay?" I ask, rushing toward her, daring to reach out and touch her arm—

Moonlight and stars and the force of an eternity split my mind. I clench my eyes against the pain slicing through me. Images flash behind my closed lids—Neph splayed on a polished floor, her eyes shut. Eirdis unconscious next to her. Tareena running. Falling. Evaluna screaming, the sound like a thousand pieces of glass bursting at once. There are two men in the room, but I can't make out their faces. Their voices are hushed, conspiring whispers.

Evaluna jerks her arm from my touch. "You're a brave one," she says, almost like she's out of breath.

Can goddesses even get out of breath?

"Yes," she answers the silent question. "We can. Especially when—" She groans, glaring up at the sky. "Damned meddling *Fates."*

"Fates. I've learned a little more about them since the last time we spoke. Especially after I visited Silvac."

She nods, flashing me an impressed look. "Did you explore the interior gardens in the Sanctuary?"

"We only saw the exterior gardens, the library, and the meditation room. We didn't have much time."

"I understand not having time," she says. "Tareena would kill me if she knew I risked this as often as I have, but being the goddess of night has its advantages. Like dreamwalking." Her eyes meet mine, something unspoken there.

My head spins.

"Listen to me," she says.

I widen my gaze at her. "I am." She eyes me, but I shrug. "Apparently, I've dreamed you up, so I'm not exactly afraid of your wrath."

She laughs, moving to lean against the balcony. "I do love your fearlessness. It certainly helped win my son's heart, but be careful. That same fearlessness could get you killed."

"There are a lot of things trying to kill me right now. Plus, as you know, I've already died once."

"Would you be so flippant as to do it again? Put my son through that torture—"

"Never." I dare to cut her off. "Of course I wouldn't want to put any of them through that. It's hard enough being away from them now, and they're merely doing princely duties."

"Exactly. Listen." Evaluna takes a breath. "Pierce is close to finding everything you need—" She groans again. Her eyes close for a moment, like she's calculating what she can and can't say. "Universal punishments for the sake of balance are so damned frustrating."

I frown. "I want to help you. I know you need it. I just don't know what to do."

She smiles softly at me. "Keep being you," she says. "Never forget who you are, Rylee Gray."

Okay? "I hadn't planned on it?"

"When you wake up," she says, testing her words carefully, "I need you to do exactly what I say."

I remain silent, intently listening.

"Take a left, go down the long corridor, and take the first right. Then, immediately left. There, you'll find a painting I hate. It's the palace when it was in the process of being built. Move it to the side. Behind it, you'll find a door." Victory glitters in her eyes as she gets the words out quickly. "Go through it. You'll find a small alcove, a hallway, and then another painting. Don't move it. Barely breathe. You'll be able to see through it."

My heart is racing now.

"And then what?"

"You'll need to—" She gasps, flinching again. Wrath contorts her features in such a way that I bow again.

"Fucking. Fates." She blows out a breath. "The journal you found," she says. "You're missing a page."

And then she's gone.

I stand there blinking, wondering—

I startle awake in an instant, my mind whirling from the transition from balcony back to bed. My feet still feel cold, like I was standing outside just now.

Ash growls from where he sits near the balcony, his tail twitching back and forth in an irritated way.

I blink a few times. Was that real? Or did I just spiral down a maddening dream again?

The balcony doors are wide open, though there's no sign of Jax's mother.

I look toward my door and move before I can stop myself. I slide into a pair of slippers, shoving my arms through my black silk robe as I peer into the hallway.

No enforcers.

I hurry, following every direction Evaluna gave. It'll be easy enough to prove it was just a dream if I take the path she spoke of and don't find any hidden doors.

I pause, adrenaline coursing through my veins as I spot the painting she mentioned. It's a monstrosity of a piece, almost as big as the wall. It depicts the bones of the palace, and all the people, mostly Ashlanders, building it. I hate it, too. It's devoid of life, of hope and color.

Okay, just because the painting is here doesn't mean there's a hidden door behind it. I hesitate, biting my lower lip as my heart thuds against my chest. I could've seen this during my exploration of the palace and it simply popped up in my dream.

I reach for the edge of the gilded wooden frame but hesitate. If I move this and there's a door behind it, then my dreams of Evaluna aren't just dreams.

If I move it and there's a wall here, I might be descending into madness.

I'm not sure which outcome I dread most.

I shift the frame.

My breath stalls at the sight of the carved door hidden behind the painting. I reach for the knob, fingers shaking as I turn it and push. I grab a lone candle burning atop a decorative table in the hallway, then step into the tunnel and quietly shut it behind me.

Wind softly spirals around my body as I step in to the small, slightly uneven hallway, ducking my head to follow its path. Pierce's power is still his, far down our bond and tightly sealed. The effort is like constantly flexing a muscle I never knew I had. It's draining at times, but a victory all the same. I ignore the instinct to yank it toward me, to fill myself with as much power as possible.

I have no clue what Evaluna is leading me toward. What if it's another test? Some otherworldly trial I have to face? *Again?*

The notion doesn't stop me, but *when* will I be done proving my worth?

I pause as an end to the tunnel comes into view. It's not a stone wall or a dead end. A thin canvas is stretched and supported by thick wooden beams that are built into the rock. It's the back of another painting, the details illuminated by the soft, golden light from the candle. I slow my breathing as best I can, making my footsteps lighter than the air in my blood.

I cover the small flame flickering, just in case someone on the other side of this painting looks my way.

Nerves tangle with each second that goes by, silence buzzing in my ears. Did Evaluna want me to merely uncover this secret passage's existence? Will it help me somehow in the future—

Two shadows move just beyond the canvas, halting all my thoughts.

"What's so important you drew me from bed?" Baydel's voice is angry. "I have company."

Eww.

"He calls," Frenrick, Baydel's Occuli, says, and a spark of green flame bursts beyond the painting.

"He what—"

"You broke your promise." An eerie voice reverberates in the space beyond the painting, though I see no one else. Frenrick lifts his palm higher, the green flames sparking brighter with each word from the mystery voice.

Baydel's shadow straightens at the sound.

"What?" Baydel sputters, his tone agitated and fearful.

"Do you deny it?" the voice calls, the power in it shaking me to my core.

I clamp my lips shut. The last thing I need is a gasp giving me away.

"I . . . I . . ." It's like Baydel has forgotten how to speak.

"You broke your promise," the voice calls again. "I've given you the time we agreed upon. Now you're suffering the consequences."

Baydel clears his throat. "I haven't," he argues. "The payment is on its way. Call off your dogs."

"I don't think I will," the voice finally says. "In fact, I think I'll double my efforts. Perhaps I should rescind my help as a punishment for your lack of fulfilment."

A burst of pure, undiluted fear rattles me so hard, I almost cry out. I grip my mouth harder, curling in on myself to stop the onslaught of panic rippling across Jax's power.

For as much as I hate Baydel, I would've thought his fear would taste better.

It doesn't. It's an acidic, sour sensation that stirs my stomach.

I take a deep, quiet breath, shoving the emotion back, separating it from mine.

"Don't," he says. "Please."

Holy fucking shit, I've never heard him beg.

"I promise your payment is on the way. I sent it. There's no need for anything more."

"I will determine that when the payment arrives. Until then, I suggest you calculate other ways to satisfy our bargain. I've grown terribly bored over here, and you know exactly what happens when my hands are idle."

Another burst of fear slices through me.

The flames disappear, and Baydel falls against the wall, using it to hold himself up.

What the actual fuck?

"What's the status on the payment?" he asks, his voice so thin. As if the conversation with whoever that was just stripped him of all his narcissistic bravado.

"Within the day," Frenrick says.

"Let's hope so," he says, as if he's uncertain. "If it doesn't . . ." His voice trails off. "Come." He shoves off the wall. "We need to prepare."

The two whisk down the hallway at a speed that's uncanny for this late hour.

I stand frozen behind the painting far longer than necessary, not wanting to risk running into them in the hallways, should they walk near my chambers.

Luckily, the space is clear when I return, shutting and locking the door behind me like I'm chased by their ghosts.

I curl into my bed, beckoning Ash in a desperate plea for comfort. He doesn't budge from his spot sprawled on the stone floor near the balcony. Sleep is long forgotten, but the sun is so far from rising. I tug the covers over me, my mind whirling.

Two things are certain.

One, Evaluna has been speaking to me through my dreams, and she *wanted* me to see Baydel's interaction. Two, there's someone out there more powerful than Baydel, and he's *terrified* of him.

And I have no clue what I'm supposed to do about it. Because if Baydel, the most powerful king in Lumathyst, is afraid of this person, then we most certainly should be, too.

CHAPTER 42

Rylee

"A payment?" Ivy asks, all but forgetting her half-eaten breakfast. "For what?"

"I don't know," I admit, sipping my second mug of coffee. I couldn't sleep last night, not after the orders from Evaluna and the dream that wasn't a dream.

"I can't tell what's more disturbing, the goddess Evaluna talking to you through your dreams or that there's something out there Baydel is afraid of," Layce adds after chomping into a bite of bacon.

"I agree," Mirren says from where she fusses in my wardrobe. "I've been here long enough to know that's not normal."

I flash her a look. "You've never seen Baydel deal with anyone like that?"

She shakes her head. "All the kings have enemies. That comes with the territory, but . . ." She tilts her head like she's trying to recall a memory from long ago. "I can't remember him acting afraid. Ever. Not even when Evaluna would get cross with him."

My eyebrows rise at that. "She'd get cross?"

Ivy physically shivers. "I can't imagine angering her."

"They were mates," Mirren replies. "Of course they grew cross with each other at times. You're in the early stages of your mating," she says to me. "Can you not imagine arguing with any of the princes?"

"Jax and I are practically pros at it," I admit. "And I've argued with each of them. It's a give-and-take. I know that. But I'm not a goddess. Wouldn't Baydel be worried about upsetting her?"

Mirren shrugs. "They were mated. He knew she would never harm him."

"Is that a mating bond thing we don't understand?" Layce asks, then finishes her eggs and fruit.

"I'm still learning," I answer, putting my coffee cup down to turn another page in Erin's journal, careful to not get any crumbs on it. "But the idea of physically harming any one of them is abhorrent." Just the thought produces a visceral reaction that has my stomach churning.

"The history says it's in the magic," Mirren explains. "The Fates choose mates based on compatibility and strength of matching. It would be easy to weave magic into the bond to ensure no harm can come to one by the other's hand, but I'm not sure if that theory has ever been tested."

"Weird," Ivy says. "I don't like the idea. Sorry, Ry, I'm glad you're happy, but I'd hate to have my future laid out like that."

"It was my choice," I remind her. "I didn't have to go through the Athanry."

"If you hadn't, you wouldn't be mated to them?" Layce asks.

I shake my head. "A part of me knew," I say. "Something inside I can't explain, but no. If I'd refused to go through the Athanry, our bonds wouldn't have been solidified by the goddesses. It may be the Fates that find the matches, but the goddesses were the ones who played with the magic to only allow their sons to have one mate instead of four, like they had."

"But didn't they choose their mates?" Ivy asks, sipping her coffee. "Not the Fates?"

I turn to Mirren, standing by the wardrobe.

"Legend says as much," she answers. "But for a goddess to choose a mortal male . . . you have to assume the Fates had something to do with that."

"At least you chose them," Layce says. "In the end, like you said, you had the choice. You made it."

A yearning awakens inside me. "I'll always choose them."

Layce reaches across the table and squeezes my hand.

I smile at my friends, grateful for their support. And their presence. If they weren't here . . . if Mirren wasn't here with me, too, I don't know what I'd do.

"So, back to what you saw last night," Ivy says. "Do you think it's some sort of bribe? Maybe Baydel buys the alliances he secures?"

"I wouldn't put it past him." I turn another journal page. The sketches are so familiar now, I could probably draw them myself. "And you know how wealthy Lumathyst is. They cart precious materials in and out of the Ashlands daily. There would certainly be enough to entice other realms to be our allies."

"Maybe he sent such a payment with Jax to Keleshore?" Layce asks.

My throat tightens. "Maybe. Either way, I'm dying to hear from Jax. The dream . . ."

"That wasn't exactly a dream?" Layce offers.

"Yes," I say. "It started with him calling out to me."

"Maybe that was actually a dream," Ivy says. "And the rest wasn't."

A headache forms behind my eyes. I turn to Mirren. "Should I ask Baydel what he sent over with Jax?"

Mirren's eyes widen. "Do you need a bigger target on your back when it comes to him?"

"He started it," I say.

"I wouldn't push it," Mirren says, opening the door to the hallway. "There's too much at stake. Your main focus should be winning the Royal Authority Council's support. You already have Jullian in your favor. That much is clear with his support every time you're put on the spot. And now an alliance with Silvac. You're collecting allies like a queen."

"Was that a compliment?"

With an undignified snort, she closes the door behind her.

CHAPTER 43

Rylee

My dinner plate sits with only a few crumbs left on the nightstand next to my bed. I ate it all. Despite not having much of an appetite after everything that's happened, I refuse to *not* eat. Where I come from, having anything to eat at all is a privilege, let alone the gourmet meals the palace chefs prepare. I won't take these gifts for granted regardless of how unmotivated I feel.

I fold my legs beneath me, propping Erin's art journal in my lap for the umpteenth time. The sky is turning a soft shade of purple as the sun sets, the light pooling in from my open balcony doors.

You're missing a page.

Evaluna's words haunt me as I flip through page after page of Erin's artwork. I can practically taste the paint and charcoal through my fingers.

And all roads point to my sister holding every answer I seek.

Ironic, since she's the reason I snuck into the Choosing event in the first place. Everything leads back to her, and I'm terrified of what I'll do when I find her. But I must.

I touch the delicate lines on the last page, tracing the outline of an illustration of Ash, who sleeps soundly next to me. In the picture, he's sitting outside our hovel in the Ashlands, a sunbeam drenching him in golden light. I flatten my hand on the opened back portion of the book, using my free one to stroke Ash a couple of times.

He grumbles a bit, then settles back into his soft purring, too tired to protest. I've followed him on his nightly strolls occasionally, secretly hoping his adventures might lead me to Erin. Ivy and Layce have searched all the old spots we used to hit across the cities. We've all come up empty in our efforts to find her.

What am I missing? The question repeats over and over, my mind threatening to fracture—

A cool wave crashes down Axl's bond inside me, making me gasp.

Warm heat, like sunshine, ripples over Kal's bond, and my hand clenches against the book. My heart races as I dive internally, searching the strength of our connections, checking the sensations humming from them.

Warmth, hope, excitement?

I blow out a breath as the feelings' intensity settles to a soft buzzing. What just happened? Maybe they've finally secured their deals and are on their way home? Maybe they are near. Is that why I felt—

The book in my hand grows unnaturally hot, and every thought empties from my mind as I look down.

There's an almost imperceptible tear in the binding of Erin's journal. I must've ripped it when the bond sensations shook me. As I examine the tear, the book cools. I peel the corner back before ripping the entire thing off.

I stop breathing and drop the book, holding only the torn cover.

A small painting has been concealed behind the now-shorn backing. One I've never seen before.

I slip the painting out and bring it close, studying every line. It's the depiction of a small wooden building near the royal docks, just outside the royal city's border. Technically, it lies in Obsidian where the two cities meet, which is why I recognize it. Jax and I have made that walk a dozen times together on nights we couldn't sleep.

Why would she paint this one specific building? There's nothing else beyond the structure itself. No illustration of Ash or any people wandering nearby. Not even other buildings. Why would she hide this painting?

There's nothing illegal in it, no depictions of Ashlanders dressed above their station or memories of us crossing borders. It's just . . . a building. Boring compared to her other work.

I run my fingers over the painting, and adrenaline races through my veins, propelling me off the bed and into my leathers and Legend jacket.

I should tell someone where I'm going, should tell Mirren or Ivy or Layce, but I don't want to wake them up in the middle of the night for something that could turn out to be nothing at all. No doubt they'd want to debate the merits of visiting a building in a painting, insisting I go during daylight hours, and honestly, I'm not in the mood for debate. Of course, Layce and Ivy would insist on going with me, but some part of me wants to do this alone—*needs* to do this alone—as foolish as that seems.

I slip on my boots and sneak through the palace, ensuring no enforcers spot me. It feels like old times when I'd do my best to hide while sneaking across borders.

I head to the stable where they keep the Legends' velomages and take Axl's, since it's the closest. I start the magic contraption, navigating it onto the palace roads the way Jax taught me, heading at top speed to the location in the painting.

My heart thuds harder against my chest the closer I get, my mind spinning with possibilities. She painted it for a reason. Hid it for a reason. Maybe she's left a letter there. Another clue in the form of a painting. *Something.*

I have to see it for myself.

The powers inside me stretch and press against my bones. Axl's water and Kal's flight are particularly fidgety, pulsing with a need for attention. I breathe around the sensation, loosening my hold on their powers just enough to get some air.

My fingers are cold as I bring the velomage to a crawl on the main road, the cool air wafting off the royal docks not far away. So many nights before this, I'd take the same path and sit on the docks, watching the waves in hopes of a ship sighting, but instead, I'm here, chasing my sister's ghost.

The roads are quiet as I park the velomage. There are very few citizens walking along the edge between the Obsidian and royal cities. I eye the smattering of people heading toward the club district in the Obsidian City, then, unnoticed, take the pathway down a small hill on foot.

At the bottom stands the building from Erin's drawing. It's a simple wooden structure used for storage by Obsidian City keepers who maintain the streets' cleanliness. There aren't any workers here at this hour, but I scan the area for observers or anything amiss.

I dip into the powers pulsing around my bonds, feeling their connection instantly. I graze my mental fingers over them, just in case I need to access them quickly. My own power leaks from me on instinct, a small wind blowing my hair away from my cheeks.

Lifting the handle on the lone door to the building, I step inside. A puff of dust falls from the door, which is painted an oddly vibrant shade of purple—Erin's favorite color. Chills chase down my spine as I study the room, illuminated by the soft moonlight beaming in from the lone window on the right wall.

The shelves are packed with cleaning supplies—brooms and trash bins, buckets and solutions. I walk around the cramped space. The structure is so small, I can circle it in a dozen paces.

I search through the supplies, hunting for a piece of parchment or scroll, anything Erin might've left behind. I shift things to the sides, scanning the walls behind stacks of cloths in case she painted something on the wood. I do this over and over again, until I'm certain I've done everything but tear up the wooden floor planks. If I have to, I'll dismantle this entire place—

"Took you long enough." My sister's familiar voice hits me like a hammer.

CHAPTER 44
Rylee

"Goddess *damn* it, Erin," I snap, my hand splayed over my chest. "I *hate* it when you do that." My knee-jerk reaction to her ability to become invisible immediately fades the moment I meet her eyes.

They're the same, but . . . different. Heavier. Tired. Her blond hair is slicked back and tied in a tight braid that she's spun in a knot on the top of her head.

She's here. She's really fucking here.

"Hey, sis," she says.

I swallow hard, a million emotions rushing through me—relief, hope, anger, heartbreak. I try to catch one and stick to it, but it's impossible.

She shifts her weight, wearing the Fader uniform, the full-face mask in her right hand.

Tears prick my eyes. I've imagined finding her for over a year. Imagined wrapping her in my arms and crying in relief that she's safe, alive. And after the Athanry, I imagined strangling her, yelling at her, convincing her to stop this madness.

Now, confronted with her, I'm frozen.

"How did you know I was here?" I blurt out the first question that springs to my mind. I've had her journal forever. There's no way the leader of the Faders has been waiting around for me to show up.

"Magic," she says with a shrug. "I was alerted when you disrupted the endpaper of the journal."

Which explains the weird heat emitted by the book.

I grit my teeth. The betrayal of what she is, what she's *done*, burns me from the inside out. "So, you have Occuli working for you, too?"

"I thought you'd find my journal a lot sooner," she says, avoiding my question, and her voice pricks my heart with a love it has no business feeling. My sister . . . *left* me.

She left me to join a group trying to kill the princes and innocent people of Lumathyst. I can't be happy to see her. I *can't*.

"You could've just sent me a message telling me to meet you," I snap, anger flooding my veins. "You know I would've met you anywhere—"

"I couldn't," she fires right back. "Actually." The word looks like a struggle, and she shakes her head. "You're constantly surrounded by . . . *them*."

"Them?"

"The Legends."

"My *mates*," I correct her. "And I've been alone for more than a week now. You could've sought me out."

"I couldn't," she says again.

The weight on my chest grows heavier. "What are you doing, Erin?"

She opens her mouth like she's going to say something, flinches, then tries again. "What I have to," she says on a released breath.

"You don't have to," I argue. "Hurting innocent people? Those dying in the streets? That's not you. That's never been you. The leader of a radical group?" I take a step closer to her. "That's *not* you."

Erin presses her lips together, shrugging.

That shrug makes me see red. I mimic it theatrically. "That's it?" I ask, tears stinging the backs of my eyes. "All this time. And that's all you have for me?" My entire body trembles with anger and grief. "Why did you want me to find you, then, if you have nothing to say?"

She parts her lips, agony contorting her features before she blows out a breath. A flash of anger before she settles into cold resolve. "Are you taking care of Ash?"

The question gives me whiplash. She's worried about her fucking *cat*?

"Of course I am," I snap. "He's gorging himself on fish in the palace."

A small smile. "Thank you."

I gape at her.

"The enhancement," she says, glancing to the side as if she's waiting for something.

"The shit you're peddling to innocent people? Hooking them on it in the hopes they'll join your cause?" I grumble. "Who's your baker?"

She groans, looking like she's trying to lift something heavy as she speaks. "Ivy," she says. "Get some to Ivy."

"And just how am I supposed to get some?"

She opens and closes her mouth, then shakes her head, clearly torn, but unable or unwilling to say more.

"Who are you working with, Erin?" I ask, my voice softening at her obvious discomfort. "Tell me. I have . . . I'm in a position to negotiate now. We can end this. Start again. Find a peaceful way to move forward for Lumathyst."

"The kings are the problem," she says.

"The Legends aren't the kings," I argue. "They'll take the thrones, and we'll work together to implement the changes we've always dreamed about—"

"They won't! They stand for everything we hate, Rylee. How can you not see that?"

"You don't know them," I say. "Do you think for one second I would've chosen them had they been anything like the people we've fought our whole lives? Do you think I would've gone through the Athanry? Dying for them? They sacrificed their powers to bring me back—"

"Dying?" She gently clenches my arms. "You what?" She blinks rapidly, her hands dropping as she takes a step back. "And they . . ."

Shit. I shouldn't have said that. I just want her to understand how deep our love is, how wonderful they are. *They're* the change Lumathyst needs.

"They . . ." She lowers her voice to barely a whisper. "They gave you their powers." She looks me up and down, something like devastation crumpling her face.

"It's complicated," I say. "Tell me who you're working for. I know you didn't come up with this scheme. It's too predatory. Tell me who's at the head of this. Who's supplying the weapons, the enhancements. I'll make sure we can end this. *Together.*"

Erin parts her lips. Shuts them again. What's wrong with her? Does she not trust me?

My stomach plummets.

"You don't trust me." A knot forms in my throat. I'm the princess of Lumathyst. Mated to the Legends. Would I have trusted anyone with those titles a year ago?

No. Probably not.

But I'm her sister.

And she's mine, but it's hard to recognize who stands before me.

"Rylee." She says my name like a plea. "I need you to . . ." She pauses. "Wake . . ."

My body tenses.

"Up." She exhales the last word like she had to climb a mountain to say it.

"I'm not asleep," I say confidently, despite reaching down to pinch myself. I've gotten too lost in dreams lately that keep turning out real anytime Evaluna shows up in them. My nightmares? They're all of Erin. Either I can't find her, or I do, and she betrays me all over again. "If I was, you'd have stabbed me in the back already," I add.

"I wasn't the one who threw blades at you," she deadpans. "That would be the Nightmare."

The Athanry.

The night I found out who she was.

It seems like an age ago.

"*My* Nightmare," I say, possessive bite peeking through. "And he was aiming for you."

"You shouldn't have stepped in the way." She sounds utterly defeated. "Should've just let the blades hit their mark."

"Erin." The words aren't her, either. She loves life, even the small, fractured one we had. She would never be so cavalier about her death.

"I'm tired." It's almost like an explanation.

"Then come back with me," I say, hope rising in my chest. "Come home with me and tell me who is doing all this, and we'll stop it. Ivy and Layce are at the palace. They're with me. And I have powerful friends now. Please, come home with me."

"Home?" She tilts her head. "You call the palace home now?"

"I call wherever my mates are home."

"I'm happy for you," she says, and it sounds genuine. "I want you to be happy, Rylee. Safe. I want you to wake . . ." She hisses like she's been hit with something. "Up. *Goddesses*," she says, exasperated.

I scrunch my brow. "I'm awake," I snap. "You're the one who won't just *talk* to me. And I'm so tired of proving myself to people. The last person in the realm I should have to earn trust from is *you*."

"You've changed."

"So have you! We should be together on this, not on opposite sides. Tell me who you're—"

A loud boom cuts me off, followed by sounds of chaos.

"Shit!" Erin snaps. "I told them to hold."

I glare at her. "An attack?" I growl. "You set up another attack?"

"No, I didn't. I—"

I'm already moving for the door, instinct propelling me toward the sound of breaking glass.

"Don't." Erin grabs my arm, hauling me back.

I whirl on her, jerking out of her grasp. My hand drops, my entire soul drowning at the sight of her already wearing her mask.

Fader.

Princess.

Two sides of the same coin.

"We can stop this," I say. "Together. We can end all of this." I extend my hand, trying one more time to reach for the sister I once knew.

She doesn't take it.

A fearful cry splits the air, and I'm out the door.

Dipping into Kal's power and racing through the streets, I follow the sounds, then come to a screeching halt amidst the chaos.

A dozen Faders tear through the streets in the club district of Obsidian City, blasting those magical weapons at anything that moves. I see a green flame hit someone in the leg, hear their agonized scream and the *thwack* as their body hits the cobblestones.

Power consumes me, building like a storm beneath my skin. I'm instinct and anger and pure survival. I move, a collective power on the tip of my fingers—

Heat bursts against the side of my head, spinning me around with the impact. A Fader punched me from behind. I'm stunned, wobbling on my feet, scrambling internally for my power. Wind slips through my fingers, flighty and hard to grasp.

The Fader throws something at me. I brace myself for the blow, only for a rain of white powder to hit my face instead. I cough, wiping frantically at the substance burning my skin. It coats my fingers, which shake uncontrollably as I scramble backward, away from the Fader. My legs become lead weights, and I hit the ground with a smack.

The nullifier. The one Atlas nicknamed Tox. I can feel it hit my system, draining me. It locks on to every ounce of energy I possess and tears it away. I cough again, trying to force the stuff from my lungs. The Fader bears down on me, grabs me by my hair, and drags me toward the fray. I reach for my power, *any* power, and hit a dead wall.

It's gone. All of them are gone.

"I've got something here," the Fader calls out, drawing the attention of the others as he drops me in the middle of the street.

I huff, cringing against the sting of the fall.

All twelve Faders head over, their attention on me. Good. At least they're no longer shooting at innocent people. That's something. Hopefully the people can use the distraction to get to safety.

I scan the uniforms, looking for my sister's build. She's nowhere among them.

She's supposedly their leader, and she left me for dead.

I didn't think my heart could break any more, but it does.

Shatters into a thousand pieces I'm sure will never fit together the same way again.

CHAPTER 45

Rylee

"Such a pretty little treasure," the Fader says as the rest form a circle around me.

"You know the boss will want her," another one says. A woman this time, though it's not Erin.

"She'll have her," the other one says. "After we've had some fun." He jabs a finger toward me. "This is the one who killed a bunch of us months ago. Saw it with my own eyes."

"To be fair," I say, shifting on my knees, wobbling a bit but regaining my balance as I hold up a finger of my own. "They were being real dicks—"

His hand cracks across my face so hard I taste blood. I spit a mouthful of it onto his boots.

"Mouthy little *bitch*," he fires right before landing a punch to my stomach that has me doubling over. I can't breathe for a full thirteen seconds.

I cradle my ribs, instinct tunneling inward, reaching for powers that aren't there.

"I'm going to track her down," the woman says, shaking her head. "Boss!" she yells, running down the street. A few follow her, leaving me with the guy who loves to hit and seven of his fucking friends.

Running on pure adrenaline, I manage to shove to my feet. It's slow and not at all graceful, but I'm standing. I shift into a defensive stance. I'm not going down without a fight.

The Fader laughs. "Can't tell if you're brave or stupid," he says, motioning to his friends. "There are eight of us and one of you."

"I've had worse odds," I lie. I've never faced this many without a scrap of power to use. But how long can this stuff really last? It has to wear off quickly, or else those without powers wouldn't go looking for another hit.

Another wave of laughter echoes through the group, the sound as enraging as it is ominous. Ice sluices through my veins. Jax will kill me if I die out here. Kal would meet his mother and beg for my life. Axl would raze the Fader organization to the ground while Pierce would melt their minds.

A shiver races down my spine at the thought of what they'll do.

There's no stopping it, though. Not when they have me so vulnerable.

I slip my hands inside my open jacket, pulling out two small blades gifted to me by the Nightmare.

"You throw those," the Fader says, "you better make them count. Because it'll be your last free move."

I point the tip at his neck, then move it down. "Your throat or your balls?"

He takes a step toward me, and I brace myself, lifting both blades—

"Enough!" Erin's voice is authoritative in a way I've never heard it before. It's enough to halt the Fader.

The rest immediately back up, parting enough for her to come through. She's wearing her mask, but even if she hadn't spoken, I'd recognize her gait. It's so obvious to me now, I don't know how I ever missed it before. The four that left walk behind her, the group looking ominous as all those masked faces are focused on me.

"We were going to bring her to you—"

"Shut up," she cuts him off as she strides up to me, examining the wounds on my face. "You dosed her?"

He looks down at his booted feet.

"She's not a Legend, idiot. You wanted her *enhanced* for some reason?" she fires at him, and I do my best not to look confused.

Wait. Of course. No one knows I have powers. And Tox gives bursts of power to users who don't have any.

"Figured it couldn't hurt," he says, motioning to me. "She did that weird magic thing with the fucking princes. Who knows what she can do now?"

"That wasn't her," Erin hisses. "It was clearly the Mind's powers. You were seeing things. And you know *he'll* want her."

He? He who?

"She's invaluable." Erin turns toward me. "Can you imagine what the princes will offer to get her back?"

I can't move. Is she seriously planning on using me as leverage?

A rumble of excitement and chatter rolls through the group.

I take a step back, only to run into the two Faders behind me. The Tox is still in effect, numbing my insides in the most hollow way. It's all I can do not to panic at the fact that I can't connect with my bonds, let alone my power.

"Get some chains," Erin orders, and four of them head in another direction. "You five, finish sweeping the perimeter for any supplies we need. And get a body count. You know he likes specifics." More rush off, leaving Erin and three others.

I move again, this time toward her. "If you think for one *second* you're putting me in chains—"

A swift move, and I'm on my back, my head rattling from the impact. Erin is atop me, hand at my throat, face so close to mine our cheeks are practically touching.

"Shut your mouth, princess," she snaps, then dips her head closer.

I don't struggle, because she's not actually choking me, and it confuses the shit out of me.

"You three," she says to the final Faders. "Has there been any progress on the temple?"

"Group B is there now," a man answers. "I can send a runner—"

"Send yourself," she barks. "I need to know if it's been successfully planted or not. If this trial doesn't work, we might not get another chance with the other temples."

I hang on every word she says, noting how easy it is for her to speak directly to her minions, as opposed to me, her own sister.

The Fader hesitates. "What about her?"

"All of you can go," she says. "I've got this one. She's got nothing left. They'll be back with the chains in minutes. Go. Don't make me ask twice."

They fucking bolt. It would be funny if I wasn't so damned confused.

She looks in their direction. "We don't have much time—"

Hollers sound in the distance. From the corner of my eye, I can see the Faders with chains, whooping and heading toward us.

"Shit," Erin mutters.

I knock her off me, scrambling to my feet. "You're not taking me." I point my blade toward her.

I can't see her face, but her body language says she's rolling her eyes. "You need to listen—"

A chain wraps around my throat from behind, hauling me to my knees. The shock of the blow has me dropping my blades.

"Easy!" Erin commands, a tiny hint of desperation in her voice. "He won't want her damaged!"

"That's owed," the man from before says. "She spit on me."

"Fucking *coward*." I force the words out, my fingers tugging at the chain tightening around my neck.

Black dots my vision.

"Let her go," Erin commands. "Or I will end you myself."

The chain loosens a fraction.

A loud, thundering *impact* shakes the ground beneath my feet, a blur of red slamming into the space next to me.

One second, I'm struggling to breathe; the next, the chain is lifted from my throat and the Fader holding it is soaring through the air like he can fly.

He can't. He lands headfirst with a sickening crack across the street.

A rush of blue accompanied by the sound of roaring water soars by me, too fast for me to follow. A wall of ocean sweeps the rest of the Faders off their feet, sending them spiraling away.

Including Erin.

"Rylee." Kal's voice matches his touch, which is soft as he cradles my face.

"Kal?" I take him in, eyes scanning his face as he kneels in front of me. "You're here?"

"I'm here," he says, drawing me against him as he pulls us to our feet. His scent envelops me, relief coursing through me so much it hurts.

I turn, following the sound of water, and *panic*.

"Don't drown them!" I yell at Axl.

He immediately drops the wall, rushing over to me. "Kitten," he growls, golden eyes on my neck. I must look like a wreck, because his expression is murderous.

I reach for him. "Please," I say, barely able to get the word out. "She's out there."

He looks to the group now scattering in different directions, then returns focus to me, tracing the sore patch of skin on my neck. He cringes. "Sorry we didn't get here sooner."

Kal shifts behind me, scooping me up and cradling me against his chest. "Home or chase?" he asks, almost like he can't form a coherent thought.

"They're gone," Axl answers for me.

"You have your powers?" I ask, still unable to feel them.

"They hit us the second we docked," Axl explains. "Thought you did that."

I shake my head, wincing when the motion hurts. Kal looks down at me, concern shaping his features. "They hit me with Tox," I explain.

"Home." Kal nods. "You need a healer."

"Axl, your velomage is by the keepers' supply building," I tell him seconds before Kal launches us into the sky, flying swiftly to the palace. He doesn't let up on the speed until we're in my room.

"Get Dalfon," Kal demands of the enforcer standing guard in my hallway.

The guard doesn't hesitate to run.

Kal sits me on the edge of my bed, agony flooding his blue eyes.

"I'm okay," I assure him even though my lip feels swollen and my neck is on fire. "You're here."

"I'm here," he says, kneeling so he can be eye level with me. "I felt you," he says. "When we were close to shore. Axl did, too. His ship docked at the same time as mine. We were so worried, especially when our powers came back."

I blow out a breath, tears spilling over my lashes as I lean my forehead against his shoulder. Kal holds me, gently stroking my hair.

"What happened?"

I don't even know where to start. My head is still spinning.

"Rylee?" Dalfon calls from the doorway.

"Hurry," Kal says, shifting out of the way so the healer can look at me.

Dalfon immediately cringes.

"That bad?"

"Sometimes I think I should shadow you," he says, shaking his head before approaching me. He eyes Kal. "Are you going to behave while watching? I know you've been separated from your mate for a lengthy time."

Kal takes a step back, balling his hands into fists. "I'm fine. Heal her."

Dalfon nods, studying me with his black eyes. His palms ignite, blue flames roaring to life. He points them at me, hovering them above my wounds. Tingling relief knits me back together, my head swimming with how good it feels.

"They dosed you with something?" Dalfon asks.

I nod. "That enhancement that's been affecting people."

A low growl from Kal.

Dalfon rakes his cool flames over me again. And again.

"I can't undo the enhancement's effects." He shakes his head. "With those afflicted by the same, we've only been able to stabilize them while it leaves their system. Her injuries are healed, but it'll be a few hours before it wears off."

"That's unnerving," I say, feeling so much clearer now that I'm not in pain. The powers are dull and numb inside me. I hate it. After becoming so accustomed to them filling me, it's a hollow sensation to be without them.

"I apologize."

I wave him off. "You fixed this." I motion to my face and neck. "I'm grateful."

Axl rushes in, breezing past Kal and Dalfon, yanking me off the bed and into his arms. "Missed you so much. I get back and you're playing with the Faders without me?"

I laugh, giving another grateful look at Dalfon, who quietly leaves, shutting my door behind him. "Wasn't a game I signed up for," I assure him. "Well, not exactly." I blow out a breath. "At least we know that me getting hit with Tox doesn't affect your ability to access your powers like Baydel's binding tonic did in the experiment."

"Now who is finding the bright side?" Kal asks, eyeing me where Axl still holds me against him.

"Have to try," I say.

Axl sets me on my feet, and Kal steps up to his side. The two of them are breathtaking. My heart hiccups at the sight of them staring down at me, hanging on my every word.

Ash hisses from his spot on the bed behind me, bowing his back at them.

Axl growls right back. The cat scoffs before hopping off the bed and slinking out of sight. I spare a moment to think how pissed he'll be when I tell him I saw Erin without him.

"Did you get the agreements?" I ask, reaching out for each of them with a hand. Now that they're here and I'm healed, I can think of little else but touching them. It's been too long. It's hard to think around the need crashing inside me to be close to them.

"Yes," Kal says, taking my hand in his.

"Mine too," Axl says, dragging his hand up my other arm, drawing me closer to both of them.

I'm like a coiled spring the more their eyes are on me, studying and attentive. The more their hands explore and urge me closer. I could've died tonight, if the Faders had decided to kill me while I was vulnerable. Or I could've been captured. Taken to whoever my sister referred to. Knowing that certainty makes these moments with them so much more precious. I've missed them so much. And it feels like time is never on our side.

"There's . . . much to discuss," Kal says as I draw up on my tiptoes, brushing my lips over his.

"So much," I say, turning to Axl to kiss him, too. "But I don't want to talk right now."

"Fuck it," Axl growls, his massive hand cupping my hip. "We can talk later." His mouth presses against mine so intently I whimper, gripping Kal harder as Axl claims me with his kiss.

I melt beneath their touch, a ball of sensation building in my core as we become a flurry of movements—shedding clothes, frantic kisses, and greedy touches. They walk me back to the bed, neither of them hesitating to lay their mouths upon me.

"I dreamed of you every night," Kal says as he trails his lips along my neck.

I arch into the touch, gasping as Axl kisses his way down my stomach, then lower.

"Have you touched yourself while I've been gone?" Axl asks, his voice pure gravel before he licks me.

I gasp, fire streaking through my veins. "No. There's been little time for such luxuries."

I can barely form words as he does it again.

Kal's mouth moves lower, kissing my breasts. I can't breathe, they feel so good. So right.

"Poor kitten," Axl says. "You need a release."

"Yes." I breathe the answer. "I need you both."

Kal sucks my nipple into his mouth, the sting rippling pleasure beneath my skin.

The way the two focus on me shifts my entire being to them. To what they're doing to me. To how they make me feel. Nothing else exists outside the need we have for one another. It's consuming. Primal. Ethereal.

"Missed you both so much," I say, my breath hitching as I touch every part of them I can reach. It's hard with the way they're devouring different pieces of me like they've been starved.

"Hated every second of it," Axl murmurs against my warmth, the vibrations making me tremble against the edge he's keeping me on.

"Hated it," Kal agrees, drawing up to look down at me. He's stunning. Those blue eyes sear before he takes his time kissing his way down my jaw and neck—

"Axl!" I gasp as he sucks and licks at me until I see stars. The move sends me flying over a sharp edge with no end, my orgasm ripping through me in a white-hot burst.

"Mmm," he mumbles against my flesh before drawing back. "So damn delicious."

Jax's power perks up, arching like it wants to play, shocking me. Dalfon was wrong; it didn't take a few hours for the nullifier to wear off. Maybe I didn't get hit with as much as I originally thought. I grasp Jax's power on instinct, relishing the loving, passionate emotions radiating from my mates. I send it right back to them, fill them to the brim with everything I'm feeling in return.

"Kitten," Axl groans when the emotions wash over him. "You have the powers back. You're so damn strong."

"My turn." Kal gently grips the backs of my knees, dragging me away from Axl. "You can wait," he fires playfully at Axl, who laughs.

"I love watching you fuck our mate." Axl shifts off the bed, backing up until he drops into the armchair near it.

"Rylee." Kal says my name with an air of reverence as he kisses his way up my stomach, over my chest, and finally to my lips before he settles between my thighs. "Need you."

"Yes." I wholeheartedly agree, arching as he drags his hard length through my wetness.

"So fucking slick." Kal gently presses in an inch before turning to look at where Axl is sitting. "You made her liquid for me."

Fire flickers beneath my skin at their communication, at the way we're both looking at Axl while Kal slides inside me another inch.

"You're welcome." Axl's grin is pure pride as he nods toward us. "Fuck. Her."

I tremble at his words, then gasp as Kal fills me, holding me there in the sweetest anticipation. I look up at Kal, heart full, as he dips down and kisses me. His lips are warm, soft, and explorative. I close my eyes, losing myself in the way he holds me, kisses me.

And then he drags himself out of me only to slide in again, warm shivers dancing over my skin at the move.

"Kal. Yes. That feels so good." I breathe the words as he does it again, his confident, sure strokes winding me up again so quickly, I'm dizzy.

Kal shifts, tucking one of his arms beneath my lower back and holding me even more tightly against him as he takes control, pumping into me so closely, there's no part of us that's not touching. He's the very thing holding me together while he does his best to break me into pieces.

"Fuck, yes," he groans, feeling me tighten around him. "She's right there." He flashes a grin to Axl, and I follow his line of sight, my eyes locking with Axl's. He's watching intently, his massive thighs spread as he patiently waits his turn. Knowing that, seeing him like that only heightens the pleasure careening toward release down my core.

"Kal!" I gasp, my body clenching around his as I come. Waves of pleasure ripple over me, sparks crackling along our bond as he finds his release, too.

Kal gently pulls out of me, and I've barely caught my breath before Axl is there, climbing onto the bed and lying beside me, shifting me toward him. "Can you handle some more?"

I shiver as his hand roams down my side. "Yes."

He grins, hooking his fingers behind my knee and hitching it over his hip. The position has his hard length gliding through my ultra-sensitive heat, and he slicks himself with the remnants of me and Kal. The thought alone is enough to make me feel brazen. My nerves tangle all over again, especially as Kal kisses my back before he shifts off the bed, heading to the chair Axl vacated.

"Doesn't she feel incredible?" Kal asks as Axl drags himself through my heat again, circling my aching center in teasing passes.

"She really does," Axl answers, hauling me closer against him.

We're both on our sides facing each other, but when I lift my head to kiss him, I can see Kal just over Axl's broad shoulder, content with his blue eyes on us. It's exhilarating, intoxicating. I'm reduced to pure sensation. Sparks and chills and trembles. I pour all of those sensations into Jax's power, pushing it toward them so they can both feel what I'm feeling.

"You're mine to please now," Axl says. The possessive claim only fuels the fire beneath my skin. There's something so inherently sexy about being desired by both of them in this way. I'll never get enough of it.

"Yes," I beg.

Axl smirks. "This what you want?"

I melt at the words, a burst of anticipation rattling through me as he slides inside me, filling me where Kal had moments ago.

"Yes," I say again. "Axl. More." I capture his mouth in mine, my mind spinning as Jax's power ripples from me and over them. We're lost to our desire and love now, and it's *everything*.

Lightning streaks down my core as Axl hitches my leg higher over his hip and pumps into me over and over again, each connection ramping up the flames igniting my body.

"Oh my goddess." I grip Axl's broad shoulder, rolling my hips in time with his thrusts, chasing that pleasure like my life depends on it. Axl's mouth is on mine, swallowing my gasps as he pumps into me in a steady rhythm.

A whimper tumbles from my lips, warmth flooding to my core as he presses tighter against me.

"That's it," Axl groans. "Come for me."

"Axl." I clench around him, dragging my mouth over his before my eyes flash behind him, to Kal, who's watching us with lust-filled eyes.

Home. This feels like coming home.

They're here. They're safe. They're *mine*.

Axl builds my pleasure brick by brick, lightning and fire and warmth and happiness as he glides in and out of me. I'm a maelstrom of bliss created by their combined storm. Sea and sky come alive, rippling along my bonds. They gleam, glistening as bright as stars as we crash together.

"I'm . . . I'm . . ."

I'm theirs. Wholly. Irrevocably.

"I've got you," Axl growls, stroking that spot deep inside me.

I combust in a wave of pleasure that crests and trembles, melting my mind in the best possible way. Axl follows me over the edge, losing himself inside me until we're nothing but panting breaths and soft, lazy kisses.

"That's so fun to watch," Kal says as he comes to the side of the bed. He helps us clean up, the two of them working so well together as they see to my care. After they're satisfied all my needs have been met, we get back into my bed, exhaustion settling over all of us.

And I fall asleep between them, feeling safe and untouchable in the best way.

CHAPTER 46

Axl

I shift off the bed in Rylee's chambers in the palace, doing my best not to disturb her and Kal sleeping on the other side.

Predawn light trickles in from the balcony doorways, casting the room in a soft glow. When I glance down at Rylee, my heart is full.

It was fucking torture being away from her. A kind of agony I'm not used to. Usually, I'm a go-with-the-flow guy, but the kings forcing me to separate from her so early in our mating process, and during such a tumultuous time, was rough.

Coming home and finding her in the midst of a Fader battle? I've never known an anger like I felt last night.

We have to end this.

I tear my eyes away from her, rummaging around the pile of clothing that's tossed carelessly along her floor. We were all in a hurry last night. I'm not mad about it. We needed her like we needed air. And now that we're back, I don't have any intention of ever leaving her like that again.

I slip into my pants as Ash decides to stroll out of the darkened closet across the chamber, narrowing his cat eyes at me.

I mimic the look, not breaking his stare. The creature tolerates me but loves Rylee—though she denies it—so someday we need to find a common ground.

After a few seconds with neither of us breaking, he snorts, dismissing me, then heads out through the balcony doors.

"Good morning to you, too," I softly grumble to his back before searching for my shirt.

I see a peek of it beneath Rylee's Legend jacket and lift the thing so I can grab it. Something falls out of her jacket pocket with the motion, and I raise a brow. Shirt forgotten, I bend to scoop up the small brown paper.

"What the fuck?" I say out loud, all but forgetting Kal and Rylee are still asleep.

Rylee mumbles something, stretching awake as she sits up. Kal follows shortly after.

"What is it, Axl?" she asks after she yawns. Fuck, she looks incredible with nothing but a sheet wrapped around her. The tops of her full breasts peek out in a way that begs to fill my hands.

Focus.

Right.

I head over to the bed, gently extending the small brown paper toward her. "Careful," I caution as she takes it. "It's folded that way for a reason."

Rylee's brow pinches together, the look similar to Kal's as he watches her crack the paper open a fraction.

Her eyes widen as she looks at me. "Where did you get this?"

I motion to the pile of clothes on the floor. "It fell out of your jacket pocket."

"That's not possible—" She cuts herself off, her shoulders dropping. *"Erin."* She looks down at the white substance in the paper. "She slipped it to me."

"Why?" I ask, unable to keep the sharpness from my tone. "Why let the Faders chain you only to give this to you?"

"They'd already dosed you with it, right?" Kal asks.

"Erin didn't," she says. "But her minions did." She shrugs, eyes contemplative as she shifts off the bed, laying the paper on the bedside table.

"I've been looking for some," Rylee continues. "While you were gone. After I got back from Silvac. If we can study it, I'm hoping Ivy can help us come up with an antidote."

I glance around, my mind clearing. "Yeah, remind us why you're here alone again? Where's Pierce? Is Jax not back yet, either?"

Rylee slips on her clothes as she relays to us the events since we left. By the time she's done, we're all dressed and full from breakfast, and we're ready to meet with Ivy.

"So, technically, Pierce should be home in two weeks?" Kal asks as we move to the sitting area in her chambers.

She tucks herself between the two of us on the couch, nodding as she takes another sip of her coffee. "Should be," she says. "But I haven't heard anything. Not from him or Jax. Even though Baydel said he made it."

Something churns in my gut. I do my best to not let that emotion head down our bond. She's dealing with enough. I don't need to add to it. And surprisingly, I still have my powers.

"Side note," I say, cocking a brow as I look down at her. "My powers are still with me. Are you doing that?"

"Same," Kal adds.

She smiles. "I'm getting better at keeping them on the other ends of the bonds, with you. Pierce has his, too. It's hard to explain. It's exhausting, but if I keep that part of me tense, flexed, they stay. Some times are harder than others, like when we're in danger, but right now, it's not too difficult."

"I'm so proud of you, love," Kal says, nuzzling her neck. "But if it's exhausting or a strain on you, don't do it. Keep them for yourself if it's easier."

I grin down at her. "We'll be fine, kitten."

"I'm okay," she assures us both.

She's incredible. If roles were reversed, I don't know that I'd adapt as well and as brilliantly as she has.

"I'm here!" Ivy says as she rushes into the room, Layce and Mirren behind her. She spots both of us and gives us a polite nod. "What's happened?"

Rylee explains last night in detail for her friends, then pushes the paper packet toward Ivy. "Do you think you can work your magic on this?"

Ivy eyes the Tox studiously, then nods. "I'll do everything I can, but I'll need a space to work. And access to gardens with healing plants. I'll have to test several."

"I've been thinking about that," Rylee says. "You should go to Pierce's place in the Emerald Wood. It's secluded, and he already has everything you need there."

"And you can have access to my mother's gardens," I add. Rylee's eyes meet mine, gratitude spilling from them in a way that makes my chest puff out slightly. "It has some of the rarest flowers and healing herbs. Take whatever you need."

"Thank you." Ivy carefully pockets the Tox. "I'll go right away."

"I'll fetch you a carriage," Mirren says. "Layce, you should go with her. You two can tell anyone who bothers asking that Rylee ordered you to get Pierce's home ready for his return."

"Good idea, Mirren," Rylee says, nodding. She hops up to hug her friends. "Be careful with that stuff."

"You know us," Ivy says, smiling. "We'll figure this out."

Relief is visible on Rylee's features. "This is the first solid clue we've had in months," she says. "I'm hopeful."

Ivy and Layce hug her one more time before following Mirren out of the room. It grows quiet as Rylee sinks onto the couch again.

"If we can get an antidote, we'll have an edge against the Faders," she says. "Maybe finally stop them."

I wrap my arm around her, drawing her closer. "What about Erin?" I ask.

She shakes her head. "I don't know what to do about her," she admits. "She barely told me anything but slipped me exactly what I've been searching for? Even Jax's contact, Atlas, couldn't do that."

"That's surprising," Kal says. "About Atlas. He's Jax's go-to source for a lot of things, not just enhancements."

"Mirren tried to find him, but she couldn't. And maybe he didn't want to approach me without Jax present," Rylee says. "Either way, Erin is a wild card. I asked her to come with me, to help me put an end to this. She wouldn't."

My heart sinks. "I can't imagine how bad that stung."

She nods, then leans farther into my chest. "Helps that you're both here now. If we can just get Pierce and Jax back, maybe we can figure out who the *he* Erin kept mentioning is."

She mentioned an interaction with Baydel, too, of him being afraid of someone. It's almost hard to believe. If it was anyone else telling me the story, I wouldn't.

"Wonder if it's the same person," I say. "That Baydel spoke with through his Occuli?"

"I was wondering the same thing," Kal says, tilting his head. "And if it is, maybe this person has something on your sister," he continues. "That's forcing her hand?"

Rylee worries her lip between her teeth, then shakes her head. "There's nothing," she says. "We have nothing left for anyone to use against us. Our parents died on a Never List mission. I'm here." She waves to Ash, who lies in the sun on the balcony floor. "She cared enough about that damned cat to ask about him last night, and he's here safe, too. What else could anyone possibly have on her?"

I look down at her empathetically. She doesn't want to hope it's that. Not when she's already had her heart broken by her sister so many times.

And I really can't blame her. I just hope, for her sake, when it comes to a head—which I know it will—she's not the one who has put her sister's antics to an end.

Ivy works at rapid speed, returning to us only two days later.

"I broke down the properties," she says, motioning to the Tox now perfectly concealed inside a glass vial. "First, I had to track down its source. You won't believe it, Rylee, but it makes perfect sense."

Rylee visibly swallows where she sits next to me. "What is it?"

"You remember those stones that used to make you sick in the Ashlands? The one you brought to me to study all those months ago?"

"Yeah," Rylee answers.

"Didn't you say those stones were imported?" Kal asks.

Rylee nods. "They weren't from our mountains," she explains. "We'd get shipments in crates, but there was never a seal or anything. We were only told to break them down. They came incased in a gray, hard exterior, and the milky white stone inside is what the enforcers said the royals wanted. We were told it was for medicinal purposes."

"Well, that's what this stuff is made of." Ivy points to the vial.

Rylee shakes her head. "I didn't make the connection. The effects of the Tox felt so different from how dealing with the stones made me feel."

"That's likely because the raw form wasn't as potent as this refined version," Ivy explains.

"Do you two know where it's from?" Layce asks Kal and me.

I shake my head. "Sapphire Cove gets imports all the time from Cardrayton. Steel and spirits. We trade with them monthly or if demand is high, biweekly. The imports always come with a seal and a letter of inventory."

"Same with Ruby." Kal casts me a curious, concerned look. "Did you ever see anything indicating where it would be from?"

"No. And when I brought the enhancement issue up with Erin . . ." Her words are cold, disappointed. "She wouldn't tell me anything. It's like she didn't trust me with the information."

I wrap my arm around her shoulders, a silent show of support. I don't have a brother by blood, but the Legends are closer than any blood relationship could ever be. Still, I can't imagine them betraying me as deeply as Rylee's sister has betrayed her.

I keep hoping that I'm wrong, that all these instances with her sister are some big misunderstanding, but everything is pointing to her sister not giving a shit about her well-being. Which is not fucking okay with me.

"But Erin slipped you this." Ivy points to the vial. "This is the only reason we know what it is now. And thanks to our access to Axl's mother's gardens, I was able to get what I needed. It was easy once I knew what it was. Nature always offers a balance." She nods her thanks to me, then motions to the other vials she's brought with a golden powder nestled inside.

The vibrant color comes from the flowers she used to create the antidote—the same ones that only grow in my mother's gardens. Her favorite. I take some pride in that, knowing my care of those gardens over the decades was worth every ounce of grief that it triggered. My mother . . . I think she'd be proud to know that, too. That something she planted helped us so much.

We've already started mass producing the antidote, entrusting it to Jullian and our chancellors to distribute it to those still in the healers' quarters suffering from the effects. Jullian is the only king any of us even marginally trust right now, despite my father desperately trying to reconnect in the last two days. It's strange, the way he worried over my return, but I haven't had time to figure it out.

"I know," Rylee says. "When it comes to her, nothing makes sense. She wanted me to find her and meet her at that spot but then couldn't tell me anything concrete. She stopped the Fader group from going further with me but then claimed she was going to hand me over to 'him.' Someone higher than her, clearly. So, who's behind all of it? And is she truly with them? Or was she trying to help me? Or was she only doing that because she wanted to convert me to her way of thinking?"

Rylee pinches the bridge of her nose.

"I don't know," Ivy says. "But I'm glad she slipped it to you. To me, that's a sign she knew we'd do the right thing with it. If she wanted to dose you with it again, she wouldn't have wrapped it up like that."

Rylee nods. "Regardless of her intentions and cryptic messages, we can go to the kings and the Royal Authority Council now and give them our findings."

I nod. We've already distributed the antidote, but we haven't officially declared we completed one of the kings' tasks yet. Priorities.

"After that," Rylee continues, "we just have to hope Jax comes home with the alliance. After meeting every task, there's no way the Royal Advisory Council *can't* vote you all in as the new kings."

"I agree," Kal says. "We've met their terms and then some." He sighs. "We need Pierce and Jax home, though."

"We do," I say. "They have to be close."

"I hope so."

"What are we going to do to pass the time when all this is over?" Layce asks, trying to lighten the mood like she often does. "You'll have so much free time on your hands when you're not battling the kings, the Faders, and everything else in between."

Rylee smiles at her friend. "Eat?"

Everyone laughs at that, the tension in the room cracked for just a moment.

I hold Rylee close, relishing the light laughter, and know exactly what I'm going to do once I claim the throne.

Put her on it.

Worship her like she deserves.

And spend the rest of my days watching her turn Lumathyst into the realm we always hoped it would be.

CHAPTER 47

Rylee

I've only ever been to the temple of Eirdis once before, during Pierce's and my first time together in the Emerald Wood.

Today is vastly different.

I've spent over an hour in the temple, combing it for anything out of place, and coming up empty. I came to the Emerald Wood to collect another batch of the antidote Ivy has been endlessly producing and deliver another three bundles of Tareena's golden flowers she needs to create it. It's the last we can spare without eradicating the plants. We'll have to wait for them to regrow before we can make more, but this will help.

I stopped here afterward. I had to, after what Erin said to her people about the temple. She could've meant Evaluna's, but I went there yesterday, and everything was normal. Neph's, too.

Same here.

I intend to check on Tareena's temple tomorrow.

Kal and Axl are currently finishing up visiting the healers' establishments, ensuring the sick are getting the antidote they need. But here I am, standing on the balcony that wraps around Eirdis's middle, my neck arched so I can look up at her pristine face.

Something inside me *pulls*, almost reminiscent of the bonds. The unbreakable connections that tug at me even now—two in the direction of the Ruby Aire, one toward the west, where Silvac lies, and one so faint I can't pinpoint where he is. I focus on the separate connection to stop me from spiraling about Jax.

No word, no inkling, nothing.

I feel so out of control when I think about him, it's all I can do to not rip my hair out.

I take a deep breath, closing my eyes as I center myself like Pierce taught me. Thinking about him, about the statue of his mother before me, has that connection flickering to life. Almost like an acknowledgment or a way to get my attention.

I could be imagining it, but after the dreams I've had with Evaluna and the events that follow them, I don't discredit any instinct fluttering through my body. I died, and thanks to my mates' sacrifice, the goddesses brought me back. Did that create a connection, too? The same one that allows Evaluna into my dreams? Or is that merely a facet of her power, like she spoke about?

"Are you trying to tell me something?" I whisper to the sleeping goddess, feeling rather foolish. Who do I think I am? Some special chosen one to interpret messages from them?

I shake my head, blowing out a breath. I think I'm so desperate for answers, I'm conjuring connections in the search for solace.

"The first time I saw her, I couldn't remember how to breathe." The king's voice cracks the silence in the temple.

I whirl around and spot Pierce's father, Brooks, strolling up the last few steps to this middle balcony, heading my way. He wears a pair of crisp black trousers, a shirt of emerald stretching tight over his chest. He's casual today, his curly black hair longer than it was the last time I saw him.

"Your majesty," I say, bowing properly. He's certainly not the worst of the kings, but he doesn't hold my trust, either. I take a casual step away, toward the stairway, in case I need to make a quick exit.

Brooks dips his head toward me, then looks up to the face of Eirdis.

"We'd all heard of the goddesses' arrival in Lumathyst," he continues, leaning against the balcony railing. "They'd walked among us for quite some time, blessing people, enriching the lands with their powers, but I'd never seen her up close until after a few months. I was working in a bookshop near what is now the Emerald Wood, poring through titles like I would any other day. It was raining, and she came in to get out of it." He smiles. "I was dumbfounded. A goddess, in my shop, looking regal and yet . . . simple in the most fascinating way. She had a thirst for knowledge that outweighed mine, which was saying something, and once I remembered how to breathe, we spoke about many things. Books and teas and her affinity for lemon cakes." He chuckles. "I told her I didn't expect a goddess to be so easy to talk to."

I swallow hard, unable to stop the warmth spreading through me at his words. The look in his eyes. There's a youthfulness there that looks like *love*.

"I knew when she walked out of my shop what she was to me," he continues. "Not that I knew the term for it or the magic behind it. I certainly didn't expect her to feel it the same way I did. But . . . *mates*. Such a tangible, undeniable situation. She returned the next day. And the next. Until neither of us could deny what the Fates had clearly deemed."

"The Fates," I say. "I've learned more about them, but I fear there is still a great deal I don't understand."

"Give it time. There's much to learn when it comes to our kingdom's foundations." He nods. "Eirdis spoke of them often," he says. "Sometimes in favor. Other times, not so much." He smiles again. "They're the ones who granted them permission to leave their ethereal domain and come to these lands," he says, tilting his head. "Didn't you know that?"

I part my lips, ready to explain that Ashlanders aren't given the same history lessons as those in the royal cities, but I stop myself. "It's wild to imagine her needing permission for anything," I say instead.

"I often said the same thing." He sighs. "I miss her."

Shock rattles through me at the confession, at the confused and longing look he casts upward.

"I rather thought she'd return to me by now," he continues, almost under his breath.

I recognize that longing, empathize with the ache. I miss Pierce, and we haven't been separated nearly as long.

I can't imagine decades of time. I almost feel sorry for him, but the notion is easily quashed when I remember the lack of trust between us. The hoops he's made me jump through before and *after* being mated to his son.

"Are you here to offer me something else?" I ask. Last year, during the time I spent in the Emerald Wood with Pierce, Brooks sought me out and offered me a new life as long as I stayed away from his son. "Or another task from the list, perhaps?"

"I deserve that," he says, then waves me off. "Believe it or not, I come here quite often."

I blink a few times. I didn't expect that answer.

"It's true," he says. "Not that many people are aware of it."

"The kings, you mean," I say.

"We all handled them going to sleep in different ways," he says. "Some took it better than others."

Baydel. He took it very well, I imagine.

I don't say as much.

"I'll leave you with her, then," I say, heading toward the stairs. I need to meet with Kal and Axl instead of chasing instincts with no rationalization.

"I'm happy you didn't take my offer the last time we met privately," he calls to me.

I pause on the first step, my hand on the marble railing as I tilt my head at him.

"Anyone who would've taken that offer wouldn't be worthy of my son," he continues with a shrug.

"While I agree with you, your majesty," I say as kindly as I can manage, "there will come a time when I'm no longer keen to perform for any of your tests." I plant him with a serious look. "There will come a time when proving myself to you or the RAC will no longer hold the weight it does now." Something flickers inside me, a sense of pride I can't quite place.

Brooks tips his chin, glancing up at Eirdis before focusing back on me. "Let us all hope it doesn't come to that, my dear," he says.

I don't bother bowing before I leave him there, staring up at the statue containing his mate's essence and body—a mausoleum of sorts. A reminder of all he lost.

It's sad, when thinking about it like that, but it's hard for me to linger on pity for the king too long.

CHAPTER 48

Rylee

I freeze just outside Tareena's gardens.

Lucas is there, his fingers sunk into the dirt where we've been safely gathering Tareena's golden flowers for Ivy's antidote.

Is he destroying the rest of the roots we have?

Panic fuels my instincts. I race toward him, seeing him no longer as a king but as a threat to all we're working toward. I grip his shoulder, yanking him backward so hard, his hand comes out of the soil, and the two of us topple onto the paved walkway surrounding it.

"What the—" He grunts as he spots me.

"You can't!" I huff, scrambling to my feet, positioning myself between him and the patch of garden.

Lucas looks up at me like I've spoken a language he doesn't understand.

"I can't what?" he asks, shoving to his feet. I rarely get this close to him. Sometimes I forget he's almost as big as Axl. Power flares to life beneath my skin. I really don't want to have to fight him.

"Destroy her gardens," I answer, raising a hand like I'm imploring him, but really, I'm readying my wind, reaching for his airways.

He scrunches his brow. "I'm not." He wipes his hand, soil falling from his fingertips. Just as quickly, he snaps them. "Look."

I whirl around, scared I missed something—

"Oh," I say, my shoulders dropping. Sprouts that weren't there moments ago creep up from the dirt. I lower my hand, turning back to him. "You're . . . helping?"

"Axl told me about the antidote. Said you found it in her flowers," he explains.

I part my lips. Shut them. His power is tied to the earth, close to Ivy's but infinitely deeper. I never thought he'd be on our side. Still, I'm wary, not taking my eyes off him as he cautiously steps around me, crouching and touching the soil again.

The sprouts stretch toward the sun, the green stems curling and spiraling until buds form. A few of them bloom, the stunning golden petals shimmering.

"That's incredible," I say, unable to hold back the wonder in my voice. "Thank you."

He clears his throat as he draws his hand back. "We built this space together, my mate and I," he says, eyeing the massive gardens around us. His gaze lingers in the distance, on the back of Tareena's temple. "Surely Axl told you that."

"He did," I answer. "The first time he brought me here." We both stand again, looking over the lush space. "He also told me he's been taking care of it alone."

Lucas nods. "I was angry with her when she went to sleep. It took me a decade to get over it," he says, then shrugs. "I'm not sure if I've ever really healed from losing her. I . . . Coming out here brought all that back."

"I understand that." I agree with the king, a shocker to all. "If one of my mates left me to protect the realm . . . I know it's an admirable thing, but I'm selfish enough not to care about such honors."

Lucas flashes me a half smile. It looks genuine. He studies me, searching for something long enough that I throw up internal walls to contain the power rumbling inside me. I long for the day I don't have to hide who I really am anymore. For a time when no one has to live in fear just for being born different from others.

"Brooks mentioned he spoke with you at Eirdis's temple yesterday."

I nod.

"He trusts you," he says on a breath. "I have a harder time opening up."

I arch a brow. "I gathered that." I also thought he had little care for anything other than himself, and yet he's here helping replenish the flowers we need.

"My son loves you," he says, eyeing the token on my wrist.

"And I him," I say.

Lucas glances at the flowers again. "I remember that kind of love," he says, his smile widening. "She came into my life like a thunderstorm over the ocean, wild and unpredictable. Addictive. I couldn't get enough of her. She opened my mind to a world I couldn't imagine. Sometimes I wonder why I ever let her go to sleep in the first place."

I stay quiet, instinct prickling on the back of my neck. I casually glance behind me, worried some danger lurks at the garden's edge, but I see nothing.

"Sometimes I wonder why I didn't *fight* her on it. Tell her that sacrifice for the realm wasn't worth it."

That gets my attention, and my heart actually aches for him in this moment. Again, I can't imagine any one of my mates doing anything like that. And it might make me a selfish asshole, but I wouldn't trade any of their lives for the entire universe.

"Did you?" I carefully ask. "Did you try to talk her out of it?"

It's likely a fool's question. He doesn't have to answer me. He doesn't even have to speak to me. This is the longest conversation we've ever had.

Lucas's eyes wax over a bit as he turns inward. He shakes his head. "It's murky."

"What do you mean?"

He shrugs. "That entire time feels like a dream," he explains. "Axl was young and wild. He rarely slept. We were tired, despite our powers. But even with all that . . ." He stops himself, then shrugs another time. "I can't quite grasp onto the memory. I don't even remember what I said to her before she went to sleep."

I swallow around the knot of emotion that lodges in my throat. That's sad. How can he not remember? Though, I know trauma like losing a loved one can be suppressed in different ways. There are things I can't remember about my parents because of the pain stitched around their memory.

"I'm sorry." I say the words before I can stop them. Before I can remind myself that this is Lucas Dawson, one of the four kings of Lumathyst. A king who ate dessert while his fellow king forced a demi to dance themselves to death in front of me. A king who seems to too often turn away when horrendous acts are taking place. "I truly am," I continue, because it's honest. To not be able to remember that last moment with his mate . . . The notion makes me shudder.

Lucas blinks a few times, then clears his throat. "I'll come back tomorrow," he says, nodding to the flowers. "I don't want to overdo it and have them overgrown and killing each other."

"Flowers can do that?"

"Sometimes," he says. "It's all about balance." His words remind me of Ivy, and for half a second, I wonder if the two would get along. Bond over their similar powers.

"Thank you," I say, but it sounds almost like a question.

He laughs, and it reminds me of Axl's laugh, which causes a kernel of trust to grow between us even though I know it shouldn't. "Give me time," he says, heading past me. He stops at the edge of the garden path. "Once you're queen, I'll try to prove to you that I'm not as big a dick as I seem."

Shock keeps me rooted in place, speechless as he turns down the path and out of sight. Was that his way of telling me I've earned his vote?

CHAPTER 49

Rylee

"You're pacing again, love," Kal says from where he sits on a crimson cushion near the pool in his sitting room.

I pause, turning to look down at him.

He's right. I'm pacing. I've *been* pacing.

"What can we do?" Axl asks, sitting on the opposite side of the small pool.

"Voting Day is *two* weeks away," I say by way of answer, plopping down on a cushion near the edge of the pool. "Pierce and Jax aren't home yet. We've helped cure those sickened by Tox but don't know why Tox was created in the first place. Is it just to hurt people with powers and boost those who don't? Or is there more? I'm no closer to stopping the Fader attacks, and I can barely sleep from dreams of Evaluna." I tuck my knees against my chest and prop my chin atop them. "I don't know what we're going to do."

Kal and Axl share a look, some silent communication as Axl nods to Kal.

"This is what we're going to do," Kal says, setting his drink down and shifting to fully face me. "We're going to face Voting Day together, no matter if it's just the three of us or not. We've done absolutely everything the

RAC and kings have asked us to. Risen to every trial and test and request. There's nothing more we can do now to secure votes. We have the majority favor in our cities, and you've garnered favor in every city you've visited." His words are calm and confident, helping unwind the knots of tension in my chest.

"We will face Voting Day," he continues. "And we will win."

My eyes meet his, hopeful. "And then what?" I dare to ask.

"Then we live happily ever after," Axl says with a laugh.

"Then we get to work," Kal says, smiling at him, then me. "We take the thrones. Our fathers take up the annual offerings to the goddesses. Our chancellors will fully transition into positions of power for our cities as we move into the palace. From the royal city, we will work to make the changes we've always dreamed about. Starting with elevating the lower classes, giving them rights that never should've been stripped from them. We'll work on programs to help the process run smoothly, and we'll make sure demis understand there is no need to fear or hide anymore. We'll announce your powers, the one you were born with and those you've acquired. And during all that, we will put an end to the Fader atrocities, one way or another."

"And then we'll live happily ever after," Axl says again as he crawls over to my cushion, nudging my legs down so he can rest his head in my lap. I laugh at the attention-seeking move, running my fingers through his long silken hair. "We'll travel during peace times," he says. "And eat ourselves silly. There will be weeks we won't leave the palace, because we're insatiable for you."

Heat streaks through me.

"We'll take to the skies at midnight," Kal offers, scooting closer to smooth his hand down my back. "Where I'll worship you under the stars."

"Lumathyst will prosper," Axl adds. "Because there's no other option with a queen like you."

I'm blushing now, my heart thumping with hope.

But it's just a hope, which makes my soul hesitant to allow myself to dream.

"That sounds truly beautiful," I say. I won't voice the alternatives. Won't mention that so many things must go right in order for all those beautiful dreams to come true. Because what would be the point? Kal is right. We've done everything we can. Now we just have to wait.

Have to wait for the vote.

Have to wait for the kings to willingly give up their thrones.

Wait for Pierce to come home.

Wait for Jax.

A knife slips into my heart. A sense of foreboding I can't shake any time I think of him.

No word. I know he's not usually big on communication, but I would've thought he'd write by now. At least to let us know he's all right.

He hasn't. I can still feel the bond between us, stretched thin across the distance, but it's there. That alone gives me hope that he's okay. If he weren't . . . I'd *know.*

I'd feel it.

I just have to be patient, but with Voting Day approaching, I have little patience left.

CHAPTER 50

Rylee

I'm out the door of Kal's home before I fully register what I'm doing. One second, we were all having a quiet, comfortable brunch on the terrace, and the next, I'm racing toward the gates.

"You're home!" I call out, my voice cracking the second I get the gates open. My bond is flaring, pulsing, *begging*.

"Darling," Pierce says, catching me as I launch myself against him.

I wrap my arms around his neck, trembling with excitement. I draw away enough to meet his eyes, and we share a silent moment before his lips find mine.

The kiss is an awakening, a deep breath after being underwater for too long. Sparks erupt down my back as we connect, our bond glittering to life.

He finally sets me on my feet, scooping up the leather satchel he dropped earlier, and we head back to Kal's home, where Kal and Axl linger in the entryway, giving us our time.

Once we cross the threshold, it's their turn to hug Pierce and clap him on the back with relieved smiles.

"Come. I must show you all something." Pierce glances between the three of us, then heads to Kal's study.

Ash barely acknowledges Pierce from where he's plopped in one of the chairs in the study, merely lifting his head before laying it back down. He looks more annoyed at us disturbing his nap than anything.

Pierce unbuckles the satchel, then pulls out iron canisters, placing them on Kal's large desk.

"I got to know Gem and Eni a little better," he says, unscrewing the canisters and carefully slipping out the scrolls nestled inside. "They granted me access to the extensive libraries we only got a glimpse of while staying there," he says, fingering a scroll, then unrolling it. "And I found myself . . . intrigued."

"Uh-oh," Axl says, looking over Pierce's shoulder and down at the parchment. "When the Mind says he's intrigued, it either means infinite boredom for us or equally as much trouble."

"Which is it?" Kal asks, a crease forming in his brow as he looks at the parchment, too. "Histories of Lumathyst?" He glances at Axl.

"Boring, then," Axl says.

"You would think," Pierce counters, beckoning me over. He's got that look in his brown eyes, that twinkle of a mystery. I understand his excitement, especially when there's not much he doesn't solve with his powers. "But look at this," he says, shifting so I can sit in the chair at Kal's desk, the three of them standing behind me. Pierce points to a section of the parchment.

I read the inked script carefully. Some of the words are faded with age. "What am I reading?" I ask when I've skimmed over the recounted agriculture advances, goddess decrees, and demi risings. "Nothing I haven't heard about before."

"Exactly," he says, as if that is answer enough.

Axl rolls his eyes before nudging me. "He does this all the time," he says. "You get used to it."

I smile.

"Note the date, darling," Pierce urges me.

I do. Another bolt of confusion hits me. "That year . . ." I scan the text over and over again. "Isn't that the year we went to war with Erithmore?"

Pierce claps his hands, nodding. "It is."

"But the historians aren't mentioning it?"

"They're not just 'not mentioning it,'" he says. "There's no mention of a war with Erithmore at all."

Kal takes a step back, folding his arms over his chest as he eyes Pierce. "How is that possible?"

"I don't know," Pierce says. "At first, I thought I had the date wrong. Or perhaps the historians filed it wrong. I pored through every record Silvac has. There's no mention of a war with Erithmore at any time in Lumathyst's history."

My blood runs cold.

"Could Silvac's records have been destroyed?" Axl asks. "That happens all the time. Written claims are lost to time or natural disasters. We had an entire rare section lost to a coastal storm a decade ago."

"I wondered that, too," Pierce says. "But there are records upon records of the happenings of Lumathyst during and around that time frame. Nothing ever mentions a war with another realm."

"But *our* records do," Kal counters.

"Yes, they do," Pierce says. "And where do we get our historical texts from?"

"Shit," Axl says.

"The kings' scribes and Occuli have always kept the historical texts up to date," Kal answers.

"What about the demis?" I ask. "That was around the same time. And the goddesses went to sleep to protect us from that uprising. There has to be an account of that." I tap the parchment before me. "The historian here mentions Goddess Tareena's blessing of the harvest that year, for fuck's sake."

"Precisely my thought," Pierce says, unscrewing another canister and unraveling another scroll. He places it gently atop the other one. "Which is why I went digging for this," he explains, taking a step back for the three of us to read it.

"The Goddesses of Lumathyst." I read the bold script aloud. "Chose four mortal mates . . ." I go on, recounting the tale of them choosing their mates, embodying them with powers, having children, and creating the Choosing. "Wait," I gasp, turning to look up at Pierce. "There's a huge section missing here." I point to where the script simply disappears. Stops mid-sentence, and the page ends.

Pierce fingers the ends of the scroll. "You see this?" he asks.

"It's rigid," I say, heart thumping against my chest. "Torn?"

Pierce nods.

I sink back into the chair.

"Wait," Axl grumbles. "You're saying the best historians across the realms, the *Occuli*, who protect their libraries with ancient magic, don't have a record of the war with Erithmore or the goddesses acting as wards in order to protect us from that war?"

Pierce's shoulders drop as if all the tension has flown right from his body. "Yes," he finally answers.

I push out of the chair, turning to face him. "What does that imply?"

"That someone wanted to bury the history," he answers. "You see why I couldn't leave until I searched everything?"

I nod, fully understanding. "Did you ask Gem and Eni?"

"I did. They were unaware of our histories. Their parents didn't pass down the information to them, and they never thought it pressing to look into ours beyond our peace treaties."

"Is that normal? For other realms to not know each other's history? Especially when it comes to wars?"

"Sometimes," he explains. "But it would make sense, if someone wanted to bury our history."

"Who would benefit from wiping that away?"

"That's the question," he says.

"Another fucking question," Axl grumbles. "Add it to the massive pile of shit we don't understand already. It's growing daily. I'm over it."

"Welcome home," I say with a half-hearted laugh.

Pierce draws me against him, holding me close. "I'm glad to be home. We'll get to the bottom of this. It's a low priority, in the grand scheme of things."

"Unnerving," I say.

"Quite."

That buried instinct inside me feels like a plucked string of an instrument, a sound reverberating inside me, beckoning me to explore it further.

The door to Kal's study closes, the sound alerting me to Kal and Axl's quiet exit.

Pierce looks down at me longingly, tipping my chin up with gentle fingers. "I missed you," he says.

"So much," I agree, heart thumping against my ribs.

He dips down, brushing his lips over mine in a teasing kiss as his hands roam to my hips. He walks me backward, picking me up and putting me on the edge of the desk so we're closer to eye level. My hands splay against his chest as he kisses me more deeply.

I breathe him in, flames igniting beneath my skin. "We have so much to catch up on," I say between his kisses.

"Later?" he asks, drawing away to scan my face.

"Later."

His lips are on mine in another breath, and I forget everything I'm supposed to be worrying about.

CHAPTER 51

Rylee

"You're running out of time." Evaluna's voice rings through the recesses of my mind.

I slowly sit up, blinking the sleep from my eyes.

Pierce is asleep next to me, Kal and Axl having retired to their rooms in Kal's home hours ago.

"Voting Day?" I ask, finding Evaluna on the balcony.

It's always the balcony. The moon is always in view.

"Can you blame me?" she says, motioning to the moon and stars.

I'm sure it glows brighter at her attention.

"No," I say honestly. "I've always loved the night." I always felt freer with the darkness shining over me. No daylight hours threatening to break me in the Ashlands. "You keep coming to me in my dreams," I continue. "And then what you say usually turns out to be true."

"Is there a question in there?"

I shake my head. "I feel so lost."

Evaluna looks at me with pity. "All do who are put in your situation."

"What can I do to help you?" I ask, urgency rising inside me. "To help the others? I feel like that's what I need to do. But I don't know how." I shake my head. "Also, it seems grandiose of me to assume you need help from me."

Evaluna's eyes widen as she nods.

I don't know what she's agreeing with.

She opens her mouth, then shuts it. The same strangled speech I've seen her do before. The Fates preventing her from—

A memory slashes through my mind. One of my sister acting the same as Evaluna. Like she couldn't tell me what she wanted to. I thought it was a show of mistrust, but . . .

"Something is preventing you from speaking plainly to me." I don't ask. She's said as much before. "The Fates."

She nods.

"Could that be the same for regular people in Lumathyst?"

"Your sister," she says, nodding again. "Though it's not the Fates that tie her tongue."

Cold shock trickles through me. "You were able to confirm that just now," I say, tilting my head. "Some things you've been able to work around in telling me."

"Some things aren't forbidden to say . . . if one asks correctly."

"No offense, but the Fates and whoever is stopping anyone else are a real pain in the ass."

Evaluna's lips twitch into a smirk that reminds me of Jax.

That hollow space in my soul aches.

"What else can I be missing?" I mumble to myself. "The Faders?"

She blinks.

"My sister?"

Evaluna's eyes flare, flecks of starlight flickering in shining silver.

My sister. Evaluna says I'm running out of time when it comes to my sister.

"Is everything connected?" I ask. "All the questions we keep running into?"

Another small, almost imperceptible nod.

"It would be much easier if you could just wake up and tell me this in person." I laugh. "It's hard to get people to believe me when I tell them you visit my dreams." I run my fingers through my hair. "Can Jax dreamwalk?"

"Jax is my son," she says with ease, relief lining her gorgeous features as she speaks freely. "He can do a great many things, if he decides to."

"I miss him."

"I know you do. He misses you," she says, shocking me.

"You know?" I ask, hopeful. "Is he okay? Why isn't he home yet? Is he on his way?" The questions pour from me quicker than water through a net.

Evaluna opens her mouth, then closes it again. "He misses you. You're running out of time."

Right. Can't stand here and steep in my separation from her son. I need to move. She's hinting all this has to do with my sister, even going so far as to suggest something is preventing her from talking to me, too.

Hope threatens to build in my heart, but I keep it latched down.

"You keep much under lock and key," she says on an exhaled breath. "It's like you don't trust yourself."

"I've made mistakes before," I say. "I don't want to again."

She tilts her head. "And yet," she says, "sometimes trusting yourself is the only way to truly understand yourself." She casts her eyes toward the sky. "Hurry."

My eyes open, and I'm back in bed with Pierce. No longer on the balcony.

Ash meows at the foot of the bed, grumbling as I shift the covers aside, slip out of bed, and get dressed.

I cast a look at Pierce, contemplating waking him. Waking the others.

Something gives me pause. If Erin is being forced to not tell me certain things, then she certainly won't open up if I bring them with me.

The last time I ventured out like this, Faders attacked. I have to hope that won't happen again. Especially with Evaluna's urgency.

I leave a note and head out of the Ruby Aire, bound on velomage toward Obsidian City. As I ride there, I unlock the doors on the powers rippling along the bonds. Pierce's snapped back to me sometime in the night when we were lost in each other. Same for Axl and Kal. I don't let them fully free, but I can feel them awaken beneath my skin.

I don't want to be caught unaware again, and now that the antidote runs through my veins, I have no fear of Tox.

I park the velomage, heading to the small hut in the hopes she'll be there. It's a fool's hope, but I have to try.

"Pushy, for a goddess, isn't she?" Erin's voice fills the small space the second I close the door behind me.

"Evaluna told you to come here, too?" I ask.

"Clearly."

"I could strangle you," I say, heart thudding against my chest. "For last time."

"I saved your life," she fires back.

The fight goes out of me. Erin looks worse than before, her features haggard, her shoulders tense, purple beneath her eyes.

"What's happening to you?" I ask softly.

She forces out a laugh. "Lot more than I bargained for, that's for sure."

"What did you bargain for?" I ask.

She flinches, then shakes her head.

Right. If something is preventing her from speaking, I have to be smarter about the way I ask.

"You dreamed of Evaluna, too. Is this the first time?" A casual enough question.

"Yes," she says. "Honestly, I thought I'd come here and you wouldn't. That it was just a dream."

Chills erupt on my skin. If Evaluna wants us to speak, she can't fully hate Erin for her role. Hope builds again, and this time I let myself feel it.

"I could strangle you for a lot of things, you know," I say.

"Are you keeping a list?" she asks.

"I'm not really a fan of lists," I answer. "Seems like any time I end up on one, I get hurt."

"I understand that more than you know."

"Did you enjoy the Choosing? I was a fan of the strawberries."

Erin laughs. It's almost healing to hear it. "I went for the art."

We share a smile. Hers is slightly broken, but I can see reflections of the sister I knew in her features. "Yours is better. I've already picked out spots for the pieces I'm going to have you paint me once you come to your senses."

Her eyebrows draw together, sadness replacing the familiarity. "Ry . . ."

"After the Choosing," I hedge when she doesn't finish. "You went to the Ruby Aire?" I ask, remembering her painting of Ash near the library.

The light drains from her features. "No."

"Emerald?"

She shakes her head.

"Sapphire?"

Another shake.

"One of the lowers?"

"No."

"Obsidian?"

Another shake.

"You went *nowhere* after the Choosing?"

Erin visibly swallows. "Not for a while. Then I did."

"Where did you go after?"

She parts her lips, then furrows her brow.

"This is asinine."

Erin laughs again, and I smile at her.

"Do they treat you well?" she asks, startling me.

"My mates?" I ask.

"Yes. The Legends of Chaos. Only you would go to the Choosing a single time and suddenly become queen."

"I'm no queen," I say. "And yes, they treat me well. Better than I could've ever imagined. They're mine, and I'm theirs. It's hard to explain how well we fit together."

"That's . . . I understand that."

I tilt my head, taking a step closer to her. "You do?"

She nods.

"Their . . . fathers," she says, almost like she's testing the words. "How do they treat you?"

I shrug. "Some are kind, others less." Though Lucas's help with the flowers has gone a long way in my opinion of him.

"Others."

"Yes, Baydel isn't my biggest fan."

"Baydel." She says his name with emphasis, and I understand that she may not be as intimately familiar with his name as I am.

"Yes, Jax's father."

Erin nods, her eyes widening. "Jax's father," she says.

Instinct has everything inside me narrowing to her body language. The powers inside me twist and push, Pierce's practically begging for attention.

I draw it toward me, holding it fully, and push it toward her mind. She might kill me for it if she knew, but I don't stop until I'm in her mind.

It's *silent*.

Visions flash so quickly I gasp. All through a dense fog that's hard to clearly see through. The palace's balcony. Groups of royals in their finest gowns. The Choosing. Her sneaking in and out of palace rooms, stuffing her pockets with jewels. A shadow looming in the hallway.

The vision speeds up. Stops.

She's slipping on a Fader outfit. Bruises dust her cheek. The heavy sensation of sheer exhaustion and terror. She's drained. So drained. Baydel. He's in a darkened room, in the farthest corner. Erin is looking at him, but he's not looking at her. He's looking at his Occuli, those green flames flickering once more. One is there, standing behind Baydel, his diamond helmet tilted in Erin's direction.

I draw myself out of her mind when the images repeat. No words, no thoughts, just images. I haven't explored enough minds to know if that's normal or not, but I hardly have a second to figure it out. Not when I can't stop the image of Baydel replaying in my mind. Him looking agitated, much like the time Evaluna sent me to find him in secret.

"Will you come back with me?" I ask just as I did last time.

"I can't."

"*Would* you?" I swallow hard. "If you could?"

She parts her lips, then blows out a breath. "Sometimes, I have this dream," she says. "It's the night before the Choosing. The last one I attended. Instead of getting ready for the ball, I pack a bag. Then I pack yours. We say goodbye to Ivy and Layce, grab Ash, and we leave. Sneak aboard a ship heading for Cardrayton or Vleyica. We get seasick," she says, a broken chuckle leaving her lips. "But we manage. And when we set foot in the new realm, we're no longer Erin and Rylee Gray. We're . . . free." Tears make her eyes glisten. She angrily swipes them away. "Then I wake up."

A heaviness tugs at my heart. I can't imagine a life that looks like that. I can't imagine a life without Axl or Kal or Pierce or Jax.

I refuse to believe the price of that happiness is my sister's absence.

"Wake . . . up," she says, the words broken and stuttered.

Their previous sting doesn't hit me. Not now. Not when I have perspective. "What word aren't you able to say?" I whisper under my breath. I even peek into her mind again, hopeful I can glimpse what she's not saying, but it's nothing but the same visions on repeat.

"Jax's father," she says, and I blink. "Do you ever do the same to him?"

A crease forms in my brow.

She taps her temple.

Holy shit, can she sense when I'm entering her mind?

"I'm your sister. I always know when you're spying on me." A soft smile.

I'm frozen. Because what she's implying . . .

She wants me to read Baydel's mind?

"It's an important day today," she says, casting a look out the window at the predawn light filtering through as the sun starts to rise.

"Voting Day," I say.

And Jax has yet to return.

The idea of hearing the vote, of possibly ascending the thrones without him, seems so vehemently *wrong*.

"Busy day," she says. "Lots of action at the palace."

I swallow hard. "Action?"

"Lots of people to see. Uninvited guests might attend."

My blood runs cold. An attack? She's warning me about a Fader attack on the palace.

"When will I see you again?" I ask for confirmation.

"Soon, sis," she says. "Very, very soon."

I silently thank her for the warning, then hug her quickly. "We will end this," I whisper into her ear. Then I push further, into her mind, weaving my words there. *Whoever has a hold on you, who's forcing you to do all of this, I'll find them and end them. You'll be free soon enough. I promise you.*

She hugs me tighter, then releases me. There's a tense look to her eyes, and she parts her lips before closing them.

"Erin?"

"I have to go."

"Wait—"

She flickers out of sight, and the door opens and closes before I can try to follow her. I push through the door, scanning the area despite knowing I won't spot her. She's never found if she doesn't want to be.

There's so much more I wanted to ask her, but now, I have to get home.

Because today is Voting Day. Not only a day that will most certainly change my future, but one that, if my sister's warning is true, will be a massive battle.

And somehow, unsurprisingly, Baydel is right at the head of it.

CHAPTER 52

Rylee

"So, all you have to do is slip into his mind," I say at the tail end of my rant. I started relaying the information I learned immediately when Kal opened the door for me. "He'll be distracted because of the events of Voting Day." It will be an all-day affair, packed with food and drink and dancing, all while the RAC and kings deliberate and hash out who they will be voting for.

"Darling," Pierce says to me with a shake of his head. "Baydel and the other kings have blocked me out since they learned of my powers. I've tried many times to penetrate his mind. He always senses me coming and reinforces his mental shields."

My shoulders sink, the hope disintegrating inside me. "He's at the heart of this," I say. "He always has been." I just didn't know the *why* behind it. Or the endgame. I still don't.

In the beginning, sure, the motivation pointed toward him remaining in power. But now that his son is mated? He doesn't stand a chance. Well, that he knows of. So what's his goal now?

"We don't doubt you," Kal says. "But I've seen it in real time, love. Baydel always blocks him."

"He's on guard whenever he's around," Axl adds.

My eyes widen. "He's always on guard when *you're* around," I repeat, standing from where I'd settled on Kal's couch in the sitting area. "Because he knows how powerful you are. And since the Athanry, he's been playing mostly nice because he fully believes you've all come into your full powers."

"Correct," Pierce affirms, but it almost sounds like a question.

"He wouldn't be on guard for a *nobody*," I say, my heart racing. "For someone who doesn't have power like yours."

Pierce's lips part, as if he wants to argue. "Going into his mind is dangerous."

"Everything we do is dangerous," I counter. "Everything since the Choosing has been a risk. And I'm perfectly fine continuing to take those risks. Especially if it earns us answers. An edge. *Peace*."

Kal shifts on the chair, shaking his head. "I don't like the idea."

I know he doesn't. He never likes anything that puts me in harm's way.

"She can handle it." Axl nods to me.

"Of course she can," Pierce adds.

"I know she can handle it," Kal says. "I just said I don't like it."

I laugh softly, reaching for Kal's hand. He takes mine in his, squeezing it. And as I look at the three of them, concerned gazes and curious intrigue, I wish so badly for Jax to be here.

If he were, he'd be encouraging me to break into his father's mind and leave it in ribbons behind me. But he's not here. And the longer I go without hearing from him, the more nervous I grow.

"He won't expect Rylee," Pierce finally says. "He'll never see her coming."

"He's still one of the most powerful people in Lumathyst," Kal counters.

I press my lips together, hating that *they* should be the most powerful, but aren't, because they gave it all to me.

Gave me all their powers, which I've worked hard to give back permanently but still haven't figured out yet.

"Hedge the bet, then," Axl says with a shrug like it's obvious. Ever the Player looking at all the angles.

"How so?" Pierce asks.

Axl points to me. "I'm sure Ivy has something in her greenhouse. Something easily poured into a drink to loosen him up. Get his defenses down. We could use Tox if need be."

I cringe at the thought. "I'm not comfortable with that," I say. "I know he deserves it, but the idea of doing that . . . it goes against everything I stand for."

"You'll be slipping into his mind," Pierce says gently. "The lines of consent will be crossed."

Oil, thick and grimy, sludges through my veins.

"He shows no regard for consent on a daily basis," Pierce continues. "And you're within your rights to look into his mind. Especially when we have a lead that says he's at the head of all this."

"What if he's not?" I ask, perching on the armrest of Kal's chair. "What if I'm wrong? What if Erin is leading me in the wrong direction?"

"If he's not," Axl offers, "then back out and don't go in there again."

"Set those boundaries," Kal says. "So you can live with them."

I blow out a breath. "This was easier when I thought you'd be doing it," I admit, looking to Pierce. "A coward's admission, but still."

"Not cowardly," Pierce says. "Courageous. And moral. Baydel has never given you any reason to care for his feelings or well-being, and yet here you are, worried about crossing lines. Especially when he gave you no such regard after the Choosing."

The memory of his power sliding over me, of what he tried to do to me and what he tried to force me to do to him, makes me flinch.

"If I could spare you from this," Pierce says, "from seeing what actually is going on in his mind, I would." He shakes his head. "But if I could've done it successfully, I would've already. You're our only shot at this, but if you choose not to do it, we're with you. Either way. We face today together."

"As Legends," I say after a slow breath. "As mates."

They nod, and I focus on Pierce.

"Do you think I can do this?"

"Without a doubt," he says. "But I admit I'm afraid of what you'll see."

I swallow hard. "And if I see nothing indicating he's anything other than a narcissistic prick?"

"Then you leave his mind, return to us, and we continue along the path we've been set upon."

"Okay," I say. "I can do this . . . but can we do a practice session first?"

Pierce nods. Already the power that had partly remained with him is pulsing back down the bond, filling me up so much it's hard to breathe around.

"You can use my mind for practice any time you want," Axl says, that playful smile on his face.

"And mine," Kal offers sincerely.

"You already know the access you have to mine," Pierce says.

I smile at all of them, my heart racing against my chest. I'm really going to do this. I'm going to go into Baydel's mind and hope to survive it.

And my mates are here, encouraging me, willing to let me slip into their consciousness, the most intimate parts of them laid bare for me.

"Okay," I say again, confidence building with their support. "Let's do this."

CHAPTER 53

Rylee

I never truly allowed myself to visualize this day.

Voting Day.

The day we've been careening toward since the Athanry. The day my mates deserve to take their rightful place as rulers of Lumathyst. The day that will, hopefully, change our realm's future for the better. I certainly never imagined I'd wake up with the intent to slip into the mind of one of the most powerful people in Lumathyst.

"I might throw up," I say, half jokingly, as Ivy and Layce help me get ready in the morning.

"That rug is a thousand years old," Mirren calls from across the room. "Don't."

I laugh, the action helping wash away some of the churning in my stomach.

Layce is applying my makeup. Ivy is selecting a gown. It all feels so familiar.

A full-circle sensation, yet everything is upside down. I'm no longer a girl sneaking into a party I shouldn't be at in the hopes of finding her missing sister. I'm a princess of Lumathyst, mated to the Legends of Chaos, boldly going into an event with the intent to put an end to the injustices within the kingdom.

"You all need to arm yourselves," I say once I've slipped into the flowing black gown Ivy has chosen for me. The yards of featherlight fabric flare at my waist and hang down, easily concealing the dark leggings I wear beneath it, along with the boots and the blades strapped to my thighs.

On the outside, I look like a princess awaiting the approval of a group of people I never should've needed it from. Beneath the surface, I'm armed with more than just steel. My mates' barely contained powers roam beneath my skin. Pierce's are dominating my soul the most in this moment.

"You really think Erin was giving you a warning?" Layce asks, selecting a few knives from the chest I have in the corner and hiding them beneath her skirts, too.

"I do," I say. "If I'm wrong, then you're armed for no reason. If I'm right and the Faders decide to attack the palace today, then the last thing I want is you unprepared." Acid bubbles up the back of my throat. I hope I'm wrong. "Don't hold back," I say because I can't stop myself. "If you need to use your powers, do it."

Ivy arches a brow at me. "You're serious?"

"Dead serious," I say. "One way or another, we're coming out of the shadows. Either we win the vote and my mates become kings, or we lose it, and . . ."

Goddess, if we lose it and the kings deny them their seats . . .

"You'll challenge them," Layce finishes for me.

I nod, a knot of guilt forming in my throat.

"The princes don't know that," Mirren says, stepping toward me with her head tilted. "Do they?"

I shake my head. "They wouldn't let me take the risk if they did," I say. "And I hate keeping anything from them. You *know* I do. But they deserve those thrones. Lumathyst deserves them as kings."

"And you," Mirren says. "Stop leaving yourself out of the equation. You aren't some tool the princes needed. You're their mate. Lumathyst needs you as their queen."

I open and close my mouth a few times. I don't know what to say to that. "Be on your guard," I say, then turn to Mirren. "Please?"

"I've lived a good long life, girl." Mirren smirks. "I'm always on my guard."

The elevator doors glide open, revealing the glorious glass balcony, the sun glittering off its smooth surface. There are a lot of people up here for the voting event, though not as many as the Choosing. The kings, the Royal Authority Council and their families, and a few exclusively invited guests. The elite enforcers and a dozen or so regular ones. My friends will join us momentarily.

After a deep breath, I take the first step out of the elevator, donning a mask of gratitude and civility as we weave through the crowd. It's not that I'm not grateful for the Royal Authority Council; I *am*. The idea of a group of elected officials to check the kings is a wonderful one. I'm more upset that they never truly served a purpose until it came time for my mates to ascend the throne. They were complicit in the atrocities some of the kings' laws enforced, and while it may have been out of fear, it's still wrong.

Another change we'll have to make.

Change. The most important motivation driving all of this.

Change for Lumathyst. For the better.

I focus on that as we mingle, sampling the food prepared for the event while music filters through the space, casting an upbeat backdrop to my increasing fear.

I glance over at Pierce, Axl, and Kal, all remaining nearby, covertly watching me as they pretend to be interested in the small talk around them.

We have a plan. In and out. A small glimpse of what's in Baydel's head, and that's it. Then, at the first sign of the trouble Erin hinted at, I'm to join the three of them, none of us left vulnerable or alone this time.

Ivy and Layce and Mirren join the event soon after, eating and sticking to the shadows, ever watchful.

After an hour of this farce with no attacks or hints of one, I'm hopeful Erin was wrong or I misunderstood.

I've had my eye on Baydel the entire time, watching him carefully. He's barely left Margreet's side, like the past events. She's hanging on his every word, looking up at him like he created the stretch of endless blue sky above us.

My stomach turns.

It's now or never. He's fully immersed in conversation with her, her father, and a few other members of the RAC, his Occuli not far away. And One. The elite is there, motionless as he watches his charge.

Luckily for me, I won't be waging a physical attack today. I would hate to die by One's hand. He wouldn't make it quick.

I have to hope no Occuli up here, Baydel's or otherwise, senses my invasion.

"Come, mate," Pierce says, guiding me to a table near the edge of the balcony. "Let's sit and play while we wait for the verdict." He's speaking louder than he normally would, drawing just enough attention for the guests to see us sit down, a game board between us.

A task to cover for my deep concentration. After all, anyone brave enough to take on the Mind needs to focus.

Ivy, Layce, and Mirren also head over to us, sitting near Kal and Axl, creating a half circle that helps keep me from view but looks natural enough.

Adrenaline spirals through me now that we're all set. Pierce will make comments on my plays, but he'll really be playing solo. It's the perfect time.

The *only* time.

My stomach rolls, nausea washing over me in a wave. I might actually throw up.

Later.

I can break down and panic later. Right now, the clock is ticking.

And I don't have much time. The most powerful king in Lumathyst will only be distracted for so long.

I swallow down the panic, the icy fear threatening to freeze me to the spot, and cast Pierce's power toward Baydel's mind.

CHAPTER 54

Rylee

Baydel's mind is a fortress, a mass of steel doors and black rock. Everything about his mental shields is a warning I feel in my bones: Run away. Run *far* away.

I don't. Can't. Instead, I use Pierce's power, slipping inside the cracks like the tiniest of spiders.

Glistening silver doors line the pathways of his mind, everything locked up tight. Frost crackles along the outside of the doors, icicles dripping from the tops like tears.

I shiver, my mental presence feeling the cold bite.

There must be a hundred doors that I can see, all down different hallways that spread out into four sections.

I blow out a breath. Of course the answers wouldn't be sitting here like floating visions, immediately pointing to whatever it is I need to know. Goddess *damn* it. I'm tired.

I reach for the door nearest me, pushing it open with little effort. My fingertips sting from the snap of cold, but I immediately forget it as the door shuts behind me.

"Please, stop!" A little boy is crying, writhing on the ground as another young boy stands over him.

They look alike—one is slightly taller, but they share the same features. Elongated face, green eyes, blond hair.

Recognition hits me after another moment. The crying boy is Baydel.

And the boy above him must be his brother, from how alike they look.

"Please," he cries again.

The older boy slaps him across his face so hard it splits his lip.

I flinch, backing away from the scene as if that will help the hurt.

"Weak," the older boy says. "That's all you'll ever be. Even Mother thinks so. You're nothing like us. Too much like our father."

Baydel wipes the blood from his mouth. He's trembling, tears streaking down his face. He doesn't attempt to get up. It's like he's done it before and knows exactly what will happen.

"I do like using you for practice, though. Mother says it's important to practice." The boy leans down, his face an inch from Baydel's. "You like to help me practice, don't you, Baydel?"

Baydel doesn't meet the boy's eyes but dips his head. "Yes, brother."

"Say it."

"I love to help you practice."

The boy smirks, satisfied with himself. "Good. We'll begin again. This time, try not to shit yourself."

I swallow hard, emotion clogging my throat as the brother closes his eyes.

Baydel screams, his eyes glazing over as he sees something I can't. Terror rolls off him in waves. Sticky, heavy terror. The suffocating kind.

Young Baydel soils himself.

The brother laughs.

Either emotion or mind control, I'm not sure which. He was born with this power?

What—

I fall backward through the door, something forcing me out. My heart is heavy, but I push on to the next door. My hand shakes as I shove it open and walk through.

"You're excited, right, Baydel?" An older man sits in a small boat, smiling down at a young Baydel, though a few years older than the last memory. The two

are looking toward the horizon as the boat dips with the waves of what looks like the ocean of Sapphire Cove.

"I am," Baydel says.

"We'll do well here," the older man says. "We'll do well and then come back. It'll make your mother and brother so proud. You'll see."

Baydel turns away from the man, who can't see the darkness lining his youthful features as he shakes his head. "I don't ever want to go back," he says under his breath—

I'm shoved out again, the effect jarring like a punch. I pick a different hallway, assuming this one is comprised of more of Baydel's past. It's not what I'm here for.

I go to the second hallway, electing to go to the farthest door, hoping there's some semblance of order here. I shove through it.

"You can't possibly expect me to go along with that," Baydel says. He looks much like the man I know as he speaks to . . .

Evaluna.

"Don't you want better for him?" she asks, a soft, loving smile on her face. That smile and the simple nightgown she wears, her hair down and freshly brushed, make her look almost mortal. She stands before him in a bedchamber. "This will ensure there's not an imbalance. I've told you before, the Fates will not take kindly—"

"Damn the Fates," Baydel cuts her off.

"Baydel," she says in warning. "For Jax. We can give our power to the realm. Enrich its soil, its waters, the very atmosphere even more than we already have. It will level the balance for everyone. No more power struggle. No more infighting. You know I don't want him to grow up in that kind of world. For any of them to."

"You and the others have already created the terms of the Choosing for them, and they're barely three years old," Baydel argues. He's pacing now. Visibly agitated. "There won't be an imbalance then. Isn't that enough?"

"I thought it might be," she says, looking like she's questioning herself.

"It will be," he says, returning to her. He takes her hands in his. "We don't need to abandon our power to live a good life with our son."

"But the fighting," she says. "Between all of us, and now with the whispers of unrest with the demis . . . I can't stand it."

"I know," he says. "But they will not struggle with such things. When the time comes, they'll have one mate. No power struggles. She'll ground them, just like you and the others intended it."

Evaluna doesn't look convinced. "We sense more," she says. "Something awful is coming. I can't risk Jax—"

"You won't. He's safe. I would never let anything happen to him."

She studies him, then her shoulders drop. "Will you think about it?" she asks. "Please, Baydel? I know in my heart it's the right path."

He nods. "I will consider living as a mortal with you," he says. "But only if the time should come that we truly need to—"

I'm shoved out again, my head spinning. Evaluna wanted to abandon her powers and live as a mortal with Baydel? For Jax? What awful danger could she sense? The war with Erithmore? The one we can't find record of? Or was it the demi uprising?

I swallow hard, racing to the next hallway. I dip into the first door—

"You found me," Baydel says, standing in a darkened alleyway in what looks like Obsidian City.

"I never lost you, baby brother." The boy from before, Baydel's brother, is older. While he looks like Baydel, there's something about him, something . . . other. Maybe it's his eyes? They have a sheen to them that's almost gray over the green now.

And there's a man between them, on his knees, bound and gagged.

"Why are you here?" Baydel asks, barely acknowledging the other man. "Never mind. Release him." He points to the man, who is staring up at him imploringly.

His brother shakes his head, stepping around the man and toward Baydel. "Not so scared anymore, are we, little Baydel?" He smirks. "Smart move, mating a goddess. Never thought you'd manage to gather powers of your own. But I'm still Mother's favorite."

Baydel rolls his eyes. "You always will be."

He reaches out a gloved hand toward Baydel, who jerks away from his touch. "Relax." He laughs. "If I wanted your measly body control powers, they'd be mine." He slips off the glove, waggling his fingers at him.

What? What does he mean, his powers would be his?

"Why are you here?" Baydel asks again.

"Why wouldn't *I be here?" he asks, turning back to the man on his knees. "Lumathyst has prospered. And your mate and her friends have made this an absolute breeding ground for powerful beings. Demis, you call them?" He sucks in a loud breath, reaching his hand toward the man's neck. "I can practically taste them." He eyes Baydel. "Let's see if I'm right."*

"Don't—" Baydel is cut off when his brother grabs the bound man by the throat.

The man seizes, as if the touch is lightning. Then his eyes roll back in his skull, his entire body convulsing. He's not making a sound; he's clenching his jaw too hard against whatever Baydel's brother is doing to him.

He releases him, and the man falls to the ground in a heap, his skin leeched of color in the most unnatural way.

Oh my goddess. He looks exactly like the people we've been finding throughout Lumathyst. The ones we assumed had taken too much Tox. But this . . . What did he do to him?

"Mmm," he moans, head tipped toward the sky. When he looks back at Baydel, his eyes are brighter green than they were before. "Tasty." He snaps his fingers, and fire dances on the tip. "Look at that," he says. "What a useful tool that demi possessed."

That demi . . .

He . . . he drained his power?

How can he do that?

"Think of the feast me and mine will have."

Apprehension bursts on the back of my neck.

"You can't," Baydel says, flicking his wrist.

The brother flinches, then laughs maniacally. "Not bad, baby brother. But not good enough. You're still weak."

Anger rages over Baydel's features. "I'm no longer the brother you once knew."

"Sure," he says.

"Leave," Baydel demands. "You've had enough fun. Take your people out of my kingdom and go back to Erithmore. You've already left too many bodies—"

"Or what? You'll sic your mate on me?" He tilts his head. "You haven't yet," he continues. "There must be a reason."

"I don't need her to fight my battles—"

"But you do," he cuts him off. "That must sting. Having your power so easily stripped from you."

"How did you know she could do that?"

"I know a great many things," he says. "Siphons know all about taking power."

Siphon? That's what he is? He mentioned his people . . . Are there more like him?

"She's not a siphon. She's a goddess," Baydel argues. "There's a difference."

"Power is power. She giveth, she can taketh away." He eyes him. "I bet she already has."

Baydel is silent.

Another laugh. "How that must irk you. To taste greatness, and then poof—nothing. Think of what she'll do if you upset her. If she grows bored *with you."*

"Enough."

"I could help you with that problem," he says.

"I don't need your help."

"Sure you do. That's why you haven't told her about me. Told her about the presents I've been leaving in your streets." He casts a look toward the dead demi behind him.

Baydel narrows his gaze but doesn't argue.

His brother grins. "What if she decides your thirst for power is too much? What if the others decide they're done with this realm and return to the celestial plane with the Fates? They'll take your powers with them." He tilts his head. "You'd beg for my help then."

"Help with what?"

"With keeping you in power," he answers. "I could do it. You know I can."

Baydel scoffs. "What would be your price?"

He points at Baydel before slipping his glove back on. "You remember how much I love bargains—"

I'm shoved out of the doorway, like some magical force has thrown me from it. My head burns. Baydel's brother is a siphon from Erithmore? And there are more like him? My knees shake as I stumble, running right into another door . . .

Baydel is in a room I've never seen before, lifting the lid on the decorative box holding the Athanry elixirs. He picks up the first vial, uncorks it, and spills a clear liquid inside. He gently swirls the mixture, then recorks it and places it back in the box.

"Are you sure?" Frenrick asks him.

"Yes," he says. "She's defiant. She fights me at every turn. She's unwilling to pay the price for greatness. She has no concept of sacrifice." He shakes his head. "Had they only Chosen Margreet, we wouldn't be in this situation."

"If the princes find out—"

"They won't," Baydel snaps. "It's miraculous to survive the transformation into immortality. They'll think she perished in the process. They'll have another Choosing. And I'll make sure they Choose right this time."

The Occuli dips his head—

I'm pushed out of the doorway and drop to my knees in the hallway.

Baydel's memories spear me from every direction. The conversation with his brother. The bargain they were preparing to strike. The poison. His mention of sacrifice.

A deep sense of foreboding chills me to my bones, the questions swirling into a whirlpool of terror.

I squeeze my hand, concentrating on drawing myself back and back, as far away from here as I can.

I open my eyes, no longer in Baydel's mind.

I'm at the table, playing a game with Pierce.

I stand up so fast I knock the chair over.

"Darling?" Pierce is on his feet, Axl and Kal coming toward me, too.

I don't really see them. Not as I spin around.

Not as I shove past the other kings and knock Margreet out of the way.

Not as I grab Baydel's throat with both hands and squeeze with all the force of Kal's power.

CHAPTER 55

Rylee

"What did you do?" Wrath undulates from every fiber of my being. "What was the price?" I squeeze his neck harder. "What was it? What did you bargain for?"

I can't think straight. Not when every instinct is roaring at me.

Baydel's mouth opens and shuts as he gapes for breath, his hands floundering against mine as he tries to free himself of my grasp—

A hit to the chest sends me flying backward. The invisible force of Baydel's power. I crash against Kal, who topples with me to the ground, breaking most of my fall.

"You've gone mad!" Baydel gasps as he clambers to standing. "You see this? *This* is what you're about to vote in for the throne? One. Do your fucking job!"

One steps in front of Baydel, a hand on the hilt of his sword as the other elites take a stance in front of their kings, like I'm a threat to them all.

Maybe I am. But whatever bargain Baydel made . . . I know it has to do with everything that's happened. I just don't know how.

Kal helps me to my feet. Power ripples along my skin. I curl my fingers, poised to *make* him tell me—

An explosion rocks the balcony so hard cracks spiderweb their way beneath our feet. Smoke covers everything. My ears ring, my vision sparkling before it clears.

Faders.

Three dozen of them.

Magical blasters blister the air, hitting targets at random. I see one of the potentials' fathers, Duke Windsor, go down like a stone. Screams erupt among the chaos, the Royal Authority Council and their families scrambling, terror lining their features as they try to dodge the shots, ducking behind overturned tables or racing for the elevators.

I step toward the fray, halting in my tracks when I see a Fader who's not wearing any gloves. He grabs hold of Duke Windsor's wife, who still clings to his lifeless body, and she immediately seizes. Seconds. It takes her *seconds* to slump over her husband, joining him in death.

I gape, noting the other six Faders not wearing gloves.

"Siphons," I mutter, ice splintering my veins. "They're siphons."

"What?" Kal asks, hauling me backward as a shot snaps by us.

"I—" The explanation lodges in my throat. "Layce, no!"

She doesn't see the gloveless Fader behind her. She's too focused on helping Beatrice Windsor to the cover of an overturned table.

The Fader grabs her bare arm. Her body twists at an awkward angle, her toes pointing in her shoes as she fights against his hold.

"He's draining her." The words leave me on a breath.

Ice fills my veins. My heart. My *mind.*

I'm frozen, watching the gruesome scene before me. Layce growing more limp the longer he holds her. The battle behind and around her, the attack Erin warned me about. Axl and Pierce are fighting hand to hand because they don't have their powers.

Because . . . they're *mine.*

The realization hits me hard and sharp like a lightning bolt. Since they sacrificed their powers to save me, I've been trying to give them *back* to them. Been locking them up, afraid of what and who I'll become if I trust myself with them.

But they are *mine*.

As I'm theirs.

Keep being you. Never forget who you are, Rylee Gray. Evaluna's demand rings in the back of my mind.

I trust myself. I've *always* known who I am. I've let other people make me doubt it too much. Not anymore.

One by one, I flick the locks on the doors I've kept the powers behind, letting them fully fly open with an acceptance I've never had before.

I'm worthy of these powers.

I deserve them.

We deserve each other.

Sea and sky and energy and emotion flood my body, my *soul*. Washing over me, filling me to the brim so much I can taste it on my tongue. I'm no longer afraid of who I'll become, because these, just like my mates, were always *meant* for me.

And I'm the embodiment of pure, white-hot wrath as I step toward Layce and *explode*.

CHAPTER 56

Rylee

Cries ring out as green bands of energy spear from me with such force, I have to bend my knees to stop from toppling over.

The first one hits the Fader gripping Layce. He immediately releases her, and they both hit the ground. Layce is twitching involuntarily. Ivy races to her, gathers her in her lap, tears in her eyes as she finds me across the chaos. She must see the power all around me, must see it radiating in my eyes, because she gives me a nod of approval that provides me with all the reassurance I need.

I send the rest of the energy bands sprawling, each one finding a Fader, an elite enforcer, a regular enforcer, the kings. My bands wrap around them, hold them aloft, subduing all of them in a matter of *seconds*.

"Ivy?" Her name is a panicked, strained cry from my lips.

"She's okay," she calls to me. Layce is coughing in her lap, raising a weak hand toward me. "She's *okay*."

Relief is a tangible thing that sharpens my focus. I shift my arms, the energy bands moving with me as I force the struggling group to the ground. Another band easily silences their pleas as I turn and walk toward Baydel.

He thrashes against the bands, eyes wide and feral as he sees me. He yells behind the energy gag I've given him, his power lashing out at me.

I flinch against it as it slams into me, doing its best to lock onto my body and halt me. It's no match for the combined wealth of power now flooding my veins unhindered.

Half a thought, and I drop him to his knees. I step to tower above him.

I could kill him.

I *want* to kill him.

I could kill them all.

It's taking a great deal of effort not to.

"Rylee." Kal says my name with such softness, I blink out of my murderous thoughts enough to *see*.

All the Faders and enforcers struggle against my bonds. The guests are staring at me in hope and terror. Lucas and Jullian and Brooks are on their knees, too, confused but not fighting their restraints.

Kal approaches me, then Axl and Pierce.

I close my eyes, and it's as easy as breathing to send them pieces of their power. An open current between us. We can freely take and give as we please.

I just needed to accept them as *mine*. To trust myself. To accept who I am.

I'm Rylee Gray. Ashlander. Legend. Mate. Queen of Lumathyst.

I turn back to Baydel. "You will tell me everything you know, or I will make your death last an eternity." I remove his gag.

"I didn't—" His eyes flare in terror as I send a wave of ice-cold fear straight into him. "How?" he gasps through the panic. *"How?"*

I bend down to meet him at his level. "You couldn't kill me," I whisper. "Though you tried to poison me. You failed."

Baydel's eyes fill with anger as I take the fear out of him. "You stupid, *stupid* girl. You have no idea what game you're playing."

A fist cracks into Baydel's face, snapping his head sideways. "You fucking did what?" Axl growls. "You poisoned her?"

Baydel spits blood on the cracked floor, his lip split.

The action drags up the memory of Baydel as a child, his brother hitting him just the same way. My heart squeezes with an involuntary ache.

I ignore the empathy. He doesn't deserve it.

"I tried to save you from her," Baydel barks. "You have no idea how badly she's messed things up."

"Coward," Kal seethes as he and Pierce rush toward him, but I stop them with one upraised hand.

"I know about your brother," I say, relishing the moment when Baydel turns a shade whiter. "The siphon." I look to the struggling Faders. The ones who don't wear gloves. "He's sending them. But you knew that, didn't you?"

The night Evaluna sent me to find him. He was talking to someone through his Occuli. He said *call off your dogs.*

I shake my head. "All this time," I continue, "you were making us chase a group of people you allowed in."

"I did no such thing!"

"You did," I say. "I know you did."

He tips his bloody chin. Defiant. "You don't know *anything*."

I hate that he's right. I have pieces of the puzzle. Not all of them.

I turn to my mates, hurrying to show them exactly what I saw in Baydel's mind. I can't risk uttering it out loud. I have *no* idea who we can trust.

Kal, Axl, and Pierce keep their outward reactions locked up, but I can feel the ripple of emotions through my and Jax's power. Anger, confusion, betrayal. More confusion.

At least we're on the same page there.

"Mirren." I spot her near Ivy and Layce. She has a nasty cut across her forehead that threatens to send me spiraling again, but I manage to breathe. "Can you help get the RAC off the balcony and inside to the healers? Yourself, too."

She looks like she might argue, but she nods, helping Layce to her feet. I send her a look that promises hugs and tears and explanations later before Mirren takes her inside first. The rest who are able form groups and follow her inside.

Ivy comes to stand near me, supportive and at the ready. I want to crumble. I want to lie down. I want to do anything other than what I'm doing right now. Which is try to unfuck this entire situation.

But right now, I have to see if one of the pieces of the puzzle is what I think it is.

I look to the Faders, then render them, the enforcers, and the elites all unconscious. They slump in their restraints to the cracked glass floor.

All except one.

"Erin." I don't need to say her name more than once. I know exactly what her mind feels like, knew her the second my energy bands touched her. I release her from them now.

She steps over the bodies, ripping off her mask. "I did warn you about this."

"You should've stopped it," I fire at her, noting the dead who were victims of the attack. The lifeless bodies strung along the once-beautiful glass floor of the balcony.

"I can't—"

"His brother," I cut her off, nodding behind me to Baydel. "Is he the one who tied your tongue with his power?" I saw him control Baydel's mind in his memory.

She nods, confirming my assumption.

"And you work for him," I say. "I can't pretend to know why. I don't care anymore." I sigh. "Ivy, take her to my chambers and don't let her out of your sight. Please," I add. Ivy nods, flashing me a concerned look. "Erin, I swear on the goddesses above, if you try anything, I will *kill* you."

Her eyes widen, almost like she doesn't recognize me. She looks down, spotting One on the floor, unconscious near Baydel's feet, like she can't bear to look at me.

I don't feel the sting. Not when I don't know if I can truly trust her. She may have warned me about this attack, warned me about Baydel, but she's never done anything to help stop this violence. She's actively been a part of it, and Layce almost died as a result.

But I *need* Erin. She knows more about Baydel's brother, and since he's clearly the one behind the recent deaths, the Faders, and who knows what else, I need all the help I can get.

I turn, eyeing the other kings, then my mates. "I don't know if we can trust them."

Kal looks to his father, pain shaping his features.

"And I don't have time to figure it out," I continue, then go quiet, slipping into my mates' minds.

If we can, we'll go into their minds and figure out if they're on our side or not. But right now, we don't have time. We need to secure them. And the elites. Their Occuli. Anyone who would be loyal to them and not to us.

They nod.

I need to go deeper into Baydel's mind to find out the pieces we're missing, I continue. *Or force it out of him. Something . . . something about all of this. It's wrong. Way more wrong than I think we understand.*

That cold apprehension claws at my spine. Erin being here, warning me about the attack. The way she let Ivy take her so easily. Something isn't right.

None of it is.

"Do we have room in the dungeons?" I ask Kal aloud, motioning to the unconscious group, then the kings.

I can't have them interfering when I question Baydel.

Kal nods, drawing from our connected power, using it to speedily secure them all in the dungeons over the course of a few trips.

"I'm going to need each of your help," I say when it's just us and Baydel left.

"We're here," Kal says. "Tell us what you need."

Each one steps around me as I look down at Baydel, our bonds strong, unbreakable and trembling with power. I wish Jax was here. He'd want to see this.

"I need to know everything he knows," I say.

"We'll help you," Pierce says.

"Whatever you need," Kal adds.

"Together," Axl says.

Baydel glares up at me, shaking his head. "I'll never tell you anything," he says. "You'll have to kill me first."

I shape my lips into a smile my Nightmare would be proud of. "We'll see about that."

CHAPTER 57

Rylee

"I should go back." I breathe out the words. "Try again."

Pierce settles me back down on the sofa in his palace chambers. "You have nothing left. You need rest."

I blow out a breath. He's not wrong. My mind feels like a bowl of mush, sweat dots my skin, and my muscles are trembling. The result of hours spent trying to reenter Baydel's mind.

The prick is powerful. Now that he knows I'm coming, he blocks me at every turn. I broke through a few times only to get a glimpse of something before he shoved me out. I thought about killing him again.

Thought about it a lot.

He still breathes. For now.

"Drink this." Axl hands me a cool glass, the liquid inside a light pink shade. "Ivy sent it," he says. "One of her tonics."

I nod, gulping down the contents. It loosens the ache in my muscles.

Ivy. She's in my chambers with my sister and Layce, who's been healed by Dalfon. I've only gone as far as checking on Layce, to hug her and feel her alive in my arms. I almost lost her. Because of Erin. Because of an attack she led.

That's what kept me from going to see my sister.

Kept me from trying to talk to her.

I will. I'm just . . . I need time.

She's the other piece to this puzzle. A vital one.

Once I rest, she'll be the next one I question.

The thought makes acid churn in my gut. It shouldn't be hard to talk to my sister. But I don't know her anymore. At least not whoever she's become.

"I brought food," Kal says as he comes through the doors, a tray in his hands. "What would you like first? Bread? Chocolate? Fruit?"

I smile up at him as he sets the tray on the table in front of the couch.

Pierce settles on my left, Axl on my right. Kal crouches down to my eye level before me, hands on my knees. "Tell me, and I'll fix it up for you."

I swallow the emotion clogging my throat. The love fueling me, soothing my soul when everything seems upside down. They're my constant. If Jax were here, it would be perfect.

"Thank you," I say. "I don't know what I'd do without all of you."

"We're here," Kal says.

"Always," Pierce adds.

"You're going to be begging for space soon," Axl says. "Cause I'm going to annoy the shit out of you with how attached I'm going to be."

"You could never annoy me." I laugh, shaking my head. "I wish Jax was here."

"He has to be getting close," Pierce says. "Keleshore is known for their slow decision-making process, but he's been gone a great while."

"Maybe he's already on his way back," Axl says.

"I saw Mirren a little while ago," Kal says. "She was heading to mail your letter to Keleshore."

Hope fills my chest. I demanded his return, in the nicest way possible. Maybe it will be enough. And once he's home, we can start making the changes we need to.

With the capture of my sister and Baydel and the other kings, too . . . we can finally put an end to the Faders. Sure, we have his brother to contend with, the siphons of Erithmore, and whatever bargain Baydel made with him in the memory I saw, but now that we know what to watch for, there's hope for an end to it all soon.

And then . . .

Then my mates take the thrones, and we get to live happily ever after.

Just like Axl always says.

"I love you all," I say. "Have I told you that today?"

Axl grins. "I never hear it enough."

Pierce squeezes my hand. "And we you."

Kal smiles and turns, fixing me a plate. "I'm going to feed you, love."

I chuckle, settling deeper into the couch. For the first time in I don't know how long, I feel like we're finally in control.

Mirren hurries through my open door, a package in her hand. Her urgency has all of us sitting up straighter. *"Rylee."*

My blood runs cold. She never says my name like that. Not so serious, so . . . distraught?

"Mir?" I ask, eyes wide as she gets closer. "Are you crying?"

"This . . ." She holds the package, which I can now see is open, the brown paper torn to reveal an intricately carved wooden box the size of my hand. "It came for you. I opened it like I do all your packages to make sure it wasn't something . . ." Her voice cracks. She's *shaking*.

Everything slows around me as I shove off the couch, walking past Kal to stand before her. I take the small box from her hands. My heart barely beats as I open the lid.

"No." The word is a cry, a plea, a promise.

"Rylee?" Axl is at my side, his words clipped as he sees the opened box. Kal and Pierce come, too, Kal holding me up when my knees buckle.

"No," I say again, my entire being focused on the contents of the box.

A *finger*.

One with a tiny inked butterfly beneath the knuckle.

And a lone piece of parchment.

IF YOU WANT HIM, COME AND GET HIM, PRINCESS.
LEST I SEND HIM TO YOU IN PIECES.

CHAPTER 58

Jax

My mouth feels like it's caked in sand.

Fuck, it's hot in here.

And it smells like piss and vomit.

Not mine. I hold *some* pride there. Though I couldn't stop the groan that tore from me when he took my finger. The loss hurt more than the physical pain. The representation of what that finger meant to me. The tattoo Rylee had given me. Fucking prick.

I thought my father was bad. I had no idea I have an uncle who is much worse.

I groan as I shift my weight, my toes barely scraping the sodden ground in this forsaken cell. My wrists are bleeding beneath the iron chains they've strung me up with, and from the pulsing heat coming off the wounds, I'm pretty sure they're infected.

My head swarms, another rush of dizziness making my eyes roll back. Everything hurts, like acid pumps between my joints. They dosed me with something. Tried to get me to talk.

I refused.

"Drink," a female voice demands.

I open my eyes. Can't remember shutting them.

I turn my head away from the wooden ladle the woman holds up to my lips.

"It's water," she snaps. "Drink it."

I press my lips together tightly, turning my head away as far as I can in the chained position. One thing I've learned: they're fond of poisons and other awful concoctions here.

"I'm trying to help you, you stubborn-ass prince." The way she says that has something prickling the back of my neck. Some sense of familiarity I can't place. I turn to look at her finally, squinting because the damn room won't stop spinning.

My heart stops as I meet familiar blue eyes. "Rylee—"

She shoves the ladle against my open mouth, and a sugary sweet water spills in that I instinctively swallow.

The pulsing ache behind my eyes fades to a dull pain, my eyes clearing as the room stops spinning.

It's not Rylee. Of course it isn't. She's safe in Lumathyst, where she belongs.

I wonder what story Baydel will spin for them. Will he say I died in a storm among the sea? How tragically boring.

"What did you call me?" the woman asks, her eyes wide. She's older, looking closer to Mirren's age, but who's to really say? I'm in a realm I know nothing about. Everything I thought I knew is a web of lies to serve a purpose I'm still not clear on.

"What was in that water?" I ask, the pain in my wrists ebbing, too.

"Tonic—"

A clang on the cell bars makes her jump, and then she glares behind her.

"No talking," a guard grumbles at the woman.

She looks back at me, studying me for a moment.

I stare right back, something itching my brain.

"Prick." She spins toward the guard, who lets her out of the cell.

"Think of what you'll call me when I get out of here," I threaten, then laugh. Low. Slow. The laugh of Nightmares.

She doesn't look back.

I don't question why she gave me a tonic. Not when my uncle has proven his sadistic side. He wants to heal me so he can break me again. Hate to say it, but I've used tactics like this before—only when they were deserved, though.

I suppose some would say I deserve worse.

I swallow hard, hissing against the burn in my arms from being suspended this long.

Time passes. I'm not sure how long. I measure it in moments of pain—a guard comes in, breaks my nose, asks me some questions, then leaves again.

Over and over.

And it's only when they beat me into unconsciousness that I gain relief.

A sharp crack startles me awake.

I groan. The taste of metal fills my mouth.

"There he is." My uncle's voice sounds before my vision clears. "Looking rather bleak today, aren't we?" He paces before me, dressed in a fine suit of purple. He looks so like my father, only taller and a little slimmer. It's unnerving. His eyes have that gray sheen to them today. The last time I saw them, they were as bright a green as my father's.

I motion in the chains with a shrug. "Not my best lighting."

He glances at the lone torch outside illuminating the cell, then laughs and shakes his head. "You're certainly hard to crack," he says, wagging a finger at me. "Violence and torture do nothing to you. I don't know what to do with a man like that." He grins. "Then I got to thinking about that mate of yours, the one you won't tell me anything about. The one I suspect got in the way of you having full powers, or I would've already drunk from you."

I glare at him. "Fuck you."

His smile deepens. "Funny, I honestly wouldn't have pegged you for a romantic." He pops his lips. "I, on the other hand, *am* a romantic. I sent your mate a gift." He reaches for my wounded hand, gripping the stump that used to be my ring finger.

Panic claws up my throat.

No.

"It should've arrived today," he continues, releasing me so hard I swing back in the chains. The motion sparks blinding pain along my body. He claps his hands together, looking downright giddy.

"I'm going to kill you," I say as calmly as I can.

"I doubt that, nephew. We're going to become friends. You'll see. You and I have a long life ahead of us." He huffs. "Especially when I get my hands on her. My person on the inside is close. I wonder if she appreciated my thoughtful gift."

Adrenaline crackles to life in my blood. I yank against the chains, growling like a wild animal.

He laughs. "I like you, Jax. And if she's anything like you, I'll *love* her."

"You touch her, you *die*."

"Now, that's not very kind," he says, tsking at me. "And to think, I was going to let you two share this cell together."

Everything in me goes cold as he spears into my mind. Weaves a vision of Rylee in this cell, strung up in chains in the worst possible way. Bruised, broken, bleeding. Begging me to help her.

"Stop!" I demand. *"Stop!"*

He doesn't relent. He shows me all the ways he intends to hurt her. It kills something inside me to watch it. He only pulls out of my mind when a guard storms into the cell and whispers something in his ear.

His smile widens, and my stomach plummets.

"Call off your source." I force the words out. "I'll tell you anything you want to know. Just leave her alone."

"It's too late for that now," he says. "You had your chance to behave. You didn't." He looks down his nose at me. "It appears your beloved is on her way to rescue you."

TO BE CONTINUED

ACKNOWLEDGMENTS

My first thanks will always be to you, the reader. Without you, this story wouldn't be what it is. I'm so grateful to have had the chance to meet so many of you this past year, and I can't wait to meet even more of you soon. I appreciate each and every one of you.

To my amazing husband, thank you for always being an inspiration and for allowing me to put so many pieces of you into these incredible book boyfriends. I couldn't do what I love without your support. Thanks for making me fall in love with you a little more every single day and for giving me the two best kids on the planet.

To Liz Pelletier, thank you for the home you've given me at Red Tower. Your insight and advice are always spot-on. I've learned so much from our chats, edits, and the projects we've worked on, and I can't thank you enough for that. This series means so much to me, and I'm so glad you love these characters like I do.

To Mary Lindsey, I'm not sure how to put into words how much I appreciate you. You see me, understand my voice, and help me sharpen it in the best way. I couldn't imagine working on these stories without you! With each edit we do, you teach me something new that I'll hold on to forever. Thanks for all the texts, calls, and edits. I'm so grateful to be a part of your team.

To Hannah Lindsey, I absolutely adore you. Without you, there would be way too many instances of "furrowed brows" and all the other bingo words I never seem to notice LOL. I'm forever in your debt for everything you catch and help unpack in these stories. You ask all the tough questions that make me dig deeper and I'm forever grateful for you.

To the friends I've made at Red Tower—Mai Corland, Abigail Owen, Hannah Nicole Maehrer, Geneva Lee, Rachel Howzell Hall, Cecy Robson, Tracy Wolff, and more—I'm so honored to know you. Thanks for all the chats, support, and encouragement! It means the world to me. And thanks for letting me pick your brains about all the characters you create. True fangirl for life.

Thank you to Justine Bylo for coming to this story with fresh eyes. You helped shape it into the sparkly version it is now, and I'm so grateful you did!

To the Red Tower team—Lindsey Staub, Heather Riccio, Curtis Svehlak, Melanie Smith, Victoria Chew, Meredith Johnson, Cai Cramer, Nicole Resciniti, and so many more—I'm grateful for your support! Working with you is always a joy, and I can't thank you all enough.

To the in-house readers, the copyeditors, assistant editors, proofreaders, and beyond, thank you! I appreciate every second you've spent on this book.

To the amazing artists—LJ Anderson, Bree Archer, Liz Wayant, Amy Acosta, Gabrielle Ragusi, Britt Marczak, Serene Illustrations—I'm so blown away by your work, and I'm always amazed at what you come up with. Thank you for bringing my fantasy worlds to life.

To everyone on the Kaye Publicity team, thank you so much for all you've done for me and this story that I'm so in love with! You're all amazing!

To my sister, for the support, the hours spent laughing as you explore this new-to-you genre, and for giving me the coolest niece and nephew who bring joy to my life every single day, thank you!

To my agent, Beth Davey, thank you for always being in my corner! Your support means the world to me. Thanks for always being there for a call and advocating for my work in every way.

And lastly, again, to you the reader. If you've made it this far, I want to genuinely thank you one more time. You're what brings books to life, and none of this would be possible without you.

PROPHECY INSISTS THAT NOBODY WILL DEFEAT THE GODDESS OF WAR.

For a hundred years, Altarra has burned. The goddess of war, Morrigan, has conquered kingdom after kingdom, leaving only ruin in her wake. Every prophecy says the same thing—nobody can defeat her.

And after a century of failure, someone finally takes that literally.

When the goddess Artemisen chooses Soli Graymind—a nobody from the lowest caste who suffers from chronic depression—to lead one last desperate quest, the world laughs. But Soli won't be alone. She's joined by five others just as broken, just as lost:

A thief with no Guild.

A noble with no wealth.

A sorcerer with no hope.

A warrior with no morals.

And a prince with no kingdom—the one man she can't stop thinking about, even when hope itself is dying.

Together, they are Altarra's last chance.

Because maybe being a "nobody" is more powerful than anyone imagines—including themselves.

Available Soon in Paperback

IT'S THE SEASON FOR TREASON . . .

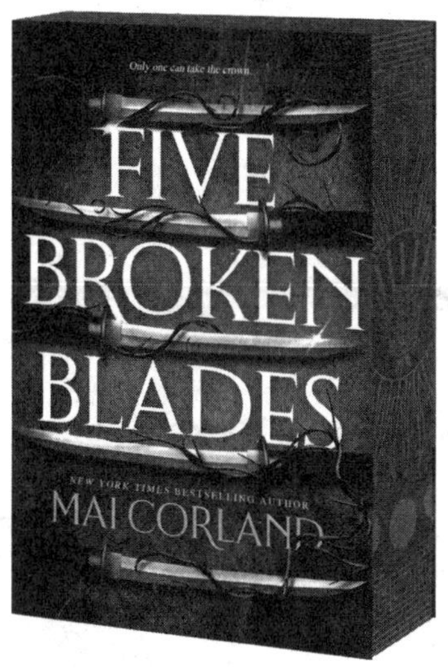

The king of Yusan must die.

The five most dangerous liars in the land have been mysteriously summoned to work together for a single objective: to kill the god king Joon.

He has it coming. Under his merciless immortal hand, the nobles flourish, while the poor and innocent are imprisoned, ruined . . . or sold.

And now each of the five blades will come for him. Each has tasted bitterness—from the hired hit man seeking atonement, a lovely assassin who seeks freedom, or even the prince banished for his cruel crimes. None can resist the sweet, icy lure of vengeance.

They can agree on murder.

They can agree on treachery.

But for these five killers—each versed in deception, lies, and betrayal—it's not enough to forge an alliance.

To survive, they'll have to find a way to trust each other . . . but only one can take the crown.

Let the best liar win.

Doubling the Trees Behind Every Book You Buy.

Because books should leave the world better than they found it—not just in hearts and minds, but in forests and futures.

Through our Read More, Breathe Easier™ initiative, we're helping reforest the planet, restore ecosystems, and rethink what sustainable publishing can be.

Track the impact of your read at:

CONNECT WITH US ONLINE

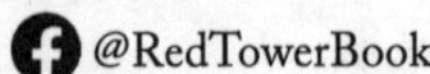

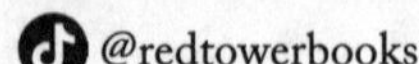

@redtowerbooks

@RedTowerBooks

@redtowerbooks

Join the Entangled Insiders for early access to ARCs, exclusive content, and insider news! Scan the QR code to become part of the ultimate reader community.